Cancer and Nutrition

A Ten-Point Plan
to Reduce Your Risk
of Getting Cancer

Cancer and Nutrition

A Ten-Point Plan
to Reduce Your Risk
of Getting Cancer

Charles B. Simone, M.D.

Foreword by
Robert A. Good, M.D., Ph.D.
Former Director,
Memorial Sloan Kettering
Cancer Hospital

SIMONE HEALTH SERIES

AVERY PUBLISHING GROUP INC.
Garden City Park, New York

Cover Design: Rudy Shur and Martin Hochberg
Cover Photographer: John Harper
In-House Editor: Cynthia Eriksen
Typesetters: Bonnie Freid and Antoinette Mason
Printer: Paragon Press, Honesdale, PA

Library of Congress Cataloging-in-Publication Data

Simone, Charles B.
    Cancer and nutrition: a ten-point plan to reduce your risk of
getting cancer / Charles B. Simone : foreword by Robert A. Good.
      p. cm.
    Includes bibliographical references (p.   ) and index.
    ISBN 0-89529-491-5
    1. Cancer—Prevention. 2. Cancer—Nutritional aspects.
    3. Cancer—Risk factors. I. Title.
    RC268.S53 1992
    616.99'4052—dc20   91-46670
                                         CIP

Printed in the United States of America

20 19 18 17 16 15 14 13 12

Contents

To my family.

Foreword

When asked what they fear the most, many Americans say cancer. This dread disease is the number two killer in the United States. Because of the nature of the disease, and also because of the drastic methods currently needed for effective treatment—surgery, radiotherapy, and chemotherapy—incredible suffering is experienced by Americans and people throughout the world as a consequence of cancer. With the use of antibiotics to control most infections—previously the major cause of disease, suffering, and death— cancer and the other diseases associated with aging, including heart and blood vessel disease, have become more and more prominent in our lives. Now, even in China, a developing country, cancer and heart disease vie for the position of number one killer. We all pray for the day when we will understand cancer and doctors can give us a cure, such as the antibiotics they found to treat tuberculosis, pneumonia, and meningitis. That day will come—hopefully very soon. But since many discoveries will be needed, we can't count on it in our immediate future.

Too few of us realize that the tremendous increase in deaths from cancer in the United States can be halted. Perhaps the preventive measures are too simple. In this refreshingly straightforward and easy-to-read book, Dr. Simone summarizes current information that promises prevention of many, if not most, cancers. We must stop smoking of all kinds, especially that of cigarettes; indeed, we must avoid using tobacco completely. We must exercise regularly, eat a prudent diet, avoid known cancer-causing chemicals, and take rational amounts of certain vitamins and minerals. We must insist that our work places are safe from exposure to chemicals known to be hazardous and to those that may be harmful. Developing lasting love relationships also seems to be important to maintaining good health. These are simple preventive measures, and abundant experimental epidemiological and clinical evidence indicates that these relatively minor adjustments of lifestyle, initiated as early in life as possible, could reduce the frequency of cancer dramatically.

Why don't we all make these relatively minor changes in our lifestyles? I have asked myself this question over and over again. I guess it is because as a species, knowing full well that we are mortal, we have the need to deny our mortality and pretend we are immortal for as long as possible. I took Simone's test for cancer risks and scored well—only a very few adjustments still to make. Unfortunately, I have perhaps made many of the changes in lifestyle a bit late, but *I am convinced that if everyone could read Simone's book early enough in life and take it seriously, we would make major strides toward putting the cancer doctors out of work and approach the legacy of health that is within our reach.*

Robert A. Good, Ph.D., M.D.
Former President and Director,
Memorial Sloan-Kettering Cancer Hospital,
New York City

Introduction

Cancer is the most feared of all diseases. People immediately associate cancer with dying. Unlike other killer diseases, cancer usually causes a slow death involving pain, suffering, mental anguish, and a feeling of hopelessness. It is the second most common cause of death in the United States and will affect one out of every three Americans during his or her lifetime. By the year 2000, two of every five Americans will be affected. The number of new cancer cases has been increasing over the past nine decades; the accelerated rise in lung cancer, for example, is alarming. According to the U.S. Bureau of the Census, in 1900, 47 people out of every 100,000 died of cancer, making it the sixth leading cause of death. Today, 173 people out of every 100,000 will die of cancer, ranking it second.

In 1971 the United States declared war on cancer with the following statement from President Nixon: "The time has come in America when the same kind of concentrated effort that split the atom and took man to the moon should be turned toward conquering this dread disease." In that year 337,000 people died of cancer, and about $250 million was spent on cancer research.

Since then, tens of billions of dollars have been invested over the years in cancer research. Approximately $75 billion is spent on cancer treatment each year: about $25 billion for direct health care, $9 billion in lost productivity due to treatment or disability, and $41 billion in lost productivity due to premature death.[1] Each month, it seems, new therapies are trumpeted. Some show promise, others fizzle quickly.

So intense is the concern to find "the cure for cancer" that more money is collected each year than can actually be spent responsibly on meaningful research. Much of these funds should be directed to cancer prevention instead of the National Cancer Institute's current allocation of less than 5 to 7 percent.

Despite this enormous effort to combat cancer, the number of new cases of nearly every form of cancer has increased annually over the last century. (See Table 1 and Figure 1.) Still worse: from 1930 to present—despite the introduction of radiation therapy, chemotherapy, and immunotherapy with biologic response modifiers, despite CT scans, MRI scans, and all the other new medical technology— lifespans for almost every form of cancer except cervical cancer and lung cancer have remained constant, which means that there has been no significant progress in cancer treatment.[2] The incidence of stomach cancer has gone down probably due to the advent of refrigeration in the 1930s and the consequent removal of carcinogenic chemicals as food preservatives. And worse yet, perhaps even deceptively so, is

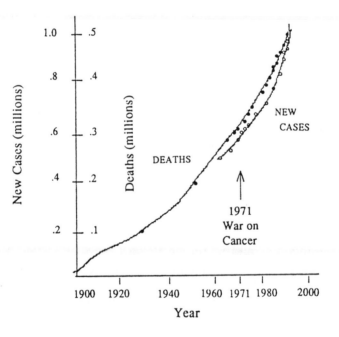

Figure 1 Cancer deaths and new cases. Note the sharp rise in new cancer cases and cancer-related deaths despite billions of dollars in research.

the unrealistic goal set by the National Cancer Institute and American Cancer Society of a 50 percent reduction in cancer mortality by the year 2000. [3-9] Looking at the almost vertical rise in the number of new cancer cases each year in Figure 1, I am convinced that the goal cannot be attained.

The chilling prospect remains: one out of three Americans alive today will develop cancer, and the majority of them will die from it. By the year 2000, two of every five will develop cancer.

Cancer research and treatment are extremely complex fields of study because the exact nature of the single cancer cell is so elusive. Cancer is many diseases with many different causes. We cannot expect miracle cures just because so much money has been poured into cancer research. At the same time, we should not expect miracles from "cancer-cure" facilities that take money from cancer victims desperate to try any treatment in hope of another chance at life.

After collating the existing cancer data, I found that 80-90 percent of all cancers are produced as a result of dietary and nutritional practices, lifestyle (smoking, alcohol, etc.), chemicals, and other environmental factors. [10] This information has now been corroborated by other major agencies: the National Academy of Sciences, [11] the U.S. Department of Health and Human Services, [12] the National Cancer Institute, [13] and the American Cancer Society.

Since nutrition, lifestyle, and the environment are the most common risk factors for cancer, many of these cancers can be eliminated or substantially reduced in number if you can identify the risk factors and modify them accordingly. Many people have the fatalistic attitude that anything and everything can cause cancer, and believe there is no use in trying to do anything about it. That attitude is unwar-

Table 1   U.S. Cancer Incidence

	1900	1962	1971*	1995
Total Cases	25,000	520,000	635,000	1,252,000
Leading Cancers				
Prostate	N/A	31,000	35,000	244,000
Lung	N/A	45,000	80,000	186,000
Breast	N/A	63,000	69,600	185,000
Colon/Rectum	N/A	72,000	75,000	158,500
Uterus	N/A	N/A	N/A	48,600

* The year Nixon declared war on cancer.
N/A=Not available.
Data from U.S. Bureau of Vital Statistics and *CA—A Cancer Journal for Clinicians.* See References 14 and 15.

ranted and fosters even more apathy. Everything does not cause cancer.

The Dietary Goals for the United States, published by the Senate Select Committee on Nutrition and Human Needs (Senator George McGovern, Chairman), states that Americans eat too much, and, specifically, that they eat too much meat, too much fat, too much cholesterol, too much sugar, and too much salt. The American diet was found to be lacking in fruits, vegetables, and grains. The committee recommended that current fat consumption, which comprises 40 to 45 percent of the calories in the American diet, be reduced to about 30 percent; that calories derived from sugar be reduced to 15 percent from the current 15 to 25 percent; and that salt consumption be substantially reduced. Since 1981, I have recommended that fat consumption be reduced to 20 percent of total calories, that sugar calories be reduced to 10 percent, that no table salt be used, and that 25 to 30 grams of fiber foods be consumed daily.

The type of diet we eat today and its preparation are proving to be a major risk factor in the development of certain cancers, a risk factor that can definitely be modified. Nutrition is a very complex topic— one that is not well understood by the public or even by some physicians. Americans need to know the role that nutrition plays in major diseases.

Diet and nutrition appear to be factors in 60 percent of women's cancers and 40 percent of men's cancers as well as about 75 percent of cardiovascular disease cases. Tobacco is a factor in about 30 percent of human cancers. Other known risk factors associated with the development of cancer are alcohol, age, immune system deficiencies, chemicals, drugs, and other environmental factors. You have total control over most of these risk factors, including the major two, diet and tobacco.

Exposure to one or more of these risk factors does not mean that cancer will necessarily develop. It simply means that a person exposed to risk factors has a greater than normal chance of developing cancer.

Physicians in our country too often wind up treating the cancer rather than the whole cancer patient. Much has been learned since 1981 about the role of nutrition, the immune system, and the patient's mental state in the healing process. Because these issues are not addressed properly by the medical community at large, many patients with advanced tumors seek alternative treatment. At great financial and emotional cost to themselves and their families, they resort to quack remedies, get-healthy-quick schemes, and practitioners and "health" centers that claim to reverse or eliminate chronic diseases easily and quickly.

It is *your* responsibility to learn about the risk factors involved in cancer development and then modify those risk factors accordingly. In order to prevent cancer, you should devise your own anticancer plan based on risk factor modification. In addition, your family, and particularly your children, should be taught about risk factor modification. If nutritional and other risk factors are modified, the benefit will be evident in all people, but especially in the young and in the following generations. Obviously, there are some risk factors, like air and water, that you cannot control; therefore, your community must also devise a plan to modify environmental risk factors.

We must eliminate or modify all known risk factors so that we will eventually be able to prevent cancer and heart disease more effectively. Nutritional factors and tobacco smoking, for example, are major risk factors, which, if modified or eliminated, could dramatically reduce the number of cancer as well as heart disease patients. Our health care system emphasizes expensive medical technology and hospital care. It does not emphasize preventive medicine and health education. *It is your responsibility to learn about these risk factors and then modify them.* Good health does not come easily—you must work for it.

You have almost total control over the destiny of your health and the health of your family! Do something about it.

PART ONE

Cancer Today

1

The Scope of Cancer

One of every three Americans will develop cancer during his or her lifetime.[1] Second only to cardiovascular disease as the leading cause of death in the United States, cancer accounts for 23 percent of all deaths, with 547,000 mortalities.[2] By the year 2000, two of every five will develop cancer, and one third of all deaths in America will be caused by cancer. These figures do not even include an estimated 400,000 patients with nonmelanoma skin cancers.[3] Other than the skin, the four organs of the body most affected by cancer are the lungs, the colon and rectum, and the breasts. Table 1.1 shows the estimated incidence of cancer in various sites in the body for both men and women and the estimated percent of deaths in each category.

Carcinoma *in situ* of the cervix and skin cancers other than melanoma (a deadly skin cancer) have not been included in the statistics. If they were, the percentages in Table 1.1 would be much higher for skin and uterine cancers. The word "incidence" means the *number of newly diagnosed cases of a specific disease*, not the number of deaths. For example, in the United States, the estimated incidence, or number of new cases, of breast cancer in 1995 is 183,400: 1,400 male and 182,000 female cases. The estimated mortality, or number of deaths, from breast cancer in 1995 is 46,300: 300 male and 46,000 female deaths.

Table 1.1   1995 Estimated Cancer Incidence
And Death for Each Site and Sex*

Organ Site	% Incidence		% Deaths	
	Male	Female	Male	Female
Skin	3	3	2	1
Mouth structure	3	2	2	1
Lung	17	12	34	22
Breast		32		18
Colon and rectum	13	13	10	11
Pancreas	2	2	4	5
Prostate	28		13	
Ovary and uterus		12		9
Urinary tract	9	4	5	3
Blood and lymph glands	8	6	8	8
All other	14	14	19	22

*From Boring 1995. See References.

The death rate for lung cancer has been rising for both the male and the female population since 1940, and the rate of rise for females is much greater now than ever before. By contrast, since 1930 the death rate has been decreasing for cancer of the uterus and for stomach cancer in both males and females.

However, for most cancers, the death rate has remained approximately the same since 1930,[4] which indicates that little or no real progress has been made in survival from these cancers (breast cancer, ovarian cancer, leukemia, bladder cancer, prostate cancer, colon and rectal cancer, and esophageal cancer). This information is quite disturbing because it indicates that there is no effective treatment for the three cancers that cause 50 percent of all cancer deaths—lung cancer, which has an increasing death rate, colon and rectal cancer, and breast cancer.

These cancer statistics concern the United States as a whole. When each state is examined individually, we find that the states in the Northeast and other heavily industrialized states have the highest number of deaths from cancer. This pattern has remained quite consistent for many years, so a map constructed for the current year would be similar to the one in Figure 1.1, which illustrates geographically the death rates from cancer from those states with the most deaths due to cancer to those with the least for the year 1988.

Table 1.2 lists the states in decreasing order of mortality due to cancer, the actual cancer death rate per 100,000 population, and the total number of deaths in the year compared with the total number of newly diagnosed cancer cases in the year. These data are not age adjusted, which means that the figures do not reflect whether the population in the state is evenly distributed according to age. For example, over the years Florida has had one of the highest cancer death rates in the country. The reason is that so many of our senior citizens retire to Florida from the Northeast. In addition, Washington, D.C., has consistently had the highest death rate per 100,000 in the country. This region has a high concentration of indigent people who consume a high-fat diet and use tobacco and alcohol products.

Table 1.2 Estimated U.S. Cancer Statistics, 1991			
State	Death Rate per 100,000	Number of Deaths	Number of New Cases
1. District of Columbia	227	1,600	3,500
2. Delaware	196	1,700	3,800
3. Louisiana	193	9,200	21,200
4. Maryland	192	10,500	24,100
5. Kentucky	191	9,300	21,300
6. Maine	185	3,200	7,100
7. New Jersey	185	18,700	43,300
8. Nevada	183	2,900	6,400
9. West Virginia	182	4,700	10,900
10. Ohio	181	25,000	57,600
11. Alabama	180	9,100	21,400
12. Illinois	180	25,900	58,500
13. Mississippi	180	6,100	13,600
14. Pennsylvania	180	31,200	71,500
15. Virginia	180	12,800	29,200
16. Massachusetts	179	13,800	32,300
17. New Hampshire	179	2,400	5,200
18. Rhode Island	179	2,400	5,700
19. Tennessee	179	11,400	26,300
20. Indiana	178	12,500	28,600
21. Arkansas	178	6,100	14,100
22. Michigan	177	20,200	46,100
23. South Carolina	177	7,800	17,600
24. Georgia	176	12,200	28,400
25. Missouri	176	12,600	28,500
26. New York	175	38,500	88,100
27. North Carolina	174	15,300	34,500
28. Vermont	174	1,100	2,700
29. Alaska	173	500	1,200
30. Connecticut	169	7,000	16,200
31. Oklahoma	169	6,900	16,400
32. Oregon	168	6,900	15,500
33. Florida	167	39,100	88,700
34. Texas	166	33,100	74,600
35. California	165	51,200	120,000
36. Wisconsin	165	11,100	25,300
37. Washington	164	10,300	23,000
38. Montana	161	1,800	4,100
39. Iowa	159	6,500	14,700
40. Kansas	159	5,600	12,800

41. Nebraska	158	3,400	7,700
42. North Dakota	158	1,500	3,400
43. Arizona	157	8,300	18,500
44. Minnesota	157	8,800	20,200
45. Wyoming	155	800	1,900
46. South Dakota	151	1,500	3,400
47. Idaho	148	1,900	4,400
48. Colorado	148	6,000	13,300
49. New Mexico	146	2,600	6,000
50. Hawaii	137	1,800	4,200
51. Utah	125	2,200	5,000
52. Puerto Rico	128	4,800	10,600

The table below ranks forty-eight nations from highest to lowest based on cancer deaths for both men and women.* The cancer death rates of some countries will surprise you; others will not.

Table 1.3   Cancer Death Rates Worldwide

Male Deaths	Female Deaths
1. Hungary	Denmark
2. Czechoslovakia	Scotland
3. Belgium	Hungary
4. Luxembourg	England and Wales
5. Netherlands	Ireland
6. France	Northern Ireland
7. Scotland	New Zealand
8. Uruguay	Czechoslovakia
9. Italy	Luxembourg
10. Denmark	Uruguay
11. England and Wales	Costa Rica
12. Poland	Austria
13. Switzerland	East Germany
14. East Germany	Chile
15. Austria	Belgium
16. Singapore	Netherlands
17. Northern Ireland	Canada
18. Soviet Union	Iceland
19. New Zealand	United States
20. Ireland	Switzerland
21. Finland	Singapore
22. Canada	Poland
23. Hong Kong	Norway
24. Australia	Australia

25. West Germany	West Germany
26. United States	Italy
27. Costa Rica	Malta
28. Spain	Sweden
29. Norway	Israel
30. Malta	Argentina
31. Japan	Finland
32. Argentina	Hong Kong
33. Chile	Cuba
34. Greece	France
35. Yugoslavia	Ecuador
36. Sweden	Soviet Union
37. Iceland	Yugoslavia
38. Portugal	Portugal
39. Cuba	Bulgaria
40. Bulgaria	Spain
41. Puerto Rico	Kuwait
42. Israel	Japan
43. Romania	Puerto Rico
44. Kuwait	Greece
45. Ecuador	Suriname
46. Suriname	Romania
47. Mauritius	Panama
48. Panama	Mauritius

*Nations ranked in order of age-adjusted cancer death rates per 100,000 population based on information from 1984 to 1986.

Source: Boring, C.C., et al. 1991. Cancer statistics, 1991. *Ca–Cancer Journal for Clinicians*. See References.

2

Risk Factors—
An Overview

You will learn that most of the risk factors for cancer are the same risk factors for cardiovascular disease. Learn about them, modify them, and your risk for both illnesses will be greatly reduced.

DIET AND NUTRITIONAL RISK FACTORS

There is a strong correlation between diet and/or nutritional deficiencies and many cancers (see Table 2.1). The National Academy of Sciences and others estimate that nutritional factors account for 60 percent of cancer cases in women and 40 percent in men.[1-3] Cancers of the breast, colon, rectum, uterus, prostate, and kidney are closely associated with consumption of total fat and protein, particularly meat and animal fat. Other cancers that are directly correlated with dietary factors are cancers of the stomach, small intestine, mouth, pharynx, esophagus, pancreas, liver, ovary, endometrium, thyroid, and bladder.[4-9] Aflatoxin, a fungus product that is found on certain edible plants (especially peanuts), is related to human liver cancer.[10,11]

Table 2.1   Cancer Risk Factors

Risk Factor	Associated Human Cancer
Nutritional factors	
High-fat, low fiber	Breast, colon, rectum, prostate, stomach, mouth, pharynx, esophagus, pancreas, liver, ovary, endometrium, thyroid, kidney, bladder
Iodine deficiency	Thyroid, breast
Aflatoxin (fungus product)	Liver
Obesity	Breast, endometrium, colon
Tobacco use	
Smoking, chewing, snuffing	Lung, larynx, mouth, pharynx, head and neck, esophagus, pancreas, bladder, kidney, breast
Passive inhalation	Lung, cervix, breast, oral
Alcohol	Mouth, pharynx, esophagus, gastrointestine, pancreas, liver, head and neck, larynx, bladder
Age greater than 55	Many organ sites
Immune system malfunction	Lymphoma, carcinoma
High blood pressure	Breast, colon
Environment	Leukemia, lung, skin, other sites
Sedentary lifestyle	Breast, colon, other sites
Stress	Implicated in multiple sites
Hormonal	
Late/never pregnant	Breast
Fibrocystic breast disease	Breast
DES (diethylstilbestrol)	Breast, vagina, cervix, endometrium, testicle
Conjugated estrogens	Breast, liver
Androgens (17-methyl position)	Liver
Undescended testicles (especially after age 6)	Testicle
Sexual-Social	
Female promiscuity	Uterine cervix
Poor male hygiene	Penis
Male homosexuality (promiscuity, amyl nitrite)	Kaposi's sarcoma, anus, tongue
Radiation	
X rays, etc. (ionizing)	Skin, breast, myelogenous leukemia, thyroid, bone
Sunlight (UV) excessive in fair-skinned people who burn easily	Skin
Pesticides	Lung, prostate, liver, skin
Occupational	
Petroleum, tar, soot	Lung, skin, scrotum
Boot and shoe manufacture and repair	Nasal sinus
Furniture and cabinetmaking industry	Nasal sinus
Rubber industry	Lung, bladder, leukemia, stomach
Chemists	Brain, lymphoma, leukemia, pancreas
Foundry workers	Lung
Painters	Leukemia
Printing workers	Lung, mouth, pharynx
Textile workers	Nasal sinus

At one time excessive consumption of coffee had been correlated with cancer of the pancreas,[12] but considerable doubt has been cast upon this correlation.[13,14] Obesity is also an independent risk factor for cancer. Cancers and their relationship to diet and nutritional factors will be discussed in Chapter 8 and other subsequent chapters.

CHEMICAL RISK FACTORS

Chemical and environmental factors, including diet and lifestyle, may be responsible for causing 80 to 90 percent of all cancers. Theoretically, then, most cancers could be prevented if the factors that cause them can first be identified and then controlled or eliminated. Throughout their lives, people are exposed to many chemicals and some drugs in small amounts and in many combinations unique to their culture and environment. Many chemicals and drugs are now known to cause human cancer, and many more are suspected carcinogens.[15] Table 2.2 lists chemicals, their uses, and the human cancers associated with them. People who are exposed to these chemicals either directly, such as those who work in the particular industry shown, or indirectly, such as firefighters exposed to burning objects made from these chemicals, are at increased risk of developing the cancer listed in the table. The incidence of certain cancers in particular populations reflects prolonged low-level exposure to many *carcinogens* (chemical substances that cause cancer), *cocarcinogens* (sub-

Table 2.2   Drug and Chemical Cancer Risk Factors

Risk Factor	Use	Associated Human Cancer
Drugs		
Chlorambucil	Anticancer	Leukemia
Chloramphenicol	Antibiotic	Leukemia
Cyclophosphamide	Anticancer	Bladder
Dilantin	Anticonvulsant	Lymph tissue
Melphalan	Anticancer	Leukemia
Phenacetin	Relieves pain	Kidney
Thiotepa	Anticancer	Leukemia
Chemicals		
Acrylonitrile	Raw material for synthetic fibers, rubbers, resins, and pharmaceutical, dyes, and surfactants	Lung
4-Aminobiphenyl	Organic rubber, dyes	Bladder
Aniline	Manufacture of dyes, pharmaceutical, photographic chemicals, rubber, herbicides, fungicides	Bladder

Risk Factor	Use	Associated Human Cancer
Arsenic	Alloy additive, certain glass, doping agent in silicon solid state, some solders, in some drinking water	Skin, lung, liver
Asbestos	Insulation, cements, brake lining, fireproofing gloves and clothes	Lung, pleura, gastrointestine
Auramine	Dye for paper, textile, leather, corrugated cardboard; antiseptic	Bladder
Benzene	Manufacture of medicine, chemicals, dyes, insecticides, paint remover, rubber cement, antiknock gasoline	Acute myelogenous leukemia
Benzidine	Dyes, some rubbers, detects blood	Bladder
Beryllium	TV phosphors, computer parts, aerospace industry, rocket fuels, alloy	Lung
Cadmium industry	Electroplating, alloys, electrical equipment, solar batteries, fire protection, TV phosphors, pigments, rubber and plastics, control of atomic fission in reactors, fungicide	Prostate, lung
Carbon tetrachloride	Solvent, refrigerant and propellant, semi-conductors, fumigant	Liver
Chlormethyl ether	Solvent, refrigerant	Lung
Chloroprene	Manufacture of synthetic rubber	Skin, lung, liver
Chromate	Catalyst, chromium plating, tanning, pigments, pharmaceuticals	Lung, nasal sinus
Isopropyl alcohol (acid process)	Intermediate for solvent, antifreeze, preservative; perfume; cosmetic	Nasal sinus, larynx
Mustard gas	Pharmaceutical industry	Lung, larynx
Nickel	Raw material for alloy, alkali batteries, ceramics, coins	Nasal sinus, lung
Radon (hematite mining)	Paints, abrasives, metals, pharmaceuticals	Lung
Vinyl chloride	Plastics, cooling medium	Lung, liver, brain

stances that activate carcinogens), and *promoting factors* (substances that facilitate the action of carcinogens).

The mortality rate from lung cancer has been increasing since 1968, even though it has been known throughout that period that cigarette smoking is the major cause of the disease. It has been estimated that 30 percent of all cancers may be related to smoking, either directly or indirectly. The incidence of cancers of the lung, head and neck, esophagus, pancreas, kidney, and bladder is increased in people who smoke. The fifteen carcinogens that have been found in tobacco smoke include hydrocarbons and aromatic amines. People who work with asbestos or uranium or who drink alcohol have an increased risk and incidence of cancer if they also smoke. (This is called synergism, an action of two or more substances achieving a result of which each substance individually is incapable.) It seems reasonable then to explore ways to decrease the number of cancers related to smoking and other known human carcinogens by reducing the number of new smokers, encouraging current smokers to quit, and eliminating the other carcinogens altogether from our diet or eliminating our exposure to them.

Due to differences in their genetic make-up, individuals exposed to a carcinogen will not all have the same probability of getting cancer. Certain proteins from the liver, called enzymes, can break down or activate the carcinogen at different speeds in different people to either render it harmless or promote it to cause cancer. These enzymes will either destroy or activate carcinogens to varying degrees according to inherited tendencies. Some foods can induce certain enzymes to destroy certain carcinogens. The most potent food sources to induce these enzymes are vegetables of the *Brassicaceae* family, which includes Brussels sprouts, cabbage, and broccoli.[16]

ENVIRONMENTAL RISK FACTORS

Environmental factors may be just as important as genetic factors for cancer. For example, Japanese men and women who leave Japan and settle in Hawaii or the continental United States have a lower risk of stomach cancer than those who remain in Japan. Stomach cancer in the United States has been steadily decreasing with the advent of refrigeration and the consequent removal of carcinogenic chemicals as food preservatives.

Air pollution may be a risk factor for cancer, especially lung cancer. Those living in cities encounter many sources of pollution. More people in cities smoke cigarettes than in rural areas. Carcinogens derived from car emissions, industrial activity, burning of solid wastes and fuels remain in the air from four to forty days and thereby travel long distances.[17] And asbestos, a potent carcinogen, can also be found airborne in cities.

Our drinking water contains a number of carcinogens, including asbestos, arsenic, metals, and synthetic organic compounds.[18,19] Asbestos and nitrates are associated with gastrointestinal cancers; arsenic is associated with skin cancer; and synthetic organic chemicals are associated with cancers of the gastrointestinal tract and urinary bladder.

As with many carcinogens, the time between exposure to the carcinogen and actual development of cancer may be quite long. Hence, the cause of a cancer initiated by trace amounts of either airborne or waterborne carcinogens years before the cancer appears may be attributed to an unrelated or unknown cause at the time of diagnosis. We are able to detect many carcinogens in our environment, but many others exist in low concentrations. These environmental carcinogens may themselves cause cancer in certain individuals, or they may interact with other risk factors to initiate, or promote, cancers. Therefore, our imperfect environment, a risk factor for cancer, must be modified. If we avoid introducing harmful substances into the environment, it will remain clean.

RADIATION RISK FACTORS

Human studies show that the more radiation a person is exposed to, the higher is the risk of developing cancer, especially if the radiation exposure is to bone marrow, where the blood cells are made. People who received radiation to shrink enlarged tonsils or to treat acne have a higher risk of developing cancer of the thyroid and parathyroid glands located in the neck. Survivors of the bombings of Hiroshima and Nagasaki have had an increased incidence of leukemia, lymphoma, Hodgkin's disease, multiple myeloma, and other cancers. People who used to paint radium on wristwatch dials have a high incidence of osteogenic sarcoma, a bone cancer. Chronic exposure of fair-skinned, easily sunburned people to sunlight (ultraviolet light) will lead to a higher rate of skin cancer.

There has been mounting concern that people who work in or live near nuclear power plants have a higher risk of developing cancer. In the United Kingdom a higher incidence of childhood leukemia has been reported in children living near several nuclear facilities, most notably a fuel reprocessing plant located at Sellafield in northwest England.[20] The results of another study involving over 8,000 men who worked in the Oak Ridge National Laboratory in Tennessee between 1943 and 1972 show that these men had a higher risk of developing cancers, especially leukemia.[21] Another study shows no such increase in cancer incidence.[22]

Women with tuberculosis who received many chest X rays to follow the progress of treatment had an increased incidence of breast cancer with as little as 17 cGy total dose. A cGy, or centiGray, is a defined amount of energy absorbed by a certain amount of body tissue. One chest X ray using modern equipment delivers about 0.14 cGy. Riding in an airplane at 35,000 feet for six hours exposes a person to 0.01 cGy.

A study by Matanoski published in the *Proceedings of the 1980 International Conference on Cancer* indicates that radiologists, besides their well-known increased risk of developing cancer, may also have a 30 percent increased risk of death from cardiovascular disease and stroke due to radiation exposure. Workers in many industries are chronically exposed to low-dose radiation and hence may be at risk for heart disease and cancer. We may therefore have to reexamine standards for acceptable radiation levels in industry.

OCCUPATIONAL RISK FACTORS

About 10 percent of all cancers are related to exposure to carcinogens on the job. The relationship between a person's job and cancer was noted in the eighteenth century when it was observed that the incidence of cancer of the scrotum was very high in chimney sweeps. Many associations between exposure to carcinogens at work and cancer have been made since then. Most recently, the boot and shoe manufacture and repair industry and the furniture and cabinetmaking industry were shown to be risk factors for cancer of the nasal sinuses.23

Preliminary studies indicate that butchers and slaughterhouse workers are at risk for lung cancer and cancer of other parts of the respiratory system as well as some leukemias.[24,25] However, these findings need to be confirmed and controlled for those persons who also smoke before this industry can be labeled as a definite risk factor for cancer. Other occupations and their associated human cancers are listed in Table 2.1.

AGE AS A RISK FACTOR

The older you get, the higher is your risk of developing cancer. Your risk for cardiovascular disease also increases with age, but to a greater degree. The Biometry Section of the National Cancer Institute has presented studies which show that with every five-year increase of age there is a doubling in the incidence of cancer.[26] The elderly often suffer from nutritional deficiencies, and they have an increased number of infections, autoimmune diseases, and infantile disease patterns, as well as cancer. Werner's syndrome, which prematurely ages very young children so that they die in early adolescence, is characterized by an impaired immune system. These facts suggest that the immune system (see Chapter 4) in the elderly is working inefficiently, partly due to poor nutrition.[27] Because the gastrointestinal tract absorbs nutrients less efficiently with age, the elderly need more nutrients in their diets.

As you get older, your risk of getting cancer increases not only because of your age but also due to the amount of time you have been exposed to external risk factors. For example, cigarette smoking increases your chances of getting lung cancer. The longer you smoke, the greater is the likelihood and incidence of lung cancer. For men between 55 and 64, the annual lung cancer mortality rate is five times higher if they started to smoke before age 15 than if they started to smoke after age 25.[28] If a person stops smoking, there is a decreased risk of developing lung cancer, but this risk does not go back to zero.

Table 2.3 lists the number of people aged 65 or more for approximately each decade beginning with 1980. By 2030 the number of Americans in this age bracket will more than double the number in this group today.

GENETIC RISK FACTORS

Cancer is usually characterized by abnormal genetic chromosome material in the affected cancer cell. A cancer cell does not have the proper amount or type of genes, or, more specifically, DNA (deoxyribonucleic acid). People with certain inherited diseases are more prone to getting cancer. There are over 200 genetic conditions that have an increased incidence of cancer,[29] including mongolism or trisomy 21 syndrome, the immunodeficiency syndromes, Gardner's syndrome, and many more. *These genetic abnormalities, although important for the physician to recognize, account for only a small fraction of all human cancers.*

Table 2.3 Number of Persons Aged 65+ in the United States	
Year	Millions
1980	25.7
1989	31.0
2000	34.5
2010	39.4
2020	52.1
2030	65.6

Source: American Geriatric Society. 1991. *JAMA* 265(23):3092.

ATHEROSCLEROSIS AND CANCER

Atherosclerosis and its many complications are the most common cause of death in the United States. Atherosclerosis, commonly called "hardening of the arteries," is a disease that narrows the inside diameter of the artery. This narrowing restricts the blood flow beyond the narrowed portion, therefore less oxygen can be delivered to those tissues by the red blood cells. Death of tissues occurs when they receive little or no oxygen. The less oxygen, the more dead tissue. Pain is a symptom of either very low oxygen supply to tissues or outright death of tissues. This is why a person having a "heart attack" is in a lot of pain: some tissues are dying and others are not receiving enough oxygen. What does atherosclerosis have to do with cancer? Well, cancer may be responsible for the development of heart and vessel disease in a way, and conversely high blood pressure (a form of blood vessel disease) may lead to the development of cancer under certain circumstances.

The first step in the formation of a narrowed artery is the manufacture of cells (endothelial cells) which line the inside of the artery. Then cholesterol gets deposited in these cells after they have increased in number. The increased cells together with cholesterol is called a plaque. There is good evidence that these cells come from a single cell, that is, they are cloned from one common cell. Cloning is a form of cancer.[30] This situation can be produced in chickens by feeding them carcinogens (benzo(a)pyrene and dimethylbenzanthracene), chemical substances that produce cancer. These particular carcinogens cause an increase in the number and rate of formation of plaques without altering the blood level of cholesterol. In humans, these types of carcinogens (hydrocarbons) are carried by certain proteins (low-density lipoproteins) which also carry cholesterol. More curiously, an enzyme called aryl hydrocarbon hydroxylase, present in cells of the inner walls of arteries, can activate hydrocarbon carcinogens to start proliferating the lining cells.[31] Therefore, if we eat food contaminated with these hydrocarbons or are otherwise exposed to them so that they get into our bloodstream, atherosclerosis may begin to develop. Of course this is just one of many factors involved in the development of atherosclerosis.

R.W. Pero and colleagues have shown a relationship between high blood pressure and cancer.[32] The study shows that the higher the blood pressure and the older the person, the more alterations of DNA that occur in cells. The more abnormal the DNA content of a cell, the more often it will lose control and develop into a cancer. There is some evidence that people with high blood pressure have an increased risk of developing breast cancer,[33] colon cancer, lung cancer, and other cancers.[34]

HORMONAL RISK FACTORS

Hormones influence a cell's growth and development, so if there is an excess or deficit of hormones in the body, then cells will not function properly and may grow abnormally or aberrantly and become cancer cells.

Women who have never been pregnant have a higher risk of developing breast cancer than women who do have children; and women who become pregnant before age 20 have a reduced risk. Women whose mothers or other close relatives have breast cancer have three times the normal risk of getting breast cancer. Women who do not menstruate during their lifetime have a three to four times higher risk of developing breast cancer after the age of 55. A lower risk of breast cancer is seen in women whose ovaries cease to function or are removed surgically before age 35.

There has been considerable controversy over whether oral contraceptives can cause breast and liver cancer. Many studies seem to indicate that hormones used in birth control pills are a risk factor for breast or liver cancer.[35,36] Estrogens in these oral contraceptives can cause benign liver growths as well, which can bleed extensively and cause problems related to bleeding.

Daughters of women who received DES (diethylstilbestrol) therapy during pregnancy have developed cancer of the cervix and vagina. Sons of women who took DES have a higher risk of developing cancer of the testicles because DES causes urinary tract abnormalities including undescended testicles, which, if not corrected surgically before age 6, can develop into cancer of the testicles.[37] Furthermore, women exposed to these same synthetic estrogens in adult life have a higher risk of developing cancer of the cells that line the inside of the uterus (endometrial cancer). Male hormones can predispose to both benign and malignant liver tumors.

Obesity is directly correlated with breast cancer[38-41] and endometrial cancer.[42] This subject will be discussed in Chapter 9.

Fibrocystic breast disease, a benign disease that affects 50 percent of all women sometime during their lives, probably represents a hormone imbalance. If a woman has had the disease over many years, she is at an increased risk of developing breast cancer.[43,44] Recently, as will be discussed in Chapter 6, fibrocystic breast disease has appeared to respond to certain nutrients and dietary modification.

SEXUAL-SOCIAL RISK FACTORS

Cancer of the cervix is associated with having sexual intercourse at an early age and with having multiple male sex partners. The earlier the age of the female when she first has sexual intercourse, and the greater the number of male partners she has, the higher is her risk of getting cancer of the cervix. Sexual intercourse with uncircumcised male partners may also contribute to a woman's risk of developing cervical cancer.

Cancer of the penis is a very rare disease in the United States. There is almost universal agreement that one primary risk factor is responsible for this cancer—poor hygiene, especially in the uncircumcised male. Secretion and different organisms retained under the foreskin produce irritation and infection, which are thought to predispose to cancer cellular changes.[45]

There is an epidemic outbreak of Kaposi's sarcoma in sexually active male homosexuals.[46-48] Kaposi's sarcoma is a cancer of the skin, mucous membranes, and lymph nodes. Those affected have an acquired immunodeficiency syndrome (AIDS). In addition to Kaposi's sarcoma, male homosexuality is a risk factor for two other cancers: cancer of the anus[49] and cancer of the tongue.

Sexually active male homosexuals in good health can have a normal or abnormal immune system. Many with an abnormal immune system appear quite healthy. Some with a malfunctioning immune system have had Kaposi's sarcoma and/or fatal or life-threatening infections caused by *Pneumocystis carinii*.[50,51]

The immune impairment from AIDS seen in sexually active male homosexuals, intravenous drug users, prostitutes, and heterosexuals is now clearly related to infection by the HIV virus. Other risk factors leading to human susceptibility to HIV include amyl nitrite, a drug used as a sexual stimulant. Amyl nitrite produces a profound impairment of the immune system, especially the T lymphocytes.[52] Also, immunological abnormalities are seen more often in homosexuals who have many sexual partners than in those who have only one partner.[53]

VIRAL RISK FACTORS

Viruses have been shown to directly cause cancer in fish, birds, frogs, and almost every mammal. Over one hundred viruses capable of causing cancer have been identified. Two human cancers, T cell leukemia and T cell lymphoma, have been shown to be *caused directly* by viruses. Perhaps all the other white blood cell tumors will also be shown to be caused by viruses.

In the following chapters we will review nutritional risk factors, other risk factors that can lead to the development of cancer, and ways that the risk factors can be modified.

WHERE DO YOU STAND?

My Cancer Risk Factor Assessment test found on page 27 has been designed to assess your own risk factors based upon diet, weight, age, lifestyle, and other variables covered in this chapter. Take the test to evaluate your risk. We define risk for potentially developing cancer based upon the following letter combination totals:

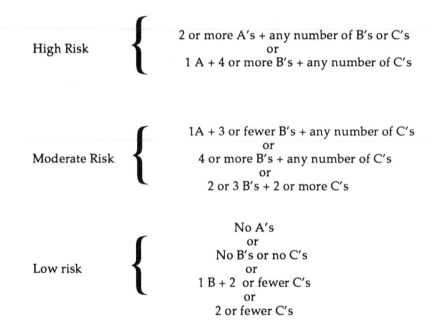

High Risk
$$\left\{\begin{array}{l} \text{2 or more A's + any number of B's or C's} \\ \text{or} \\ \text{1 A + 4 or more B's + any number of C's} \end{array}\right.$$

Moderate Risk
$$\left\{\begin{array}{l} \text{1A + 3 or fewer B's + any number of C's} \\ \text{or} \\ \text{4 or more B's + any number of C's} \\ \text{or} \\ \text{2 or 3 B's + 2 or more C's} \end{array}\right.$$

Low risk
$$\left\{\begin{array}{l} \text{No A's} \\ \text{or} \\ \text{No B's or no C's} \\ \text{or} \\ \text{1 B + 2 or fewer C's} \\ \text{or} \\ \text{2 or fewer C's} \end{array}\right.$$

A person in a high-risk category will not necessarily develop cancer. The high-risk category indicates only that a person in it is more at risk than a person in another category.

Following are a few examples of persons with various risk factors, their relative degrees of risk for developing cancer, and what they should do to modify those risks and thereby reduce their chance of developing cancer (and/or cardiovascular disease). After each risk factor the score is indicated in parentheses.

Consider Linda, a 56-year-old (C) New Jersey (B) housewife (0). She is 5 feet 5 inches tall, weighs 160 pounds (B), eats red meat daily,

SELF-TEST

What is your risk of developing cancer? Take the following Cancer Risk Factor Assessment Test to determine your risk according to your diet, weight, age, lifestyle, and other factors discussed in this chapter. After you assess which factors pose a risk, you can begin to modify them according to my recommendations. Then take the test again to see if your overall risk has been reduced.

The test consists of a list of cancer risk factors, several statements associated with each risk factor, and a specified score associated with each statement. Choose the statement that most nearly applies to you and write its score in the blank. After going through the questionnaire, add up your scores. The zero scores won't count in the total.

Cancer Risk Factor Assessment Test

Risk Factor	Score
1. Nutrition	
• If during 50% or more of your life two or more of the following apply to you:	
(1) one serving of red meat daily (including luncheon meat);	
(2) 6 eggs per week;	
(3) butter, milk, or cheese daily;	
(4) little or no fiber foods (3 gm or less daily);	
(5) frequent barbecued meats;	
(6) below-average intake of vitamins and minerals.	Score A __
• If during 50% or more of your life two or more of the following apply to you:	
(1) red meat 4–5 times per week (including luncheon meat);	
(2) 3–5 eggs per week;	
(3) margarine, low-fat dairy products, some cheese;	
(4) 4–15 gm of fiber daily;	
(5) average intake of vitamins and minerals.	Score B __
• If during 50% or more of your life two or more of the following apply to you:	
(1) red meat and 1 egg once a week or none at all;	
(2) poultry or fish daily or very frequently;	
(3) margarine, skim milk, and skim milk products;	
(4) 15–20 gm of fiber daily;	
(5) above-average intake of vitamins and minerals.	Score 0 __
2. Weight	
Ideal weight for men is 110 lbs plus 5 lbs per inch over 5 ft. For women, ideal weight is 100 lbs plus 5 lbs per inch over 5 ft.	
• If you are 25 lbs overweight.	Score B __
• If your are 10–24 lbs over.	Score C __
• If you are less than 10 lbs over.	Score 0 __
3. Tobacco	
• Smoke 2 packs or more per day for 10 years or more.	Score A __
• Smoke 1–2 packs for 10 years or more, or quit smoking less than a year ago.	Score A __

- Smoke less than 1 pack for 10 years or more or smoke
  pipe or cigar.   Score B ___
- Smoked 1–2 packs per day, a pipe, or a cigar but
  stopped 7–14 years ago.   Score B ___
- Chew or snuff tobacco.   Score B ___
- Inhaled others' smoke for 1 or more hours/day up
  to age 25.   Score B ___
- Inhaled others' smoke for 1 or more hours/day from
  age 25 on.   Score C ___
- Never smoked, quit smoking 15 years ago, or never
  inhaled others' smoke.   Score 0 ___

4. Alcohol

- If you drink 4 oz or more of whiskey daily or
  equivalent alcohol content in other beverages.   Score B ___
- If you drink 2–4 drinks per week.   Score C ___
- If you drink 4 oz or more of whiskey daily or the
  equivalent alcohol content in other beverages *and* also:
  Smoke less than 1 pack per day, or chew
  or snuff tobacco   Score B ___
  Smoke 1–2 packs per day, pipe, or cigar.   Score A ___
  Smoke 2 or more packs per day.   Score A ___
- If you do not drink at all.   Score 0 ___

5. Radiation exposure

- If you received multiple X rays or radiation treatments,
  or if you were exposed to radioactive isotopes used
  for diagnostic workups, or radioactive weapons.   Score C ___
- If you are fair-skinned and sunburn easily.   Score B ___
- If neither applies.   Score 0 ___

6. Occupation

- If you are a radiologist, chemist, painter, uranium or
  hematite miner, luminous-dial painter, or a worker in
  the following industries: leather, foundry, printing,
  rubber, petroleum, furniture or cabinet, textile, nuclear,
  slaughterhouse, or plutonium. (The longer your
  exposure, the greater your risk.)   Score B ___
- Never was one of the above workers.   Score 0 ___

7. Chemicals

- If you have worked directly with one of the following
  chemicals: aniline, acrylonitrile, 4-aminobiphenyl, arsenic,
  asbestos, auramine manufacturing, benzene, benzidine,
  beryllium, cadmium, carbon tetrachloride, chlormethyl
  ether, chloroprene, chromate, isopropyl alcohol (acid
  process), nickel, mustard gas, or vinyl chloride. (The
  longer your exposure, the higher your risk.)   Score A ___
- If you have worked indirectly with one of the above
  chemicals.   Score C ___
- Never worked with one of the above.   Score 0 ___

8. Sexual-social history

- If you are a female who started having sexual intercourse before age 16 and has had many male partners,
  particularly uncircumcised.   Score C ___

- If you are a sexually active male homosexual who has had many male partners and/or uses amyl nitrite.   Score C ___
- If neither applies.   Score 0 ___

9. Immunity, drugs, and hormones
- If your physician said you have a severe deficiency in your immune system, or you have received an organ transplant.   Score A ___
- If you've taken 1 or more of the following for a prolonged period of time: chlorambucil, cyclophosphamide, melphalan, or high-dose steroids (anticancer drugs).   Score A ___
- If you have taken one or more of the following for a prolonged period of time: phenacetin, thiotepa, diethylstilbestrol (DES), birth control pills (conjugated estrogens), or 17 methyl-substituted androgens.   Score B ___
- If you had early onset of menses or late onset of menopause, or never had menses at all.   Score B ___
- If you were first pregnant late in life or never at all, or had fibrocystic breast disease.   Score C ___
- If none of the above apply.   Score 0 ___

10. Geography
- Based on Figure 1.1 in Chapter 1, if during most of your life you lived in one of the states with the most cancer deaths.   Score B ___
- If during most of your life you lived in a state that has a moderate number of cancer deaths.   Score C ___
- If during most of your life you lived in a state with the least number of cancer deaths.   Score 0 ___

11. Age
- If your age is 70 or more.   Score B ___
- If your age is 55 to 69.   Score C ___
- If your age is 55 or under.   Score 0 ___

12. Personal history
- If you had cancer.   Score B ___
- If you never had cancer.   Score 0 ___

13. Family history
- If one or more close family members had cancer.   Score B ___
- No family history of cancer.   Score 0 ___

14. Exercise
- If you exercise very little or not at all.   Score C ___
- If you exercise 3 or more times a week and get your heart rate 50% higher than normal for at least 20 min.   Score 0 ___

15. Stress
- If you are frustrated waiting in line, easily angered, and unable to control stress.   Score C ___
- If you are comfortable when waiting, easygoing, and able to control stress.   Score 0 ___

TOTAL SCORE: ___ A's; ___ B's; and ___ C's.

To evaluate your score, see page 26 under "Where Do You Stand?"

eats several eggs per week, drinks milk daily, consumes very little fiber-containing foods, and does not eat a balanced diet (A). She also smokes two packs of cigarettes a day, which has done for over fifteen years (A). Linda drinks socially (0) and has never had cancer (0), but her mother had breast cancer (B). She started having sexual intercourse at age 20 (0), first got pregnant at age 24 (0), has a history of fibrocystic breast disease (C), never had any radiation (0), and is relatively easygoing (0).

Linda's total score is 2 A's, 3 B's, and 2 C's. She is in the high-risk group. What can she do to modify her risk factors? She directly controls the most serious ones. I would advise her to terminate cigarette smoking abruptly and completely. Then I would suggest that she permanently modify her diet in order to reduce two other serious risk factors: her high-animal-fat, high-cholesterol, low-fiber diet, and her overweight problem. This would serve also to counter any weight gain that may occur when she stops smoking. Linda has no control over her age, the state in which she has lived, or her history of fibrocystic breast disease; but these are minor risk factors. By modifying the risk factors that she directly controls, over the course of time she will lessen her overall risk category and reduce her risk of developing cancer or cardiovascular disease.

The second example is Dave, a 24-year-old sexually active male homosexual who has many male partners and uses a drug called amyl nitrite (C). He smoked two packs of cigarettes a day for eleven years but quit one year ago (A). Up until a few months ago, he ate red meat daily, ate cheese daily, ate very few fiber-containing foods, and took no vitamins (A). His weight is normal (0), and he has never had cancer (0) nor have any of his family members (0). Until Dave was 21 years old he lived in Alaska (0), but he has since lived in New York City.

Dave's total score is 2 A's, zero B's and 1 C. He is in the high-risk group, but by continuing not to smoke and by modifying his diet, he can dramatically lessen his overall risk.

Next is Nancy, a 27-year-old woman who smoked two packs of cigarettes a day until she quit eight years ago (B). She eats a well-balanced diet consisting of red meat five times a week, low-fat dairy products, and an average intake of fiber (B), and she is 20 pounds overweight (C). As a lifelong resident of Vermont (C), Nancy has been working in the furniture industry for the past seven years (B). She is taking birth control pills (B) and has been doing so for the past ten years. She is fair-skinned, sunburns easily, and enjoys sunbathing and using a suntanning booth year-round (B).

On the surface of things it looks as though Nancy's overall risk is not so bad, but when you examine the whole picture, you find she is in the moderate-risk category. Her total score is 5 B's and 2 C's. However, she is on the right track. She should do the following to modify her risk factors and thereby reduce her overall risk: continue not to smoke, lose 20 pounds, modify her nutritional status, seek another means of birth control, use sun screens to sunbathe, and avoid suntanning booths.

The last example is Bob, a 50-year-old (0) male chemist (B) who is 25 pounds overweight (B) and a meat-and-potatoes man all the way (A). He has smoked two packs of cigarettes a day for the past thirty years (A), drinks 4 ounces of whiskey every day (A), has lived in Illinois most of his life (B), and is easily angered (C). His father died of lung cancer (B).

You know that Bob is in the high-risk category: 3 A's, 4 B's, and 1 C. As you can see, he does have risk factors that he can directly control. He should do the following: stop smoking, drastically modify his diet and lose weight, consume alcohol in moderation, and learn how to relax. All these modifications will greatly reduce his overall risk.

What can *you* do to reduce *your* risk for cancer? You have now identified the problem areas that need modification. Simple preventive measures can be taken to help you reduce your chances of developing cancer or cardiovascular disease. This book will show you how you can make relatively minor adjustments in your lifestyle to lessen your risk. Maintaining a good weight, eating a healthful diet (one that is low in animal fat, low in cholesterol, and high in fiber), choosing not to smoke or drink alcoholic beverages, avoiding or limiting exposure to the sun—all of these are just a few of the ways you can protect yourself from cancer. You must strive to maintain good health. Good health is no accident.

PART TWO

The Body's Defenses

3
The Backbone of Nutrition
Proteins, Carbohydrates, and Lipids

Nutrition is a complex subject, confusing to the public and to some physicians as well. Since roughly half of all cancers are related to nutritional factors, it is important to understand the role that diet plays in the development of cancer.

Food may contain carcinogens, chemicals that can cause cancer, either as natural components of the food or in the form of additives. Carcinogens may be inhaled or may be found in our drinking water. Carcinogens may be present in food that is spoiled by bacteria, fungi, or chemicals, food that is improperly washed, or food contaminated with industrial pollutants. Processing or cooking may activate existing carcinogens in foods. Food products may contain nitrite preservatives, which can form an extremely potent carcinogen, nitrosamine. Intestinal bacteria may be altered by diets high in animal fat and cholesterol, and these altered types of bacteria may activate or produce carcinogens from the ingested food or bile acids. If you have insufficient protein, carbohydrates, vitamins, or minerals in your diet, you will be particularly susceptible to the effects of carcinogens because your immune system will be impaired. Obesity is a risk factor for many cancers and is associated with several women's cancers. People who develop heart disease have many of these same dietary risk factors in common. Nutritional deficiencies can cause damage to genetic material and then repair it abnormally, which may lead to the development of cancer. Furthermore, food, drugs, and hormones (especially estrogens) that we ingest for various reasons may alter body tissues in such a way as to predispose the tissue to cancer development. If all these nutritional risk factors can be identified, then preventive measures can be taken to avoid, eliminate, or at least reduce them. But first, let's review the three main components that make up the backbone of nutrition.

PROTEINS

Proteins are extremely important. Every cell in the body is partly composed of proteins. Each cell is constantly exposed to wear and tear and eventually dies, only to be replaced by another cell. Proteins contribute about 10 to 15 percent of our total energy needs. Enzymes, which are proteins, help most of the body's chemical reactions to proceed quickly. Some very important hormones that are made in the body are proteins as well. In addition, the transport system of the blood is composed of proteins that act as vehicles to carry necessary substances to all parts of the body. Therefore, a constant supply of proteins is required so that the body can build tissues and function properly. Our only source of proteins is the food we eat. Proteins are complex structures consisting of amino acids, some of which cannot be made by the body at all and therefore must be supplied exclusively by the diet. (These include valine, leucine, isoleucine, threonine, lysine, phenyl alanine, tryptophan, methionine, and histidine.) When proteins are eaten, they are broken down into amino acids in the stomach by digesting enzymes and then used by the body to build whatever proteins are needed.

Children and adolescents tend to need more protein than adults, but the amount required varies from one individual to another. A person suffering from burns, bedsores, or other open wounds loses a great deal of protein from these sites. This loss has a deleterious effect because protein is needed to heal wounds in addition to its other functions. An active athlete needs slightly more protein per day than a normally active person because he loses protein through his sweat glands.[1] A pregnant woman also requires more protein than a non-pregnant woman.

A healthy man weighing 140 pounds requires about 28 grams of protein per day, equivalent to about 100 to 115 calories. The source of protein does not have to be animal meat, a fact that is aptly demonstrated by pure vegetarians who are active and have normal life spans. Seventh-Day Adventists, a religious group composed of many pure vegetarians, have a very low incidence of cancer and heart disease compared with nonvegetarians.

Some sources of proteins are much better than others. Table 3.1 lists food sources and the percentage of usable energy derived from them.[2] Foods high in fiber, like rice, provide less energy; they are mostly bulk. Fish, on the other hand, has a higher percentage of usable energy.

Protein Deficiency. Kwashiorkor, an example of extreme protein deficiency that occurs in 1- to 3-year-old children, was first described by C. Williams in West Africa in 1933. The patient is weak, is emotionally upset, and has no appetite; growth is retarded; and there is considerable swelling all over the body. Victims also frequently have vitamin deficiencies and anemia. Another syndrome, called nutritional marasmus, results from a very low intake of all nutrients, including protein. This disorder commonly affects infants during their first year of life and is comparable to starvation in adults.

Table 3.1 Energy From Protein Food Sources	
Food Source	**% Usable Energy**
Sweet potatoes	4
Rice	8
Wheat flour	13
Peanuts	19
Cow's milk (3.5% fat)	22
Beans and peas	26
Beef	38
Cow's milk (skimmed)	40
Soybeans	45
Fish	62

CARBOHYDRATES

Carbohydrates provide most of the energy in almost all human diets. They account for 90 percent of poor people's energy needs (poor people consume more junk foods, which have a great deal of simple carbohydrates) and 40 percent of affluent people's energy needs. Carbohydrates have an advantage over fats in that they contain less than half the number of calories per ounce. Food carbohydrates consist of complex polysaccharides, starch, glycogen, sucrose, and lactose. Green plants use sunlight to make carbohydrates from carbon dioxide and water. Man has always been able to seek out and grow seeds, fruits, and roots that have concentrated supplies of carbohydrates. Unlike ruminants such as cows, which cannot conserve vegetable foods (cows eat what is available; humans can grow and then store vegetables), humans have been successful in selecting and growing carbohydrate foodstuffs like cereal grain. Complex carbohydrates such as beans, peas, nuts, fruits, vegetables, and whole-grain breads and cereals not only provide calories and essential nutrients but also increase dietary fiber. Dietary fiber, such as lettuce, if eaten daily, can absorb some gastrointestinal carcinogens, increase stool weight, and induce bowel movements daily—all of which decrease the risk of colon cancer. There are some saccharides in certain plants that may be eaten but cannot be digested or absorbed. Our intestinal bacteria can feed on these and produce great amounts of gas as a by-product.

Starch, a complex polysaccharide, is made up of glucose. When ingested, it is broken down into disaccharide and other components that are then further broken down into single glucose units by special enzymes. Cellulose is another polysaccharide found in plants that cannot be digested; it provides most of the roughage in human diets.

Eighty percent of the carbohydrate absorbed from the intestine is in the form of the simple sugar glucose. The main role of glucose is to provide energy for immediate needs. The unused excess glucose is taken to the liver and a small amount is resynthesized into glycogen. Glycogen accumulates in all major muscle bundles and is used for its energy. During exertion, glycogen is broken down in the muscle for energy use, and lactic acids builds up as a waste product. This acid causes the pain perceived in muscles during intensive exercise. Most unused glucose is converted into fat and stored in fat cells called adipose tissue. The larger the fat cell, the quicker the conversion of glucose into fat.[3] In people who are obese, only the size of the fat cells is increased, not the number. The number of fat cells in a person is determined by about age 2 and from then on remains constant. Hence it is important to keep a child 2 years old or under from becoming obese.

When a person ingests carbohydrates, the hormone insulin is released from the pancreas to help utilize the glucose molecules. Obviously, the more times you eat carbohydrates in day, the more often the pancreas has to work. In some people, insulin is released later than normal and/or over a prolonged time. Insulin in these situations results in a low blood sugar after even a moderate ingestion of carbohydrate.

Diabetes mellitus is a constellation of signs and symptoms that are the result of high blood sugar due to defective insulin release from the pancreas. There is evidence to implicate a number of causes of diabetes: hereditary factors, obesity, chronic alcoholism (which causes pancreatic disease), and a virus. Contrary to a popular old wives' tale, too much sugar in the diet probably does not cause diabetes mellitus.

Carbohydrates available to us in processed foods in the United States are generally depleted of vitamins, minerals, and fiber. (Processing food, per se, can deplete it of vitamins, minerals, and fiber.) You can, however, supplement the diet with vitamins and minerals.

LIPIDS

The word "lipid" is the biochemical term used to denote what is commonly called fat. Lipids are very important chemical substances; they include cholesterol, triglycerides, fatty acids, phospholipids, and sterols. Lipids provide a concentrated source of energy, delay the emptying of the stomach, stimulate the gallbladder to empty its contents, and provide the materials for the absorption of fat-soluble vitamins and other dietary substances. Lipids are by far the most important form of storage fuel we have, and they also act as insulation for the body.

Other functions and processes that lipids participate in are much more complex than those of either proteins or carbohydrates. Lipids provide the structure of the brain and all nerve tissue, and they are the major components of all cell membranes and the membranes of structures inside cells. As fatty acids and cholesterol esters they store energy in adipose tissue. When energy is needed, free fatty acids are released by the action of stress or epinephrine (adrenaline).

The body can make lipids from carbohydrates and amino acids if enough fats are not supplied from the diet. This is usually not the case in the American diet, though.

Adipose tissue is composed of 60 to 90 percent triglycerides. Triglycerides are one major group in the lipid family. The normal serum (blood) level of triglycerides ranges from 10 to 150 mg/ml. Triglycerides and cholesterol, another lipid, are of major clinical significance in the development of heart and vascular disease. Lipoproteins (proteins coupled to lipids) are important in relation to heart disease, also. The following terms are frequently used when discussing the causes of heart disease, colon cancer, and breast cancer: chylomicrons, very low and low-density lipoproteins, and high-density lipoproteins. *Chylomicrons* are large particles in which cholesterol and other lipids in the diet are transported from the intestine into the blood. *Very low density lipoproteins* (VLDLs) are proteins in the blood that transport triglycerides made in the body. VLDLs are broken down into *low-density lipoproteins* (LDLs), which are thought to cause atherosclerosis. *High-density lipoproteins* (HDLs) contain cholesterol and aid in the chemical reaction that modifies cholesterol. HDL is the most important of these proteins for our discussion because it correlates fairly well with heart disease.

For an analogy of HDL's importance and function, consider that each HDL is a street bus, each blood vessel a street, and each cholesterol molecule a person. Now consider that there is only one bus (one HDL) to pick up one hundred people (one hundred cholesterols) along the street. Well, obviously, not all the people can be transported by the bus, and many people have to stay in the street. In this situation, with only one HDL, the cholesterol molecules that were not picked up get embedded in the blood vessel and start to cause narrowing and hardening of the artery—atherosclerosis is the medical term. If there are two buses (two HDLs), then more people (cholesterol) can be transported and fewer are left behind to stay in the street (get embedded in the artery). If four buses are available, all the people can be transported and none are left behind (all the cholesterol is transported and none embed in the arteries). Cholesterol is crucial to the development and progression of atherosclerosis. The level of HDL is important only if the cholesterol level is high. With very high cholesterol (people), you would want to try to raise the HDL level (buses). The HDL protein can be raised by vigorous exercise, by administering small amounts of alcohol, and by decreasing substantially the total intake of cholesterol in your diet.

Cholesterol exists in all animal cells. Everyone requires cholesterol in correct amounts for good health, but too much can lead to the development of heart and blood vessel disease. It is a precursor substance needed for the manufacture of sex hormones and some adrenal hormones that regulate many phases of salt, sugar, protein, and fat metabolism in the body. Part of the cholesterol in your body comes from food of animal origin, and part is made in your body. Cholesterol content is very high in many foods, including eggs, milk products, and organ meats such as liver. It is moderately high in shellfish.

The normal cholesterol range is 150 to 200 mg/ml. One third of the U.S. male population 25 years old and older has serum cholesterols over 250 mg/ml and is at risk for coronary heart disease and vascular disease. Table 23.1 in Chapter 23 provides a comprehensive list of foods and their cholesterol contents. There is no cholesterol in foods of plant origin—fruits, vegetables, grains, cereals, and nuts.

Fatty acids are part of the lipid family also. There are three types.

First there are the saturated fatty acids, which consist predominantly of saturated fats hardened at room temperatures. Saturated fats tend to raise the blood cholesterol level and should be restricted or totally eliminated from your diet. Most Americans eat foods that are high in saturated fats and high in cholesterol, and therefore they tend to have high cholesterol levels. People who eat high-cholesterol, high-saturated-fat foods have a greater risk of having heart attacks than people who eat low-fat, low-cholesterol diets. Eating extra cholesterol and saturated fat increases blood cholesterol levels in most people, but there are wide variations among individuals due to inherited tendencies and the way in which the person uses cholesterol. It appears that some people can eat diets high in saturated fats and cholesterol and still maintain normal blood levels of cholesterol, while other people cannot. Unfortunately, some people have high blood cholesterol levels even though they eat low-fat, low-cholesterol foods.

Saturated animal fats are found in beef, lamb, pork, and ham; in butter, cream, and whole milk; and in cheeses made from cream and whole milk. Saturated vegetable fats are found in many hydrogenated and solid shortenings; and in coconut oil, cocoa butter, and palm oil (used in commercially prepared cookies, pie fillings, and nondairy milk and cream substitutes).

The other two groups of fatty acids are the monounsaturated fats, with a single unsaturated site, and the polyunsaturated fats, which have two or more unsaturated sites in the fat chain. An unsaturated site does not have hydrogen in it; if enough hydrogen were added, the fat would then become saturated or hydrogenated. Fats with a high proportion of unsaturated fat sites, such as cod liver oil, olive oil, and whale oil, are usually liquid at room temperatures. There is only one essential fatty acid: arachidonic acid. This can easily be made in the body from linoleic acid, which is widespread in nature. In reality, a deficiency of fatty acids is very rare in humans.

Polyunsaturated fats are liquid oils of vegetable origin. The following oils are high in polyunsaturated fats: corn, cottonseed, safflower, sesame seed, soybean, and sunflower seed. These lower the blood cholesterol level by eliminating newly formed excess cholesterol. Peanut oil and olive oil are vegetable oils and are low in polyunsaturated fats. Polyunsaturated fats can be attacked chemically by free radicals because they have empty or "unsaturated" chemical bonds that can "accept" the extra electron of the free radical. These free radicals can damage cells and lead to the development of cancer. There are, however, agents that neutralize free radicals—beta-carotene, vitamin E, vitamin C, and selenium, for example—that we can take daily to aid in our defense. (See Chapter 5 for an in-depth discussion of free radicals.)

All fats, then, whether saturated or unsaturated, should be severely restricted or eliminated to reduce your risk of developing cancer as well as heart disease. The next chapter will discuss how certain nutrients can help build a strong immune system and protect against cancer and other illnesses.

4
Nutrition, Immunity, and Cancer

Poor populations around the world that suffer from malnutrition are more susceptible to infection than those who receive adequate nutrition. Investigators studying the relationship between the immune system and nutrition have found that nutrition affects immunity[1,2] and also affects the development of cancer[3,4] either directly or indirectly via the immune system.

The immune system is a complex interaction of blood cells, proteins, and processes that protects you from infections, foreign substances, and cancer cells that spontaneously develop in the body.

In 1989, research at the Shriner's Burn Institute in Cincinnati showed that administration of a special liquid diet to severely burned patients begun the day they were burned reduced the risk of infection by 50 percent. The special diet consisted of protein, vitamins including A and E, minerals, and iron, as well as omega-3 fatty acids.

White blood cells and antibodies are two major armies of the immune system. These armies arise separately but are related and dependent upon each other for their development and maturity. The lymphocyte, a specific type of white blood cell, is the main cell involved in cellular immunity. Lymphocytes make up only a small portion of the blood, comprising only about 15 to 20 percent of all white cells. The lymphocyte population is divided into two large groups, based on particular markings on the outer surface membrane of the cell.

T lymphocytes, or T cells, are one group of lymphocytes. They are derived from or are under the influence of the *thymus*, which is an organ in the neck and front part of the chest that is functionally active in early childhood. T cells are responsible for your defense against cancer, fungi, certain bacteria (intracellular), some viruses, transplant rejections, and delayed skin reactions (tuberculosis skin test). T cells are further divided into several subpopulations: helper T cells and suppressor T cells, those which either help or hinder normal immune cellular function.

Proteins called antibodies or immunoglobulins are produced by the other major group of lymphocytes, the B lymphocytes, or B cells. B cells may have their origin in the *bone* marrow, from which they derive their designation. Antibodies are formed by the B cell in response to a foreign substance introduced into the body. For example, when a person is given a vaccine against polio, antibodies to this foreign substance are made by the B cells. If the polio virus enters the body in an infectious state after a person has been vaccinated, the previously formed antibody, which is circulating in the blood, will attach to this foreign intruder and dispose of it with the help of

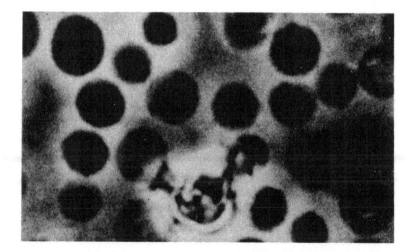

Figure 4.1   White blood cell (center) killing several cancerlike cells. Notice that the white blood cell extends feetlike processes which aid in killing the targets.

defending white blood cells or other proteins called complement proteins or a combination of both. The same process of antibody production is initiated by some cancer cells. Killing white blood cells or complement proteins, when activated by an antibody, destroy a foreign-appearing cell by making holes in the foreign cell's membrane, thereby allowing water to rush in and explode the cell. In 1980, I showed how a white blood cell kills a foreign cancerlike cell. Figure 4.1 shows a white blood cell (center) killing several cancerlike cells. Notice that the white blood cell extends feetlike processes that aid in killing the targets.[5]

Phagocytes are another group of white blood cells that reside in the blood and body tissues and are part of your defenses against foreign invaders. These also act as policemen to recognize and dispose of abnormal cancer cells and other foreign substances. Phagocytes can perform this task alone or can recruit antibodies and complement proteins to aid in the disposal.

IMMUNOLOGY AND CANCER

The immune system is extremely intricate and finely tuned. If any one aspect of the system malfunctions because of poor nutrition, or if it is destroyed, you may become susceptible to cancer and foreign microbial invaders. The white blood cell army and the antibody army must be functioning perfectly to destroy any cancer cell or foreign invader and prevent either one from gaining a foothold in your body.

The major histocompatibility complex is part of your genetic make-up and is another component of the immune system, acting as a commander of the white blood cell and antibody armies. This complex allows the immune system to recognize the parts of your body so that it does not destroy them as it would destroy foreign substances. At the same time, it can recognize a substance or tissue (histo-) as not belonging to its body and subsequently take the necessary steps to destroy it. The histocompatibility complex is responsible for rejection of transplanted organs such as kidneys and hearts. If the histocompatibility complex is not working properly, a virus capable of converting normal cells to cancer cells may enter the body without being attacked because the immune system did not recognize it as foreign. The virus, if not destroyed, will convert normal cells to cancer cells in a process called transformation, and the cancer will multiply and eventually kill the person.

In 1970, F.M. Burnet introduced the concept of immunosurveillance, which states that killer cells of the immune system watch, or keep a surveillance on, all cells in the body and immediately destroy any cells that start to have a malignant or cancerous potential.[6] There is a lot of evidence to support this concept. The most clear-cut and convincing evidence comes from observations of patients with suppressed immune systems caused by drugs or radiation or an inherited disorder. Patients with inherited immunodeficiencies, whose immune systems do not function normally from birth, or patients whose immune systems acquire a malfunction later in life have one hundred times more deaths due to cancer than the expected cancer death rate in the normal population.[7,8] Kidney transplant patients, who receive drugs to suppress the immune system's ability to reject the new kidney, also have a higher rate of cancer than would be expected.[9,10] The cancers most frequently seen in these cases are the lymphomas and epithelial cancers; however, all other types of cancers have been reported as well.

The immune system is relatively immature in infancy, and then runs down and does not function well in old age. These two times of life have the highest incidence of lymphocytic leukemia. Other immune-deficiency states that can lead to cancer are seen with malaria, acute viral infections, and malnutrition.

NUTRITION AND THE IMMUNE SYSTEM

Nutritional deficiencies decrease a person's capacity to resist infection and its consequences and decrease the capability of the immune system.[11] In old age, there is a decrease in skin hypersensitivity reactions,[12-14] a decreased number of T cells,[15,16] and impairment of some phagocytic functions. Surveys of the population have discovered nutritional deficiencies in senior citizens that also lead to impairment of the immune system.[17] It is possible that the gradual impairment of the immune system associated with aging may, in fact, be due to one or more nutrient deficiencies. Poor nutrition adversely affects all components of the immune system, including T cell function, other cellular-related killing, the ability of B cells to make antibodies, the functioning of the complement proteins, and phagocytic function. When several of these functions or processes are impaired, the ability of the entire immune system to keep a watchful eye for cancer cells, abnormal cells, or foreign substances and to dispose of them is also markedly impaired.

Protein deficiency affects all the organs in the body. The number of digestive enzymes produced is reduced, and absorption of nutrients is impaired. With severe chronic protein deficiency the heart muscle atrophies. The immune system is also severely affected. In diets that are only moderately deficient in protein, phagocytes and T cells are reduced in number,[18] and their ability to kill cancer and other abnormal cells is impaired.[19] The amount of antibody is slightly reduced as is the speed with which it attaches to an "enemy."[20] The complement proteins also have impaired function in this state. Hence, a person who is not consuming the proper amount of protein will have a malfunctioning immune system that will not be able to deal effectively with cancer cells or infection.

The immune system is affected by both hypoglycemia (low blood sugar) and hyperglycemia, as in diabetes mellitus. C.J. Van Oss has found that phagocytic function in humans is impaired if the blood sugar level is very low.[21] Much more research has been done concerning the function of the immune system in diabetes. The number of T and B cells is normal in diabetes, but their functions are impaired: phagocytic function as well as cellular killing.[22,23] The degree of impairment correlates very well with the fasting blood sugar level and then improves when the sugar level becomes normal.

Lipids have a significant effect on the functioning of the immune system. Cholesterol oleate and ethyl palmitate inhibit antibody production, probably because these lipids do not allow the immune system to recognize the foreign substance.[24] Researchers E.A. Santiago-Delpin and J. Szepsenwol wanted to know what effects lipids had on T lymphocytes.[25] They first grafted pieces of skin from one mouse to another of dissimilar genetic make-up and found that the grafted skin was rejected in a very short time. They then fed the recipient mouse a high-fat diet and found that it accepted the graft for a very prolonged time, indicating that the high-fat diet impaired the ability of the animal to reject the foreign graft. The T cell is involved in this kind of rejection as well as in cancer cell rejection, and its ability to function is impaired if you eat a high-fat diet. In other experiments, phagocytosis was studied. Another saturated fat, methyl palmitate, was found to markedly impair phagocytosis for at least seventy-two hours after a single injection.[26] There is great controversy and discrepancy among experiments dealing with polyunsaturated fats and their effect on the immune system. Some investigators report that a diet low in polyunsaturated fats enhances the immune system,[27] and some show no such enhancement.[28] In all these studies, it must be kept in mind that the significance of the results is unclear because large amounts of lipids were used. It has not been determined whether physiological doses of the same lipids have similar effects on the immune system as do these large amounts of lipids.

The Epstein-Barr virus may manifest itself as entirely different diseases in different people as a result of varying degrees of impairment of the immune system. The extent to which the immune system is weakened or damaged is partly determined by the nutritional status of the individual prior to infection. Epstein-Barr virus is implicated in a relatively benign disease, infectious mononucleosis; a slow-growing cancer, nasopharyngeal cancer; and a rapidly growing, usually fatal cancer, Burkitt's lymphoma; as well as other diseases. Why does one person's immune system permit infectious mononucleosis to develop and another person's immune system permit a fatal cancer to develop? The answer is very complex and not well defined at all, but nutritional status is a factor. Your *nutritional status* is determined by how well your diet and supplementation program is meeting your nutritional needs. The better your nutritional status, the better your immune system, and the better off you will be.

5

Free Radicals

Free radicals are made in our bodies all the time and, if not destroyed, can lead to the development of cancer. By definition, free radicals are chemical substances that contain an odd number of electrons. Every atom has a nucleus and a certain number of electrons that orbit around the nucleus. This setup is very much like our solar system, with the sun in the middle and all the planets orbiting around the sun. The nucleus has a positive charge, and the electrons have a negative charge. The negative charges of electrons balance out the positive charge of the nucleus to give an overall charge of zero. Hence, the energy of a single atom is very stable at zero.

When high energy in any form (light, radiation, smog, tobacco, alcohol, polyunsaturated fats, etc.) hits an atom, an electron is kicked out of orbit. All of the energy that forced the electron out of orbit is transferred directly to the electron, making it highly energetic and unstable. Because it is so unstable, this electron quickly seeks *another* atom to reside in. This excited high-energy electron transfers very high energy to the new atom, which then becomes extremely unstable because of the newly acquired high energy. (An analogy to this state is a nine-month-old child who has a great deal of energy but is extremely unstable if left unattended.) This excited high-energy atom with its extra electron is called a free radical. (See Figure 5.1.)

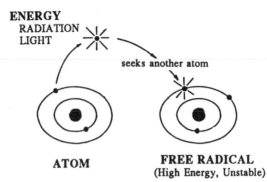

Figure 5.1   Free radical formation. When high energy from any source hits an atom, it knocks an electron out of orbit. This high-energy electron goes into another atom, making it extremely unstable.

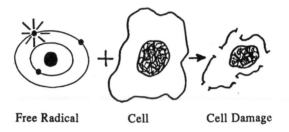

Figure 5.2   Cell damage by free radicals. Free radicals can destroy the layer of fat in the cell membrane.

A free radical is unstable and must get rid of all the extra energy for the atom to become stable once again; hence the radical transfers its energy to nearby substances. (All these reactions take place within a fraction of a second.) When free radicals are made in the body, the high energy is transferred to body tissues, particularly to the polyunsaturated fats found in the cell membranes. The more unsaturated fats you eat, the more of them will be absorbed by the cell membranes and the higher the risk will be for membrane disruption by free radicals. (See Figure 5.2.) If not counteracted, this process can lead to the development of cancer of the tissue affected by the radical.

FORMATION OF RADICALS

Oxygen

There are many processes in the body that initiate destructive radical reactions. Oxygen is crucial to us because it is required for all animal life. In certain instances, however, oxygen can be activated or split with high energy into very potent damaging radicals (superoxide) or a high-energy, unstable non-radical called singlet oxygen. Singlet oxygen has extremely high energy and is very unstable, and thus is very destructive to normal body tissues and cells.

Oxygen radicals can be both beneficial and harmful to us at different times under different circumstances. It is a beneficial reaction when a phagocyte kills an invading bacteria.[1] This destruction is accomplished by oxygen radicals, which are made by the phagocyte when a foreign substance like a bacterium is ingested and taken inside the phagocyte. On the other hand, oxygen radicals can produce hydroperoxides, which are chemicals that form more radicals and damage cell membranes, thereby altering the cell's function.[2] This can lead to the development of cancer. Singlet oxygen, a very-high-energy form of oxygen, has a shorter life than an oxygen radical but damages cells and tissues much more quickly. Not only does singlet oxygen have the potential of causing cancer by itself but it also activates carcinogens.

Lipids

Another group of substances that encourage the formation of destructive free radicals is the polyunsaturated fatty acids. As you recall, saturated fats are to be avoided, and polyunsaturated fats are to be consumed only moderately. The reason for recommending minimal intake of polyunsaturated fats is that when oxygen or enzymes react with polyunsaturated fats to release their energy, a free radical is made. This free radical reacts with another polyunsaturated fat to produce a lot of hydroperoxide.[3,4] The more unsaturated the fat is, the more hydroperoxides are made. And hydroperoxides produce more radicals, damage cell membranes, and can lead to the development of cancer.

Metals

Certain metal accumulations in the body can also initiate free radical formation by activating oxygen. Iron is one example of a metal that can form extremely potent hydroxyl radicals if found in excessive amounts in the body.

Radiation

Ionizing radiation produces radicals and electrons that react to yield many different kinds of free radicals. Background radiation in the atmosphere at sea level probably does not produce free radicals in the body, however.[5] Radicals produced in the body and by pollutants are much more important than those caused by radiation unless, of course, a person is receiving large doses of radiation for the treatment of a disease. At high levels of radiation, hydroperoxides are produced in addition to all the other free radicals.[6]

Light From the Sun—Photolysis

All life on earth requires the sun's energy. But sunlight also has a harmful effect on our skin. Excessive sunlight can cause several types of skin cancer. Since millions of people enjoy getting a dark suntan, it is important to review this topic. We are exposed to an increasing number of chemicals in our foods and in the environment that make. our skin more sensitive to the damaging effects of sunlight. Ultraviolet light inhibits DNA (genetic material) synthesis and protein synthesis, interrupts normal cell replication, and causes skin cancer. Free radical formation by ultraviolet light may be involved in producing all these effects on the skin's cells. Ultraviolet light has been shown to produce free radicals in skin cells in the test tube,[7] and free radicals are probably responsible for the damaging effects on the skin, including skin cancer. These light rays represent only 0.1 percent of the total energy that comes to us from the sun. Chronic sun exposure in Caucasians directly damages the uppermost skin cells and results in wrinkling, the formation of tiny networks of blood vessels, and the appearance of discrete small raised bumps on the skin called actinic keratosis (which are precancerous).

Ultraviolet light affects the immune system in several ways. A mild sunburn decreases the function of circulating lymphocytes for as long as twenty-four hours. In animals ultraviolet light suppresses the entire immune system so much that skin tumors grow uninhibited.

A fad that has swept the country in past years is suntanning booths that offer "year-round" suntans at a minimum charge. The ultraviolet light used in many of these booths is of higher energy (wavelengths of 270 to 350) than the ultraviolet light that we receive when we sunbathe naturally. This higher-energy ultraviolet light is worse for the skin than the light ordinarily received from the sun.

Skin cancers in Caucasians occur most often in those who work out-of-doors and in those who live in areas like the tropics which have intensive sunlight most of the year. Skin cancers are very rare in black people and in other people with deeply pigmented skin. Their dark skin protects them against ultraviolet-light damage. The Scottish and Irish, who are the lightest-complexioned peoples, have the highest incidence of skin cancer if they live in areas of the world with high ultraviolet-light exposure. Skin cancers usually arise in areas of the body that are exposed to the sun, except in blacks, in whom skin cancers occur anywhere on the body when they do occur.

Skin cancer is the most common of all human cancers. There are three main types: basal cell cancer, squamous cell cancer, and melanoma. Squamous cell cancer is directly caused by sun exposure, and about 66 percent of all basal cell skin cancers occur in areas of the body exposed to sunlight. The influence of sunlight on forming melanoma, a very deadly cancer, is not conclusively established, but a number of surveys do suggest that sunlight does cause the development of some melanomas.

F. Urbach and others point out that skin cancers develop with three primary factors.[8] The total sunlight exposure in a lifetime is an important factor for developing skin cancer. The more time the body is exposed to sunlight, the higher is the incidence of cancer. (People living in Texas and Australia have more skin cancers than people living in North Dakota and Germany.) It has also been found that the total time of exposure at one sitting and the frequency of these sittings (especially at wavelengths 290-320, as in many suntanning booths) increase the risk of developing skin cancer. And finally, there are certain inherited diseases, such as xeroderma pigmentosum, that predispose to developing skin cancer. In addition, people without any apparent diseases are prone to developing skin cancers if they have light eyes and light hair color, a fair complexion, and a poor ability to tan, and get sunburned easily with a repeated history of sunburning.

As was pointed out before, certain chemicals (tars, petroleum products, etc.) can also cause skin cancer. What triggers this is not clear, but free radicals may be involved.

What defenses do we have against the harmful and cancer-producing effects of sunlight? There are many common-sense preventive measures that we can take to lessen our risk for skin cancer. First of all, before sunbathing, use one of the several commercially available sunscreens on areas of your body that will be exposed. Don't stay out in the sun for a prolonged period of time at one sitting. If you work out-of-doors, wear protective clothing to minimize the chronic prolonged exposure to sunlight. Don't seek a suntan from a suntanning booth, because the rays it usually emits are more damaging on the whole.

Eat carrots! Carrots contain a chemical substance called carotene. Carotene is one of the most efficient scavengers of singlet high-energy oxygen. When you eat carotene, it also localizes to the skin cells and partially protects them from light damage. Eating carrots or ingesting carotene in quantities large enough to color the skin slightly orange is well tolerated by the body. Vitamin E similarly works to stop high-energy oxygen (singlet oxygen) damage.

Smog

It has been shown by R.E. Zelac et al. that the amount of ozone in smoggy air causes more tissue damage than does background radiation.[9] Ozone reacts with almost every type of molecule in the body to form free radicals, which then damage cells. Ozone in normal amounts in the air can even form radicals with polyunsaturated fatty acids.[10] One other component of smog, peroxyacetyl nitrate, can break down and produce singlet oxygen. Again, free radical scavengers or antioxidants will neutralize and inhibit ozone-induced radicals. These include vitamin E, vitamin C, selenium, and carotene.

Smog also contains nitrogen dioxides, which, like ozone, can form free radicals but to a lesser extent. These nitrogen oxides react with unsaturated fats of human cell membranes to form radicals that can damage the membranes. Antioxidants or radical scavengers like vitamin E can protect the membrane against radicals.

The components of smog, tobacco smoke, and other air pollutants can form radicals, especially in the lungs. Lung cancer is the leading cause of cancer deaths and is most common in the heavily industrialized areas of the country.

Alcohol and Carbon Tetrachloride

It is now known that excess alcohol and *certain* chloride-containing compounds (vinyl chloride, chloroprene, carbon tetrachloride) react with some enzymes (specifically microsomal mixed function oxidase system) in the liver to produce free radicals.[11,12] These radicals can then locally damage liver cells and potentiate liver cancer or other deadly liver diseases.

FREE RADICALS AND DISEASE

It has become quite clear that free radicals play an important role in the development of many human diseases. The free radical connection to human diseases is so exciting that two new medical journals which deal solely with this subject have been created. It is now thought that once free radicals are made, they are the primary cause of certain human diseases involving many organs. This theory is supported by a multitude of data.[13,14] The following are medical conditions associated with free radical formation:

- Heart and cardiovascular disease
  Alcohol heart condition
  Selenium heart condition
    (Keshan disease)
  Atherosclerosis
  Adriamycin toxicity
  Heart attack

- Cancers: all types

- Lung disease
  Emphysema
  Pneumoconiosis
  Respiratory distress syndrome
  Cigarette smoking effects
  Bleomycin toxicity
  Air pollutant toxicity

- Alcohol-related diseases

- Immune system related diseases
  Glomerulonephritis
    (kidney disease)
  Vasculitis (inflammation of
    blood vessels)
  Autoimmune diseases: lupus,
    Sjögren's, etc.
  Rheumatoid arthritis

- Eye diseases
  Cataracts
  Retinal damage

- Central nervous system diseases
  Senile dementia
  Parkinson's disease
  Hypertensive stroke
  Encephalomyelitis
  Aluminum overload
  Worsening of traumatic
    injury
  Ataxia-telangiectasia
    syndrome

- Iron overload

- Radiation injury

- Kidney diseases

- Gastrointestinal diseases
  Free fatty acid induced
    pancreatitis
  Nonsteroidal anti-inflam-
    matory drug lesions
  Liver injury from toxins
  Carbon tetrachloride injury

- Skin diseases
  Solar radiation
  Thermal injury
  Contact dermatitis
  Dye reactions

- Aging

Free radicals cause damage to the nucleus of the cell and subsequently to the DNA. When certain segments of the DNA are affected, a malignant change occurs, altering the genetic code and leading to cancer.[15,16] It is thought that substances called antioxidants can protect against agents that cause cancer. (See Chapters 6 and 7.)[17-19] Antioxidants work against (anti-) oxidation (the process in which oxygen reacts with another chemical) and thereby prevent the harmful effects of oxygen on tissue via free radical formation. These protective substances occur naturally in the body, and various nutritional supplements also act as antioxidants (see next section).

The preponderance of evidence suggests that free radicals damage the cells that line the inside of all blood vessels.[20] Due to this initial injury, fats and fibrin and other elements of the blood ultimately form clots and block the arteries.[21] It has also been shown that once a person sustains a heart attack, the injury that occurs within the first 12-24 hours is secondary to free radical damage.[22,23] Therefore, antioxidants (also called free radical scavengers because they neutralize the free radicals) may have an important role not only in the prevention of cardiovascular disease but also at the time of an ongoing heart attack.

OUR BODY'S DEFENSES AGAINST RADICALS

We know that all life requires oxygen, but sometimes oxygen can produce radicals and high-energy (singlet) oxygen. Because of this, most animals have developed many lines of defense against free radical formation to preserve their very existence and to lessen the chance of abnormal cell (cancer) development.

There are many mechanisms that prevent or decrease the occurrence of radicals and the formation of hydroperoxide and thereby decrease the amount of cell membrane damage. The most obvious one is the *protective protein coat* that lines the surface of the cell membrane. This protective coat prevents oxygen from directly reacting with lipids in the membrane, which otherwise would produce many free radicals. In this situation the protein coat is an antioxidant, which protects the body from the formation of free radicals by preventing oxidation.

A second defensive mechanism involves the *protective enzymes* that float around in all cell membranes. These enzymes also act as antioxidants, preventing radical formation and also converting existing hydroperoxyl radicals into stable oxygen and hydrogen peroxide. They eliminate the danger of radicals and prevent radical damage to the cell membrane. These protective enzymes are small proteins that swim in the membrane fluid around polyunsaturated fats and hence are in close proximity to them. They include *superoxide dismutase,*[24] *catalase,*[25] and *selenium-containing glutathione peroxidase.*[26] Figure 5.3 represents a gross simplification of the cell membrane. The enzymes are denoted by a dark dot. Glutathione peroxidase, which is the main enzyme that destroys hydroperoxides, contains the metal *selenium* in very small amounts. Without selenium, glutathione peroxidase will not function properly. So if there is a slight dietary deficiency in selenium, glutathione peroxidase will not destroy hydroperoxides and a great deal of tissue damage will result from radical formation.

There is a very narrow but equal space between polyunsaturated fat molecules. One *vitamin E* molecule just fits snugly between them. This location and closeness to the polyunsaturated fats is extremely

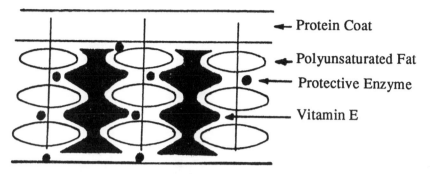

Figure 5.3 Simplified membrane structure.

important. Vitamin E is also an antioxidant and is the third mechanism that inhibits radical formation and thereby prevents their destructive damage. Vitamin E competes with the polyunsaturated fat for free radicals that are formed when polyunsaturated fats react with oxygen. This means that if there are more vitamin E molecules than polyunsaturated fat molecules, the radicals will be taken out of the system and neutralized by vitamin E. The more polyunsaturated fats you eat, the more vitamin E you will require. On the other hand, if the number of vitamin E molecules is low, then the radicals that are formed will not be neutralized and will proceed to cause membrane damage. Vitamin E also destroys hydroperoxides and therefore prevents more radical formation. Vitamin E and selenium also protect vitamin A because vitamin A is a polyunsaturated compound. W.L. Wattenberg has reviewed lipid antioxidants and demonstrated their role in preventing cancer.[27] The process of aging is also most probably related to hydroperoxide action on lipids. Aging is thought to be due to the process of oxidation.

Free radicals are unstable chemical substances with high energy. Normal enzymes can produce free radicals, which can form more radicals and singlet oxygen (very-high-energy oxygen). Oxygen reacting with lipids to free its stored energy may also produce hydroperoxides. All of these will cause tissue damage and may lead to the development of cancer. As already discussed, the body does have defenses to protect itself against these, including the protective protein coat of the cell membrane, protective enzymes (catalase, superoxide dismutase, and selenium-containing glutathione peroxidase), and vitamin E. We will investigate the vitamins and minerals and their role in protecting us in Chapter 6.

6
Vitamins, Minerals, and Other Nutrients

Living cells contain proteins, nucleic acids, carbohydrates, lipids, and certain organic substances that function in very small amounts, called vitamins. It has been known for centuries that many diseases are directly related to diet. Night blindness was cured by eating liver. In the eighteenth century, cod liver oil was used to treat rickets. The juice of limes was found to prevent the symptoms of scurvy among British sailors in the late eighteenth century (and from then on, the sailors were known as "limeys"). F.G. Hopkins in England proved in 1912 that animals require certain "accessory factors" in addition to proteins, fats, and carbohydrates. In the same year, Casimer Funk lessened the symptoms of beriberi among Japanese sailors by giving them an extract of rice husks, which was an amine. He was the first to denote this essential amine as *vitamine* (*vita* means life). Shortly thereafter, a scientist in the United States named E.V. McCollum showed that animals need both water-soluble and fat-soluble vitamins to maintain proper existence. Then it was discovered that bacteria which normally live in our intestines to help with food digestion can produce some of the vitamins that we require.

Vitamins are divided into two groups: those that are soluble in fat and those that are soluble in water. Fat-soluble vitamins are vitamins A, D, E, and K. And those that are soluble in water are thiamine (B_1), riboflavin (B₂), nicotinic acid, pantothenic acid, pyridoxine (B₆), biotin, folic acid, vitamin B₁₂, and ascorbic acid (C).

Vitamins are essential to life and play a crucial role as helper enzymes in important chemical functions of the body. If there are deficiencies of vitamins, a variety of diseases may occur, and the immune system will not function properly.

Vitamins interact with each other, and a few are toxic in high doses. Some vitamins can be stored for long periods of time, while others have to be supplied on a daily basis. We now know that certain drugs and hormones can produce a gradual vitamin deficiency by interfering with the ways in which vitamins are broken down for use in the body. Vitamins are also needed for normal prenatal development. They are of great interest because of their interplay among all organ systems of the body, especially the immune system.

What are the proper amounts of vitamins that we should ingest daily? The 1990 Recommended Dietary Allowances were published by the National Academy of Sciences. Recommended Dietary Allowances (RDAs) are the levels of intake of essential nutrients considered to be adequate to meet the nutritional needs of most healthy people in the United States, as judged by the Committee on Dietary Allowances of the Food and Nutrition Board. Individuals with special nutritional needs are not covered by the RDAs.

Recommended Dietary Allowances were established in 1943 to be used as a guide for planning and purchasing food supplies for the armed forces. RDAs are recommendations for the average daily amount of nutrients that healthy people should consume over a period of time and are estimated to exceed the requirements of most individuals. The RDAs are revised every five years. Needs for extra nutrients arise from such problems as inherited disorders, infections, cancer, chronic diseases, and the use of some medications. The current RDAs are listed in Tables 6.1 and 6.2.

After the food for our American diet has been harvested or slaughtered, it is prepared in large volume for sale and loses much of its nutritional value. You see, the RDAs represent the minimum nutrient levels needed to prevent obvious signs of vitamin deficiencies. These recommended levels are probably *not* the maximum needed for good health. Dr. Linus Pauling, a Nobel laureate, has recently shown in animal studies that the levels of vitamins required to maintain good health varied by 2,000 percent from one animal to another of the same species. Dr. Pauling extrapolates from this study that human requirements may vary just as greatly, and therefore the RDA for a given food may be one person's exact requirement but not the next person's. Dr. Pauling is quoted by the *Washingtonian* magazine in March 1981 as saying that today's diet does not provide as many vitamins as the diet of two generations ago. Over the past seventy-five years people have increased their consumption of fat by 30 percent and sugar by 50 percent, and have decreased their consumption of vegetables, grains, and fruits by 40 percent. In fact, Dr. Pauling found that 110 raw, natural foods eaten by our grandparents contained two to five times more vitamin A, thiamine (B_1), riboflavin (B_2), and pyridoxine (B_6) than these same foods contain today.

It is more difficult to identify a person who is only marginally deficient in vitamins than someone who is obviously deficient. Whereas a person who is grossly deficient in vitamins demonstrates many physical problems and complains about specific symptoms related to the deficiencies, a person with only marginal deficiencies demonstrates no such signs or symptoms and does not appear to be ill. The RDAs were designed for healthy people, and the values recommended may not be adequate for persons developing undetected marginal deficiencies.

Do you consider your diet to be well balanced? Do you think it is meeting your nutritional needs? Although you may believe it is fulfilling your requirements, you will most likely find that your diet is deficient in at least one nutrient. Consider the following sections.

MARGINAL DEFICIENCIES

Marginal deficiencies of micronutrients produce no frank symptoms of deficiency diseases; however, they do affect your mental acuity, your ability to cope with stress, and your body's ability to resist disease and infection and to recover from surgery. Marginal deficiency is defined as a state of gradual vitamin depletion in which there is evidence of personal lack of well-being associated with impairment of certain biochemical reactions.[1,2] There are several lines of evidence that a large number of people suffer from marginal deficiencies: biochemically measured data and data from dietary assessment studies.

Several biochemical studies revealed marginal deficiencies of vitamins and minerals among substantial portions of the population, including schoolchildren, elderly people, newborns, and mothers at time of delivery, among others.[3-5] Fifty percent of the population surveyed was below RDA levels for calcium, iron, vitamin A, and vitamin C. All socioeconomic groups were surveyed in the HANES II study.

New York City's schoolchildren were found to have low serum levels of thiamine, riboflavin, folic acid, and iron as well as zinc.[6] A study of teenagers in Miami revealed that 15 percent had deficient

Table 6.1   Food and Nutrition Board, National Academy Recommended Dietary Allowances,[a]
Designed for the maintenance of good nutrition

		Weight[b] (kg)(lb)		Height[b] (cm) (in)		Protein (g)	Water-Soluble Vitamins						
	Age						Vitamin C (mg)	Thiamine (mg)	Riboflavin (mg)	Niacin (mg NE)[c]	Vitamin B6 (mg)	Folate (µg)	Vitamin B12 (µg)
Infants	0.0-0.5	6	13	60	24	13	30	0.3	0.4	5	0.3	25	0.3
	0.5-1.0	9	20	71	28	14	35	0.4	0.5	6	0.6	35	0.5
Children	1-3	13	29	90	35	16	40	0.7	0.8	9	1.0	50	0.7
	4-6	20	44	112	44	24	45	0.9	1.1	12	1.1	75	1.0
	7-10	28	62	132	52	28	45	1.0	1.2	13	1.4	100	1.4
Males	11-14	45	99	157	62	45	50	1.3	1.5	17	1.7	150	2.0
	15-18	66	145	176	69	59	60	1.5	1.8	20	2.0	200	2.0
	19-24	72	160	177	70	58	60	1.5	1.7	19	2.0	200	2.0
	25-50	79	174	176	70	63	60	1.5	1.7	19	2.0	200	2.0
	51+	77	170	173	68	63	60	1.2	1.4	15	2.0	200	2.0
Females	11-14	46	101	157	62	46	50	1.1	1.3	15	1.4	150	2.0
	15-18	55	120	163	64	44	60	1.1	1.3	15	1.5	180	2.0
	19-24	58	128	164	65	46	60	1.1	1.3	15	1.6	180	2.0
	25-50	63	138	163	64	50	60	1.1	1.3	15	1.6	180	2.0
	51+	65	143	160	63	50	60	1.0	1.2	13	1.6	180	2.0
Pregnant						60	70	1.5	1.6	17	2.2	400	2.2
Lactating 1st 6 months						65	95	1.6	1.8	20	2.1	280	2.6
2nd 6 months						62	90	1.6	1.7	20	2.1	260	2.6

[a]The allowances, expressed as average daily intakes over time, are intended to provide for individual variations among most normal persons as they live in the United States under usual environmental stresses. Diets should be based on a variety of common foods in order to provide other nutrients for which human requirements have been less well defined.

[b]Weights and heights of Reference Adults are actual medians for the U.S. population of the designated age, as reported by NHANES II. The median weights and heights of those under 19 years of age were taken from Hamill et al. (1979). The use of these figures does not imply that the height-to-weight ratios are ideal.

levels of folic acid and another 30 percent had low levels. Fourteen percent of the girls had low levels of iron. In addition, low hemoglobin levels were found in 18 percent of the boys and 34 percent of the girls.[7] The Texas Nutrition Survey found that 30 percent of individuals had two or more deficiencies of seven different biochemical nutrients assayed.[8] Other studies[9-12] demonstrate similar findings—namely that subclinical micronutrient deficiencies are prevalent among significant segments of the population even though there are no demonstrable clinical signs.

Dietary assessment is another means of evaluating nutritional status. At least one nutrient was found to be inadequate in 30-35 percent of the U.S. diets in the USDA's Market Basket Survey of 1965.[13] Diets of both adolescent girls and women were below the recommended amounts of calcium, iron, and thiamine. For some age

of Sciences—National Research Council
Revised 1989
of practically all healthy people in the United States

Fat-Soluble Vitamins				Minerals						
Vitamin A (µg RE)[d]	Vitamin D (µg)[e]	Vitamin E (mg α-TE)[f]	Vitamin K (µg)	Calcium (mg)	Phosphorus (mg)	Magnesium (mg)	Iron (mg)	Zinc (mg)	Iodine (µg)	Selenium (µg)
375	7.5	3	5	400	300	40	6	5	40	10
375	10	4	10	600	500	60	10	5	50	15
400	10	6	15	800	800	80	10	10	70	20
500	10	7	20	800	800	120	10	10	90	20
700	10	7	30	800	800	170	10	10	120	30
1,000	10	10	45	1,200	1,200	270	12	15	150	40
1,000	10	10	65	1,200	1,200	400	12	15	150	50
1,000	10	10	70	1,200	1,200	350	10	15	150	70
1,000	5	10	80	800	800	350	10	15	150	70
1,000	5	10	80	800	800	350	10	15	150	70
800	10	8	45	1,200	1,200	280	15	12	150	45
800	10	8	55	1,200	1,200	300	15	12	150	50
800	10	8	60	1,200	1,200	280	15	12	150	55
800	5	8	65	800	800	280	15	12	150	55
800	5	8	65	800	800	280	10	12	150	55
800	10	10	65	1,200	1,200	320	30	15	175	65
1,300	10	12	65	1,200	1,200	355	15	19	200	75
1,200	10	11	65	1,200	1,200	340	15	16	200	75

[c]1 NE (niacin equivalent) is equal to 1 mg of niacin or 60 mg of dietary tryptophan.
[d]Retinol equivalents. 1 retinol equivalent = 1 µg retinol or 6 µg beta-carotene.
[e]As cholecalciferol 10 µg cholecalciferol = 400 IU of vitamin D.
[f]α-Tocopherol equivalents. 1 mg d-α tocopherol = 1 α-TE.

groups, vitamin A and riboflavin were also insufficient, as determined by the Nationwide Food Intake of Individuals.[14] The same study showed that older men also have diets that are low in vitamin A, riboflavin, vitamin C, and calcium.

Among females 15 years old and older, vitamin B6 intakes were 30 to 40 percent below RDA levels as determined by the 1977-78 Nationwide Food Consumption Survey by the USDA.[15] The 1985 Nationwide Food Consumption Survey showed more of the same: most people surveyed had a low intake of vitamin B6 and consumed less than 50 percent of the RDA of folic acid; 41 percent of the women consumed less than 70 percent of the RDA for vitamin E; only 2 percent were consuming the RDA for folic acid; and only 6 percent consumed the RDA for vitamin B6.[16]

Data from the Ten State Nutrition Survey showed that "significant numbers of people in the populations studied had intakes below the RDA for calcium, iron, and vitamin A; and that pregnant and lactating women tended to have low intakes of protein."[17] The above studies did not assess all micronutrients; therefore the findings could be even more extensive than what was actually reported.

Table 6.2   Estimated Safe and Adequate Daily Dietary Intakes of Selected Vitamins and Minerals[a]

Category	Age (years)	Vitamins	
		Biotin (µg)	Pantothenic Acid (mg)
Infants	0–0.5	10	2
	0.5–1	15	3
Children and	1–3	20	3
adolescents	4–6	25	3–4
	7–10	30	4–5
	11+	30–100	4–7
Adults		30–100	4–7

Category	Age (years)	Trace Elements[b]				
		Copper (mg)	Manganese (mg)	Fluoride (mg)	Chromium (µg)	Molybdenum (µg)
Infants	0–0.5	0.4–0.6	0.3–0.6	0.1–0.5	10–40	15–30
	0.5–1	0.6–0.7	0.6–1.0	0.2–1.0	20–60	20–40
Children and	1–3	0.7–1.0	1.0–1.5	0.5–1.5	20–80	25--50
adolescents	4–6	1.0–1.5	1.5–2.0	1.0–2.5	30–120	30–75
	7–10	1.0–2.0	2.0–3.0	1.5–2.5	50–200	50–150
	11+	1.5–2.5	2.0–5.0	1.5–2.5	500–200	75–250
Adults		1.5–3.0	2.0–5.0	1.5–4.0	500–200	75–250

[a]Because there is less information on which to base allowances, these figures are not given in the main table of RDA and are provided here in the form of ranges of recommended intakes.
[b]Since the toxic levels for many trace elements may be only several times usual intakes, the upper levels for the trace elements given in this table should not be habitually exceeded.

Marginal deficiencies of protein, vitamins A, C, E, and B6, and folic acid have been shown to result in greater vulnerability to a number of viral and bacterial processes.[18] Inadequacies of these nutrients can impair the body's ability to resist disease since these nutrients are known to help maintain the immune system. With the recent discovery of a viral etiology for two human cancers and AIDS, marginal deficiencies take on an added significance. Proper wound healing requires adequate amounts of vitamins C, A, D, and K, the B-complex vitamins, and the minerals zinc, iron, and copper.[19]

Lifestyle and Eating Patterns

Lifestyle and eating patterns can also lead to nutrient deficiencies. Years ago, the homemaker was the person who planned the meal; today more than half of adult females are in the labor force and half of married women have children under the age of 18.[20] In 1982, 32 million children or 55 percent of all children under 18 had working mothers. In addition, the number of single-parent households is increasing at twice the rate of two-parent households. These changes have an impact on our eating patterns. There is now an increased demand for convenience foods, and the fast-food market is very successful because the married working woman has less time to spend in the kitchen. Cost is another factor, especially in households with single working women as their heads.

Eating patterns have also changed. A nine-year study conducted by the National Center for Health Statistics has shown that 26 percent of the population say they never eat breakfast, and 60 percent of those who do eat breakfast tend to be older.[21] The USDA Nationwide Food Consumption Survey (USDA-NFCS) supports those findings: breakfast skipping is prevalent in 19-22 year olds (29 percent) and 23-34 year olds (25 percent), as compared with 14 percent of the population overall. In addition, 23 percent of the groups surveyed admitted to skipping lunch.[22,23] Sixty-one percent of the people surveyed by the USDA-NFCS and 38 percent of the people surveyed by the National Center for Health Statistics reported that they snack.[24]

Eighteen percent of the people said they ate away from home once in the twenty-four-hour period, and most of these were young adults. Sixty percent of the men aged 23-24 and 50 percent of the women aged 23-24 had eaten away from home on the day of the survey.[25] Poor food choices and processing of foods are other areas of concern.

In the HANES II study, people were asked to choose a food that they liked and considered "balanced." For a "balanced" vegetable, the majority chose French fries over broccoli; for meat/legume, hot dogs over split peas; and for grain, white bread over whole wheat. In the same study, favorite foods included coffee, doughnuts, soft drinks, and hamburgers. The percentage of calories in the American diet derived from fat is 42; from sugar, 24.

In addition, to eat well you really have to take the time and have the knowledge to plan proper meals. When caloric intakes fall below 1,600 calories, there is no guarantee that all nutritional guidelines can be met. In the menus published by the U.S. Department of Agriculture in "Ideas for Better Eating" in which meals were planned by competent professionals, the diets consisting of 1,600 calories fall short of the recommended level of some essential nutrients.[26] As was stated before, the average caloric intake of women in this country is at or around this level, as is also the case for the elderly and many dieters.

Data from the national HANES II study show that the median caloric intake of the general population is 1,831 calories, which suggests that 50 percent of the population surveyed take in less than that amount. At that level, trained nutritionists have trouble designing meals to provide the minimum RDA.[27] According to the 1985 Nation-wide Food Consumption Survey, significant percentages of the population were consuming less than 70 percent of the RDA for the nutrients listed in Table 6.3.[28] These data demonstrate that today's eating patterns and preferences do not afford people a "well-balanced diet."

Table 6.3 America's Poor Nutrient Intake	
Nutrient	**Percentage of Individuals Deficient***
Vitamin B$_6$	51%
Calcium	42%
Magnesium	39%
Iron	32%
Vitamin A	31%
Vitamin C	26%
Thiamine	17%
Vitamin B$_{12}$	15%
Riboflavin	12%

* Deficiency = Intake less than 70% of RDA.

Outright vitamin deficiencies occur in two groups of people. In the first group, an individual is unable to buy the right kinds of food either because of the expense or because he is not knowledgeable about the proper foods. It is estimated that 25 percent of U.S. households do not have nutritionally balanced diets because people do not know what foods to buy or because vitamins and minerals are lost through cooking. The milling process used to make white flour has been reported to remove twenty-two nutrients from the wheat, including about 90 percent of the vitamin E content. When flour is labeled "enriched," usually only four of these nutrients are replaced: thiamine, riboflavin, niacin, and iron. Sugar refinement also removes most of its vitamins and minerals. Cooked and reheated potatoes are reported to have only 10 percent of the vitamin C content of raw potatoes. The second group consists of people whose nutrient deficiency occurs as the result of a specific disease or a drug or other treatment therapy.

The results of a study on the incidence of low blood levels of vitamins in a randomly selected group of hospitalized patients are listed in Table 6.4.[29] The table lists the vitamin and the corresponding percentage of people with a deficiency. Only 12 percent of 120 patients had normal vitamin levels (RDA standards); 88 percent had at least one vitamin deficiency. What is even more interesting is that many had more than one vitamin deficiency. In spite of this, 61

Table 6.4   Vitamin Deficiencies in Hospitalized Patients

Vitamin	Percentage of Individuals Deficient
Folic acid	45%
Thiamine (B$_2$)	31%
Nicotinic acid	29%
Pyridoxine (B$_6$)	27%
Pantothenic acid	15%
Vitamin A	13%
Vitamin E	12%
Riboflavin (B$_2$)	12%
Vitamin C	12%
Vitamin B$_{12}$	10%
Biotin	1%
Multiple Vitamin Deficiencies	
Two deficiencies	38%
Three deficiencies	14%
Four deficiencies	6%
Five deficiencies	10%

percent of the total group of 120 patients were eating what is considered to be a normal American diet!

GROUPS AT RISK FOR NUTRIENT DEFICIENCIES

There are several segments of our population that may not be "healthy" and that may be considered to be "at risk" for inadequate nutrient intake. The RDAs do not take into account the special needs of these people. The greater requirements of the groups listed in Table 6.5 need to be recognized and addressed.

Alcohol Drinkers

Approximately 90 million Americans drink alcoholic beverages, and 10 million of these are considered to be alcoholics.[30] Heavy alcohol consumption has been shown to adversely affect levels of beta-carotene, folic acid, thiamine, riboflavin, niacin, vitamin C, vitamin B$_6$, vitamin B$_{12}$, magnesium, and zinc.[31-44] Consuming three or more drinks a week can lead to deficiencies of these nutrients.

Smokers

There are 50 million cigarette smokers in the United States. Studies have shown that the plasma level of vitamin C in heavy smokers may be 40 percent lower than in nonsmokers.[45-48] The levels of other anti-

Table 6.5   U.S. Nutrient Supplementation Candidates

Risk Group	Million	Nutrient Deficiencies
Alcohol Drinkers (3+ drinks/week)	90	Beta-carotene, vitamins A, B_6, D, folate, thiamine
People With Allergies/ Food Intolerance	80	Any or all
Cigarette Smokers	50	Beta-carotene, vitamins C, E, B_6, folate
Dieters	45	Any or all
Hospitalized Patients	36	Any or all
People With Infectious Diseases	5	Any or all
Osteoporosis Patients	34	Calcium, vitamin D, others
People With Chronic Diseases	31	Any or all
Elderly Patients	25	Folate, vitamins C and D
Surgical Patients	23.5	Any or all
Oral Contraceptive Users	18	Beta-carotene, folate, vitamin B_6
Teenagers	17	Vitamin A, folate
Stressed People	*	B vitamins, any or all
Athletes/Exercisers	*	B vitamins, or any
Consumers of High-Fat Foods	*	Any
Diabetics	11	Vitamins C, D, B_6, magnesium
Pregnant Women	7	All
Strict Vegetarians	1	Vitamins B_{12} and D

*Unknown millions.

oxidants, like beta-carotene,[49-51] vitamin E,[52] and B_6,[53] have been shown to be low as well.

Dieters

An estimated 40 or 50 million Americans are dieting at any given time.[54] In some age groups of women, this figure is even higher than 50 percent of the total female population.[55] Whenever the dieter's total caloric intake drops below 1,400 calories a day, it is almost impossible to obtain most vitamins and minerals in adequate amounts. Your vitamin requirements remain the same despite your caloric intake, even during total fasting.[56,57] Hence, dieters not taking supplemental vitamins and minerals are at risk for nutrient deficiency. Dieting in the form of skipped meals or fad diets is common in the United States and almost guarantees inadequate intakes of vitamins and minerals without supplementation. None of eleven published reducing diets provides 100 percent of the U.S. RDA for vitamins.[58]

People With Chronic Illnesses

There are an estimated 31 million people in this country with serious chronic illnesses. This group is "at risk" for inadequate nutrient intake because of interactions of medications with micronutrients or because of the effects of various diseases themselves, like cancer. The incidence of these chronic illnesses increases yearly, especially cancer, with about one million new patients developing cancer every year. About 36 million people are hospitalized yearly, and the nutritional status of seriously ill hospitalized patients is very poor. Their disease or injury increases their nutritional needs, which can precipitate malnutrition and impair the immune system.[59-66]

People Undergoing Surgery

There are 23.5 million patients who undergo surgery every year, and their nutritional status is compromised by the trauma of surgery. Some operations interfere with the ingestion, digestion, and absorption of food as well. Trauma and wound healing require that you take certain nutrients in amounts exceeding the RDA.

People With Infections

Approximately 5 million patients are in the hospital yearly with infections. The majority of these patients have little or no appetite and a marked reduction in food intake. The tenth edition of the U.S. RDA states, "Infections—even mild ones—increase metabolic losses of a number of vitamins and minerals." In addition, acute or chronic infections of the gastrointestinal tract impair the absorption of nutrients.

The Elderly

There are a little over 25 million elderly citizens in the United States, and this segment of the population is growing. Various factors affect their nutritional health. Nutritional problems in this age group occur mainly as a result of decreased caloric intake, impaired absorption, poor dentition, drug/nutrient interactions, limited activity or handicap, low income, altered taste perception, loneliness, lack of transportation, or any combination of these. Nutrients most often identified as deficient in the elderly include calcium, vitamin B_6,[67,68] thiamine, folate, riboflavin, niacin,[69-71] vitamin C (to a point of unrecognized scurvy),[72-76] and vitamin D.[77]

Teenagers

There are approximately 17 million teenagers in our country, and the 1985 USDA Nationwide Food Consumption Survey indicated that the diets of adolescent girls who consume foods that satisfy less than 70 percent of their energy requirements met the RDA requirements for only one of twelve nutrients studied—and that was protein, not any of the vitamins or minerals. The prevalence of nutrient deficiencies in female teenagers may result from constant dieting for weight control. Iron, magnesium, and vitamin C were identified as problem nutrients among 20 to 40 percent of male teens studied.[78] Folate[79] and vitamin A [80,81] were also found to be deficient in a significant number of adolescents. Many teenagers skip meals, snack, and often eat meals away from home. About 50 percent of all teenagers report that they are not concerned about nutrition, and only 33 percent say that they try to eat correctly. Many favor junk foods and soft drinks.

Diabetics

Another group that has an increased need for some nutrients is the estimated 11 million diabetics in the United States. Diabetics have low levels of thiamine[82] and other B vitamins, vitamin C, and vitamin D.[83]

Pregnant and Lactating Women

Substantial numbers of American women have demonstrated marginal intakes of vitamin A, vitamin C, vitamin B_6, calcium, iron, and magnesium.[84] Pregnant and lactating women require nutrients in greater amounts than the RDA. Unfortunately, these women do not have a sufficient intake. In healthy pregnancies, at the time of delivery, 25 percent of mothers had at least one nutrient deficiency.[85]

Premature Infants and Toddlers

Babies and toddlers are also at risk for nutrient deficiencies. Premature infants have low levels of vitamins A,[86] C,[87] and E.[88] The USDA Nationwide Food Consumption Survey showed that iron and vitamin C were problem nutrients among infants and youngsters. Vitamins A and C were insufficient among many children aged 1-5 in the HANES I study, and children aged 1-5 were shown to be at greater risks for niacin insufficiency in the HANES II study.[89-91]

Low-Income People

Low-income populations have been shown to have deficiencies of vitamin C, thiamine, riboflavin, niacin, and iron.[92] Those who bought food with food stamps had 10 to 20 percent lower amounts of eleven nutrients studied than households not needing food stamps. Only 12 percent of those with food stamps met the RDA criteria for all eleven nutrients.[93] Spanish-Americans have been shown to have a deficiency of vitamin A, a state that is probably due to insufficient vitamin A food sources in their cultural diet. And, as was stated before in the Ten State survey and HANES I Survey, vitamins A and C, riboflavin, niacin, and iron were problem nutrients among lower income blacks.

Stressed People and Osteoporosis Patients

Countless millions of Americans also have an increased nutrient need because of stress. As recommended by the ninth edition of the RDA in 1980, you should increase your intake of various nutrients when you are under stress. Approximately 34 million people have osteoporosis, a condition that also necessitates a larger intake of many nutrients.

Users of Medications and Oral Contraceptives

Another segment of the population at risk for nutrient deficiencies is the millions who use therapeutic drugs that directly interfere with nutrient levels. Very common drugs such as laxatives and mineral oil deplete your body of fat-soluble vitamins; aspirin impairs the utilization of vitamin C and folic acid; and oral contraceptives deplete your body of folic acid, vitamins B_6, B_{12}, and C, and beta-carotene.[94-98] A recent article in the *British Medical Journal*[99] reviews the entire subject, and well over fifty to sixty commonly used drugs are listed as interfering with vitamins and minerals; hence, these drugs increase your micronutrient requirements.

Children With Low IQs

One of the most exciting areas of nutrient investigation is that of intelligence quotient. Many studies have been conducted on the effects of nutrients on intelligence. When children's diets were supplemented with vitamins and minerals, their IQs were raised.[100-103] The implication is obvious: the marginal deficiencies seen in some young children are enough to hamper neural function in these children. Other studies have shown that marginal vitamin and mineral deficiencies are associated with poor motivation,[104,105] abnormalities in attention and perception,[106-109] and personality changes.[110,111]

Summary

Americans continue to eat foods that are sprayed with chemicals, refined, processed, frozen, canned, stored, and trucked around the country. Many of our meats contain the hormones and chemicals that have been fed to animals. All of these foods have been depleted of nutrients to varying degrees. Some methods of cooking can destroy nutrients or deplete the food of them as well, and some nutrients are not stable in heat or boiling water. As a result Americans do not or cannot eat a healthful balanced diet.

The average American consumes about 60 pounds of sugar each year and four to five times the amount of salt necessary, favors carbonated drinks to others when not consuming 2.6 gallons of alcoholic beverages each year (if of drinking age), and usually gets about one third of his total calories from sources of little or no nutrient value.

In short, it is very difficult to find an individual who consistently, on a daily basis, eats a "well-balanced diet"—that is, one containing foods that are freshly prepared, varied, and nutritionally adequate.[112]

DEFICIENCY SYMPTOMS

Specific nutritional deficiencies are associated with abnormal behavior and learning disabilities. The classic example of this is pellagra, caused by a lack of niacin or certain proteins. Pellagra is characterized by mental derangement (psychosis) and several other symptoms including skin inflammation and diarrhea, and can result in death. A number of vitamins are necessary for normal functioning of the nervous system. For instance, thiamine (B_1) deficiency results in convulsions in infants; pantothenic acid deficiency causes sensory losses in the arms and legs; niacin deficiency causes pellagra; folic acid deficiency causes unclear thinking; vitamin C deficiency causes fatigue; vitamin E deficiency in animals causes brain degeneration; and vitamin A deficiency causes night blindness. Many other medical illnesses may be responsible for these symptoms or behaviors, and all such possibilities must be entertained and excluded by proper workup. However, assuming all other medical illnesses have been ruled out as possible causes, a marginal deficiency of a vitamin may cause subtle early symptoms of these abnormal brain functions.

You should ingest the proper amount of vitamins and minerals daily, through a well-balanced diet and supplementation, because vitamins and minerals play a vital role in all organ functions of the body; a marginal deficiency cannot be readily detected in an apparently normal individual; certain vitamins and minerals are antioxidants and help rid the body of free radicals that can lead to the development of cancer; and certain vitamins may have direct anticancer properties.

Table 6.6 is an easy-reference guide to the vitamins, with a brief description of their function and their food sources. The remainder of the chapter will discuss nutrients individually.

Table 6.6 Vitamins: Their Functions and Sources		
Vitamin	Function	Food Source
Fat Soluble		
Vitamin A	Has anticancer properties. Essential for normal immune function. Prevents night blindness. Vital for normal growth, good vision, healthy skin and hair.	Tomatoes, milk, eggs, liver, kidney, fortified margarine, leafy green and yellow vegetables.
Vitamin D	Prevents rickets. Helps body use calcium and phosphorus. Needed for strong teeth and bones.	Milk, tuna, cod liver oil, salmon, egg yolk.
Vitamin E	Is an antioxidant and as such protects against free radicals. Protects against polyunsaturated fats. Vital for red cell function.	Leafy vegetables, wheat germ, whole-grain cereals, vegetable oils.
Vitamin K	Essential for normal blood clotting.	Fresh green leafy vegetables, beef liver.
Water Soluble		
Thiamine (B$_1$)	Prevents beriberi. Essential for normal function of heart and nervous system.	Bread, flour, enriched cereals, fish, lean meat, liver, milk, pork, poultry, whole-grain cereals.
Riboflavin (B$_2$)	Helps to degrade drugs and foreign substances. Prevents light sensitivity of eyes. Builds and maintains body tissues like skin, brain, blood.	Leafy green vegetables, enriched bread and cereals, lean meat, liver, milk, eggs.

Table 6.6—*Continued*		
Vitamin	**Function**	**Food Source**
Niacin	Prevents pellagra. Helps convert food into energy. Vital for nervous system.	Lean meat, liver, eggs, enriched bread and cereals.
Pantothenic acid	Helps body to use fat, proteins, and carbohydrates.	Virtually all edible plant and animal food.
Pyridoxine (B₆)	Deficiency leads to decreased antibodies and T cells, lowering the body's ability to reject transplants and cancer cells. Necessary for teeth and gums, red cells, nervous system.	Vegetables, whole-grain cereals, wheat germ, meat, bananas.
Vitamin B₁₂	Prevents certain anemias. Essential for the nervous system and proper growth in children.	Lean meat, liver, kidney, milk, saltwater fish, oysters.
Folic acid	Prevents certain anemias. Needed for certain functions in intestinal tract.	Fresh green leafy vegetables, lean meats.
Biotin	Deficiency results in anemia and depression. Essential for chemical reactions involving fats, proteins, carbohydrates.	Green vegetables, milk, liver, kidney, egg yolk.
Vitamin C	Antioxidant. Inhibits certain cancers and carcinogens. Deficiency results in decreases in T-cell number and phagocytic function. Prevents scurvy. Essential for gums, teeth, bones, body cells, blood vessels.	Citrus fruits and fruit juices, fortified juices, tomatoes, berries, green vegetables, potatoes.

FAT-SOLUBLE VITAMINS

Carotene

Beta-carotene is the chemical precursor that the body uses to make vitamin A. Carrots account for the major source of beta-carotene in North American diets, yellow-green vegetables in Japan, and red palm oil in West Africa. Studies have indicated that people who consume higher than average amounts of beta-carotene have a lower incidence of cancer, and "it is most unlikely that this association will disappear entirely with future observational studies."[113] It appears that this lower incidence of cancer is attributed to beta-carotene itself, rather than to its conversion for vitamin A. Beta-carotene may inhibit the development of cancer in the following ways: It greatly enhances the immune system.[114] It is a powerful antioxidant, free radical scavenger. Beta-carotene is the most efficient neutralizer of singlet oxygen, the high-energy, destructive molecule.

The normal range of human intake of beta-carotene is a few milligrams per day. However, large daily intakes of beta-carotene appear to be harmless and do not cause vitamin A toxicity. Beta-carotene is converted to vitamin A only as the body requires it. One or two hundred milligrams per day are regularly prescribed for the treatment of a disease called erythropoietic protoporphyria without causing vitamin A toxicity, liver problems, or any other apparent side effects. The World Health Organization Expert Committee on Food Additives estimated the acceptable daily intake of beta-carotene for a 140-pound adult to be about 350 milligrams per day.[115] In several studies, supplemental beta-carotene in the amount of 30 milligrams per day has been used without harm but has caused oranging of the skin in a select few persons.

Several leading government agencies and I have recommended diets high in beta-carotene ever since the association was made between diets high in beta-carotene content and low rates of cancer. The diet that I recommend contains about 15-20 milligrams of carotene, while the diets recommended by the agencies suggest that a person obtain 5-6 milligrams per day.[116] However, studies done by the U.S. Department of Agriculture Food Intake Survey show that the average American diet provides only 1.5 milligrams of beta-carotene a day, an amount that is much less than that recommended to prevent cancer.

Good sources of beta-carotene include carrots, kale, pumpkins, spinach, sweet potatoes, Swiss chard, apricots, cantaloupes, papayas, and peaches. These can be eaten on a daily basis. Beta-carotene is extremely safe and is not toxic in any amount;[117]; however, most people do not consume foods containing beta-carotene daily—or at least not enough of them·

Vitamin A

The recommended dose for vitamin A is given in terms of international units (IU). Little of this vitamin is lost in normal cooking, but prolonged or repeated cooking will result in significant loss. The absorption of vitamin A and other fat-soluble vitamins requires bile acids, which are specific types of fat compounds stored in the gallbladder. Without these bile acids, all fat-soluble vitamins do not get properly absorbed into the blood, resulting in a vitamin deficiency. Table 6.6 shows which food sources contain vitamin A.

There are many benefits from a diet containing sufficient vitamin A, among them:

- Vitamin A is effective in the treatment of chemically (methylcholanthrene) induced cancers in experimental animals and lung cancer in mice.[118,119] The growth of human breast-cancer cells is decreased by vitamin A.[120] Vitamin A also inhibits the growth of human melanoma cells, a deadly skin cancer.[121] Several different clinical trials using vitamin A treatment for patients with skin, cervix, or lung cancer have been done in Europe and show very promising results.[122] Another study shows that vitamin A protects both smokers and nonsmokers from lung cancer.[123] Presently, there are clinical trials ongoing at the National Cancer Institute in Bethesda, Maryland, and other centers involving retinoic acid (a vitamin A derivative) and its effect on patients with many types of cancer.
- It maintains the integrity of the skin and all inner linings of the airways and gastrointestinal tract, the first line of defense against invading bacteria and other microorganisms.
- A vitamin A deficiency results in decreased production of antibodies to certain foreign substances like diphtheria and tetanus.[124] By giving enough vitamin A, antibody production is increased substantially. Impaired production of antibodies to cancer cells is also a possibility if vitamin A is at low levels in the blood.
- A vitamin A deficiency also causes a decrease in T cells, which consequently renders the person vulnerable to cancer cells. Without a sufficient number of T cells to kill the cancer cells, the cancer may grow unchecked.
- A deficiency of this vitamin enhances the binding of a certain carcinogen benzo(a)pyrene to respiratory cells' DNA in our lungs,[125] which in turn can transform the normal lung cell into a cancer cell.
- Vitamin A is needed for proper color vision and night vision. Deficiency is the principal cause of blindness in the world.
- This vitamin is required for proper growth and maintenance of bones, teeth, glands, nails, and hair.
- Vitamin A is crucial for fetal development.

Vitamin A is one of the few vitamins that may lead to toxicity if taken in great excess. Typical symptoms include drowsiness, headache, vomiting, and drying of the skin, and it may raise blood cholesterol and triglyceride levels. Daily doses of 100,000 IU (30 milligrams of retinol) have been given to adults for many months without serious side effects.[126] But children who ingest 50,000 to 500,000 IU (15 to 150 milligrams of retinol) per day do exhibit toxicity.[127] Researchers have extensively reviewed the safety of vitamin A.[128]

Vitamin D

Vitamin D (cholecalciferol) requirements are expressed in international units (IU). Ten micrograms of cholecalciferol equal 400 IU of vitamin D. There are several types of vitamin D. Some become activated when minimal ultraviolet light reacts with them in the skin; other types are activated by the liver or kidney. So if a person does not get minimal sunlight, or has liver or kidney disease, that person will be deficient in vitamin D (cholecalciferol). Most people get little or no vitamin D from their diet, but rather obtain their supply from production by skin cells after activation by ultraviolet light. Table 6.6 lists food sources for vitamin D.

Vitamin D performs many important functions, including the following:

- It helps the body use calcium and phosphorus to build, form, and maintain all bones and teeth.
- It prevents rickets, a disease in which the bones are deformed. (Cod liver oil was used as a folk remedy in Scotland in the eighteenth century and ultimately was found to have beneficial effects in the treatment of rickets.)
- Vitamin D enhances the immune system.[129]
- It aids in cell growth and maturation.
- It inhibits the oncogene c-myc.[130]
- It inhibits cancer-cell growth.[131]
- Vitamin D decreases the risk of colon cancer.[132]

Toxicity may occur with large amounts of vitamin D. Fat-soluble vitamins, in contrast to water-soluble vitamins, are not rapidly broken down and disposed of quickly by the body. The earliest toxic symptoms are loss of appetite in children, nausea and vomiting, thirst, and constipation alternating with diarrhea. However, a daily dose of 100,000 to 150,000 IU of vitamin D (250 to 375 micrograms of cholecalciferol) for many months can be tolerated by a healthy adult.[133] Even so, there is no need to exceed the RDA of 400 IU of vitamin D (10 micrograms).

Vitamin E

Vitamin E requirements are given as international units in which 1 IU equals 1 milligram of dl-tocopherol. As we discussed in Chapter 5, "Free Radicals," vitamin E is very important to us because it is an antioxidant. There is no difference between natural vitamin E and "d" vitamin E. The "d" denotes the chemical structure of the vitamin E molecule. Two preparations that contain identical amounts of natural vitamin E and dl-tocopherol are identical in their tocopherol content. (The natural preparation is usually more expensive.)

There are a few myths about vitamin E that need to be cleared up. Vitamin E has been touted as the great "sex vitamin." There is no absolute proof that this vitamin affects sexual competency except that rats deficient in vitamin E fail to reproduce. Vitamin E has not been shown to make a man more potent or to increase a woman's sex drive. As you know, sexual performance is a complex interaction between psychological and physical factors. In addition, vitamin E probably does not slow down the aging process per se; there is certainly no strong evidence for this. But it is a potent antioxidant, and aging is thought to be a process of oxidation (oxygen reacting with body tissues). Finally, there is some evidence that the elderly can walk longer distances after six months of supplemental vitamin E, but good studies concerning this have not yet been done.

Vitamin E has many important functions:

- It is a potent antioxidant and, as such, acts as a scavenger, damaging free radicals that may produce cancer. Many studies have been done concerning the effect of vitamin E on the inhibition of cancer.[134-136] The results show that vitamin E can inhibit the growth of certain cancer cells.
- As an antioxidant, it may protect you from the cancer-inducing effects of smog. This protective quality of vitamin E has already been shown in animals.
- It protects the body against the oxidation of polyunsaturated fatty acids. Therefore, it is essential that you take enough vitamin E if your diet contains polyunsaturated fats. As you recall, polyunsaturated fats help to reduce the amount of blood cholesterol.
- Vitamin E is essential for the normal function of red blood cells. A deficiency causes an anemia in children.
- Vitamin E, among other nutrients, is beneficial for a very common breast disease, fibrocystic breast disease, which affects 50 percent of all women. This is a benign condition in which cysts develop, usually in both breasts, giving the breasts

a granular consistency, and often associated with pain. However, women with fibrocystic disease have a two- to eightfold greater risk of developing breast cancer.[137,138] Several recent studies report that 85 percent of women (twenty-six in the study group) with fibrocystic disease who took 600 IU of vitamin E daily for eight weeks experienced relief of the pain associated with their disease, and some of these women had demonstrable regression of disease.[139,140] The women whose disease did not respond had lower vitamin E levels when checked, suggesting poor vitamin E absorption.

- Vitamin E reduces LDL levels (lipids involved in atherosclerosis) and increases HDL levels (lipids that protect against atherosclerosis).
- Supplementing with 600–1,200 IU of vitamin E daily may help prevent diabetic complications.[141]

There is no case on record of vitamin E toxicity nor any indication of vitamin E toxicity. A daily intake of 800 IU of vitamin E per 2.2 pounds of body weight for five months has not been toxic. This amounts to 56,000 IU (56,000 milligrams) for an average man weighing 140 pounds, or about 5,600 times the RDA. A good dose of vitamin E seems to be 400 to 600 IU (400 to 600 milligrams) daily.

As ridiculous as it may sound, some people, including some physicians, *believe* that vitamin E causes cancer. They reason that since the molecule of vitamin E looks similar to estrogen, it can cause breast cancer. This is absolutely absurd! There are hundreds of molecules in the body that are formed from the same basic cholesterol ring structure. The body is able to discriminate one molecule from another even if there is only a slight difference between their structures. For instance, what differentiates men from women is a mere methyl group, CH_3, on two different cholesterol rings. Obviously, mother nature has this under control.

Vitamin E is safe and has never been shown to cause cancer or changes in the DNA or RNA, nor has it ever been shown to cause changes in fetal development—even at very high doses of 3,200 IU.[142,143]

Vitamin K

Vitamin K is essential for normal blood clotting. After vitamin K gets into the blood via the bile fats, it helps manufacture clotting proteins in a normal liver. Bacteria that normally inhabit our intestine also make vitamin K, and we get much of our needed vitamin K from their production. If the liver is not working properly (as in alcoholism), clotting factors are not made, and the person is at risk for bleeding to death in certain circumstances. Anticoagulant drugs such as Coumadin are purposely given to interfere with the action of vitamin K in those patients who are generating blood clots that may lodge in their lungs and cause death.

Vitamin K may enhance the immune system. It, too, has not been shown to be toxic in large doses.[144]

WATER-SOLUBLE VITAMINS

Thiamine (B₁)

Thiamine deficiency causes beriberi, a disease that was more prevalent when the rice-milling industry spread across Asia. Thiamine is easily destroyed by heating, and grain and cereal foods may lose quite a bit of thiamine when they are milled. In the United States, thiamine deficiency syndromes occur almost exclusively in alcoholics because of poor diet, or, for that matter, in any person who does not consume a good diet.

Thiamine food sources are listed in Table 6.6. It is important that your diet contain plenty of thiamine; otherwise you may suffer from deficiency symptoms.

- Immunologically, animals show an increased risk of infection with certain bacteria if they are deprived of thiamine.[145]
- It helps the body to fully utilize carbohydrates by interaction with enzymes.
- Thiamine deficiency causes a loss of appetite, mental depression, a "pins and needles" sensation in the feet and hands, as well as other sensory losses. If severe, it will cause beriberi.
- Thiamine is required for the proper function of the heart.
- A deficiency of thiamine and folate leads to specific DNA changes that have been correlated with cancer.[146,147]

There are no recorded cases of thiamine toxicity. Supplemental thiamine is recommended for all persons who are eating a poor diet.

Riboflavin (B₂)

Riboflavin is important because it is involved in so many chemical processes and functions in the body. Dietary riboflavin must first be converted into an active form in the body before it can be used. Several drugs and diseases interfere with this conversion and hence will cause riboflavin deficiency.

Consider the following facts about this important B vitamin:

- Riboflavin deficiency results in a decrease in lymphocytes and an increased susceptibility to certain infections.[148] With T cells decreased, a person could also be more susceptible to cancer development.
- It is essential for building and maintaining body tissues including the brain, blood, and skin.
- It helps to transform proteins, fats, and carbohydrates into energy.
- Riboflavin protects the body from skin disorders as well as cataracts and other corneal disorders.
- Its deficiency can result from a low-protein diet and can cause lip, mouth, and tongue soreness and burning.
- Excess thyroid hormone can use up riboflavin quicker than normal.
- Boric acid, which is a part of some mouthwashes, suppositories, and some important foods, helps riboflavin to be secreted into the urine and thereby causes partial riboflavin deficiency.

Niacin

A diet deficient in niacin produces pellagra in humans. At one time, pellagra was endemic in Europe and America because the main diet consisted of cornmeal, molasses, and pork fat almost exclusively.

Niacin performs the following functions:

- Niacin converts food to energy.
- It prevents pellagra, a disease that affects the central nervous system, skin, and gastrointestinal tract.
- It reduces cholesterol and triglyceride levels and has been shown to be beneficial to cardiac patients. The Coronary Drug Project Study showed a decrease in mortality of 11 percent in cardiac patients given niacin.[149]

Those using niacin should take only the immediate-release form. The timed-release form can damage your liver. Do not exceed 1,500 milligrams of niacin per day. Take it with food to decrease flushing. Niacin may aggravate diabetes, gout, and stomach problems.

Pantothenic Acid

Rarely is a human diet ever deficient in this important vitamin, because pantothenic acid is distributed in almost all plant and animal tissues. It has the following functions:

- It is required in almost all energy-producing reactions in the body involving fats, carbohydrates, and proteins.
- It is required for the formation of some hormones and nerve-regulating substances.
- It helps to regulate the blood-sugar level.

Pyridoxine (B₆)

Like most other B-complex vitamins, pyridoxine is not stored in the human body to any great extent. But even so, a deficiency in this vitamin is extremely rare. It has the following uses:

- Pyridoxine has a marked effect on the immune system. Its deficiency inhibits the formation of antibodies, decreases the number of T cells, and decreases the ability of the immune system to reject foreign tissues like transplants[150] and to destroy cancer cells.[151]
- It is important in the formation of certain proteins and in the use of fats in the body.
- Pyridoxine is essential for the proper function of the nervous system.
- It is needed for the formation of red blood cells and for healthy gums and teeth.
- More than the normal amount of pyridoxine is required by women who are using oral contraceptives containing estrogen.

Vitamin B₁₂

Vitamin B₁₂ has been known for over fifty years. Information on this B vitamin includes the following:

- It is needed to make hemoglobin and other parts of the red blood cell.
- B₁₂ is required for healthy nervous tissue and normal growth.
- A deficiency causes anemia and mental changes.
- Many alcoholics develop vitamin B₁₂ deficiency.

Folic Acid

Sufficient folic acid is important for the following reasons:

- Folic acid is essential for forming certain proteins and genetic materials in the body.
- Its deficiency results in an anemia.
- It is important during the last three months of pregnancy.

Biotin

Biotin has only recently been discovered, but much is known about its functions and deficiency symptoms, including the following:

- It synthesizes fatty acids, metabolizes carbohydrates for energy use, and makes the body use protein properly.
- It aids in maintaining muscles, the circulatory system, nervous system, hair and skin, reproductive system, adrenal glands, and the thyroid gland.
- Its deficiency results in depression, anemia, sleepiness, muscle pain, hair loss, and increased cholesterol levels.

Vitamin C

Vitamin C is a major factor in controlling and potentiating multiple aspects of human resistance to many agents including cancer. Much work concerning vitamin C and its effects on infections and cancer has been done by Dr. Linus Pauling. However, some of the studies concerning vitamin C and cancer are controversial. Vitamin C is an antioxidant and, as such, has tremendous implications in the management of free radicals, which can lead to the development of cancer. Curiously, we are one of the few animals that do not manufacture their own vitamin C.

What is known about vitamin C is the following:

- Vitamin C prevents the formation of nitrosamines (a potent carcinogen) from nitrites and amines, both in the test tube and in the body.[152]
- Several studies show that vitamin C in foods like lettuce is responsible for the decreased incidence of human gastric cancer in the United States.[153]
- Numerous studies show that vitamin C protects the body against human bladder cancer[154,155] and destroys another very potent bladder carcinogen called N-methyl-N-nitrosoguanidine.[156] People who take high doses of vitamin C excrete most of it in the urine, where nitrosamines are also excreted. This high amount of vitamin C accumulating in the bladder neutralizes nitrosamines that would otherwise cause bladder cancer.
- Vitamin C protects the body against most carcinogenic hydrocarbons.
- Vitamin C is needed to produce collagen, a substance that gives structure to the bones, cartilage, muscles, and vascular

tissues. Large amounts of vitamin C may be needed to produce sufficient collagen to protect the body from cancer by forming a wall around the cancer.[157]

- Vitamin C molecules may inhibit the spread of cancer by neutralizing an enzyme (hyaluronidase) made by cancer cells that would otherwise help the cancer to metastasize.[158] It has been found that many cancer patients have low blood levels of vitamin C, but it is not known whether this is a result of poor nutrition, which is generally seen in cancer victims, or whether this is due to the fact that vitamin C is being exhausted to neutralize that special enzyme made by the cancer.

- Smoking decreases the amount of vitamin C in lung tissue and blood. Here again, vitamin C could be neutralizing the toxic carcinogens contained in cigarette smoke.

- Some animal studies by Homer Black show that vitamin C can reverse the carcinogenic effect of ultraviolet light.

- The literature is replete with studies showing that vitamin C may have a protective role in viral illnesses.

- Vitamin C greatly affects the immune system: the phagocytes require vitamin C for proper function; and a deficiency in vitamin C causes a decrease in T cells, the defensive killing cells of the immune system.[159]

The question is, how much vitamin C should a person take? It seems that large doses of vitamin C ("large" relative to that amount specified by the RDA) can be taken without serious side effects. One way to estimate the amount of vitamin C we need is to measure the amount made by an animal that can manufacture it, and then extrapolate from that figure the amount a human needs based on body weight.[160] If an animal that makes X amount of vitamin C weighs 15 pounds and a human weighs 150 pounds, then the human's need of vitamin C is ten times X. Using this comparison, the estimate for a human's need for vitamin C is 2 to 4 grams without stress and up to 10 grams with stress. These amounts are many times higher than the RDA allowance of 60 milligrams. Dr Pauling is reported to take about 10 grams of vitamin C daily. A study by Hoffer shows that doses of 3 to 30 grams of vitamin C in more than 1,000 patients since 1953 did not cause one miscarriage, kidney-stone formation, or any other serious toxicity.[161] Klenner has given patients 10 grams of vitamin C daily for over thirty years without any serious toxic side effects.[162]

DRUGS AND VITAMINS

The interaction between many drugs and nutrients has become known during the past fifteen years. Some of these drug interactions involve the absorption or utilization of vitamins by the body, and ultimately compromise a patient's health. Table 6.7, on the next page, provides a list of some commonly used prescription drugs, describes what they are used for, and lists the vitamins with which drugs interfere. A patient who is taking one of these drugs should be aware that his or her diet may have to be supplemented with the indicated vitamin. Of course, if one of these drugs (like tetracycline) is taken for just a short period of time, no vitamin supplementation is needed. However, if some drugs are taken for months or years (like anticonvulsants, oral contraceptives, high blood pressure medication, or antituberculosis drugs), then vitamin supplementation should be instituted.

MINERALS

Selenium

Selenium, a metal in our body, has three very important functions. First, selenium together with glutathione peroxidase is a major antioxidant and, as such, is a free radical scavenger. It enables organisms to survive with less oxygen. Second, selenium reacts with toxic metals to form biologically inert compounds. The metals that are toxic to our bodies but rendered harmless by selenium are mercury, cadmium, and arsenic. Third, there is a correlation between night vision and the selenium content of the retina; the higher the selenium content, the better the vision.

Rich dietary sources of selenium include organ meats such as liver, seafoods, and some whole-grain cereals (whole-grain cereals vary greatly in selenium content). It has been shown by G.N. Schrauzer and colleagues that the selenium content in pasteurized milk in Caracas, Venezuela, is ten times greater than that in milk in Beltsville, Maryland.[163] Schrauzer and colleagues also studied the number of cancer deaths related to the amount of dietary-selenium intake from food consumption in twenty-seven different countries and nineteen different states in the United States.[164] They have concluded that the higher the blood-selenium content, the lower the cancer incidence. The cancer incidence for each state, which is given in Chapter 1, correlates well with their selenium data. R.J. Shamberger has shown that selenium suppresses the development of skin tumors in animals.[165] Shamberger and Willis have shown that in 1965, the higher the soil or crop level of selenium, the lower the cancer death

Table 6.7   Effect of Drugs on Nutrients

Drug	Use	Nutrients Decreased
Antacids		
Sodium bicarbonate	Decreases stomach acid.	Folate, phosphate, calcium, copper.
Aluminum hydroxide	Decreases stomach acid.	Folate, phosphate, calcium, copper.
Antibiotics		
Tetracycline	Kills bacteria.	Vitamin C, calcium, potassium, magnesium.
Gentimicin	Kills bacteria.	Vitamin C, calcium, potassium, magnesium.
Isoniazid	Treats tuberculosis.	Vitamin B$_6$, niacin, vitamin D.
Para-aminosalicylic acid	Treats tuberculosis.	Vitamin B$_{12}$, folate.
Trimethoprim	Treats tuberculosis and bacteria.	Folate.
Anticonvulsants		
Phenytoin	Prevents seizures.	Folic acid, vitamin D, vitamin K.
Phenobarbital	Prevents seizures.	Folic acid, vitamin D, vitamin K.
Primidone	Prevents seizures.	Folic acid, vitamin D, vitamin K.
Valproic acid	Prevents seizures.	Folic acid, vitamin D, vitamin K.
Anticancer		
Cisplatin	Treats cancer.	Magnesium.
Methotrexate	Treats cancer.	Folate, calcium.
Anticoagulants		
Coumadin	Thins blood.	Vitamin K.
Antihypertensives		
Hydralazine	Lowers blood pressure.	Vitamin B$_6$.
Beta Blockers	Lowers blood pressure.	Carotene.
Anti-inflammatory		
Aspirin	Decreases inflammation.	Vitamin C, folate, iron.
Colchicine	Decreases inflammation.	Vitamin B$_{12}$.
Prednisone	Decreases inflammation.	Calcium.

Drug	Use	Nutrients Decreased
Diuretics		
Furosemide	Excretes water.	Potassium, calcium, magnesium.
Thiazides	Excretes water.	Potassium.
Triamterene	Excretes water.	Folate.
Laxatives		
Mineral oil	Stimulates bowel.	Vitamins A, K, D.
Phenolphthalein	Stimulates bowel.	Potassium.
Psyllium	Stimulates bowel.	Calcium.
Senna	Stimulates bowel.	Calcium.
Oral contraceptives	Birth control.	Vitamin B_6, folate, vitamin C.
Tranquilizers		
Chlorpromazine	Relaxes, calms.	Riboflavin.
Ulcer medications		
Cimetidine	Decreases stomach acid.	Vitamin B_{12}.
Ranitidine	Decreases stomach acid.	Vitamin B_{12}.

Table 6.7—Continued

From Ovesen, L. 1979. *Drugs* 18:278.

rate in the United States and Canada.[166] They also studied the population in several American cities and found that the higher the average blood selenium level, the lower the cancer death rate.[167]

Another study demonstrates that rats depleted of selenium and fed a diet high in polyunsaturated fats developed breast cancer.[168] My own research shows that selenium protects the cell membrane from attack by free radicals. Other research by R. Medina and colleagues shows that selenium fed daily to mice inhibits cancer from forming in them.[169] The antioxidant property of selenium protects your body against cancer especially if your diet is high in polyunsaturated fats.

Several studies indicate that selenium deficiency corresponds to incidence of heart attacks.[170,171] High rates of heart disease and heart attacks are evident in selenium-deprived children in China and in selenium-deprived adults in Finland. Deaths from heart attack are highest in Finland, New Zealand, and perhaps South Africa. These countries have widespread selenium deficiency compared to the United States. When selenium supplements are given to Chinese children, significant improvement occurs in their heart-disease rates.

Survival rates of offspring in animals is very sensitive to the amount of selenium in the mother. An average sow has four or five piglets per litter in areas of Finland with low selenium soil content. But when 0.1 milligram of selenium is added to the diet, the litter size increases to ten.

Schrauzer maintains that the average selenium intake of the American population is only one-half of the amount required "for optimal protection against neoplastic [cancer] disease."[172] The average American diet contains between 50 and 160 micrograms of selenium per day, depending on area of residence. The recent recommendation by the National Research Council for selenium consumption is between 50 and 200 micrograms per day, but Schrauzer concludes from his studies that at least 300 micrograms of selenium per day are needed for cancer protection. Selenium toxicity occurs after prolonged ingestion of 2,400 to 3,000 micrograms of selenium per day.[173]

Obviously, selenium is not the only factor involved in cancer development or its progression, and it would be unwarranted to consume a great deal of selenium every day thinking that it alone would prevent cancer. However, depending upon where you live, you could take supplemental selenium in the amount of 100 to 200 micrograms per day, assuming that you are living in an area with an adequate selenium content and assuming that you are eating a well-balanced diet. Vegetarians, dieters, and people living in areas of the country without adequate selenium stores will require about 200 micrograms of selenium per day. A study shows that a total of 500 micrograms of selenium per day is safely tolerated by people in Japan.[174] Organic selenium, as found in certain yeasts, is better than inorganic selenium for supplementation because it has less systemic toxicity at high concentrations, it resists chemical changes, and it is stable during food processing.

Zinc

Zinc is a metal that is essential for good growth and development, protein synthesis, and wound healing, and it is a functional part of many enzymes. Danbolt and Closs have shown that zinc deficiency produces the symptoms and problems of an inherited disease called acrodermatitis enteropathica, which consists of multiple skin and gastrointestinal problems.[175] This disease is completely cured by dietary zinc supplementation.

More importantly, zinc is intimately involved in immune function and the development of cancer. This subject has been extensively reviewed by Robert A. Good and colleagues.[176] Zinc has the following effects:

- Zinc deficiency decreases the number of T cells and suppressor T cells,[177,178] which could potentially lead to the development of cancer. However, phagocytes are more efficient with low blood levels of zinc.[179]
- Zinc deficiency is seen in patients with several different types of cancers, but this is related to poor dietary habits rather than to the cancer itself.
- Zinc excess and zinc deficiency have both been shown to inhibit tumor growth in animals. Whereas zinc deficiency stimulates anticancer inflammatory cells, zinc-supplemented animals have augmented T-cell anticancer activity.

Copper

The trace mineral copper is needed by the body in minute amounts. A deficiency of this nutrient results in anemia, a low white blood cell count, and bone demineralization. Copper enhances the immune system and also acts in cooperation with the antioxidants. The incidence of cardiovascular disease is increased with low levels of copper. Elevated cholesterol, elevated glucose levels, and heart-related abnormalities are seen in people who have a marginal deficiency of copper.

Calcium

The average daily intake of calcium for an American is 450–500 milligrams, an amount well below even the U.S. RDA of 1,000 milligrams per day for those under age 50 and 1,500 milligrams per day for those over 50. While it is important to include sufficient calcium in your diet, you have to be wary of dairy products, its chief source. They contain too much fat and are also highly allergenic no matter what their fat content. Fatty foods are a factor in 60 percent of women's cancers, 40 percent of men's cancers, and 75 percent of all cardiovascular diseases.

Low calcium levels are linked to:

- Osteoporosis.
- Hypertension.[180]
- Colon cancer.[181,182]

- Alzheimer's disease.[183]
- Asthma flares.
- Some male infertility problems.

It is important to get the proper amounts of calcium in your early years—the first twenty to twenty-five years of life—so that the risk of all illnesses will be greatly reduced. However, recent studies suggest that postmenopausal women should take calcium supplements because even at that age bone loss can be reduced.[184,185] These studies have important implications for osteoporosis, because it is shown that bone loss can be reduced significantly even if you begin taking calcium later in life. Osteoporosis currently affects 34 million Americans and results in 1.3 million bone fractures each year.

The safest and easiest way to obtain calcium is by taking a calcium supplement. However, calcium should not be taken by itself; rather, it should be taken with several other nutrients that aid calcium absorption and metabolism. Some of these nutrients, like vitamin D and vitamin C, should be taken only with food, and the others, like magnesium, boron, silicon, threonine, and lysine, should be taken with calcium at night.[186] Calcium and magnesium should be taken in a ratio of about three or four to one. Calcium should be taken only at night and not with food because fiber foods bind calcium and render it useless, and the body repairs itself at night using calcium, and if there is insufficient calcium available, it will be taken from the bones. Take calcium with orange or tomato juice if they do not upset your stomach because they facilitate calcium absorption.[187] The best form of calcium to take is calcium carbonate because it is absorbed better than the other forms of calcium, and the lower molecular weight of calcium carbonate allows the use of a smaller pill. And finally, calcium taken at bedtime may help you fall asleep.

Magnesium

Many processes in the body require magnesium. It is essential for all biosynthetic processes and for the formation of energy molecules.

A marginal deficiency of magnesium results in nausea, muscle weakness, irritability, mental derangement, and other muscular changes. Because magnesium assists in calcium and potassium uptake, decreased supplies of magnesium will result in lower levels of calcium and potassium. The proper magnesium concentration is needed to maintain proper heart function. Moreover, if magnesium is given to patients during the first few days following their heart attacks, a decrease in mortality is seen thereafter.[188,189] It is equally important to make sure that your magnesium levels are adequate if you are receiving digitalis, a cardiovascular drug. It has been shown that patients receiving digitalis have low magnesium levels.[190] Low levels of magnesium are frequently seen in diabetics as well. When diabetic patients were given magnesium, their glucose levels were much better controlled and less insulin was required.[191]

Fluoride

Fluoride is an essential trace element, and the U.S. Recommended Dietary Allowance is up to 4 milligrams per day. About 50 percent of the American population now drinks water that has been fluoridated. Fifty percent of those who are 17 years old or younger have no dental decay whatsoever. This was not the case in the United States just fifteen years ago.

Fluoride occurs naturally in foods and the environment. Water is the number one source of fluoride, which is also found in certain plants, such as tea, and fish products. Some areas of the United States, including the Rocky Mountain and southwestern areas, have many more times the optimal content of natural fluoride in their water. Since climate determines the amount of water children drink in a particular area of our country, the concentration of fluoride in the community water supply will vary accordingly. The United States government recommends fluoride supplementation when the drinking water contains less than 0.7 ppm (parts per million). The optimal range for drinking water should be 0.7–1.2 ppm.

High doses of fluoride (75 milligrams a day) have been used in an attempt to increase the bone matrix in patients with osteoporosis.[192] In this study and other studies, using high doses of fluoride did, in fact, make the bones appear more solid on X rays, but the bones were extremely brittle and broke. However, low doses of fluoride under the 4-milligram Recommended Dietary Allowance have been shown to enhance the entry of calcium into the bone, to form a very solid bone matrix, and to help correct the effects of osteoporosis.[193-195]

Some health enthusiasts have indicted fluoride as a trace mineral that causes cancer. A number of studies were conducted recently to address this very issue, and the data show that fluoride in low concentrations does not cause cancer.[196,197] The 1990 National Toxicology Program said that very high doses of fluoride, much higher than the amount humans are exposed to, may cause a marginal increase in cancer in test animals.

At least 51 percent of the inhabitants of more than thirty-six states are drinking fluoridated water. New Jersey, third from the bottom of the list of states drinking fluoridated water, has 15 percent of its population drinking fluoridated water. Ninety-one percent or more of the population in the following states are drinking fluoridated water: Michigan, Connecticut, South Carolina, South Dakota, North

Dakota, Georgia, Maryland, Colorado, Indiana, Illinois, and the District of Columbia.

Iron

Iron is an integral part of hemoglobin, the large protein molecule inside red blood cells that carries oxygen. This important mineral is absorbed through the intestine. Many people have a marginal deficiency in iron. Women require more iron than men; however, iron should not be taken unless there is a real need, such as when iron loss leads to anemia. Because iron is stored in the body, a high iron intake can cause problems. It has been shown that iron complexes can initiate the production of free radicals[198] and that excess stores of iron increase the risk of cancer in men and probably in women as well.[199]

LOWERING YOUR RISK OF CANCER

Cancer patients have vitamin deficiencies (in particular, folic acid, vitamin C, and pyridoxine) as well as other nutritional deficiencies.[200] There have been a number of studies of patients with proven cancer who are being treated with vitamin therapy alone. Many of these vitamin-therapy studies have recently been reviewed by Bertino,[201] who concludes that such treatment is without proven benefit to the cancer patient—and I agree with him. The cancer patient should be thoroughly worked up by an oncology specialist. I am advocating simple common sense: an apparently healthy person should take steps to avoid or eliminate risk factors that could potentially cause cancer and atherosclerosis. This includes eating the right foods and taking the right amount of those vitamins and minerals shown to have anticancer and antioxidant effects, and shown to be needed for the immune system to function well. By eliminating all known risk factors of cancer and atherosclerosis and practicing good nutrition supplemented with vitamins and minerals, your overall risk of developing cancer or atherosclerosis will be kept to a minimum.

Richard S. Schweiker, then Secretary of Health and Human Services, said in a policy statement given at a symposium on cancer research at Rockefeller University that he and the Reagan Administration endorse the research focus on cancer prophylaxis and the protective potential of vitamins and trace minerals in both normal and high-risk populations. As reported by the *Medical Tribune* on June 30, 1982, he said that enough new data have emerged in recent basic, clinical, and epidemiological studies to justify support for the hypothesis that micronutrients may prevent the initiation or development of cancer. The National Cancer Institute in Bethesda, Maryland, has allocated several million dollars for this purpose.

Schweiker stated, "This new strategy holds promise for reducing the incidence of cancer more successfully than an attempt to remove from the environment all substances which may initiate the cancer process—an approach which is not always possible or practical." In addition, he said that laboratory studies of vitamin A precursors, vitamins C and E, selenium, and certain chemicals demonstrate that these "act as preventive agents."

I recommend taking the combination of vitamins and minerals in Table 6.8 as a food supplement. These nutrients could be taken daily unless otherwise specified by your physician. Pregnant or lactating women should not follow this program unless it has been approved by their physician. The formula for younger children is also shown.

I also recommend taking as a food supplement the Calcium Formula shown in Table 6.9.

Table 6.8   Supplementation Program

Nutrient	Adult Amount	% U.S. RDA*	Child (Age 1-4) Amount	%U.S. RDA
Beta-carotene	20 mg	***	1 mg	***
Vitamin A (palmitate)	5,000 IU	1,000	834 IU	33
Vitamin D (ergocalciferol)	400 IU	100	400 IU	100
Vitamin E (di-tocopherol)	400 IU	1,333	15 IU	150
Vitamin C (ascorbic acid)	350 mg	580	60 mg	150
Folic acid	400 mcg	100	200 mcg	100
Vitamin B$_1$ (thiamine)	10 mg	667	1.1 mg	157
Vitamin B$_2$ (riboflavin)	10 mg	588	1.2 mg	150
Niacinamide	40 mg	200	9 mg	100
Vitamin B$_6$ (pyridoxine)	10 mg	500	1.12 mg	100
Vitamin B$_{12}$ (cyanobalamin)	18 mcg	300	4.5 mcg	150
Biotin	150 mcg	50	25 mcg	20
Pantothenic acid (d-calcium pantothenate)	20 mg	200	5 mg	100
Iodine	150 mcg	100	70 mcg	100
Copper (cupric oxide)	3 mg	150	1.25 mg	125
Zinc (zinc gluconate)	15 mg	100	10mg	125
Potassium	30 mg	#	2 mg	#
Selenium (organic)	200 mcg	**	20 mcg	**
Chromium (organic)	125 mcg	**	20 mcg	**
Manganese (gluconate)	2.5 mg	**	1 mg	**
Molybdenum	50 mcg	**	25 mcg	**
Inositol	10 mg	#	0	N/A

Table 6.8   Supplementation Program–*continued*

Nutrient	Adult Amount	% U.S. RDA*	Child (Age 1-4) Amount	% U.S. RDA
Para aminobenzoic acid	10 mg	#	0	N/A
Bioflavonoids	10 mg	#	10 mcg	#
Choline (choline bitartrate)	10 mg	#	5 mg	#
L-Cysteine	20 mg	#	0	N/A
L-Arginine	5 mg	#	0	N/A
Histidine	N/A	N/A	10 mg	**
Leucine	N/A	N/A	10 mg	**
Isoleucine	N/A	N/A	10 mg	**
Lysine	N/A	N/A	10 mg	**
Threonine	N/A	N/A	10 mg	**

*Percentage U.S. Recommended Dietary Allowance (U.S. RDA) for adults and children 4 or more years.
**Established as adequate and safe by the National Research Council, National Academy of Sciences; no U.S. RDA has been established.
***Can be converted to vitamin A according to body needs; 1 mg of beta-carotene = 1,666 IU of vitamin A.
No nutritional requirement established.
N/A=Not applicable

Table 6.9   Calcium Formula

Nutrient	Dosage	% U.S. RDA*
Calcium (calcium carbonate)	500 mg	50
Magnesium (magnesium oxide)	140 mg	36
Silicon	2 mg	#
Boron	2 mg	#
L-Threonine	2 mg	#
L-Lysine	2 mg	#

* Percentage U.S. Recommended Dietary Allowance (U.S. RDA) for adults and children 4 or more years.
# No U.S. RDA established.

7

Disease Prevention and Treatment Using Nutrients

By the year 2000, cancer will emerge as the number one cause of death in the United States. The successes in the treatment of cancer plateaued in the 1970s, and no real advances have been made since then. Even though much has been learned about the biology of cancer growth, there is much doubt that this information will translate into any therapeutic success. As I have said since 1981, we need to globally implement strategies like our Ten-Point Plan to reduce your risk of ever developing cancer or heart disease in the first place. Part of Point One, Nutrition, is the use of certain nutrients. Many scientists now agree that chemoprevention of a disease like cancer is a novel approach that has great promise of success. So far, the nutrients used in human chemoprevention trials include beta-carotene, selenium, the retinoids, folic acid, the B vitamins, vitamin C, vitamin A, and vitamin E. These human trials study a specific disease and the effects a nutrient has on it.

CANCER AND PRECANCER PREVENTION

Multiple studies have been done on the effects of antioxidants and B vitamins on immunity. These studies show that these nutrients can enhance the immune system, protect against free radicals, protect against carcinogens, and hence protect normal cells from transforming into malignant cells.

Over the past twenty-five to thirty years, large epidemiological studies have shown that people consuming large amounts of carotene in their diets have a very low risk of getting cancer. This information is so exciting that the National Cancer Institute of the National Institutes of Health has set up an entire Chemoprevention Program sponsoring human intervention trials with individual vitamins and minerals. By performing these trials on high-risk patients, the National Cancer Institute can see if such intervention will decrease the patients' overall risk of getting cancer.[1]

Lung Cancer Prevention

Investigators have shown that patients at high risk for developing lung cancer (heavy smokers, for instance) had their risk greatly reduced if their serum levels of beta-carotene, vitamin E, and selenium were very high.[2,3] Bronchial metaplasia, an abnormality of cells in the bronchial tubes, is considered to be an indicator of lung cancer risk in smokers. Retinoids, folate, and vitamin B12 have reversed metaplasia in smokers.[4-7] Other precancerous lung conditions are also being treated with beta-carotene, vitamin E, and other antioxidants. Zinc is being used in conjunction with other antioxidants to treat precancerous conditions of the esophagus. Many of these studies are being done in cooperation with the United States National Cancer Institute and other foreign universities, including ones in China, Finland, and Africa. Other studies show similar findings, that is, a correlation between high levels of beta-carotene and other antioxidants and a low risk of getting cancers at eight different sites.[8-10]

Colon Cancer Prevention

We have already discussed the role of calcium in the prevention of colon cancer. This has been a very significant finding given the fact that over half the population is marginally deficient in calcium due to insufficient daily intake. Patients with low selenium intake are also at risk for developing colon cancer and breast cancer, as well as lung cancer.

Polyps are growths that can occur in the rectum and colon. These can be easily removed, but they often recur. About 20 percent of all polyps transform into cancer, so it is important to try to prevent their recurrence once they have been resected. The recurrence of polyps was examined in one study sponsored by the Ludwig Institute for Cancer Research in Toronto, Canada. After surgical resection of polyps in 200 people who were then deemed free of all other polyps, one group of 100 patients was given a daily supplement of 400 milligrams of vitamin C and 400 IU of vitamin E. The other group received a placebo. After two years of treatment, a slight reduction of polyp recurrences was noted in the patient group receiving the vitamin supplementation.

Another similar study at six different research centers in the United States involved 865 people. They too had resected polyps and were deemed free of polyps at the time they were enrolled in the program. One group received supplements of vitamins C and E; the second group received beta-carotene; the third group got vitamins C and E as well as beta-carotene; and the fourth group got a placebo. This trial is still ongoing, but the results thus far are encouraging and show some promise, since the people who received vitamins C and E plus beta-carotene had a decreased recurrence rate.

Cervical Dysplasia and Cervix Cancer Prevention

Cervical dysplasia is a premalignant lesion of the uterine cervix and is associated with an increased risk of cervical cancer. Several epidemiological studies show that a person has a significant risk for cervical dysplasia or frank invasive carcinoma if that person has low dietary intakes or low blood levels of beta-carotene and vitamin C.[11-21] In one study, women consuming low amounts of dietary carotene had a two to three times higher risk of developing cervical dysplasia or cancer than women with the highest dietary carotene intake. In another study, women with high blood carotene levels had an 80 percent reduction in risk of cervical carcinoma. An evaluation of patients with cervical dysplasia, carcinoma *in situ*, and invasive cancer reveals a progressive decrease in blood carotene levels with increasing severity of disease. In another study, women consuming less than 2 milligrams of dietary beta-carotene had a sixfold greater risk of developing cervical cancer than those consuming more than 3 milligrams per day.

Vitamin C, another antioxidant, is equally important for the health of the cervix. Women with cervical dysplasia had an average daily vitamin C intake of 80 milligrams; their healthy counterparts, by comparison, had a daily intake of 107 milligrams. The risk of developing cervical dysplasia was ten times higher for women whose daily vitamin C intake was below 30 milligrams. Studies examining blood vitamin C levels reveal an association between higher vitamin C levels and a reduced risk for dysplasia. A lower incidence of cervical cancer is seen when there is a high blood level of both carotene and vitamin C.

Gastritis and Stomach Cancer Prevention

Like all cancers, stomach cancer develops in a series of stages. First, the lining of the stomach undergoes an inflammation (gastritis). Gastritis makes the stomach susceptible to further damage from certain compounds, like nitrosamines, which are powerful carcinogens. Further damage leads to a precancerous lesion called dysplasia, and then finally to stomach cancer.

Certain nutrients can prevent or reduce the risk for further development of stomach cancer at each of its stages.[22-36] Vitamins C and E reduce the risk of stomach cancer because they block nitrosamine formation. Vitamin C also decreases the ability of gastric fluids to cause genetic mutations. Antioxidants, especially vitamin C, reduce the overall risk of gastrointestinal cancers.

Atrophic gastritis is a chronic inflammation of the stomach and is considered to be a risk for stomach cancer. Atrophic gastritis is not itself a precancerous lesion but can develop into one. If you have atrophic gastritis, chronic gastritis, or recurrent gastric ulcer, you have a two- to threefold higher risk of stomach cancer.

Inadequate vitamin C intake has been correlated with a higher risk for atrophic gastritis. Studies of people with chronic gastritis found they also had low blood levels of vitamin C, and people having the highest risk for stomach cancer had the lowest blood levels of vitamin C. Dietary vitamin C was found to be protective in reducing the risk of chronic atrophic gastritis.[37]

Other antioxidant nutrients have been studied and show equally impressive results. In one study, blood levels of carotenes and vitamin E were low in people with gastric dysplasia compared to healthy controls.[38]

Urinary Bladder Cancer Prevention

Urinary bladder polyps, like colon polyps, can also become cancerous. They are easily removed by surgical procedures, but 70 percent of them will recur or new polyps will form in these patients.

Approximately 120 people have been enrolled in a study being conducted at West Virginia University to test whether four nutrients can decrease the risk of future bladder polyps after surgical removal. Patients were divided into two groups: one group took a multiple vitamin at the Recommended Dietary Allowance levels; the other group took the same multivitamin but additional doses of vitamins A, B6, and C, as well as E. B6 has been known to decrease recurrence rates in bladder cancer studies in humans. Vitamins A and C have been used in used in animal studies with very good results, but vitamin E has never been used in this setting before. While the study is still ongoing, preliminary results again indicate that the extra doses of nutrients have decreased the risk of recurring bladder polyps.

Oral Leukoplakia Prevention

Leukoplakia is a condition characterized by white patches of tissue inside the mouth that are known to be premalignant. The major risk factors for leukoplakia are tobacco use, alcohol use, dietary factors, and the chewing of betel nuts. The highest rates of oral cancer are seen in India, Sri Lanka, Vietnam, New Guinea, the Philippines, Hong Kong, Taiwan, and parts of Brazil. In the United States there are about 32,000 cases of oral cancer.

Patients who have been treated for and cured of their first cancer of the head and neck usually continue the same lifestyle, then develop and succumb to a second one.

Certain nutrients, including retinoids, carotene, vitamin A, and vitamin E, have an important role in the prevention of oral cancer.[39-53] These nutrients inhibit leukoplakia and other precancerous and cancerous lesions in animal studies and in human trials. In humans, the use of certain retinoids reversed leukoplakia, but it recurred once the retinoids were discontinued. Taking beta-carotene alone or in combination with vitamin A was found to decrease the incidence of damaged mucosal cells in populations at high risk for oral cancer.

In India, patients with oral lesions were divided into three groups: the first group received 180 milligrams per week of beta-carotene alone; the second received beta-carotene plus vitamin A (100,000 IU per week); and the third group received a placebo. Six months after treatment, complete remissions were seen in 15 percent of group one, 27.5 percent of group two, and only 3 percent of group three. New appearances of leukoplakia were strongly inhibited. In another study, similar patients were given 200,000 IU of vitamin A per week for six months; 57 percent of them responded completely and also had a complete suppression of new leukoplakia.

Of twenty-four patients with leukoplakia given 30 milligrams of beta-carotene daily, 71 percent responded completely after three to six months. The investigators of this study also showed that beta-carotene enhanced the immune system by significantly increasing the number of killer cells as well as effecting smaller increases in other immune cells. Hence beta-carotene effectively inhibits the cancer process, is nontoxic, and is readily available.

In another human study beta-carotene conclusively reversed leukoplakia.[54] The results of this study suggest that beta-carotene may not protect the body from cancer until late, when a normal cell is about to be transformed into a cancer cell. This means that the initial actions triggered by a carcinogen may not be inhibited by beta-carotene as it is by other nutrients, but rather the carotene stops the transformation of the cell from a normal one to a malignant one.

Very high doses of carotene taken by mouth appear to lower the blood concentration of vitamin E over a period of eight months,[55] and other studies show similar findings.[56] In these studies, the protective effect of beta-carotene was somewhat reduced, indicating that all of the antioxidants are needed to protect the cell.

Conclusions

At this point the bulk of scientific data, test tube and animal studies, indicates a strong correlation between certain vitamins and minerals and immunity. The data suggest that some nutrients enhance the immune system and also reduce the incidence of cancer.[57-59] Many researchers have already advocated the use of vitamin and mineral supplements in the prevention of cancer and other diseases.[60-62]

In 1987 the American Cancer Society issued statements regarding its views on chemoprevention and cancer.[63] They stated: "Cancer epidemiology provides the most compelling evidence that primary prevention is possible and that chemoprevention agents exist naturally in our diet. The growing body of evidence demonstrates the lack of past success in developing therapies that can eradicate disseminated solid tumors in the United States...There seems little doubt, if chemopreventive intervention works, it will be highly cost effective and ethically a far more desirable means of reducing mortality than treatment." We are all agreed then that the preponderance of evidence suggests that certain nutrients can, in fact, decrease your risk of developing cancer.

Ongoing chemoprevention trials are utilizing individual nutrients in specific sites. For instance, retinoids are being used in bladder cancers; vitamin C in high-risk patients for colon cancer; and topical Retin-A on oral cavity lesions called leukoplakia, skin lesions like actinic keratosis, and basal cell carcinoma. Other chemoprevention trials are studying the abilities of selenium to protect against breast, lung, and colon cancers; of vitamin A and beta-carotene to protect against cancer at all sites; and of other antioxidants to prevent gastrointestinal cancers. An attempt for a trial to decrease the recurrence rate of breast cancer was initiated using a low-fat, high-fiber diet with foods having higher amounts of vitamins and minerals. But this trial never really got off the ground because doctors did not refer patients as readily, and once patients did get into the trial, they simply did not adhere to the protocol. (See Chapter 14, Sexual-Social and Hormonal Factors, for more information.)

In addition to protecting against cancer, some nutrients help prevent the side effects commonly experienced when taking certain medications. For example, vitamin E has been shown to prevent the hair loss of adriamycin chemotherapy in one report.[64]

PREVENTION OF CARDIOVASCULAR DISEASE

Cardiovascular diseases are the leading cause of death in the United States. Two of every five Americans will develop cardiovascular illness in the form of high blood pressure, a heart attack, a stroke, or other vascular disease. Until now, however, treatment consisted largely of systematic relief; prevention of the primary cause of the illness was not terribly important. It has long been known that dietary factors, especially a high-fat, low-fiber diet, are the major cause of cardiovascular illness. This correlation was first confirmed about eighty years ago by an experiment involving rabbits fed a high-cholesterol diet. Rabbits eating high amounts of cholesterol were later found to have atherosclerosis. Although research had also focused on the link between heart disease and diet, specifically the fat and cholesterol content, major breakthroughs today show that vitamins, minerals, and other nutrients can have a dramatic and very positive impact on cardiovascular disease. Antioxidants like beta-carotene and vitamins C and E hold great promise in the fight against heart disease.

It took a long time for the medical profession to consistently inform patients that a high-fat, high-cholesterol diet leads to the development of cardiovascular illness. For decades now, the total blood cholesterol has been part of most laboratory blood diagnostic analysis. Recently, attention has been given to the various lipoproteins that carry cholesterol throughout the body. These tests also have become very commonplace in the usual blood diagnostic work-up. The most exciting aspect of this research has focused on the reaction of free radicals with low-density lipoprotein cholesterol (LDL cholesterol), or, as I commonly tell my patients to remember it, the "lousy cholesterol." As you recall from Chapter 5, free radicals are highly unstable because of the way in which their electrons behave.

They can effect dramatic changes in the molecules with which they react. Free radicals, particularly the oxygen free radical, have recently been shown to change the LDL cholesterol molecule. Once changed, it assumes different properties that promote hardening of arteries. This modification is known as oxidation.[65]

Antioxidants to Prevent Alteration of LDLs

In Chapter 5 we discussed how antioxidants rid the body of harmful free radicals. An antioxidant called probucol has been shown to retard the progression of atherosclerosis in an animal model. Since probucol has many side effects, attention has been turned to the action of dietary antioxidants on the deleterious LDL oxidative process. Inhibitors of LDL oxidation are vitamin C and alpha-tocopherol, the most abundant and active form of vitamin E. The more important of the two in this situation, however, seems to be vitamin C. Vitamin C is equal to probucol in inhibiting LDL oxidation but more effective in preserving antioxidants like vitamin E and beta-carotene in the cellular membrane. Hence, there is a positive role not only for vitamin C but also for other antioxidants as supplements in atherosclerosis prevention.

The initial process of atherosclerosis actually begins with the immune system. Macrophages, cells of the immune system, ingest low-density lipoproteins and then are unable to get rid of these fats efficiently. These macrophages, full of fat and very sluggish, collect in arterial walls and create the first signs of atherosclerosis. Curiously, macrophages do not ingest unaltered LDL but rather only LDL that has been attacked and modified by free radicals. The most common alteration of LDL takes place because of lipid peroxidation, which occurs as a result of free radicals.

When the LDL is oxidized, several reactions take place that may lead to development of atherosclerosis. Included are the following: increased cholesterol accumulation in the macrophages, recruiting of additional macrophages into arterial walls, damage to nearby cells, and altered muscular control of arterial walls.[66]

Antioxidants can inhibit atherosclerosis in rabbits without elevating plasma cholesterol levels because they inhibit the formation of modified or oxidized LDL. Epidemiological evidence also shows that there is an inverse relationship between heart disease and vitamin E levels. The greater your serum vitamin E level, the less your risk of developing coronary artery disease. Also, the more unsaturated fats you consume, the higher your risk of developing oxidized LDL. Antioxidants such as beta-carotene, vitamin E, and vitamin C lessen the risk for developing oxidized or free radical modified LDL. On the other hand, iron is a potent free radical inducer. The more iron in the system, the higher the chance of converting the LDL into oxidized form—that is, the kind leads to atherosclerosis. The higher the concentration of serum vitamin C, beta-carotene, and vitamin E, the lower the chance of developing the same oxidation state of LDL.

Theoretically, then, in order to prevent the harmful LDL, oxidation of LDL by free radicals, you should decrease consumption of unsaturated fats and increase consumption of antioxidants like beta-carotene, vitamin E, and vitamin C. Although there is no direct randomized clinical trial using antioxidation as a means of preventing atherosclerosis, animal studies and basic science indicate that antioxidants do, in fact, reverse and inhibit atherosclerosis by modifying or reversing the action of free radicals on LDL.

Within the LDL molecule there are such antioxidants as vitamin E, beta-carotene, and coenzyme Q. Surrounding this protein in the plasma is vitamin C. In a series of experiments by Frei, human plasma was exposed to many oxidizing conditions, among them activated macrophages (macrophages loaded with oxidized LDL) and cigarette smoke. The results show that vitamin C was the only antioxidant that completely protected low-density lipoproteins from oxidative damage by free radicals. The antioxidants that reside within the molecule of LDL—beta-carotene, vitamin E, and coenzyme Q—started to protect LDL from free radical damage only after vitamin C had been used up in the plasma. In another series of experiments, coenzyme Q was found to be most effective among the antioxidants that naturally reside within the LDL molecule. Beta-carotene and vitamin E were also effective but slightly less so. However, vitamin C was the most potent of the four to protect LDL from attack by free radicals.[67] Human epidemiological studies also support the fact that people who have high vitamin C plasma levels also have a low incidence and risk of developing coronary artery disease. Other human studies also reveal similar findings: high levels of vitamin E, coenzyme Q, and beta-carotene can prevent atherosclerosis or even slow down its progression by inhibiting the oxidation of LDL by free radicals.

A fair percentage of people with cardiovascular disease have relatively normal total cholesterol and LDL cholesterol values. This sector of the population undergoes bypass surgery that reveals significant disease, takes cardiac medications, and requires physical rehabilitation. Even though these people may have other risk factors, it is curious that cardiovascular disease occurs with normal blood values. It seems probable to conclude that their LDLs are attacked by free radicals, are altered, and ultimately become embedded into arterial walls by way of macrophages.

Nutrients to Prevent Hypertension

Dietary factors have been shown to be an important aspect in the development of high blood pressure. Those factors include sodium, potassium, calcium, alcohol, magnesium, and fatty acids. Vitamin C has been shown to be involved in blood pressure regulation. As you increase the vitamin C level in the plasma, you consistently decrease the blood pressure. People with high plasma levels of vitamin C have 5 to 10 percent lower systolic as well as diastolic blood pressures. The higher the blood level of vitamin C, the lower the blood pressure. There are now data to suggest that vitamin C supplementation by a person with borderline hypertension will, in fact, reduce that person's blood pressure. Three men and nine women between the ages of 35 and 74 years old were given one gram of vitamin C per day, which decreased their systolic blood pressure by about 4 percent. The diastolic pressure, however, remained unchanged. Although experimentation in humans is limited, the potential rewards are enormous. The effect of other antioxidants on blood pressure has not yet been studied.

HDL cholesterol, the protective lipoprotein or "healthy cholesterol" is thought to be responsible for protection against cardiovascular disease. Vitamin C increases levels of protective HDL cholesterol. The greater the HDL cholesterol, the less the risk for developing cardiovascular disease. The Baltimore Longitudinal Study of Aging reported that high dietary levels of vitamin C were associated with high levels of HDL cholesterol. In this study, 360 women and 511 men aged 20 to 95 were studied. Plasma levels of vitamin C and various lipids including triglycerides, LDL cholesterol, and HDL cholesterol were all measured. Intakes of vitamin C supplements were also recorded. The plasma vitamin C content was higher in women than in men, and those women who took vitamin C supplements had higher vitamin C levels also. Women had higher HDL levels than men. The higher the vitamin C level in plasma, the higher the HDL. Hence, vitamin C can reduce the risk of developing atherosclerosis by increasing the protective HDL cholesterol.

Antioxidants to Protect the Smoker From Free Radicals

Cigarette smoking increases oxygen free radicals directly and by smoke-induced inflammatory responses, which include an increased number of white blood cells, particularly the neutrophils, which, in turn, generate large amounts of reactive oxygen free radicals. Smokers, however, have very low levels of vitamin C, beta-carotene, vitamin A, and vitamin E in their plasma as well as in white blood cells. Hence, smokers probably have an increased risk of cardiovascular disease because of an increased number of free radicals being generated and a decreased blood level of the antioxidants beta-carotene, vitamins C and E, and vitamin A.

DEALING WITH EXISTING CARDIOVASCULAR DISEASE

How can antioxidants benefit a person who already has cardiovascular disease and who is symptomatic from it? Medical ischemia results when normal tissue is deprived of its regular blood supply. When there is no blood supply or a decreased amount, there is less oxygen delivered to the tissue. This can be caused by an obstruction in the blood vessel or constriction of those blood vessels. When a condition like this occurs in the heart, it can lead to angina and heart attacks.

A widely used medical technique called reperfusion actually resupplies blood to the deprived area. However, when new blood full of oxygen flows again through what was previously deprived of oxygen, a high concentration of free radicals are unleashed. This large surge of free radicals overwhelms the normal defense system of the tissue and often leads to severe damage. Cardiac arrhythmias commonly seen immediately after having a heart attack, "reperfusion arrhythmias," are mainly caused by the generation of free radicals. Studies employing free radical scavengers or antioxidants in this situation have shown a positive antiarrhythmic effect.[68,69] Vitamin E is the major antioxidant that can help prevent this reperfusion damage. Animal studies show that when vitamin E is administered orally, heart damage is prevented. Vitamin E can also dissolve blood clots in an acute heart attack. Currently, a water-soluble form of vitamin E is being developed for emergency treatment of heart attack victims.

Antioxidants also benefit patients with existing heart disease and chest pain that results from it. An important study investigated the relationship between angina and blood concentrations of carotene and vitamins A, C, and E.[70] Those who had angina also had low levels of plasma vitamins E and C and beta-carotene. Smokers had lower vitamin C and beta-carotene levels, and cigarette smoking contributed to low plasma levels of these nutrients in patients with angina. Vitamin E, however, was not influenced by cigarette smoking and was low in patients with angina. Those who had very low levels of vitamin E had a 2.7 times higher risk of developing angina. The findings suggest that people with angina and coronary heart disease benefit from natural antioxidants, particularly vitamin E. As you may remember, vitamin E can reduce the incorporation of cholesterol into arteries and decrease the damage in the heart muscle during a heart attack. This important study shows for the first time that people with angina can benefit from the intake of simple nutrients like these antioxidants.

Certain antioxidants, then, can help in some situations in the prevention of cardiovascular disease and also in the prevention of damage sustained from heart attacks and strokes. Supplementing with antioxidants is a simple measure that can help prevent cardiovascular disease and also greatly benefit a patient with existing cardiovascular disease. This along with my Ten-Point Plan, should be employed for the prevention and treatment of all heart disease.

PREVENTING NEURAL TUBE DEFECTS

A large body of evidence now suggests that women who were using multivitamins, especially those with folic acid, at the time they conceived had a much lower risk of having a fetus with neural tube defects. Neural tube defects are life threatening and occur in about 1 of every 1,000 children in the United States. That number becomes 1 in 20 for a second child. Birth defects among U.S. children cost about $1.4 billion annually due to their need for medical care. These findings should suggest the implementation of multivitamin use for women of childbearing age, especially those who have had high-risk pregnancies.[71-73]

NEUROLOGICAL DISEASES

There is a decrease in the amount of oxygen to the brain when there is heart injury, lung disease disorders, or head trauma; any condition leading to low blood pressure; or trauma such as a stroke in which blood pressure becomes severely elevated. New evidence suggests that with decreased oxygen, free radicals multiply and *promote* this damage. Therefore antioxidants or free radical scavengers may prevent damage in any of these situations.[74]

Vitamin E has been shown to be helpful in tardive dyskinesia[75] and in some cases of peripheral neuropathy.[76] Vitamin E deficiencies have also been associated with changes in the neurological status of some patients with chronic liver disease and cystic fibrosis. By adding vitamin E to the diets of animals that have these conditions, improvement was seen.

OTHER MEDICAL CONDITIONS

Skin Aging and Cataracts

A number of studies have shown that topical retinoids prevent skin aging and wrinkles.[77] Cataracts and macular degeneration are successfully treated with carotene, and vitamins E and C.[78-82]

Stomach Ulcers

Evidence also shows that stress-induced gastric mucosal injury may be prevented by using antioxidants.[83] This exciting discovery may lead to the use of antioxidants as adjuncts to other ulcer medications, and ultimately they may be used solely.

Infectious Diseases

About 20–40 million children worldwide suffer some degree of vitamin A deficiency that leads to impaired immune function. Research trials show that vitamin A supplementation prevents illness and death from infectious diseases among malnourished children. A study in southern India showed that mortality was reduced by more than half in those children with measles who were given vitamin A.[84] In a South African study the results were significant enough to suggest routine supplementation of vitamin A in children with acute measles.[85] In other studies vitamin A supplementation has reduced the mortality and morbidity in children with other infectious diseases.[86-88] Also, antioxidants can benefit patients with gram-negative sepsis, an often fatal illness.[89]

Bone Fractures

It has been found that elderly patients with fractured necks of the femur had healing of that fracture much sooner if they were fed a certain dietary supplement during their initial hospital stay.[90] The dietary supplementation included protein, carbohydrate, lipid, a certain amount of calories, 525 milligrams of calcium, many vitamins in moderate doses, including vitamins A, C, D3, and E, the B vitamins, folate, nicotinamide, pantothenate, and biotin, and other minerals. Patients who did not receive such a supplement not only required more time for their fracture to heal but also had many more other complications during the hospital stay. The differences between the supplemented and unsupplemented groups were quite significant.

Psoriasis

A study was conducted with a topical form of an analog of vitamin D, calcipotriol, on 345 patients with psoriasis. The special vitamin D ointment placed on the psoriasis was superior to the conventional medical ointment, betamethasone valerate, in reversing the psoriasis. The results of the study are particularly significant given the large number of patients who participated.[91]

TREATMENT OF CANCER

An equally exciting area of study is the use of vitamins and minerals in the treatment and control of cancers. In the early 1980s several small clinical chemoprevention trials appeared. Larger trials involving about 100,000 people began in 1985 and 1986. The sites of cancer most studied in chemoprevention are the head and neck, cervix, colon, lung, and breast. There are at least fifteen trials in the United States and five in other countries studying the effects of natural vitamins A, C, and E, the B vitamins, selenium compounds, calcium, and isotretinoin on breast cancer. Vitamin A analogue (4-HPR) is being studied in Italy as a chemopreventive agent against cancer in the healthy breast of patients treated for breast cancer.

Vitamin A, retinoic acid, and carotene have been used in the treatment of squamous cell carcinoma, basal cell carcinoma, and cutaneous T cell lymphoma of the skin,[92,93] and for the treatment of pro-myelocytic leukemia, a specific kind of leukemia.[94] However, the most solid success in human chemoprevention has been in the use of retinoic acid to prevent a second new tumor in patients with squamous cell carcinoma of the head and neck.[95]

Skin Cancer

Vitamin A and other retinoids, the large family of vitamin A analogs, have been used against basal cell carcinoma and squamous cell carcinoma of the skin. Retinoids have been very effective against these two cancers because they accumulate primarily in the skin where they act. Since these cancers, like other cancers that the retinoids have been used against, are unlikely to regress on their own, small changes have been important. In most of these studies, however, once the treatment was completed, many of the cancers returned. This observation suggests that retinoids will probably be required continuously so that the tumors do not recur. However, the problem with some of these retinoids, specifically etretinate and isotretinoin, has been that in larger doses they tend to dry the skin and also the mucous membranes.

So far, 50 percent of patients with basal cell carcinomas and about 71 percent of squamous cell carcinoma patients responded to retinoid use. It is true that basal cell carcinoma and squamous cell carcinoma are easy to cure using surgery, radiation, or other conventional means. However, most of these methods leave scar tissue; retinoids do not. Where retinoids are used, tumors shrink and the body fills that voided area back with normal tissue. Retinoids have been used also in other skin cancers. In a small group of patients with malignant melanoma, 3 of 20 people responded to retinoid use. About 78 people with mycosis fungoides or cutaneous T cell lymphoma have been treated with retinoids. Over half of them have responded somewhat to retinoid therapy thus far.

According to a study by S.M. Lippman et al., of M.D. Anderson Oncology Hospital in Texas, twenty-six patients with advanced metastatic squamous cell carcinoma were treated with a combination of a synthetic vitamin A analog (isotretinoin–Retin A) and interferon. Over 60 percent responded, which is slightly better than the response seen using aggressive chemotherapy in other studies.[96]

Leukemia

Sixteen patients with acute pro-myelocytic leukemia have been treated with retinoic acid, a member of the beta-carotene family. Twelve of these patients entered a complete remission.[97,98] This leukemia is usually refractory to all treatments. In addition, up to three-fourths of all patients treated in Chinese studies with this same disease had a complete remission. Advanced myelodysplastic syndrome is a rare but fatal disease. In one study, 3 of 6 patients with this disorder responded well to the vitamin D therapy.[99] Another study shows equally promising results using vitamin D and retinoic acid.[100]

Through studies that have been done and ones that are ongoing, we can discover what combinations of nutrients can be used to prevent cancer and other diseases. Hundreds of potential chemopreventive compounds have been identified from dietary sources like vegetables and garlic. Thousands more are being screened at the National Cancer Institute. However, the biggest drawback of all this excitement is that we are forever looking for a quick fix—one or two individual nutrients that will reduce or prevent a tumor—rather than addressing the needs of the entire individual and his or her lifestyle. A single pill simply will not do the job. What will? Begin by making changes in your lifestyle and diet, by not smoking or drinking alcohol, and by following all the other points that we will enumerate in the cogent Ten-Point Plan in Chapter 22.

DO VITAMINS OR MINERALS INTERFERE WITH CHEMOTHERAPY OR RADIATION THERAPY?

This is a question I am asked frequently by patients because their oncologists, ignorant of the subject, advise the patients not to take supplements during treatment. Many studies have been done to address this. The early studies were performed at the National Cancer Institute using an antioxidant called N-acetyl cysteine, which has a protective effect on the heart, with patients receiving a chemotherapeutic drug called adriamycin, which is toxic to the heart. The heart was protected and there was no interference with the tumor-killing performance of adriamycin. Another antioxidant called ICRF-187 offered significant protection against cardiac toxicity caused by adriamycin without affecting the antitumor effect.[101-104] Many cellular studies[105-108] and animal studies[109-113] demonstrate that vitamins A, E, and C, as well as beta-carotene and selenium, all protect against the toxicity of adriamycin, and at the same time actually enhance its cancer-killing effects.

Vitamins and minerals have also been studied with other chemotherapies and radiation. Studies using beta-carotene and other retinoids, vitamin C, or vitamin K show that normal tissue tolerance was improved in animals undergoing both chemotherapy and radiotherapy, and that tumors regressed.[114-120] Vitamin E produced similar findings: no interference with the killing of tumors by either radiation or chemotherapy in animals given concomitant vitamin E.[121-123] Animals given both beta-carotene and vitamin A with radiation and chemotherapy had more tumor killing than with chemotherapy and radiation alone, normal tissues were more protected, and there was a longer period of time without tumor recurrence.[124,125] Selenium and cysteine also heighten tumor killing by chemotherapy and radiation, and at the same time protect normal tissue.[126,127]

All cellular studies using vitamins (C, A, K, E, D, beta-carotene, B_6, B_{12}), minerals (selenium), and cysteine concomitantly with chemotherapy and radiation show the same effect: increased tumor killing and increased protection of the normal tissues.[128-137]

In human studies, vitamin E reduced the toxicity without affecting the cancer-killing performance of 13-cis-retinoic acid, used in the treatment of patients with head and neck, skin, and lung cancers.[138] At 1,600 IU of vitamin E per day, hair loss in patients receiving chemotherapy was reduced from the expected 30–90 percent.[139] Treating 190 head and neck cancer patients with vitamin A, 5FU, and radiation resulted in more-than-expected tumor killing while preserving normal tissue.[140] And vitamin A combined with chemotherapy for postmenopausal patients with metastatic breast cancers significantly increased the complete response rate.[141] In 13 patients with different cancers receiving different chemotherapies, vitamin K decreased tumor resistance.[142] Vitamin B_6 at 300 milligrams per day decreased radiation therapy toxicity.[143] In 20 patients receiving chemotherapy with vitamins A, C, and E, there was a greater response rate.[144] And studies show that WR-2721, an antioxidant, protects against the harmful side effects of chemotherapy and radiation without the loss of antitumor activity.[145]

An increase in survival for cancer patients, which is uncommon with any treatment, has been shown using antioxidants combined with chemotherapy or radiation. In fact, 11 patients who were given beta-carotene and canthaxanthin while undergoing surgery, chemotherapy, and radiation lived longer with an increase in disease-free intervals.[146] And antioxidant treatment with chemotherapy and radiation prolonged survival for patients with small cell lung cancer compared with patients who did not receive antioxidants.[147,148]

The effects of only one chemotherapeutic agent, methotrexate, can be reversed with folinic acid, which is an analog of the vitamin folic acid. Folic acid itself does not reverse methotrexate's effects. In order to reverse the effects of methotrexate, folinic acid has to be given in extremely high doses. It cannot be obtained over the counter; it must be prescribed.

All studies show that vitamins and minerals do not interfere with the antitumor effects of chemotherapy or radiation therapy. In fact, on the contrary, some vitamins and minerals used in conjunction with chemotherapy and/or radiation therapy have been shown to protect normal tissue and potentiate the destruction of cancer cells. In our own preliminary studies, we have found a decrease in side effects from chemotherapy and/or radiation therapy in breast cancer patients who followed our Ten-Point Plan, which, among other things, advocates the consumption of certain vitamins and minerals.[149]

PART THREE

The Risks

8
Nutritional Factors

It is now estimated and widely accepted that 60 percent of all women's cancers and 40 percent of all men's cancers are related to nutritional factors alone.[1-3] Overall it has been estimated that 75–90 percent of all cancers are related to lifestyle: nutritional factors, smoking, alcohol, occupational factors, chemicals, environmental factors, etc. All the major agencies in the United States—the National Academy of Sciences, the National Cancer Institute, and the American Cancer Society—have supported the fact that nutritional factors are linked to certain cancers.

Nutritional factors are most closely associated with the following cancers, listed in order of their prevalence in the United States: gastrointestinal cancers, the number two cancer; breast cancer, the number three cancer; prostate cancer, the number four cancer; and endometrial cancer, the number five cancer. With each year the number of new cancers continues to rise, and with the great majority of these being diet-related cancers, you can readily understand the enormous impact that proper nutrition could have in lowering the overall incidence of cancer in the United States and the world.

NUTRITIONAL EVOLUTION

The human race has existed for about two million years, and our prehuman ancestors for at least four million years. Today we are confronted with diet-related health problems that were previously of minor importance or totally nonexistent. Dietary habits adopted by Western society over the past hundred years have greatly contributed to the development of coronary heart disease, hypertension, diabetes, and cancer. These illnesses have dominated the past ninety-year history of humanity and are virtually unknown among the few surviving hunter-gatherer populations, like the Bantu tribesmen in Africa, whose way of life and eating habits today resemble those of man before agricultural development. Members of primitive cultures today who survive to the age of 60 or more are relatively free of these illnesses unlike their Western "civilized" counterparts.[4,5]

With the development of agriculture over 10,000 years ago, we began eating less meat and more vegetables. With less protein in our diets, our height declined by six inches. Since the Industrial Revolution, the pendulum started to swing back and we started to increase the protein content of our diets. Height increased and we are now nearly the same height as were the first biological modern men. But our diet is still very different from theirs: we are affluently malnourished.

Investigating the wild game in areas of the world where people are still quite primitive today, we find that these wild animals have less fat than domesticated ones because they are more active and have a less steady food supply. Also, domesticated animals are fed high concentrations of fat to produce tender meat. Wild game has fewer calories and more protein per unit of weight. Even modern vegetable food sources have more fat than noncommercially grown vegetables and fruits. Table 8.1 lists the various nutrients consumed by primitive man compared with those eaten by Americans today.[6]

Table 8.1 Diet Comparison of Primitive and Modern Man			
Nutrient	Primitive Man	American Man	Our Recommendations
Percentage of Total Calories			
Protein	34%	12%	10%
Carbohydrate	45%	46%	70%
Fats	21%	42%	20%
Daily Consumption			
Cholesterol	591.0 mg	600 mg	250 mg
Fiber	45.7 gm	19 gm	30-45 gm
Sodium	690.0 mg	5,000 mg	1,000 mg
Calcium	1,580.0 mg	740 mg	1,500 mg
Vitamin C	392.3 mg	88 mg	400 mg

Given primitive man's wide variety of collected plant foods, and assuming that his vitamin C intake is representative of his overall vitamin intake from foods, the diet of primitive man contained substantially greater amounts of vitamins than ours currently. The vitamin and mineral content continues to decrease in our food supply by: pesticides, processing techniques like refrigeration, freezing and thawing, transporting around the country, etc. The protein content of early man's food was nearly two to five times that of ours. The early human diet contained much less fat than ours, and the fat that it did contain was of a very different mix from ours. Its cholesterol content was about the same as ours, but its total fat was much less than ours. In addition, primitive man consumed many more essential fatty acids than we do today. Since chronic diseases have been with us for only a few decades, with the incidence of cancer spiraling ever upward, we should perhaps model our modern diet after that of our ancestors.

We have created a food supply very different from that of our ancestors with the development of food technology and the chemicals used for its growth and production. This "advancement" is costly to the human race.

EPIDEMIOLOGICAL PATTERNS

Large epidemiological studies demonstrate that a high-risk diet for cancer as well as cardiovascular diseases is one that has high-fat, high-cholesterol, low-fiber, salt-cured, pickled, charred, smoked, or burned foods, and a low consumption of vitamins and minerals. About forty years ago Dr. A. Tannenbaum showed that dietary fat significantly favored the development and growth of both spontaneous and induced breast cancer in animals.[7] Since then a high-fat, low-fiber diet has been associated with human breast cancer, colon cancer, prostate cancer, cancer of the endometrium, and coronary artery disease, suggesting that similar modifications of the diet would be beneficial in decreasing the risk of developing all these major diseases. Over the past half century, Americans have been consuming more fat, more cholesterol, more animal protein, more refined sugar, and less fiber. Likewise, an ever-increasing incidence of cancer has been seen for the same period in the United States.

Epidemiological studies are very important to assess cancer trends. The Bantu people of rural Africa have an extremely low incidence of cancer compared to industrialized nations. They have a low-fat, very high fiber diet. Except for Japan and Finland, the more industrialized a country is, the higher is the rate of "diet-sensitive" tumors, that is, colon/rectal cancer, breast cancer, endometrial cancer, and prostate cancer. People in industrialized countries usually eat a diet higher in fat than do people in nonindustrialized countries. The people in western Europe and in English-speaking countries have the highest colon cancer incidence rates, while the peoples of Asia, Africa, and South America (except Uruguay and Argentina, where the rates are similar to those of North America) have the lowest colon cancer incidence rates.

If a person emigrates from a country with a low incidence rate of colon cancer to a country with a high rate, such as the United States, the higher colon cancer rate shows up within the first generation. Japanese immigrants to the United States have the same colon cancer rate after only twenty years of consuming the American diet and have the same incidence of breast cancer after only two generations. Only 20 percent of the daily caloric intake in Japan is derived from fat compared to 40 percent in America.

About half of the Seventh-Day Adventists in the United States follow a vegetarian diet, and most do not eat pork. Their breast cancer mortality is one-half to two-thirds the breast cancer mortality seen in the United States population in general.

American-born Jews of European descent are at high risk for developing colon and rectal cancer. A twenty-year prospective study conducted in Israel has recently shown that a diet high in fiber, with foods of high vitamin C content, and with polyunsaturated fats, substantially reduces the number of colon and rectal cancer cases in that group.[8] And Seventh-Day Adventists and Mormons have a substantially lower incidence of colon cancer than the general population in the United States as well.[9-11] Both of these groups consume dietary fiber in great amounts and little or no beef or animal fat.

People in Finland have a high fat intake, with the majority of their fat calories derived from dairy products rather than beef. The incidence of heart attacks is quite high in that country; however, the incidence of colon cancer is very low. The latter statistic may seem surprising, but it is probably due, in part, to the large amount of fiber the Finnish get from rye. Hard evidence to explain this seeming discrepancy was unavailable until the recent discovery of fecapentaene. Fecapentaenes are found in the stools of people on fiber-depleted diets who have a high incidence of colon cancer. This chemical, produced by bacteria in the large bowel and then released by them when they die, is not present in fiber-eating populations who are free from colon cancer.[12,13] Fecapentaene is a very potent mutagen, as potent as one of the most potent carcinogens that we know, benzopyrene. When fiber is added to the diet, the bacteria stay healthy: they don't die and they don't release the fecapentaene.

OBESITY

Obesity affects about 35 percent of all Americans. Animal studies have shown that those animals with lean body masses have lower rates of cancer development as well as greater longevity.[14-18] Epidemiological studies also show the same correlation. In one study, when per capita total caloric intake was examined relative to cancer incidence in twenty-three countries and to cancer mortality in thirty-two countries, a significant correlation was found between total calories and each of the following: the incidence of rectal cancer in males, the incidence of leukemia in males, and the rate of mortality from breast cancer in females.[19] Another researcher found obesity to be a factor in breast cancer in the United States as well.[20] Of the postmenopausal women studied in the Netherlands, the heavier and taller ones were found to have a higher rate of breast cancer.[21] And this same correlation was seen in other studies.[22,23]

Obesity is also a major risk factor for the development of endometrial cancer in postmenopausal women. Obese postmenopausal women produce more estrone. This increased production is directly related to the number and size of the woman's fat cells since estrone is manufactured in the fat cells from androstenedione. Similarly, postmenopausal women who take estrogens daily for symptoms of menopause also have a higher incidence of endometrial cancer. The mechanism is probably the same. Most obese women have lesser symptoms of menopause than thinner women, presumably because of their increased production of estrone.

The American Cancer Society sponsored a study from 1959 to 1972 in which mortality from cancer and other diseases among 750,000 men and women was recorded and compared with their weights.[24] Those who were overweight by 40 percent had a significantly higher cancer mortality rate. For men, the mortality was from cancer of the colon and rectum; for women, from cancer of the gallbladder, biliary passages, breast, cervix, endometrium, and ovary. Many other studies confirm the relationship between obesity and increased risk of cancers in various sites.

Obesity also brings with it an increased risk of developing cardiovascular disease, gallbladder disease, and adult-onset diabetes. Obese people tend to have higher blood cholesterol and triglycerides.

FATS

Dietary animal fat is found in all red meat, luncheon meats, and all dairy products, including milk, cheese, and eggs. Dietary animal fat promotes and probably initiates carcinogenesis.[25-45] Epidemiological studies have repeatedly shown an association between consumption of dietary fat and the occurrence of cancer at several sites, especially the breast, the prostate and colon/rectal area, the endometrium, and, to a lesser extent, the ovary. The high fat consumption is related not only to the high incidence of breast cancer but also to the high mortality rates from breast cancer.[46-51] Some studies show a correlation with saturated fats, but other studies show a correlation with both saturated and unsaturated fats.[52] Low breast cancer rates are seen in peoples who consume low-fat diets, such as the Japanese, Seventh-Day Adventists, and Mormons in the United States.

Early life exposures are the important determinants of breast cancer risk for dietary fat. The studies citing changing rates of colon cancer as well as breast cancer in some Japanese immigrants to the United States suggest that the older the Japanese immigrant to the United States, the less her risk of developing breast cancer and colon cancer. However, you must remember, older Japanese women would be less apt to adopt American dietary customs.

The issue of an inverse relationship between serum cholesterol and cancer of the colon was thought to be significant at one time. However, a thorough examination of all the data revealed that the information was inconclusive and did not point to a casual relationship between low cholesterol levels and the risk of colon cancer. In fact, the National Institutes of Health Consensus Conference stated that there was no relationship between low blood cholesterol and colon cancer.

The prognosis for patients with breast cancer differs from one country to another. A better survival rate is seen in Japanese patients than in United States patients.[53-55] The differences are thought to be related to fat consumption.[56-61] Neither the clinical extent of disease nor histology was the basis for the differences seen in survival. Disease-free survival was also greater for Japanese women than American women.[62] The medical care given to Japanese women and Caucasian women in Hawaii was the same, so the differences in survival could not be attributed to differences in treatment.[63]

Several studies have indicated that increased body weight may decrease both disease-free survival and overall survival in breast cancer patients.[64-66] The lowest five-year disease-free survival in patients was noted in patients with high weights (more than 150 pounds) and high cholesterol (above median), and the highest five-year disease-free survival rate was noted in those with low weights (less than 150 pounds) and low cholesterol (below median).[67] Dietary fat and obesity clearly influences the patient's prognosis, but the mechanism by which it does is not well understood. Several theories have been put forth to explain the reactions that are triggered by increased body weight and dietary fat, including abnormalities in the pattern of prolactin secretion,[68] decreased levels of gonadotropins,[69] increased conversion of androstenedione to estrone,[70] or altered sex hormone binding globulin, free androgen, and free estrogen.[71]

Because of the preceding data, it might be worthwhile to put breast cancer patients on a low-fat, high-fiber diet to test the hypothesis. Another reason to increase dietary fiber in breast cancer patients is that it has been shown to increase the fecal excretion of estrogen and to decrease the plasma concentration of estrogen.[72] In fact, it might be wise to extend this modified diet to other diet-sensitive tumors— colon and rectal, prostate, and endometrial cancers, for example—in an attempt to increase disease-free survival as well as survival in general.

Cancer Mechanisms

There are several mechanisms by which dietary animal fat promotes and initiates carcinogenesis. It increases bile acids and bile steroids. It also significantly increases the number of colonic anaerobic bacteria, which then form carcinogens from bile acids. Certain bacterial enzymes are induced by beef for its digestion. These same enzymes can change cocarcinogens into carcinogens. As was already discussed, a potent fecal mutagen called fecapentaene probably also plays an important role in the development of colon cancer.

Dietary animal fat also weakens the immune system by decreasing antibody production and impairing the function of T cells and phagocytes.[73] Cholesterol oleate and ethyl palmitate inhibit antibody production, probably because these lipids do not allow the immune system to recognize a foreign substance.[74] In addition, the structure of a fat makes it easily susceptible to attack by free radicals and increases the cell susceptibility to carcinogens. This is more true for unsaturated fats than it is for saturated fats, because the unsaturated fats act as a natural sink for these highly unstable free-radical chemicals.

DIETARY FIBER

During the past several decades the consumption of dietary fiber has decreased in many industrialized countries, and concomitantly the consumption of dietary fat has increased. Dietary fiber includes indigestible carbohydrates and carbohydratelike components of food such as cellulose, lignin, hemicellulose, pentosan, gum, and pectin. They provide bulk in the diet, and the major categories of foods that provide dietary fiber include vegetables, fruits, and whole-grain cereals.

Fiber is important for protection against cancer. Americans typically consume three to five grams of fiber per day compared to the twenty-five to thirty grams consumed by rural Africans every day. High dietary fiber protects against colon/rectal cancer, breast cancer, heart disease, diverticular disease, obesity, and diabetes.[75-79] A low incidence of cancer is seen in people who consume large amounts of carotene-rich foods and cruciferous vegetables like cabbage, broccoli, cauliflower, and Brussels sprouts.[80-86]

Fiber's protective action is probably due to its binding of bile acids, cholesterol, lipids, poisons, and carcinogens. It also increases the weight and amount of stool, which, in effect, dilutes carcinogens. And it decreases the gastrointestinal transit time so that the carcinogens are excreted more quickly.[87-92] And finally, it keeps the intestinal flora healthy so that they do not die and excrete fecapentaenes.

PROTEIN AND CARBOHYDRATES

High amounts of daily protein cause a high incidence of carcinogenesis in animals.[93] In many animal studies carcinogenesis was suppressed when animals were fed levels of protein that were at the minimum or below the minimum required for optimal growth.

There has been a fair amount of epidemiological human data to support that total protein intake will correlate with the incidence of and mortality from cancers of various sites.[94] This correlation has been seen for breast cancer[95-97] and colon and rectal cancer.[98,99] There has also been a weaker association between high protein intake and other cancers, specifically pancreatic cancer, prostate cancer, and endometrial cancer.

Many of the studies included the consumption of fat as well as protein. Because there is not one but two variables, it is not possible to say with any certainty that high protein per se will be a factor in the cancers described.

The evidence linking pure sugars to the incidence of cancer is much weaker. A high dietary intake of refined sugar was one of the dietary components linked to the increased incidence of breast cancer in several studies.[100,101]

To date, the evidence from both epidemiological and laboratory studies is too inconclusive to suggest any role for carbohydrates in carcinogenesis. But as we have already discussed, excessive carbohydrate ingestion contributes to obesity, which, in turn, has been implicated in carcinogenesis.

NATURALLY OCCURRING CARCINOGENS AND MUTAGENS

Some foods have naturally occurring carcinogens or mutagens. Plants have certain molecules to protect them against microorganisms and insects, and some of these are carcinogenic or mutagenic in humans. The following are only a few of these foods and are listed with their carcinogens in parentheses: black pepper (piperine and safrole), bruised celery (psoralen), herbal teas (pyrrolizidine, phorbol esters), mushrooms (hydrazines), and all foods containing mold (aflatoxin) or bacteria (nitrosamines).[102-108] A complete review of these is given in the reference by Ames.[109] Many of these are occasional contaminants, whereas others are normal components of relatively common foods, as you can see. The ones that pose the greatest risk of cancer in humans are those especially from mycotoxins, that is, aflatoxin and nitroso compounds from bacteria.

Some foods also contain mutagens, which are chemical compounds that cause heritable changes in the genetic material of cells. Many vegetables contain mutagenic flavonoids, and mutagens are seen in charred and smoked foods. Mutagens can also be produced at lower temperatures, such as from the normal cooking of meat. Other commonly consumed items like coffee and horseradish also contain mutagens (quinones and allyl isothiocyanate, respectively).[110] The overall risk of developing cancer from mutagens in human beings is thought to be minimal.

FOOD ADDITIVES

The "Delaney clause" of the Federal Food, Drug, and Cosmetic Act,[111] written because of food additives, prohibits the addition of any known carcinogens to food. Currently there are about 3,000 intentional food additives. One is nitrite, which can be converted in the body to a potent carcinogen, nitrosamine. There are over 12,000 unintentional additives from packaging, food processing, and other phases of the food industry that are occasionally detected. Those in the unintentional category that are of some concern to us are vinyl chloride and diethylstilbestrol, which are used in food packaging and processing and in the foods fed to many livestocks. The overall risk of human cancer from food additives is thought to be quite minimal at this time, however.

EPIDEMIOLOGICAL STUDY OF DIETARY FACTORS

One of the largest epidemiological studies done of dietary and other factors in both China and the United States has been completed by

Cornell University. A total of 6,500 Chinese participated in the study, and each contributed 367 facts about his or her eating practices and other habits. This study was begun in 1983 and completed in 1990.

The study found that the Chinese consume 20 percent more calories than Americans but that Americans are more obese. Chinese people eat only a third of the amount of fat that Americans do and eat twice as much starch. Our government agencies recommend that Americans reduce their percentage of calories from fat to 30 percent; however, I recommend only 15-20 percent of total calories from fat. The level of 30 percent may not be enough to curb the risk of heart disease and cancer, as demonstrated by this Chinese study.

The Cornell University study also showed that Americans consume 33 percent more protein than the Chinese and that 70 percent of this protein comes from animal sources, compared to only 7 percent coming from animals for the Chinese. The Chinese who eat the most protein have more heart disease, cancer, and diabetes.

Diets rich in fat and high in calories and protein also promote growth and early menarche, which, as we discussed, has been associated with higher cancer rates, especially breast cancer. Chinese women rarely suffer from these cancers and start menstruating three to six years later than Americans.

Osteoporosis is very uncommon in China. Unlike Americans, the Chinese do not consume dairy products; instead they get all their calcium from vegetables. They consume only half as much calcium as Americans and yet do not have osteoporosis. This indicates that calcium derived from dairy products is certainly not needed, and since dairy products contribute to the fat content of your diet, it is wise to limit or avoid their consumption.

While Chinese people are a genetically similar population, there are differences in dietary habits, environmental exposures, and disease rates in China from region to region. For instance, the cancer rate varies by a factor of several hundred from one region to another. These facts make this an important study, since the genetic contribution to cancer in China is minimal. Any differences in cancer rates and other chronic illnesses, like heart disease, can therefore be attributed to dietary and other environmental exposures.

In poor areas of China, infectious disease is the leading cause of death. In areas that are more affluent, heart disease, diabetes, and cancer are more often seen. These differences are typical and confirm what we have said: chronic illnesses including cancer, diabetes, and heart disease are more prevalent in affluent countries than poorer ones.

As with most other studies, high cholesterol levels were shown to be predecessors of cancer, heart disease, diabetes, and other chronic diseases. The Chinese study showed that low cholesterol protects against heart disease and also cancer, especially colon cancer. What is considered to be a high cholesterol level in China is thought to be low in the United States. In other words, the range of normal cholesterol levels for the Chinese is much lower than our levels.

The Chinese diet contains three times the dietary fiber of the typical American diet. The average intake of fiber in China is 33 grams a day with a high of 77 grams in some regions. Those with the highest fiber intakes also had the least diseases. (See Tables 8.2 and 8.3.)

Table 8.2 Comparison of Chinese and Western Normal Blood Values

Blood Component	Chinese Range	Western Range
Cholesterol	88–165 mg/dl	155–274 mg/dl
HDL cholesterol	25–60 mg/dl	30–70 mg/dl
LDL cholesterol	41–128 mg/dl	90–205 mg/dl
Hemoglobin		
men	11–16 gm	14–17 gm
women	10–15 gm	12–15 gm

Table 8.3 Comparison of Chinese and Western Daily Nutrient Consumption

Nutrient	Chinese Consumption	Western Consumption
Total protein	40–90 gm	39–192 gm
Plant protein	31–98 gm	27 gm
Dietary fiber	8–77 gm	3–21 gm
Starch	190–610 gm	120 gm
Vitamin C	6–429 mg	7–315 mg
Calories	1,800–3,700	1,090–3,800
Fat (percentage of calories)	5.9–25%	40%

Source: Nutrition, Environment and Health Project, Chinese Academy of Preventive Medicine—Cornell-Oxford.

NATURAL FOOD PROTECTORS

For a number of years researchers, prompted by epidemiological evidence in the United States and abroad, have begun to study the importance of foods that can enhance your health. Although the research is still in progress and none of the findings are conclusive, and it is known that any substance can be toxic when taken in excess, the following are among the most studied foods today. See Table 8.4, Natural Food Protectors.

Carotene

There are now fourteen ongoing prospective randomized studies sponsored by the National Cancer Institute that look at the anticancer potential of carotene in high risk patients. Over thirty studies have shown that people who consume foods with high amounts of carotene have a low risk for developing cancer.

Carotene has also been shown to be the most potent antioxidant, i.e., which neutralizes free radicals and also single oxygen radicals. In addition, it has been shown to be one of the more important enhancers of the human immune system and can also reverse precancer conditions.

Indoles

Indoles, found in the cabbage family, can destroy or otherwise inactivate estrogen. Estrogen is known to initiate new cancers, especially breast cancer.

Isoflavones

This is one of the more exciting areas of cancer prevention. Isoflavones, predominantly found in legumes, have been shown to inhibit or block estrogen receptors thereby prohibiting the cell from its normal cellular function without estrogen. Isoflavones also inhibit estrogens from being effective in the first place, and have been shown to destroy certain cancer gene enzymes that can propagate and transform a normal cell into a cancer cell.

Lignans

Lignans are predominantly found in flaxseed, walnuts, and fatty fish. Each of these is an excellent source of omega-3 fatty acids, which are known to inhibit the production of prostaglandins, hormones that modulate cell metabolism. Numerous studies have shown that omega-3 fatty acids have been used to reduce cholesterol, hypertension, heart disease, and the risk for developing breast cancer, rheumatoid arthritis, and multiple sclerosis. Lignans have also been shown to inhibit the action of estrogens on cells that are responsive to estrogen.

Polyacetylene

Polyacetylene, mainly found in parsley, inhibits the action of prostaglandins and destroys a potent carcinogen called benzopyrene.

Protease Inhibitors

Protease inhibitors, mainly found in soybean, have been shown to inhibit the development of colon cancer, lung cancer, mouth cancer, liver cancer, and esophageal cancers in animals. Protease inhibitors do this by inhibiting the action of the enzymes chymotrypsin and trypsin, as well as by preventing the conversion of normal cells to malignant cells in the early stages of carcinogenesis, but not in the late stages. These protease inhibitors have been shown to cause an irreversible suppressive effect on the process of carcinogenesis. They can also inhibit oncogene expression.

Quinones

Quinones are mainly found in rosemary, and these chemical agents have been shown to inhibit carcinogens and co-carcinogens, chemicals that help carcinogens work more effectively to cause cancer.

Sterols

Sterols are mainly found in cucumbers, especially the skin of cucumbers. Sterols have been shown to decrease cholesterol; and by lowering the cholesterol, you lower most of the fat content that is linked and associated with multiple cancers, including colon and rectal cancer, breast cancer, prostate cancer, and cancer of the uterus, endometrial cancer.

Sulfur

Sulfur is found in large amounts of garlic. Garlic has been used in Japan as a painkiller. The National Cancer Institute, the United States Department of Agriculture, and Loma Linda University are currently studying garlic as an immune system enhancer, a cancer preventive agent, a blood clot inhibitor, and an agent to lower high blood pressure. Sulfur compounds from garlic inhibit carcinogens, and inhibit the enzymes that allow cancers to spread.

Terpenes

Terpenes are mainly found in citrus fruits. The National Cancer Institute is sponsoring studies to investigate the use of vitamin C and citrus fruits to treat certain viruses, to lower blood cholesterol, to reduce arterial plaque, and to prevent certain forms of cancer. Terpenes also have been shown to increase enzymes known to break down carcinogens.

Triterpenoids

Triterpenoids are found in licorice. The National Cancer Institute is studying the potential of licorice to fight cancer, protect the liver, and slow cell mutation. Triterpenoids inhibit estrogens, prostaglandins, and slow down rapidly dividing cells like cancer cells to prevent them from having daughter cells.

Phenylalanine and Tyrosine

Investigators at Washington State University found that cancer did not spread in animals if they were kept on a stringent diet that eliminated two amino acids, phenylalanine and tyrosine. Although these animal experiments have been repeated many times, human studies of this nature have not been done. However, the foods that have a high content of phenylalanine and tyrosine are those that are high in fats or high in protein: meats, eggs, and dairy products. Avoid or limit these, and increase consumption of fruits, vegetables, and carbohydrates.

FAST-FOOD "NUTRITION"

Fast-food restaurants are here to stay, but how nutritious are the meals they serve? Two hundred people in the United States order one or more hamburgers every second.[112] Every day of the year, one fifth of the American population eats at a fast-food restaurant, according to the United States National Restaurant Association. The number of fast-food outlets increased from 30,000 to 140,000 during the period 1970 to 1980. And most disturbing is the fact that fast-food chains have expanded to elementary and secondary schools, colleges, military bases, other countries, and even hospitals.

Fast-food restaurants have increased in number because of the growing employment of women outside the home, the increasing number of people who live alone, the prevalence of smaller families and less formal lifestyles, an increased desire for convenience, and an increase in disposable income.[113] There is a growing reliance on fast foods

Table 8.4   Natural Food Protectors

Protector	Food	Protective Action
Carotene	Carrots, sweet potatoes, yams, pumpkins, squash, kale, broccoli, cantaloupe	Neutralizes free radicals and singlet oxygen radicals; enhances immune system; reverses pre-cancer conditions; high intake associated with low cancer rate.
Indoles	Cabbage family: cabbage, broccoli, cauliflower, mustard green, etc.	Destroys estrogen, known to initiate new cancers, especially breast cancer.
Isoflavones	Legumes: beans, peas, peanuts	Inhibits estrogen receptor; destroys cancer gene enzymes; inhibits estrogen.
Lignans	Flaxseed, walnuts, fatty fish	Inhibits estrogen action; inhibits prostaglandins, hormones that cause cancer spread.
Polyacetylene	Parsley	Inhibits prostaglandins; destroys benzopyrene, a potent carcinogen.
Protease Inhibitors	Soybeans	Destroys enzymes that can cause cancer to spread.
Quinones	Rosemary	Inhibits carcinogens or co-carcinogens.
Sterols	Cucumbers	Decreases cholesterol.
Sulfur	Garlic	Inhibits carcinogens, inhibits cancer spread, decreases cholesterol.
Terpenes	Citrus Fruit	Increases enzymes to break down carcinogens; decreases cholesterol.
Triterpenoids	Licorice	Inhibits estrogens, prostaglandins; slows down rapidly dividing cells, like cancer cells.

for more than one meal a day; and because fast-food restaurants serve a need in our fast-paced society, they are probably here to stay.

Ever greater is the tremendous influence fast foods have on children who begin eating them at young ages. Because of the high fat, high sodium, low fiber, and low calcium content of fast foods, and because of their other nutrient deficiencies, we will see an increase in the development of diseases like cancer, cardiovascular diseases, obesity, and osteoporosis, as well as deficiencies of vitamins, minerals, and other nutrients.

Over the years we have recommended that Americans reduce their consumption of fat, cholesterol, and sodium, and increase their intake of fiber-containing foods, as well as certain vitamins like A and C, carotene, and calcium, among other nutrients. The fast foods that are currently available offer the reverse of the recommendations. A number of other agencies, such as the United States Surgeon General, the National Cancer Institute, the National Institutes of Health, the United States Department of Agriculture, and the American Heart Association, later concurred with these recommendations.

NUTRIENT COMPOSITION OF FAST FOODS

Fat

Most fast-food meals obtain 40 to 55 percent of their calories from fat. For example, the percentage of calories that a fast-food hamburger typically derives from fat is 40 to 58 percent. Some health-conscious people, thinking that chicken or fish would be lower in fat than a hamburger, might choose them over the hamburger; however, they also contain a great deal of fat. Six chicken nuggets have 20 grams of fat, that is, they obtain 58 percent of their total calories from fat. A fast-food chicken patty sandwich contains the same amount of fat as 1.5 pints of ice cream. Most fast-food establishments fry their chicken or fish in beef tallow, which increases the fat content of these foods many more times. On the other hand, some fast-food restaurants advertise that they fry with only 100 percent pure vegetable oil. The oils they use are palm and coconut, which contain no cholesterol but are highly saturated. Other vegetable oils used are highly unsaturated. As you may recall from Chapters 3 and 5, saturated fats cause heart disease and unsaturated fats have been implicated in cancer.

Sodium

There are between 700 and 900 milligrams of sodium in most fast-food sandwiches. If the purchaser also consumes French fries, ketchup, a milk shake, or a pastry, the amount of sodium increases dramatically. There are between 1,350 and 1,950 milligrams of sodium in each of the following foods: a triple cheeseburger, a roast beef sandwich with cheese, and a cheeseburger with bacon. The U.S. Recommended Dietary Allowance of sodium is between 1,100 and 3,300 milligrams per day.

Fiber

The fiber content of fast-food meals is extremely low. Some fast-food establishments have made a meager attempt to increase the fiber by introducing salad bars. When you examine the amount of fiber in these salads, however, you will discover that it is very little. In addition, the contents of these salad bars are sprayed with a chemical called sulfite to prevent them from turning brown, and this can also be harmful. Most people also use salad dressings that are high in calories, fat, and sodium.

Protein

The protein content of fast-food meals varies from 50–100 percent of the U.S. RDA. Children usually consume twice the RDA for protein. Concern over protein consumption has risen since we discovered evidence that high amounts of protein are linked with cancers, osteoporosis, and heart disease. If your protein consumption is double the U.S. RDA, 50 percent more calcium is lost through the urine.[114]

Calcium

Most fast-food meals are very low in calcium. As we have already learned, low calcium levels are associated with osteoporosis, hypertension, colon cancer, and perhaps Alzheimer's disease as well.

People who often eat at these fast-food restaurants should be aware of the nutritional value of these foods. As you can see by Table 8.5, found on the next page, fast foods are deficient in many nutrients. In addition, most consumers at fast-food restaurants prefer soda and coffee, which have little nutritional value, to other beverages. As was stated before, the average American has an insufficient intake of vitamins B6, C, and E, folic acid, calcium, iron, magnesium, and zinc, among others. In addition, marginal deficiencies that we have already discussed affect millions of people in our country. Moreover, the total caloric intake of most Americans exceeds what it should be, resulting in 35–40 percent of the population being obese.

Fast-food restaurant owners are not required to comply with federal laws that mandate nutritional labeling or the listing of all ingredients of the foods they sell. So even if you wanted to know what the nutrient content of the food you were being served was, you could not find out at the time of purchase. You may wish to examine the analyses of fast foods that have been published.[116,117]

One of the most disturbing things about fast-food restaurants is their presence in children's hospitals in various cities of North

Table 8.5 Nutrient Values of Sample Fast-Food Meals[115]

Sample Meal	% Fat Calories	Cal-ories	Choles-terol (mg)	Sod-ium (mg)	% U.S RDA Vitamin A	Vitamin C	Cal-cium
Double burger with sauce, milk shake, French fries, regular	46	1,275	155	1,190	10	30	80
Chicken nuggets (6), apple pie, coffee with cream	55	655	95	1,115	2	20	9
Fish sandwich with cheese and tartar sauce, soda (12 oz.), French fries, regular	53	885	73	811	2	20	19
Beef tacos(2), low-fat milk (8 oz.)	40	495	60	690	18	3	61
Single burger, tossed salad, low-fat milk	32	445	55	1,005	28	75	50
Baked potato, plain margarine (1 pat), tossed salad with low-calorie dressing, low-fat milk	18	340	10	620	28	120	45
Cheese pizza (1 slice), tossed salad with low-calorie dressing, orange juice (8 oz.)	30	310	40	500	27	233	26

America. It is this author's opinion that this is as bad as the tobacco industry's targeting of young people. Our society, I doubt, will reduce or eliminate fast-food dining. Therefore, we should aim to improve the nutritional quality of fast foods.

A large study was done to find out if dietary advice could help people who had suffered a heart attack prevent a second one from occurring. Over 2,000 patients were divided into three groups. One group received dietary advice on how to reduce fat intake, another group received dietary advice on how to increase fatty-fish intake, and the third group received advice on how to increase cereal fiber. The group given advice on fat intake had no difference in mortality (their serum cholesterols did not change). Those advised to eat fatty fish had almost a 30 percent reduction in two-year mortality compared with those who were not advised. The third group again had no difference in mortality. This study indicates that even after given advice about the proper thing to do, people rarely take it. The study group simply would not reduce their red-meat intake. One group did show that they would increase the fatty fish and benefited from that.[118] This study indicates that unless there is a strong motivating factor, and it is hard to imagine that a person's life is not such a motivating factor, people simply will not change habits even though they are told it will benefit them medically.

9
Obesity

Obesity affects about 35 percent of all Americans. Being obese carries with it a social stigma as well as a general health risk. One study calculated that there are 832 million pounds of excess fat on American men and 1,468 million pounds of excess fat on American women, for a total of 2.3 billion pounds.[1] That is a staggering amount of fat, and it has been increasing over the past several decades. More obesity occurs in middle-aged people and in people with low socioeconomic status. The percentage of black American women who are obese is greater than the percentage of white women. Obesity runs in families, and adopted children become obese if adoptive family members are obese.

The fat cell *size* is increased in all types of obesity. An increased *number* of fat cells is found in children and adults who were obese before the age of two. Statistics show that if a child is obese before he is two years old, he will likely be obese in adulthood because he already has an increased number of fat cells. It is ideal, then, not to allow a baby to become fat, because if he does, the resulting fat cells will remain with him for the rest of his life. Adult obese patients who have an increased number of fat cells acquired before age two are usually more grossly obese and will have obesity in the abdomen and chest as well as in the forearm. It is more difficult for an obese patient to lose weight if he was obese before age two; in other words, it is more difficult for an obese patient to lose weight if he has more fat cells than normal. Ninety-nine percent of all obesity is directly related to overeating—make no mistake about that! Only one percent of obesity is caused by a disease or medical problem.

Because obese individuals tend to develop a variety of diseases, some of which are life threatening, obese adults have a higher than normal death rate for their age group. The risk of death correlates almost directly with how much a person is overweight. Even if you are only a little overweight, you still have an increased risk of death compared to a person who is not overweight.

There have been several studies suggesting that longevity is correlated with factors that limit the adult body size. In 1935, C.M. McCay showed that feeding rats a low-protein diet yielded lean animals that lived much longer than animals fed high-protein diets.[2] Many more of these types of experiments were completed by Dr. Robert A. Good and colleagues at Memorial Sloan-Kettering Hospital in New York City.[3,4] They have had similar results: animals with lean body mass live much longer. Many human studies have now been done and show that obesity decreases longevity.[5] This finding has been corroborated. In addition, investigations by Tannenbaum,[6] Kraybill,[7] and others[8-10] have shown that animals with lean body masses have lower rates of cancer development as well as greater longevity. Because of all these well-planned studies, the National Dairy Council issued the following statement in 1975: "Of all dietary modification studies, caloric restriction has had the most regular influence on the genesis of neoplasms in experimental animals."[11]

Obesity is a major risk factor for the development of endometrial cancer (cancer of the inner lining of the uterus) in postmenopausal women. The reason for this is that obese postmenopausal women produce a lot more of a female hormone called estrone. This increased production is directly related to the number and size of the woman's fat cells, since estrone is manufactured in the fat cells from another hormone (androstenedione). Estrone constantly stimulates the uterus, and this is believed to cause endometrial cancer. Similarly, postmenopausal women who take estrogens daily for symptoms of menopause also have a higher incidence of endometrial cancer. The mechanism is presumably the same.

People who are obese usually consume more fats in their diet; this is a major risk factor for the development of breast cancer and colon cancer.[12] Both height and weight are positively associated with cancer in postmenopausal women. An animal study done recently showed that if food intake was reduced (the number of calories decreased) during a "critical period" after a carcinogen was given to induce breast cancer, then the development of the cancer was inhibited.[13] This may result from low amounts of two hormones, prolactin and estrogen. Leaner animals produce less of these two hormones, which in high amounts can lead to the development of cancer.

In addition, obesity can adversely affect the body's response to infection. Diets that are high in fat depress a person's resistance to tuberculosis, malaria, and pneumococcus (an often severe pneumonia). Obese animals have more severe infections and higher death rates from the infections.[14] The incidence of pneumonia is significantly higher in obese infants than in nonobese infants.[15] Adverse effects on the immune system or poor lung ventilation due to obesity have been suggested as possible reasons for severe pneumonias in these infants.

An obese person also has a two or three times higher risk of developing diabetes. Obesity interferes with the action of insulin, the hormone that normally packs sugar into the cells of the body. Hence, with interference of insulin, the blood-sugar level goes very high. If this person loses weight, insulin can then work properly and usually return the blood-sugar level to normal.

An obese person has an increased risk of developing cardiovascular disease. The reasons for increased heart attacks are not clear but may be related to increased blood lipids associated with obesity. Obese people tend to have higher blood cholesterol and triglycerides. If the obese person loses weight, the high blood levels of cholesterol and triglyceride return to normal.

A prospective study showed that even women who were only mildly to moderately overweight had an increase in their risk of developing coronary heart disease.[16] Obesity was found to be an independent risk factor again. Another study showed that men who were obese in the central portion of their bodies, that is, those who had a "beer belly," also had a higher risk of developing coronary artery disease independent of all other risk factors.[17] An older person had a twofold higher risk of death if the individual was only moderately overweight.[18]

Overweight people have a higher incidence of hypertension, which itself contributes to the risk of coronary heart disease, heart attacks, and stroke.[19] The left ventricle of the heart, which is the chamber that pumps blood into the arteries, becomes thickened in mass with hypertension and other heart diseases. Obviously, this impairs heart function and is detrimental to health. It has been found, however, that when people start to lose weight, the thickness of the left ventricle becomes less.[20]

When smokers quit smoking, they frequently gain weight. This is due to the fact that they have sweeter tastes and prefer diets with a higher proportion of sugar.[21] In addition, people who quit smoking have a much lower energy output than smokers regardless of whether they are busy at work or home or even resting.[22] It appears that nicotine is responsible for increasing the rate at which smokers burn calories. Hence, people gain weight when they stop smoking because they want sweeter foods, which are high in calories, and they burn less calories when working or resting.[23]

Obesity contributes to the development of gallbladder disease and also is a risk factor for major respiratory problems. Some massively obese individuals have trouble breathing because the weight of the chest is so great that the individual's chest muscles have difficulty lifting it. Being overweight causes too much wear and tear on bone joints and leads to the early development of joint problems.

How much should a person weigh? There is no one answer, but here is a good rule of thumb. Men who are 5 feet tall should weigh 110 pounds. For every one inch over 5 feet, add another 5 pounds. Thus if a man is 5 feet 11 inches tall, his ideal weight is about 165 pounds. Women who are 5 feet tall should weigh about 100 pounds. For every one inch over 5 feet, add 5 pounds. Therefore, if a woman is 5 feet 6 inches tall, her ideal weight is about 130 pounds.

If you do need to lose weight, you should do it gradually. Losing one or two pounds a week is safe, and that loss will probably be maintained. Do not lose more weight than called for by the formula. Successful weight loss and maintenance of that loss will be achieved only if you totally modify your eating habits. Many people are put on high-protein liquid diets consisting of 800 calories a day and lose a great deal of weight within the first few weeks. But on a long-term basis, these pounds come right back on because the person did not learn new eating habits. Diets containing less than 800 calories per day may be dangerous if the person is not closely monitored by a physician.

Most people do lose weight on reducing diets, but they invariably gain it back along with some additional pounds. This self-inflicted fluctuation in body weight usually happens many times in a person's life. A number of studies have shown that repeated fluctuation in body weight *per se* has negative consequences on a person's health.[24-26] A person whose body weight fluctuates often or greatly has a much higher risk of developing coronary heart disease and dying than does a person who has a relatively stable body weight. Those aged 30 to 44 were shown to suffer the most detrimental effects of weight fluctuation. These harmful effects of weight fluctuation were independent of degree of obesity or existing cardiovascular risk factors.

To lose weight, you must eat less and increase your physical activity. Before you start a physical exercise program, you should be checked by a physician. An exercise program should start out gradually, with new goals set every week. Walking is very good exercise. Every pound of fat you have contains about 3,500 calories.

Table 9.1 Activities and the Calories They Burn			
Activities	Calories Used Per Hour	Activities	Calories Used Per Hour
Job		*Recreation (cont.)*	
Answering telephone	50	Calisthenics	500
Bathing	100	Card playing	25
Bed making	300	Cycling slowly (5 ½ mph)	300
Brushing teeth or hair	100	Cycling strenuously	
Chopping wood	400	(13 mph)	660
Dishwashing	75	Dancing, slow step	350
Dressing, undressing	50	Dancing, fast step	600
Driving automobile	120	Fishing	150
Dusting furniture	150	Football	600
Eating	50	Golfing	250
Filing (office)	200	Handball	660
Gardening	250	Hiking	400
Housework	180	Horseback riding	250
Ironing	100	Jogging	600
Mopping floors	200	Kissing vigorously	6–12
Mowing lawn	250	Lovemaking	125–300
Preparing food	100	Painting	150
Reading	25	Piano playing	75
Sawing	500	Running, fast pace	900
Sewing	50	Singing	50
Shoveling	500	Skating leisurely	400
Sitting	100	Skating rapidly	600
Sleeping	80	Skiing (10 mph)	600
Standing	140	Soccer	650
Typing	50	Swimming leisurely	
Walking upstairs		(¼ mph)	400
and down	800	Swimming rapidly	800
		Tennis, singles	450
Recreation		Tennis, doubles	350
Badminton	400	Volleyball	350
Baseball	350	Walking leisurely	
Basketball	550	(2 ½ mph)	200
Boating, rowing	400	Walking fast (3 ¾ mph)	300
Boating, motor	150	Watching television	25
Bowling	250		

Therefore, to lose one pound, you have to burn off 3,500 calories more than you eat. You will lose a pound a week if you burn off 500 calories per day more than you consume. If you eat a diet containing 1,200 calories per day and burn off 1,700 calories per day, you will lose one pound a week. Refer to Table 23.1 in Chapter 23 for the number of calories in the various foods listed.

Table 9.1, on the previous page, shows approximately how many calories are used up by a 150-pound person performing the indicated activity. This information comes from the Department of Agriculture in a 1980 publication derived from data prepared by Dr. Robert Johnson at the University of Illinois.

If you lose weight suddenly or without a good reason, see a physician. Unexplained weight loss could be a sign of cancer or another serious medical problem.

Even though it is very difficult to lose weight, you must try if you are overweight because of the tremendous benefits of being at your ideal weight. Obesity has no benefits, and the risks are very great.

10

Food Additives and Contaminants

Chemical food additives and food contaminants have been quite extensively studied, more so than most other chemicals that come into contact with our bodies—with good reason. Only carefully selected chemicals can prevent contamination and spoilage of food that has to be produced in great quantities, stored, and transported. Chemicals are also used for flavoring and appearance. Chemical contaminants may develop as a result of food processing procedures such as irradiation, cooking, pickling, or smoking. The trouble with the use of chemicals in food is that we are exposed to them constantly, repeatedly, and at low doses. For this reason it is difficult to ascertain from tests whether these chemicals can cause cancer, and therefore laboratory investigations rather than large population studies must be conducted to find out whether the chemicals are potentially hazardous.

Chemical food additives are divided into several groups. *Intentional* food additives are chemicals that are purposely added to food. Some of these definitely produce cancers in animals, but others do not produce such clear results. Thiourea[1] and butter yellow[2] produce cancers in animals and are no longer used in food. A very important antioxidant presently used in foods, butylated hydroxytoluene, is reported to enhance certain animal cancers[3] but inhibit some carcinogens.[4] Red No. 2 and Red No. 40 dyes have both been banned because they are not safe according to the Food and Drug Administration.

Cyclamate has not been shown to be carcinogenic in humans, but its metabolite does produce testicular atrophy (shrinking) in rats. Saccharin, another highly publicized intentional food additive, does produce bladder cancer in rats when comprising 5 percent or more in the diet,[5] but epidemiological studies show that saccharin does not pose a major cancer risk to man.[6] However, it is generally agreed that additional studies are needed concerning the effects of saccharin on man before conclusive statements can be made. Xylitol, a new sweetener compound, also has been reported to give rise to bladder cancer in mice and to adrenal cancer in rats.[7]

Nitrite is a most important food additive. Nitrites are used as meat preservatives to prevent botulism; they also add color to certain meats, especially bacon and hot dogs. Nitrites can react with other compounds to form potent carcinogens called nitrosamines.[8] When bacon is cooked, nitrosamines form. Look at the label of ingredients on your package of bacon or hot dogs—nitrites are probably listed. There is a low level of nitrites in our saliva and in some vegetables, but there is no information on whether these nitrites can be activated to form nitrosamines. Vitamin C, also found in vegetables, can inhibit the formation of nitrosamines and is usually added to meat cures. Some research has suggested that nitrite itself might be carcinogenic.[9]

A certain wine additive, diethylpyrocarbonate, interacts with alcohol to cause levels of 0.1 parts per billion of another strong carcinogen, urethan.[10] This chemical is now banned in many countries.

Unintentional food additives are those chemicals used to prepare or store the food product; small amounts of these chemicals subsequently, unintentionally, become part of the food. An example of this is trichloroethylene. Decaffeinated products were made by using trichloroethylene to extract the caffeine. Trichloroethylene was found to be a carcinogen and was removed from the market. Another example of unintentional contamination of food involves certain processes used to make the paraffin wax that lines many food containers. Carcinogens were formed during certain of these processes, and once discovered, these processes were discontinued. Pesticides like DDT, aldrin, and others produce liver cancer in mice and are probably carcinogenic in other species. It is important to realize that most pesticides get into our bodies and are stored in fat cells, since they are fat soluble. These pesticide-laden fat cells can then act as reservoirs to slowly, but constantly, release the pesticide into the bloodstream. Another chemical that is used in agriculture is DES (diethylstilbestrol). DES is used for cattle and has been found in trace amounts in foods derived from cattle. DES causes human cancer: cancer of the vagina in young women and cancer of the testicles in men whose mothers had taken DES. (Cancer of the testicles is rare, however, especially in this situation.) Keep in mind that a large amount of DES is needed to cause cancer, and only a small amount is in our food. But small amounts accumulate and do affect us.

Some food contaminants, like aflatoxin, which causes human liver cancer, are of natural origin. It is a product of a fungus, *Aspergillus flavus*, which grows mainly on peanut plants. Other fungal products have been implicated in human cancers, but these findings have not yet been substantiated. *Gyromita esculenta*, a common mushroom used in cooking, contains a compound called N-methyl-N-formyl-hydrazine, which is a most potent animal carcinogen.[11] Related chemicals in other mushroom types are now under investigation. There is no current information on whether cancer incidence is related to the amount of mushrooms eaten by people in different parts of the world.

Certain food processing techniques, such as smoking and charcoal broiling, are known to produce carcinogens.[12] Smoked food is associated with an increased incidence of gastric cancer in the Baltic states and Iceland. The carcinogens that result from charcoal broiling appear to come from the fat that drips from the meat and is burned, forming the carcinogen, which then rises with the smoke back up into the meat.[13] If the fat drippings were eliminated, the carcinogens would probably be eliminated also.

As yet there are no definite proven cases of human cancers directly related to food additives, but many authorities agree that additives and contaminants do account for a very small percentage of human cancers. Those chemicals implicated in animal cancers were removed from the market for the most part. However, nitrites are bothersome sources of carcinogens and should be avoided. It is altogether possible that the reduced incidence of gastric cancer in the United States is directly related to better methods of food preparation and smaller amounts of nitrites being used in foods with the advent of refrigeration. Also it seems that certain naturally occurring food components like aflatoxins do cause human cancer and should definitely be eliminated. And finally, think twice before you make a habit of eating a great many mushrooms.

11
Pesticides

Pesticides, though not commonly used before the 1940s, are now in widespread use throughout the world. We will define pesticides as chemicals that control or kill pests or affect plant or animal life. Herbicides therefore will be included under the general term of pesticide. Pesticides are commonly used in your home to control pests and weeds. Their presence permeates many areas other than the home; they are used in agriculture, horticulture, public parks, and gardens, among others. Table 11.1 is a partial list of different types of pesticides and their functions.

Table 11.1 Pesticide Class and Function

Pesticide	Function
Insecticide	Controls or kills insects.
Herbicide	Controls or kills weeds.
Fungicide	Kills fungi.
Bactericide	Kills bacteria.
Disinfectant	Destroys or inactivates harmful microorganisms.
Defoliant	Removes leaves.
Desiccant	Speeds drying of plants.
Repellant	Repels insects, mites, ticks, dogs, cats.

THE HISTORY OF PESTICIDE DEVELOPMENT

Pesticides have been in use for centuries. In 470 B.C., the Greek philosopher Democrates used olive extracts on plants to prevent blight. Vine pests were destroyed with sulfur fumes by Cato in Italy in 200 B.C. Biological control was found effective by the ancient Chinese who used ants to protect their trees from insect pests.

Pesticide use in the early twentieth century brought with it some problems. Many of the so-called "natural" chemical pesticides in use before 1940 were extremely toxic. They included sulfur, copper, oil, nicotine, arsenates, formaldehyde, and micurate bichloride. These were all sprayed on crops, and little was mentioned of their hazards at that time.

The world market for pesticides has exploded since the 1940s. Approximately $13 billion worth of pesticides were being used every year by 1986. The breakdown of pesticide use in 1984 was as follows: herbicides, 43 percent; fungicides, 18 percent; and other pesticides, 39 percent. The United States uses more pesticides than any other country. In 1984 we used 34 percent of all pesticides; Eastern Europe and Russia used 8 percent; Latin America, 10 percent; the Far East, 16 percent; and Western Europe, 19 percent. The rest of the world used the remaining 13 percent.

Pesticides have made an important contribution to both food production and disease control. It is estimated that 45 percent of the world's potential food supply is lost to pests: 30 percent to weeds, pests, and diseases before harvest, and another 15 percent between harvest and use. Some estimate that at least one third of the crops in Third World countries are lost to pests.[1]

Despite the fact that pesticides have aided in the control of malaria, schistosomiasis, and filariasis in tropical countries, there are still 150 million cases of malaria and about 250 million cases of schistosomiasis and filariasis each year in the world. There is no way of knowing and no way to calculate how many lives will be saved or improved by the use of pesticides to control diseases and increase our food production. Likewise there is no way to calculate how many lives will be lost from pesticide use either. Some dangerous pesticides that are banned or restricted in North America and Europe have been unloaded on Third World countries.

There were about 1,200 pesticide chemical compounds, combined in 30,000 different formulations and brands in the United States in 1981. The United States used about 900 million pounds of pesticides in that year. Approximately 334 million pounds of pesticides or 5–10 percent of the entire world's supply was used by California alone in 1977.[2]

THE HIGH COST OF PESTICIDES

Companies that develop pesticides become committed to marketing them early in development for a number of reasons. First, they must test thousands of new compounds each year, among which only a few make it through the screening process. It usually takes about seven years for a pesticide to be put through the screening process and granted registration by the U.S. Department of Agriculture and the Environmental Protection Agency (EPA). Naturally, pesticide manufacturers are eager to advertise their products before they appear on the shelves because of their large out-of-pocket expense. For example, in 1987, one company invested approximately $45 million to develop one pesticide that required the screening of at least 20,000 chemical compounds before it could be identified as effective.

D. Pimentel has looked at the cost effectiveness of pesticides in the United States.[3,4] It cost approximately $2.8 billion each year to apply pesticides that prevent pest losses totaling about $10.9 billion a year. Hence, there is a return of about three dollars for every dollar invested in pesticide application. The indirect costs of pesticides are estimated to be about $1 billion and stem from human exposure to pesticides, an increase in the number of pests when the chemicals kill off the natural predator, pest resistance, pollination problems from destroying the bee population, and other problems. Pimentel's estimate for the cost of cancers in the United States is about $125 million per year. About $58 million a year is ascribed to human pesticide poisonings.

Pesticides enter your body by inhalation, absorption through the skin, or ingestion. And unlike industrial chemicals, which are used in a very controlled manner, pesticides are sprayed, powdered, or dropped as pellets or granules in and around places where the general public may walk or play. In fact, pesticide residues are commonly found in human tissue in almost everyone in the United States, averaging six parts per million (ppm) in fatty tissue.[5] Pesticide residues have been found in breast milk and cow milk and have been found to cross the placental barrier to the human fetus.[6]

THE DANGERS OF PESTICIDE USE

Because pesticides are soluble in oil or fatty tissue like that of the human breast and its milk, it is theorized that pesticides may be a contributing factor to breast cancer.[7] Incidental findings in experiments involving exposure of rats and mice to pesticides show a significant increase in breast cancer in the exposed animal group. Women are at greater risk than men when exposed to the same amount of pesticides because the Allowable Daily Intake for pesticides as determined by the federal government is calculated on the basis of a 70-kilogram man, not a 50-kilogram woman with larger breast tissue.

Some cases of Parkinson's disease as well as other neurological diseases have been linked to various pesticides.[8] Hypertension, cardiovascular disease, and abnormal blood cholesterol and vitamin A levels have been linked to pesticide exposure. Pesticides are also associated with allergies, liver disease, skin diseases, fertility problems as manifested by changes in the egg and sperm (teratogenicity), and changes in the RNA and DNA (mutagenicity). Regular spraying of pesticides in homes and gardens was linked with the development of acute leukemia in young children in the Los Angeles area.[9] Other cancers have also been associated with pesticides.[10,11]

Pesticides also pose an environmental hazard. They pollute the rain water of many U.S. states when they are vaporized or when the wind blows soil particles treated with pesticides.[12]

If you were exposed to toxic amounts of pesticide, that is, if a large dose were inhaled or made contact with your skin, you would experience acute effects. These effects usually appear within minutes to hours after contact. However, the effects of low-level or prolonged pesticide exposure, particularly to those that may have carcinogenic potential, are very different. Cancer does not appear immediately after exposure to a pesticide; it may not be apparent until long after exposure has occurred. Unfortunately, by the time the medical and scientific community becomes aware that a particular pesticide causes cancer, a large number of persons could have been exposed without their knowledge. For example, R-11, which is a chemical found in insect repellants, has just been shown to cause cancer in animals.

Dioxin, otherwise known as Agent Orange, and one of its associated contaminants, TCDD, was extensively used toward the end of the United States's conflict in Vietnam.[13] Hundreds of thousands of people were exposed to these agents, and serious allegations by Vietnam veterans and other persons have been raised that Agent Orange and TCDD[14] caused malignant tumors, sterility, spontaneous abortions, birth defects, disfiguring skin diseases, and other illnesses.

We do know that TCDD is very toxic and causes tumors in rats, in which it acts as a promoter of cancer.[15] It can also initiate carcinogenesis in animals.[16,17] A number of human epidemiological and toxicological studies have suggested an association between TCDD, or the chemicals it contaminates, and soft-tissue sarcoma,[18-20] Hodgkin's,[21] non-Hodgkin's lymphoma,[22-24] stomach cancer,[25,26] nasal cancer,[27] and liver cancer.[28,29] However, other studies did not show a correlation between TCDD and other cancers.[30-35] Most of these studies involved a short period of time between exposure and disease. It now appears that the longer the time from exposure to TCDD, the higher the risk for the development of cancer and the higher the incidence of cancer.[36,37]

Table 11.2 lists several different pesticides and their roles as human carcinogens.[38-41] Some are definitely associated with human cancer, some are probably associated with human cancer, and some are possibly associated with human cancer. You will recognize a number of them. Many other pesticides not included in this table, like malathion and Mirex, have been linked to cancers in animal studies. Some of them are also familiar to you because they are commonly used in household and garden settings. Currently there is no definite evidence that the pesticides causing animal cancer also cause human cancer. However, we should continue to be on the alert and await future studies for their possible link to human cancer.

Table 11.2   Pesticides as Human Carcinogens

Pesticide (Chemical Name)	Human Carcinogen		
	Definite	Probable	Possible
Aldrin and dieldrin			√
Amitrole		√	
Arsenicals	√		
Benzal chloride			√
Benzotrichloride		√	
Benzoyl chloride			√
Benzyl chloride			√
Carbon tetrachloride	√		
Chlordane			√
Chlorophenols		√	
p-Dichlorobenzene		√	
2,4-Dichlorophenoxyacetic acid esters (2,4-D)			√
p,p'-Dichlorodiphenyl trichloroethane (DDT)		√	
Ethylene dibromide		√	
Ethylene oxide		√	
Formaldehyde		√	
Heptachlor			√
Lindane (-hexachloro cyclohexane)			√
(4-chloro-2-methyl phenoxy) acetic acid			√
Methyl parathion			√

Table 11.2   **Pesticides as Human Carcinogens–*continued***

Pesticide (Chemical Name)	Human Carcinogen		
	Definite	Probable	Possible
Pentachlorophenol			√
Phenoxy acids	√		
2,3,7,8-Tetrachloro dibenzo-p-dioxin		√	
2,4,5-Trichlorophenol			√
2,4,6-Trichlorophenol		√	
2,4,5-Trichlorophenoxy acetic acid			√
Vinyl chloride		√	

Several human cancers are associated with pesticide use. They include the following:

- Leukemia.
- Multiple myeloma.
- Lymphoma.
- Soft-tissue sarcoma.
- Prostate cancer.
- Stomach cancer.
- Melanoma.
- Brain cancer.
- Liver cancer.
- Skin cancer.
- Lung cancer.
- Central nervous system tumors: gliomas.
- Cancer of esophagus.
- Ovarian cancers.

There is a correlation between these cancers and a variety of pesticides and pesticide uses. This does not mean, however, that pesticides are the direct cause of these cancers.

In this age of organic farming, the debate over pesticide use rages on. Othal Brand, who was recently appointed to the Texas Pesticide Regulatory Board, said of the termite killer Chlordane, "Sure, it's going to kill a lot of people, but they may be dying of something else anyway."[42] Farmer Clarence Hopmann of Dumas, Arkansas, decreased the use of agricultural pesticides because he developed an allergy to them. However, in order to qualify for bank loans, the bankers demanded that he use large doses of pesticides on his crops. He has resumed using them.[43]

There are several things that can and should be done to minimize the use of pesticides in our country and the world. Before the 1940s, pesticides were not used very much at all. Hence there have always been alternatives to the artificial chemical pesticides currently in use.

Nature provides us with biological controls, that is, natural predators that can be introduced to control insects. For example, ladybugs can be used to fight off aphid predators. Beetles were used to control weeds in the western United States in the 1950s, parasites to control the citrus fly in Barbados in the 1960s. You can also minimize the number of pests by providing food and habitat for the pest's natural enemies. Certain traditional farming practices may be employed as well. Crop residues may be removed by plowing or flooding. Pest deterrents, crop rotation, proper drainage methods, and physical controls like traps or blocking of insects and/or other pests can be used. These techniques, along with biological controls, have been used successfully by many countries, including China, Nicaragua, certain areas of England, and also some parts of America.

While chemical pesticides certainly benefit populations by increasing food production and decreasing certain diseases, it is important to use them only when they must be used and to use the pesticides that cause the least toxicity in human beings and the least damage to the environment around us. Treat them all as hazardous and minimize their use in public areas and in and around your home. For example, since the pesticide 2,4,5-T is very hazardous, substitute the less hazardous Amcide or Krenite. Silicon and soap can be used in gardens as a nontoxic insecticide rather than the other commonly used pesticides for the garden. Wasps have been controlled by parasites in greenhouses more effectively than with chemicals. And the bacteria called *Bacillus thuringiensis* has also been shown to be a good alternative to several toxic insecticides.

WHAT CAN BE DONE

The number of tons of pesticides has increased thirty-three times since 1940, and their toxicity has grown tenfold. However, crop losses to microorganisms, insects, and weeds have gone up 31–37 percent. There are a number of reasons for this. As new pesticides are developed, insects develop resistance to them. But even more importantly, the government supports prices of various crops, which encourages farmers to produce only a single crop instead of rotating crops to inhibit the pests.

By using crop rotation and biological pest control, pesticide use could be cut in half. Food prices would rise by one percent—about $1 billion a year—but the benefits would be enormous. The United States would save $4–$10 billion per year from decreased damage to fish and water supplies, decreased costs of regulating pesticides, and decreased health-care costs for the 20,000 people poisoned each year from pesticides.[44]

You should learn as much as you can about any pesticides you do use. Acquiring such information is not easy but neither is maintaining good health. Acquire information and use alternatives to the current pesticides. Exposure to pesticides can be controlled. This is yet another risk factor for disease over which you have control.

12
Smoking—
A Slow Suicide

Smoking is one of the biggest health hazards today. The scientific evidence of the dangers of smoking is tremendous. In 1979 Joseph Califano, then Secretary of the Department of Health, Education, and Welfare, wrote: "Smoking is the largest preventable cause of death in America." In 1979, over 55 million American men and women smoked 615 billion cigarettes; and worldwide consumption is about 3 trillion each year. Since then regular cigarette smoking by adults has dropped slightly from 40 percent to about 33 percent.

Projections by the World Conference on Smoking and Health sponsored by the World Health Organization (WHO) show that even if present consumption rates of cigarettes stay steady—and all data indicate a continued increase—the annual number of premature deaths caused by tobacco will rise from about 3 million worldwide in the 1990s to 10 million by the year 2025. Over half a billion people alive today, including 200 million currently under the age of 20, will die from tobacco-induced disease, and half of these will be in middle age.[1] Tobacco-related diseases will kill one-fifth of all who now live in industrialized countries. One-third to one-half of all smokers will die from smoking.

The WHO Conference said that the tobacco companies have targeted for expansion Third World countries, countries in Eastern Europe, Thailand, and other Far Eastern countries. Also targeted are women and girls, and young boys.[2]

Smoking among children has increased dramatically. Since 1968, the number of girls between the ages of 12 and 14 who smoke has increased eightfold. Six million children between the ages of 13 and 19 are regular smokers, and over 100,000 children under 13 are now regular smokers. Smoking among blacks exceeds that by whites. However, on a positive note, about 30 million Americans have become ex-smokers since massive educational warnings were issued by the federal government.

More deaths and physical suffering are related to cigarette smoking than to any other single cause: over 228,700 deaths (and rising) each year from cancer, over 325,000 deaths from cardiovascular disease, and more than 50,000 deaths from chronic lung diseases. Compare these figures with the number of people who died in the following wars (combat and noncombat fatalities): World War I (from 1917 to 1918), 116,708; World War II (from 1941 to 1946), 407,316; Korean War (from 1950 to 1953), 54,246; and Vietnam conflict (from 1964 to 1973), 58,151. The cigarette industry's own research over a ten-year period (1964–1974), which cost over $15 million, confirmed the fatal dangers of smoking cigarettes.[3] In a one-year period, a one-pack-a-day smoker inhales 50,000 to 70,000 puffs which contain over 2,000 chemical compounds, many of which are known carcinogens. A president of the American Cancer Society, Dr. Robert V.P. Hutter, said that many tobacco product ingredients, such as flavoring additives, are kept secret even from the government.

The cost of smoking-related diseases is staggering. Health care in the United States cost $817 billion in 1992. Smoking accounts for approximately $53 billion per year.[4] A great deal of this cost is paid by nonsmokers and smokers through ever-increasing health insurance premiums, disability payments, and other programs. It doesn't seem fair that nonsmokers have to pay one penny for self-induced smokers' diseases.

The longer a person smokes, the greater is his risk of dying. A person who smokes two packs a day has a death rate two times higher than a nonsmoker. The earlier a person starts smoking, the higher is his risk of death. Smokers who inhale have higher mortality rates than smokers who do not.

If a smoker stops smoking, his mortality rate decreases progressively as the number of nonsmoking years increase. Those who have stopped for fifteen years have mortality rates similar to those who never smoked, with the exception of smokers who stopped after the age of 65. Persons who smoke cigars and pipes also have an increased risk of death. Life expectancy is eight to nine years shorter for a two-pack-a-day smoker of age 30 to 35 than it is for a nonsmoker, and those who smoke cigarettes with higher contents of "tar" and nicotine have a much higher death rate. Overall, the greatest mortality is seen in the 45 to 55 age groups. Hence, death from smoking is premature death!

SMOKING AND CANCER

Lung Cancer

Cigarette smoking is the major risk factor for lung cancer in both men and women. The scientific evidence for this and for other cancers related to smoking is overwhelming. The risk of developing lung cancer is increased by the amount of smoking, duration of smoking, age at which smoking started, and content of tar and nicotine. Female lung cancer deaths are rising at an alarming rate, and lung cancer has become the leading cause of female cancer deaths. Smoking now accounts for 25 percent of all cancer deaths in women.

Evidence suggests that certain lung cancer cells come from precursor abnormal cells found in smokers.[5] These precursor cells are present for years before an overt cancer develops. A smoker who has only these precursor cells and no cancer cells can eliminate these precursor cells if he or she stops smoking. However, there is an undetermined point of no return at which time the precursor cell develops into a cancer cell—even if the person stops smoking one day before this change occurs. After a single cancer cell develops, it may be many years before the cancer is detected.

Smoking acts in combination with certain occupational exposures to produce lung diseases. The carcinogenic potential of smoking is greater when it works together with the occupational exposures than when it works alone. The cooperative action between these carcinogens is called synergism. However, in most of the studies done before 1964, adequate smoking histories were not obtained from the subjects, so many of the workers in mining industries (coal, hematite, copper) and refining (nickel, chromium) claimed that the industrial exposure itself produced the many lung diseases, from chronic bronchitis to cancer, for which they claimed compensation. It is probable that smoking had a great deal to do with the development of these "industrial diseases." There are several ways tobacco can act in combination with environmental factors to produce toxic chemicals and carcinogens. The tobacco plant itself can become contaminated with toxic chemicals such as insecticides. Some environmental toxicities, like coal, may increase a smoker's risk for developing disease. Synergism may occur: smoking and asbestos exposure may act together to greatly increase a person's risk of developing lung cancer. Also, those who smoke the most generally have the highest occupational incidence of other chemical exposure; that is, blue-collar workers smoke much more than white-collar workers.

There has been much concern about marijuana and its effects on the human body. In 1982 the National Academy of Sciences released the report "Marijuana and Health," which states that there is a "strong possibility" that heavy marijuana smoking may lead to lung cancer. In fact, marijuana tar extracts have produced genetic changes in cells, and the smoke has 50 percent more carcinogenic hydrocarbons than cigarette smoke.

Nutrition and Lung Cancer

A study done by T. Hirayama showed that for those who smoked and also ate green and yellow vegetables every day, there was a slight beneficial effect not seen in a similar group of smokers who did not consume vegetables daily.[6] This is only one study and should not be taken to mean that a smoker is "safe" from lung cancer if he eats vegetables every day.

Other Tobacco-Related Cancers

Smoking cigarettes, pipes, and cigars is directly related to cancer of the larynx in men and women, and the more alcohol a smoker consumes, the higher is his risk of developing laryngeal cancer. Asbestos exposure has this same synergistic effect. Other cancers related to smoking include cancer of the mouth, esophagus, and pancreas, and here again, alcohol acts to intensify the effects of tobacco smoking. Cancer of the kidney and the urinary bladder are also directly related to smoking. Chewing tobacco or snuff dipping in nonsmokers causes a fourfold increase of oral cancers and a sixfold increase in those who were both tobacco smokers and heavy alcohol drinkers.[7] Furthermore, countries such as India, Ceylon, China, and the Soviet Union have the highest rates of death from oral cancer because the people there combine snuff and/or chewing tobacco with other ingredients such as betel nut. A chemical in the betel nut (N'nitrosonornicotine) can initiate tumors in animals. Hence these findings should discourage the use of chewing tobacco or snuff as a substitute for smoking, because you would simply be exchanging one type of cancer risk for another.

Cigarette smoking is associated with cancer of the cervix.[8] Cigarette smoking also causes dysplasia of the cervix,[9] which is detected by abnormal Pap smears.

Carcinogens of Tobacco Smoke

There are over 2,000 chemical compounds generated by tobacco smoke. The gas phase contains carbon monoxide, carbon dioxide, ammonia, nitrosamines, nitrogen oxides, hydrogen cyanide, sulfurs, nitriles, ketones, alcohols, and acrolein.

The "tars" contain extremely carcinogenic hydrocarbons, which include nitrosamines, benzo(a)pyrenes, anthracenes, acridines, quinolines, benzenes, naphthols, naphthalenes, cresols, and insecticides (DDT), as well as some radioactive compounds like potassium-40 and radium-226.

Do you recognize any of these compounds? Some of them, already described in Chapter 2, are known to be risk factors for human cancer.

Tobacco smoke, through its many carcinogens, produces harmful free radicals, which have been shown to change the DNA. Experiments with free radical scavengers show that some of them can inhibit to a degree the radicals' damaging effects.[10]

SMOKING AND CARDIOVASCULAR DISEASE

Smoking is one of the three major independent risk factors for cardiovascular diseases and intensifies the effects of other cardiac risk factors. Dr. A. Pic of the Haut Leveque Cardiac Hospital in Pessac, France, recently reported that a majority of a group of men under 35 years old who smoked more than thirty cigarettes a day had heart attacks immediately after vigorous exercise.[11] He warns that young athletes who smoke may be at an increased risk for heart disease.

There is much evidence to show that atherosclerosis of the aorta and coronary heart arteries is more severe and extensive in smokers than it is in nonsmokers. This is probably related to the hydrocarbon carcinogens in cigarette smoke that have the potential to initiate the atherosclerotic process (see Chapter 2). Two chemical compounds in tobacco smoke, nicotine and carbon monoxide, can aggravate heart disease, chest pain, and other vascular symptoms. Carbon monoxide can significantly raise the blood hemoglobin concentration to dangerously high levels in smokers.

Cigarette smoking has been shown to be a major risk factor in men and women, especially in middle age.[12-14] Circulation in the brain can improve dramatically, even in the elderly, if they stop smoking.[15] If smoking is stopped, painful symptoms lessen, especially from compromised arteries of the legs. In addition, women who smoke and use oral contraceptives have a tenfold increased risk of cardiac disease.

SMOKING AND OTHER SERIOUS DISEASES

Chronic lung diseases related to smoking are second to coronary heart disease as a cause of disability. Chronic bronchitis and emphysema are seen much more often in smokers, and death from these diseases is higher for smokers than for nonsmokers. Respiratory symptoms, like cough and sputum production and lung function abnormalities, are seen in smokers, adults as well as young adolescents. If smoking is stopped, lung function and symptoms can improve.

Persons who smoke are two times more likely to develop peptic ulcer disease and death from peptic ulcers than are nonsmokers. Also, once an ulcer develops, smoking retards the healing process.

EFFECTS OF SMOKING ON PREGNANCY, INFANTS, AND GENETICS

While smoking does not affect fertility in males, it does affect fertility in females. It took 50–70 percent longer for female smokers to conceive than it did for female nonsmokers.[16]

The birth weight of a baby born to a woman who smoked during the pregnancy is considerably lower than the birth weight of a child of a nonsmoker. The more the mother smokes, the more the infant's birth weight decreases. This weight deficiency is due to retardation of growth, probably from the harmful effects of carbon monoxide, which decreases the amount of oxygen delivered to the fetus. Smoking during pregnancy may affect subsequent child development, physical growth, and mental development at least up to the age of 11.

Smoking during pregnancy increases the developing fetus's risk of cancer by 50 percent.[17] Other studies have confirmed this finding.

The risk of spontaneous abortion and of the fetus dying at birth are higher if the mother smoked during pregnancy, probably because there was less oxygen delivered to the fetus. There are more premature births and more deaths of these premature infants—and a higher incidence of the "sudden infant death syndrome"—in babies delivered from mothers who smoked during pregnancy.

Heavy cigarette smokers have a higher frequency of genetic abnormalities[18] and have a high frequency of sperm abnormalities,[19] the latter probably due to the genetic damage caused by smoking. In addition, smoking has a pronounced effect on some drugs, food products, and laboratory blood tests.

SMOKING AND THE IMMUNE SYSTEM

Cigarette smoking adversely affects the human immune system. It affects certain anatomical parts as well as cellular components of the immune system.

Smoking destroys the hairlike structures that line the mucosa of the respiratory tract. These hairlike structures normally beat upward synchronously to remove mucous and any microorganisms. With these hairlike cilia gone, the mucous remains in the respiratory tract and is a perfect medium for the growth of microorganisms, including bacteria and viruses.

Another finding is that smoking causes an increase in macrophages, cells of the immune system that defend the lung against invading organisms and abnormal cells. Macrophages secrete enzymes and other cellular products against the invaders, which also inadvertently causes emphysema, the breakdown of the walls of the respiratory tree.[20-22] The secretion of these enzymes and cellular products by macrophages generates free-radical chemicals, which are responsible for the breakdown of the walls. When this breakdown occurs, organisms can take hold and infect the person because the functional capacity of macrophages to kill invading microorganisms is greatly diminished. Certain micronutrients, like carotene, vitamins E and C, selenium, zinc, and copper, can neutralize free radicals and prevent the invasion of microorganisms and the breakdown of the respiratory wall.

Smoking has been shown to cause reversible changes in the immunoregulatory T cell lymphocytes.[23,24] The ratio of T4 to T8 lymphocytes is decreased in heavy smokers, as in patients with AIDS, but returns to normal six weeks after these heavy smokers stop smoking. Other studies have corroborated these findings: suppressor T cell activity is significantly enhanced by smoking.[25]

Smokers also show a significant decrease in natural killer cell activity,[26,27] which may explain the reported increase in survival of cardiac transplants in patients who resumed smoking postoperatively. Antibody levels are adversely affected by smoking as well.[28] IgA, the antibody in the mucous membranes, and one of the first lines of defense against viruses and bacteria, is decreased in smokers.[29] Other antibody classes are at lower levels also.

Studies show that smokers have lower blood levels of vitamin C and several other free radical scavengers. Nutrition in smokers is generally poorer also. Nutritional deficiencies, especially of vitamin C, compromise the immune system of the smoker. Smoking is associated with many infections, cancers, heart disease, and many other chronic illnesses. Smoking suppresses the immune system, but early data indicate that this is reversible.

PASSIVE SMOKING

A nonsmoker who is exposed to tobacco smoke from other smokers has many adverse reactions and is unjustly and unnecessarily subjected to risk factors detrimental to his or her health. The smoke that comes from the lighted end of a cigarette contains more hazardous chemicals than does the smoke that is inhaled by the smoker. It is almost unavoidable to inhale tobacco smoke because it is so prevalent in homes, work places, public areas, and private establishments. In a large study of nonsmokers and former smokers, 64 percent of the nonsmokers reported daily exposure. Thirty-five percent were exposed to secondhand smoke at least ten hours per week. Under experimental conditions, nonsmokers inhaled enough smoke to be the equivalent of one cigarette per day in England, and up to two cigarettes a day in Japan.

The Surgeon General's report in 1986 was a landmark, asserting for the first time that involuntary inhalation of cigarette smoke by nonsmokers causes disease, most notably lung cancer.[30,31] The report also states that the number of people injured by involuntary smoking was much larger than the number injured by other environmental agents that have already been regulated. The National Research Council of the National Academy of Sciences reported similar findings.[32]

The controversy over passive smoking began to heat up in 1983, and on March 19, 1984, R.J. Reynolds Tobacco Company paid for a third of a page advertisement in the *Wall Street Journal* entitled "Smoking in Public: Let's Separate Fact From Fiction." The company asserted, "But, in fact, there is little evidence—and certainly nothing which proves scientifically that cigarette smoke causes disease in nonsmokers."

Separating smokers from nonsmokers within the same physical space is not always successful because the smoke travels on the same floor and between floors. A movement to ban all smoking in public areas has culminated in the ban of smoking on all domestic flights in the United States since early 1990. Forty-two states have legislated smoking restrictions in various areas like public transportation, hospitals, elevators, indoor areas, cultural or recreational facilities, schools, and libraries.

Lung Cancer

The National Research Council has estimated the effect of passive smoking on nonsmokers to be significant in the development of lung cancer. Of the 12,200 annual deaths from lung cancer in the United States that are not due to smoking, between 2,500 and 8,400 of these may be attributable to passive smoking.[33] This equates to about 7.4 deaths from lung cancer among nonsmokers per hundred thousand person years. (Person years are computed by taking the age of each person and adding them together. For example, a 70 year old and a 20 year old would equate to 90 person years. If the study were of 1,000 people each of whom were 100 years old, this would equate to a hundred thousand person years (1,000 x 100 = 100,000).)

Over a dozen studies have been done to assess the relationship between passive smoking and lung cancer. There have been at least three significant prospective studies that show there is a higher risk of developing lung cancer in nonsmokers married to smokers. All these studies show that nonsmokers married to smokers have a greater risk for lung cancer than do those married to nonsmokers. The lung cancers most frequently seen in these studies were squamous cell carcinoma and small cell carcinoma of the lung. A review of these studies made by the National Academy of Sciences and the Surgeon General found that the risk of developing lung cancer in a passive smoker is 1.34: one hundred times higher than the person exposed to asbestos for twenty years.[34]

About 17 percent of lung cancers in nonsmokers are a result of exposure to tobacco smoke during childhood and adolescence.[35] For the first time, this study confirms that innocent children are at tremendous risk for lung cancer because they inhaled tobacco smoke in their household.

Cervical Cancer

Studies show that cigarette smoking increases your risk of cervical cancer. Passive smoke exposure for three or more hours per day has been shown to increase almost threefold a nonsmoker's risk of developing cervical cancer. It is quite alarming that this amount of exposure increases your risk of cervical cancer by such a significant factor.[36]

Cancer in Children

Smoking during pregnancy increases by 50 percent the fetus's risk of developing cancer later in childhood. This too is alarming.[37]

Bladder Cancer

Nonsmokers have a higher risk of getting bladder cancer if they are exposed to other people's smoke at home, at work, or during transportation.[38]

Other Respiratory Diseases

Nonsmokers inhaling smoke passively at the work place had a significant reduction in their capacity to expel air over the course of one second as measured by FEV1.[39] These reductions in lung function are quite significant, comparable to that experienced by light smokers (those who smoke 1–10 cigarettes per day). The exacerbation of asthmatic conditions in nonsmokers exposed to secondhand smoke also was apparent in these studies.

Cardiovascular Disease

A number of studies have been conducted to confirm the suspected association between heart disease and exposure of nonsmokers to tobacco smoke. They revealed that a man had a 2.1 times higher risk of having a heart attack if he was married to a wife who smoked. Men whose wives did not smoke, by comparison, experienced heart attacks at a rate of 1.4.

Allergies

People may have allergies to tobacco and tobacco smoke products, because there are definite antibodies made to some of these products. In addition, people who have other allergies (pollen, mold, dust) are much more sensitive to smoke than those who do not have such allergies.

Effects of Smoking on Children

It is 50–75 percent more difficult for a smoking woman to conceive than it is for a nonsmoker. The birth weight of children born to smoking mothers is significantly less than the weight of children born to nonsmoking mothers.[40]

The rate of both upper and lower respiratory problems is consistently higher among young children of smoking parents than it is among children of nonsmoking parents. Another study reported a 28 percent increase in admission of infants of smoking mothers to the hospital for pneumonia or bronchitis. These studies have been repeated.[41] The children of a mother who smokes five cigarettes a day will have 2.5 to 3.5 more incidents of lower respiratory illnesses than they would otherwise. Other studies show a significant increase in the frequency of tracheitis, bronchitis, pneumonia, and bronchiolitis, all of which are attributable to maternal smoking.

It has been estimated that 10–36 percent of all chronic middle ear infections could be attributable to smoking exposure.[42] Mother's smoking contributed more to these illnesses in their children than did father's smoking.

Chronic Respiratory Symptoms

There is also an excess of 30–80 percent of chronic respiratory disease symptoms in children of smokers. We are unaware at this point what significance these findings have on the future health of these children nor do we know the significance of the other symptoms of lung disease already discussed.

Time for New Public Policies

On the basis of the evidence citing the dangers of passive smoking, I believe it is prudent for all individuals, specifically employers and those who develop public policy, to consider tobacco smoke a threat to the health of nonsmoking adults and children alike. The data have been thoroughly reviewed,[43] and it is time now to prohibit smoking in all public areas and work places.

Not only do nonsmokers experience many harmful health effects from tobacco smoke, but they also have to pay higher health insurance premiums for diseases related to smoking (cancer, cardiovascular diseases, lung diseases, etc.). Moreover, nonsmokers subsidize the tobacco industry through their tax dollars. We should pressure our senators and congressmen to force the American government to stop subsidizing the tobacco industry.

STOP SMOKING

More than 95 percent of former smokers quit on their own, usually at the recommendation of their physician. People who follow this popular strategy outlined by the American Lung Association have had good results:

1. Set a future date when you will stop smoking, and sign a contract with yourself to that effect.

2. Make a list of:
   - All the reasons you continue to smoke ("It's a crutch," "It feels good").
   - All your bonds with smoking (coffee, alcohol, etc.).
   - All your reasons for not quitting.
   - All the reasons you should quit smoking.
   - All the rewards for becoming a nonsmoker.

- Every cigarette you smoke for the two weeks before your quit date.
- All situations you think will be difficult without a cigarette.

3. Find substitutes for cigarettes, like chewing gum.

4. Save your butts for two weeks before quitting day. Put them in a jar and then fill the jar up with water and keep it in a visible place. Every time you feel the urge to smoke, open the jar and take a whiff.

5. Be prepared for withdrawal symptoms—cough, constipation, tiredness, headache, sore throat, trouble sleeping. These last only a week at most.

6. Begin a daily exercise program (walking, etc.) and eat the proper foods.

7. Tell all the people you know that you are going to quit and tell your friends how they can help.

8. Use coping techniques to break your smoking pattern:
- "I have the strength to do it."
- Doodle, stretch, touch your toes.
- Put a rubber band on your wrist and snap it every time you have the urge.
- Take a deep breath and hold it for several seconds and then exhale. Repeat this several times until the urge disappears.
- Avoid smoking situations and places; avoid people who smoke.
- Move around, take a shower, go get a drink, etc.
- Remember: "A craving for a cigarette will go away whether or not I smoke."

9. Don't dwell on your desire for a cigarette. Simply decide you have smoked your last cigarette.

10. Don't have in mind an estimated time by which the discomfort should end. Change your routine to distract yourself.

11. Sign a final nonsmoker contract with yourself.

A common mistake a "quitter" makes is to think it is all right to have one or two cigarettes every once in a while. If you could have done that before, you would have.

Your local chapter of the American Lung Association has courses on how to stop smoking. These sessions are inexpensive and quite comprehensive. I encourage you to use them.

Smokers who have existing heart disease can reduce their risk of future heart attacks and death if they quit smoking.[44] Prospective findings in a study that involved over 7,000 people who are 65 years old or older indicate that smokers who continue to smoke will have a higher rate of mortality, but those who quit will have an improved life expectancy.[45] So it's never too late to quit.

Many people say that they do not want to stop smoking because they fear gaining weight. Weight gain may occur in those who stop smoking, but it is likely to occur only in a small percentage of them.[46] This study and others never considered the fact that people who were quitting took no measures to control their weight. It is important to guard against possible weight gain, and this can be accomplished by following the Ten-Point Plan in Chapter 22.

Many studies indicate that if a person quits smoking for at least ten years, his risk of developing coronary heart disease is the same as a nonsmoker of the same age. On the other hand, a person must quit smoking for fifteen years before his risk of developing cancer will equal that of a nonsmoker.

Federally sponsored programs support tobacco prices, benefiting allotment holders (a unique monopoly situation) and tobacco growers. In addition, other federally sponsored programs benefit the tobacco industry. The programs and their cost to the taxpayer—both smoker and nonsmoker—are the following: tobacco inspection and grading, $6.1 million; market news service, $10.5 million; research, $7.4 million; short-term credit, $69.2 million (1979). Total cost to the taxpayer: over $157 million in 1979.

On the other hand, federal funds are spent to discourage smoking, to research the health effects of smoking, and to provide a great portion of the cost of medical care for people who are suffering from and dying of smoking-related diseases. Patients with *self-induced* smoking-related diseases and families of these patients receive Social Security benefits.

The United States has adopted uncompromisingly restrictive measures concerning food additives, but only a verbal statement of caution is required on every package of cigarettes. The Delaney Clause legislation prohibits the sale of any product to the American people that has been shown to be carcinogenic to humans and animals, and thus applies to situations in which the human hazard may be minimal. Tobacco is a major risk factor for cancer, cardiovascular diseases, lung diseases, and other illnesses. If you smoke, you should stop. If you have not started, don't! Seek professional help if you must, but stop smoking.

13
Alcohol and Caffeine

THE PRICE OF ALCOHOL ABUSE

Industrial losses in the United States due to alcohol cost about $45 billion every year. Many more billions of dollars are added to this figure when you consider that alcohol is involved in 50 percent of all traffic fatalities, 30 percent of small-aircraft accidents, and 66 percent of all violent crimes. Furthermore, the totals are higher still when you consider the losses due to diseases aggravated by alcohol abuse, and losses due to alcohol-induced poor decision-making in government, industry, education, law, the military, and medicine. About 68 percent of adult Americans abuse alcohol.

It is estimated that 100 million Americans drink alcohol, and over 28 million—1 of every 8 Americans—are children of alcoholics. Alcohol-related costs total about $117 billion every year; for other drug abuse, the cost is $60 billion a year. This total of $177 billion a year represents about $63 a month for every man, woman, and child in the United States.

All of society pays for substance abuse. Employers lose productivity, you pay the tax bill for programs and services, and you also pay higher insurance premiums. You do the same for tobacco abuse as well.

Excessive alcohol consumption is a risk factor for cancers of the mouth, pharynx, larynx, esophagus, pancreas, liver, and head and neck. Alcohol acts synergistically with tobacco smoking in the development of other gastrointestinal cancers and urinary bladder cancer. A greater frequency of these cancers occurs in men, blacks, people on the low end of the socioeconomic scale, and older people. Alcohol is directly responsible for causing cirrhosis of the liver, which is the seventh leading cause of death in the United States. Fifty percent of alcoholics die from cardiovascular diseases and 20 percent from accidents, suicides, and homicides.

Nutrition and Alcoholism

Alcoholics have more nutritional deficiencies than all other groups of people.[1] Alcohol is a source of calories, and alcoholics consume this rather than foods with much better nutritional value. Alcoholics will consume about 20 percent of their total calories as alcohol.

Many vitamin deficiencies are severe in alcoholics. The most important is thiamine (vitamin B1) deficiency. A severe brain disease called Wernicke-Korsakoff syndrome can be rapidly reversed in alcoholics by the administration of thiamine. Folic acid and vitamin B12 deficiencies are seen in alcoholics due to the lack of fresh fruits and vegetables in their diets. These deficiencies are responsible for anemias, among other things. Pyridoxine (B6) deficiency is responsible for alcoholics' peripheral nerve problems. Vitamin C is normally stored and activated in the liver, but alcoholics have a deficiency of vitamin C because of their liver disease. Because of their vitamin deficiencies, alcoholics may complain of visual problems and sometimes infertility, since their sperm production may be impaired. In addition to vitamin deficiencies, alcoholics have several mineral deficiencies including calcium, zinc, and magnesium. Since alcohol can interfere with the absorption of iron from the gut, some alcoholics develop the Plummer-Vinson syndrome, which is characterized by a cluster of symptoms including difficulty swallowing; a red, smooth tongue; and iron deficiency anemia. People with this syndrome have a high rate of cancer of the mouth.

Alcohol and Immunity

Not only does consumption of alcohol rob the body of many nutrients, it also increases complications from cirrhosis of the liver, gastrointestinal hemorrhage, trauma, cancer, and infection. The high incidence of infection among alcoholics is attributed to dulled mental function; breakdown of the protective mucous lining of the nose, mouth, and airways; aspiration of saliva into the lungs; exposure out-of-doors; and malnutriton. The frequency and severity of infections are so pronounced among alcoholics that most physicians believe that alcohol itself directly inhibits the body's immune defense mechanisms. Clinical observations and laboratory studies support the long-held conviction that alcohol depresses the function of the immune system.

The clinical evidence linking alcohol intake and depressed immune function dates back to 1785. There is a strong correlation between the amount of alcohol consumed and the degree of immune dysfunction. Even moderate users of alcohol have very high rates of infections, especially pneumonia. Alcohol interferes with normal immune defense mechanisms (see Chapter 4 for a review).

The neutrophil leukocyte, a kind of white blood cell, is decreased in number and its function is retarded with chronic or acute ingestion of alcohol. As you may remember from Chapter 4, the function of these cells is to fight and kill invading bacteria. Alcohol consumption of this type also causes a decrease in the number of lymphocytes and impairs their function, especially the T cells and natural killer cells, which seek out and destroy viruses and cancer cells. Monocytes, too, are impaired by alcohol ingestion. Suppression of this cellular arm of immunity leads to a high rate of tuberculosis infection and viral infections. Because cellular killing is inhibited, latent viruses, like the Epstein-Barr virus, become activated and there is a high degree of susceptibility to all viruses.

Alcohol ingestion significantly interferes with the ability of the immune system to make antibodies against a new invading antigen, like a virus or bacterium. The complement protein defense system is also adversely affected by alcohol consumption.

Thus, both acute and chronic use of alcohol interferes significantly with our defense mechanisms. Chronice use of alcohol adversely affects the cellular arm of the immune system and increases the risk for tuberculosis, viral infection of all types, and cancer. Alcohol should be considered an immune suppressive drug with far-reaching effects.

Alcohol, Cancer, and Other Diseases

Alcohol may exert its carcinogenic effects by direct topical action on the mouth, pharynx, and esophagus. The evidence that alcohol is a topical carcinogen is that mouthwash users have a high rate of oral cancer and mouthwash is rarely swallowed. Alcohol and tobacco account for 75 percent of all oral cancers in the United States. And a considerable amount of evidence shows that alcoholism, because of the nutritional deficiencies associated with it, significantly increases the risk of smoking-related cancers.

The rate of liver cancer in alcoholics who have cirrhosis is rising. In addition, there are many other complications of cirrhosis, including varicose veins in the esophagus, which can bleed; ascites (fluid in the abdomen); muscle wasting; and kidney failure. Alcohol induces an inflammation of the pancreas and other abnormalities of the pancreas, and the heart can become severely enlarged and nonfunctional with alcoholism.

One study shows that women who consume alcohol have a greater risk of developing breast cancer than nondrinkers.[2] The preponderance of evidence also shows an association between alcohol consumption and the development of breast cancer.[3-6] A higher risk of developing breast cancer was seen even in women consuming only a moderate amount of alcohol, especially in the younger group. A moderate amount of alcohol in these studies constitutes two to four drinks a week. Moderate alcohol consumption is also an independent risk factor for the development of heart disease and stroke.[7,8]

Premature testicle and ovary shrinkage are seen in alcoholics. Peptic ulcers are also common and are often quite large. Infants born of alcoholic mothers may have a variety of problems including defects in the brain, in intellectual development and physical growth, and in the facial features. This is called the "fetal alcohol syndrome," in which alcohol acts to transform normal cells of the fetus into abnormal cells. The number of persons affected in this way is grossly underestimated.

CAFFEINE AND CANCER

Caffeine is the most popular drug in North America and in many other parts of the world. It is found in coffee, tea, cola beverages, and chocolate.

Coffee drinking may be related to cancer of the lower urinary tract, including the bladder.[9] Studies show that the risk for these cancers is independent of other factors like tobacco smoking, and these cancer rates are very high in persons who drink more than three cups of coffee a day. This risk is probably related to other compounds in coffee as well as caffeine.

It is well known that caffeine can cause damage to genetic material[10,11] and thereby potentially lead to the development of cancer by altering DNA. It also interferes with the normal repair mechanisms of DNA and other genetic material. Caffeine can act as a teratogen, which is an agent that causes mistakes in gene production leading to malformations of a fetus.

Excessive coffee consumption by pregnant mothers can lead to lower infant birth weights.[12] Pregnant women who consumed 600 milligrams or more of caffeine per day have a higher incidence of abortion and prematurity.[13]

In a study of coffee consumption in 1,130 male college graduates for nineteen to thirty-five years after graduation, it was found that those who drank five or more cups of coffee a day had a 2.8 times higher risk of developing heart disease.[14] This study also showed coffee to be an independent risk factor for the development of heart disease.

Although alcohol and caffeine are two important risk factors for cancer, the decision to consume them is *yours*. You can again decide about the status of your health!

14

Sexual-Social and Hormonal Factors

Sexual-social behavior and hormonal factors have become increasingly important in the development of cancer in modern day. The relaxation of sexual mores has increased promiscuity, which is a major risk factor for certain cancers. There has also been a concomitant increased use of hormones, which can lead to the development of other cancers.

CERVICAL CANCER

Women who start having sexual intercourse before age 16 with multiple male partners, particularly those who are uncircumcised, have higher incidence of cervical cancer. Fortunately, increased awareness of the importance of early cancer detection has led to increased Pap smears over the past two decades. As a result, cervical abnormalities have been detected in their early stages and treated earlier. Oral contraceptives and tobacco have been shown to be risk factors for cervical cancer as well. Passive smoke exposure for three hours/day increases the risk of developing cervical cancer by a factor of three.[1] A woman has a higher risk of cervical cancer if her husband had previously been married to a woman with cervical cancer.

CANCER OF THE PENIS

Although cancer of the penis is not common in the continental United States, it occurs more frequently in many parts of the world where circumcision is not performed routinely. Penile cancer has been studied extensively in Puerto Rico. The epidemiological evidence there suggests that uncircumcised males with poor hygiene techniques, that is, those who do not routinely clean beneath the foreskin, have a very high incidence of cancer of the penis. Routine circumcision almost completely eliminates the risk for this cancer.

AIDS AND CANCER

AIDS now rivals cancer as the most feared disease in the nation, and many Americans believe that almost everyone is susceptible to this deadly incurable disease (Media General—Associated Press Poll). As of late 1991, there have been over 200,000 cases of AIDS reported by state and local health departments and over 125,000 AIDS-related deaths. In 1981 only 189 cases of AIDS were reported to the Centers for Disease Control (CDC). The first 50,000 cases of AIDS were reported from 1981 to 1987, and the remaining 150,000 were reported between January 1988 and late 1991. These numbers represent the minimum number of persons with severe HIV-related disease. There is underdiagnosis and underreporting of AIDS, so the actual number of cases is much greater. Between 1 and 2 million Americans are infected with HIV but have no symptoms. The World Health Organization estimates that 1 in every 350 adults around the world is infected with HIV, the equivalent of 8 to 10 million people. By the year 2000, it is predicted that 30 to 40 million people will be HIV positive.

Because oncologists take care of patients with AIDS and because AIDS patients may develop three cancers—anal cancer, tongue cancer, and Kaposi sarcoma—a brief discussion of AIDS is warranted.

The prevalence of AIDS in the homosexual population received much media attention; however, today over 60 percent of the cases of HIV infection worldwide have been acquired heterosexually.[2] Intravenous drug users, their sexual partners, and their children represent the next largest portion of all cases. Before 1985, 63 percent of all AIDS patients were homosexual or bisexual men with no history of intravenous drug use, and only 18 percent were female or heterosexual male IV drug users. In the first six months of 1989, 56 percent of AIDS patients were homosexual or bisexual males with no IV drug use, 23 percent were female or heterosexual male IV drug users, and 4 percent were the sex partners or children of IV drug users. Blacks and Hispanics continue to have a high incidence of AIDS.

Mode of Spread

In June 1987 Dr. F. Noireau reported from the Congo that the isolation from monkeys of retroviruses closely related to the human immunodeficiency virus (HIV) strongly suggests a simian origin of this virus. HIV is widely thought to have originated in central East Africa where the virus may have existed in an endemic state for at least fifteen years. The indirect transmission of the virus from the monkey to man may have occurred through bites, through the cutting up and consumption of monkey meat, or from insects.

In a book on the sexual practices of people in the Great Lakes area of Africa, Kasharmura writes the following: "To stimulate a man or woman and induce them to intense sexual activity, monkey blood (for a man) or she-monkey blood (for a woman) was directly inoculated in the pubic area and also the thighs and backs." These magic practices could be responsible for the emergence of AIDS in man.

Homosexuality and intravenous drug use have been shown to be major risk factors for AIDS. Although AIDS is spread primarily through sexual contact and the sharing of needles by intravenous drug users, there have been five startling reports of HIV transmission merely through the skin or mucous membranes.[3] The first was in England, where AIDS was contracted by a woman whose only source of infection was a man whom she had been caring for at home. He was found to have AIDS during an autopsy. The woman recalled having had some small cuts on her hands and eczema while she had been caring for him. She was not a nurse. The second woman was not a nurse either but had contracted the virus while taking care of her son, who had gotten HIV-infected blood from a transfusion. Three others who contracted the virus were all health care workers accidentally exposed to blood from HIV seropositive patients but not via an HIV-contaminated needle. Two of the three women had an acute illness like that with early HIV infection, and all three are HIV positive. The transmissions reportedly occurred during a failed arteriocatheterization in an emergency room; an accident with a blood collecting tube in an outpatient clinic; and a spillage of blood that was being collected from an unsuspected donor.[4] One woman had chapped hands but no open wounds, and another had dermatitis on her ear. It has also been reported that a badly burned British person contracted the AIDS virus through a skin transplant in a London hospital in 1987.[5] And in early 1991, the U.S. Centers for Disease Control reported the transmission of HIV from a dentist to his patient during an invasive dental procedure.[6]

These earlier reports sent shock waves throughout the world. It was possible to get AIDS not only from a blood transfusion but also from close contact with bodily fluids of infected persons. The immunology of the skin is very delicate. To prevent invasion by microorganisms, the skin possesses Langerhans macrophages, which are white blood cells capable of migrating into the epidermis and engulfing foreign material, and the dermis, which is rich in T helper lymphocytes. Once an invading organism has been engulfed, these cells migrate to local lymph nodes where more immunocytes are recruited. Both the T cell and the Langerhans cells bear certain receptors that make them easy targets for infection by HIV.[7] The immunological activation that takes place when these cells go into lymph nodes provides an opportunity for HIV viral replication through the cell division of the lymphocyte. In other words, the human immunodeficiency virus can replicate itself only by using the machinery of a cell—in this case, the lymphocyte. When the lymphocyte goes through cell division to replicate itself, so too can the human immunodeficiency virus by utilizing the lymphocyte "machine" in motion.

Unbroken skin may well be a good defense against HIV; however, people with broken or inflamed skin are vulnerable to HIV infection. People at risk for HIV have numerous small abrasions on their hands or eczema, particularly those whose occupation involves frequent hand washing in detergent. Hence all people whose blood may need to be handled by others should be screened for HIV. Appropriate protective clothing, such as gowns and rubber gloves, should be worn when handling bodily fluids. We have already seen litigation by employees who can prove that they became infected by HIV only after accidental exposure on the job. The Centers for Disease Control concedes that "exposure of skin or mucous membranes to contaminated blood may result in transmission of HIV." And the CDC recommends that all health care workers take precautions when handling blood or other bodily fluids. The Centers for Disease Control also points out that "it has not been established that knowledge of a patient's serological status increases the compliance of the health care workers with recommended precautions, however."

AIDS has reportedly been transmitted in the following manners:

- Breastfeeding.[8]
- Oral-genital transmission.[9,10]
- Mother to child transmission via the placenta.
- Heterosexual transmission.[11]
- Blood transfusions of unscreened blood.
- Blood transfusions of screened blood.[12]

- Female to female transmission.[13]
- Transmission by human bite.[14]
- Insect-borne transmission.[15]
- Acupuncture.[16]
- Faulty condoms.[17]
- Transmission between two siblings.[18]

In addition, HIV has been isolated from dead infected patients up to eleven days after death.[19]

It appears that the risk of developing AIDS increases each year after infection by the virus. With most illnesses, on the contrary, the more time that elapses the less the risk for the illness. Evidence from San Francisco's Health Department and the Centers for Disease Control has shown that only 4 percent of those infected with the virus will develop the disease within three years. But after five years of exposure that figure climbs to 14 percent, and after seven years it jumps to 36 percent. Hence the longer you are infected, the higher are your chances of developing AIDS. The United States Public Health Service estimates that by 1992 close to 500,000 Americans will suffer from this deadly disease. The number of cases of Kaposi's sarcoma, anal cancers, and tongue cancers (the three tumors associated with AIDS) will probably rise accordingly.

HORMONES

As early as 1898, scientists recognized a connection between the immune system and the hormones of the body. More recently both clinical and experimental evidence support the hypothesis that the sex hormones regulate immune function. This is based on the following observations: (1) immune response is slightly different in men and women; (2) immune response is altered by decreasing or increasing hormones; (3) immune response is altered during pregnancy when sex hormones are increased; and (4) immunological cells have specific receptors for sex hormones. Female and male sex hormones regulate the immune system, indicating an important interaction between the nervous system, endocrine system, and immune system. The immune system, in turn, can control the circulating levels of these hormones. As we see again, the immune system is very delicate and can orchestrate a great many things.[20]

Apart from their regulatory effect on the immune system, excess hormones can increase the chance of an error in normal cell division and lead to a cancerous transformation. This occurs because hormones can affect cell division rates of normal, hyperplastic, and even cancer cells. The more often these cells try to divide, the higher the risk is for them to make a mistake and hence change or transform into a cancer cell.

NATURE'S BIOLOGICAL FACTORS

Menstrual History

A woman's reproductive history is another risk factor for developing cancer. The longer the body is bathed with estrogens, the higher is a woman's risk of developing cancer. The earlier a woman starts menstruating and the later she stops, the higher is her risk for cancer, especially breast cancer. For instance, American women typically begin menstruating around age 11 and experience menopause in their early 50s. If a woman has had few or no pregnancies and long reproductive years, she has a higher risk of getting breast cancer. Women are less at risk for developing breast cancer, however, if they have an early menopause of if they have their ovaries removed surgically so that early menopause is induced.

The older a woman is when she first becomes pregnant, the higher is her risk of developing breast cancer. A woman who delivers her first child after the age of 35 has a threefold higher risk of developing breast cancer than a woman who bears her first child before the age of 18. Women who never become pregnant and women who never menstruate have a three or four times higher risk of developing cancer, especially breast cancer. In addition, if you had an abortion in the first trimester of your first pregnancy, whether it was spontaneous or induced, you are 2½ times more likely to develop breast cancer.[21]

Cancer and Pregnancy

There are not many situations in medicine that arouse the anxiety of the physician and patient as much as the discovery of cancer in the pregnant woman. Cancer during pregnancy is not an infrequent occurrence. About 1 of every 1,000 pregnancies involves cancer, and about 1 of every 118 women who are found to have cancer will be pregnant at the time. The cancers most likely seen in pregnant women in order of their prevalence are breast cancer, cervical cancer, ovarian cancer, lymphoma, and colorectal cancer.

Cancer and pregnancy are the only two biological conditions in which foreign cells to the mother, that is, the cancer cells and those that make up the fetus—foreign because half of the genetic make-up of the fetus is from the father—are tolerated by what appears to be a relatively normal immune system. These conditions are permitted because some aspects of the immune system are not working to peak capacity. Hormones like estrogen, progesterone, alpha fetal protein, and human chorionic gonadotropin all have an immunosuppressive effect on the mother's immune system, without which the fetus would not grow. Other changes that occur during pregnancy are depression of the cellular killers, enhancement of certain blocking antibodies, and alteration of other esoteric factors of the immune system. The hormonal mechanisms that ensure the survival of the fetus and consequently suppress the immune system are the same mechanisms that also favor the progress of a cancer. However, the important point is *pregnancy, per se, is probably not a risk factor for the development of cancer nor is it likely that it will cause existing cancer to spread.*[22,23]

Poor results seen in the treatment of cancer in pregnant women have largely been due to late diagnosis or inadequate treatment. Signs of cancer can often be mistakenly attributed to changes of pregnancy or lactation. If you discover you have a cancer during pregnancy, treatment should be instituted without delay by delivering the fetus if it is viable. However, data suggest that treatment should not be delayed to obtain a viable fetus. Since the symptoms of the cancer are usually attributed to the pregnancy, the diagnosis is usually somewhat delayed, and generally speaking, the prognosis is slightly worse in patients who are pregnant and who have cancer, especially those who have breast cancer.

Should you become pregnant after having been diagnosed as having breast cancer? This is a very common question since breast cancer is one of the leading causes of death in women. A review of the data reveals that pregnancy is not associated with excessive risk of cancer recurrence; hence there is little evidence for advising against subsequent pregnancy for women who want to become pregnant and are free of any recurrences at the time. However, it is still recommended that breast cancer patients do not become pregnant. Given the fact that most cancer recurrences appear within the first two years, it is prudent to advise a woman not to become pregnant until she has been free of cancer for at least two years. Should a pregnancy occur before two years have elapsed, the decision for a therapeutic abortion should be based on the patient's treatment program and other factors.

Most of the time a physician attending a patient who has had a cancer or a patient with a newly diagnosed cancer will decide whether to recommend an abortion based on his feelings or religious beliefs. When the supporting data as outlined above concerning these patients are presented to physicians, these data fly in the smack of what has been taught, handed down, or otherwise believed. Hence abortions are commonly recommended. The data for this section involve well over 300 references and has been reviewed in two major investigations.

Cancer Risk to Fetus

There may be a link between the amount of estrogen to which a fetus is exposed during pregnancy and a later risk of developing breast cancer. An ongoing Harvard study involves Sweden's Uppsala University Hospital's records of women who delivered daughters between 1873 and 1957 and the number of breast cancer cases that occurred between 1958 and 1986. The hypothesis is that the level of estrogen during pregnancy may influence a daughter's subsequent risk of breast cancer because a female gets her largest exposure to estrogen while *in utero*, her mammary glands being undifferentiated then and very susceptible to the effects of estrogen. Symptoms related to high estrogen levels in pregnant mothers include: severe nausea, obesity, or sometimes high birthweight. A correlation will be made between these symptoms and the subsequent development of breast cancer in daughters.

Benign Breast Disease

There are many terms used to describe benign breast diseases. Fibrocystic breast disease is the most common one. A more broad umbrella term, such as "lumpy breast disorders," should be used. Benign breast disorders occur mainly in menstruating women but usually not in the teenage years. Collectively, benign breast lesions are commonly called fibrocystic disease by physicians and lay persons.[24] Some are inconsequential, others can predispose the person to breast cancer.

About 50 percent of the female population in the United States will have lumpy breast disease at one time or another. Unless the cysts are greater than 3 millimeters in diameter, they are usually not a risk factor for the development of cancer. And although smaller cysts can come and go and ultimately disappear, it is very uncommon for a cyst greater than 2 centimeters in diameter to do so. A single cyst having a diameter of 2 centimeters or more puts the patient at a higher risk for subsequent breast cancer. Also, a number of studies have shown that the more atypical the cells are in the cysts when looked at under the microscope, the higher is the risk of developing breast cancer.

Lumpy breast disease is influenced greatly by a number of factors: hormonal changes, dietary practices such as consumption of caffeine and foods high in fat and an inadequate intake of certain vitamins and minerals, and nicotine exposure. A randomized trial involving 21 patients who had painful breasts premenstrually for at least five years showed these women to benefit from a diet that reduced the fat content to 15 percent of their total calories and increased complex carbohydrate consumption to maintain the normal caloric intake. There was a significant reduction in the severity of the breast tenderness and swelling after six months. Physical examination also showed reduced breast swelling, tenderness, and nodularity in 60 percent of the patients.[25]

Since 1979 I have treated women with breast cancer and benign breast disorders, specifically lumpy breast disease. All the patients with lumpy breast disease followed my Ten-Point Plan as outlined in this book, with particular attention paid to low-fat, high-fiber foods, supplementation with certain vitamins and minerals, abstinence from alcohol and smoking, and avoidance of passive smoke. Almost 90 percent of the patients had decreased breast pain premenstrually, and about half of the patients experienced a decrease in the size of their cysts. In most cases the size of the breast diminished somewhat; however, in about 10 percent of the women, the size of the breast increased slightly.

Undescended Testicles

Undescended testicles are relatively common, occurring in about 8 of every 1,000 boys after one year of life. Half the time the testicle is in the inguinal canal, but the other half of the time the testicle is within the abdominal cavity. It is the testicle in the abdominal cavity which, if uncorrected before the age of 6, is a risk factor for the development of cancer of the testicles.[26,27] It is important, then, for a pediatrician to examine the testicles at birth to make sure they are descended into the scrotum. If one or both are not, then surgical intervention should be entertained at an appropriate time.

Prolactin

A number of studies indicate that high levels of prolactin, a hormone secreted by the pituitary gland in the brain, may be another risk factor for breast cancer. Normally, prolactin rises during pregnancy and then promotes and maintains lactation for breastfeeding. Although there is wide range of normal values for prolactin in the nonpregnant state, values 2 to 2.5 times higher than normal have been associated with breast cancer.[28]

In a provocative study, investigators have shown that a first pregnancy causes a significant decrease in the normal secretion of prolactin. This effects long-term changes lasting 12–13 years regardless of the age of the pregnant woman. Researchers have proposed that the long-term depression of prolactin after an early first pregnancy may be the protective factor against the development of breast cancer.[29]

EXOGENOUS HORMONES (HORMONES TAKEN BY THE PATIENT)

DES

A little more than 2 million women took diethylstilbestrol, commonly known as DES, to avert miscarriages in the 1940s and 1950s. Adding this figure to the number of children exposed to DES brings the total to an estimated 6 million. DES is associated with vaginal and cervical adenocarcinomas and dysplasia in women who were exposed to the drug as fetuses.[30,31] There is also a higher risk of developing breast cancer in mothers given DES during pregnancy.[32-34]

In addition, sons of DES-exposed mothers have reproductive and urinary tract abnormalities. One of these is undescended testicles, which may lead to cancer of the testes if uncorrected before the age of 6 as mentioned previously in this chapter.[35]

In Italy, between the years 1977 and 1979, there was an epidemic of breast enlargement in children which, when investigated, proved to be caused by the presence of DES in the meat the children ate.[36] Although it was known that cattle were being treated with hormones including DES, the potential consequences were not realized until the late 1970s. We must continue to keep abreast of the amount and type of hormones used in the animals we consume.

Oral Contraceptives

The risk of developing cancer, specifically breast cancer, with the use of oral contraceptives has been the focus of much controversy and media attention. It is a topic that evokes dramatic swings of emotion in patients, physicians, and newscasters. Scores and scores of studies have been done on the subject. A number of studies show no increased risk in cancer, including breast cancer, but the great majority of studies show an increased risk of developing breast cancer in those who use oral contraceptives.[37]

Recent studies show that early use of oral contraceptives is linked to a high incidence of breast cancer. Women who have used oral contraceptives with a high progesterone content, the so-called "safer pills," for five years prior to age 25 are four times more likely to get breast cancer than those who did not.[38] Another study of women less than 45 years old showed a correlation between risk of breast cancer and use of oral contraceptives. Women who used birth control pills for four or more years had a threefold increase in their risk for breast cancer.[39] The most recent study involving a large number of women has come from the UK National Case Control Study Group. The risk of breast cancer among women under age 36 was found to be increased by 74 percent by long-term use—eight years or more—of oral contraceptives. Those who took the contraceptives for four to eight years had a 43 percent greater chance of developing breast cancer. Oral contraceptive use accounted for 20 percent of all breast cancers among the women studied.[40] Two more major studies have been done that confirm this relationship: there is an increased risk of breast cancer when a person begins using oral contraceptives at an early age.[41,42] Comprehensive reviews of all previous epidemiological studies that have been reported confirm that oral contraceptives are a risk factor for breast cancer.[43,44]

Oral contraceptives have also been associated with cancer of the cervix. The incidence of cervical cancer rises increasingly when using oral contraceptives for two to eight years. In addition, oral contraceptive users have a higher incidence of carcinoma *in situ* and premalignant conditions like dysplasia of the cervix than do women who do not use birth control pills.[45] Oral contraceptives have also been linked to primary liver cancer.[46] In addition to its correlation with cancer risk, oral contraceptive use has been associated with lumpy breast disease, stroke, heart attack, pulmonary embolus, and other cardiovascular illnesses.

Oral contraceptive use does not increase the risk of all types of cancer. Two studies have reported that oral contraceptive use may marginally reduce the risk of getting ovarian cancer and endometrial cancer.[47,48]

The preponderance of evidence suggests that oral contraceptive use is a strong risk factor for the development of breast cancer. The earlier in life a woman uses it, the higher is her risk. Oral contraceptives also have contributed to other forms of cancer as well as cardiovascular illness. The *minimal* protection allegedly seen for ovarian cancer and endometrial cancer in a few studies should not entice people to use the contraceptive. The U.S. Food and Drug Administration inserts a warning in all oral contraceptive packages which states that oral contraceptive use is associated with cancer, cardiovascular disease, and other illnesses.

Progesterone as a Contraceptive

Injection of medroxyprogesterone as a contraceptive has been shown to increase the risk of developing breast cancer, cervical cancer, uterine cancer, and ovarian cancer in women.[49,50]

Estrogen Use in Menopause

Life expectancy in women today is 86. This life expectancy has increased by thirty years since the turn of the century, but the average onset of menopause is still 51½ years, which has not changed significantly. One sixth of the United States population are postmenopausal women, and the number of women age 65 or older is expected to double by the year 2000. Estrogens are used to prevent osteoporosis and minimize the effects of menopausal symptoms, like vulvovaginal dryness, urinary frequency, urgency, incontinence, dyspareunia, and skin and hair changes associated with inadequate estrogen and relative androgen excess.

Despite the benefits of estrogen use, there is also a down side. There is an increase in the development of endometrial cancer as well as breast cancer in postmenopausal women who use estrogens.[51-54] Other risks seen in postmenopausal women using estrogens have been an increased risk of myocardial infarction (heart attack), stroke, gallbladder disease, porphyria, liver disease, and other cardiovascular illnesses. Again, the risk associated with using estrogens even in postmenopausal women, I am convinced, far outweigh the potential benefits associated with their use.

Androgens

The use of anabolic androgens by athletes to increase muscle bulk and performance carry with them a major risk. Not only do androgens cause cardiovascular illnesses, but they also have been implicated in the development of prostate cancer, liver cancer, and osteosarcoma, as well as benign liver disease.[55] Because of their serious health risks, these agents must be severely restricted and not used.

15

Environmental Factors— Air, Water, and Electromagnetism

Mounting evidence suggests that our environment contains many carcinogens. The air we breathe, the water we drink, and the power lines that supply us with energy may pose threats to your health. It is important for you to understand what the dangers are so that you can work to modify them. As with many carcinogens, the time between exposure to the carcinogen and actual development of cancer may be quite long. Because of this, the cause of a cancer initiated by trace amounts of either airborne or waterborne carcinogens years before may be attributed to an unrelated or unknown cause at time of diagnosis. This is why we must detect and clean our environment of as many carcinogens as possible.

OUTDOOR AIR

The American Lung Association estimates that air pollution costs the nation $40 billion to $60 billion a year. Since the mid-1950s, it has been shown that the air in large urbanized areas is a risk factor for lung

cancer.[1-3] Collectively, the studies suggest that the increased incidence of cancer in cities is due to three factors: (1) more cigarette
smoking by the people who live in cities; (2) increased exposure of
nonsmokers to side-stream or passive smoke from lighted cigarettes;
and (3) occupational exposures.

The following occupations, involved with ambient air pollutants,
are risk factors for certain cancers. Gas production workers have a
greater risk of getting lung cancer than those who rarely work in the
gas production area, especially if they are exposed to the products of
coal carbonization. Men working at coke ovens in United States steel
factories have an excess of lung cancer compared to men working in
other parts of the steel industry. This is directly related to the exposure to the emissions from the ovens. Roofers who work with hot
pitch are exposed to large amounts of benzo(a)pyrene (BaP). They,
too, have a higher risk of getting lung cancer. So the concentration of
BaP is a significant factor in heavily polluted cities and contributes to
the excess of cancer.

The numerous atmospheric contaminants are found in one of
two forms: particulate form, in which the carcinogen adheres to
small particles in the air, or vapor form, in which the carcinogen is
in a gas form. A city's atmosphere contains more contaminants
than the atmosphere of a suburb or rural area. Many of these
contaminants have been shown to be carcinogenic in various
animals. The carcinogens found in particulate form are more important than those in vapor form because they can remain in the
air from four to forty days and consequently travel very long
distances. Carcinogens in particulate form originate mainly from
the burning of fuels. Contaminants in vapor form are derived from
the release of aerosols from industrial activities, from car exhaust,
and from natural sources.

City air pollution is derived from many sources. A large amount
of the particulate carcinogens comes from the burning of any material
containing carbon and hydrogen, including petroleum, gasoline, and
diesel fuel. A list of more than 100 different particulates containing
detected carcinogens has been compiled.[4] A great many more exist,
but detection of additional carcinogens in low concentrations is difficult because existing instruments are incapable of doing so.

In order to have a means of discussing carcinogenic air pollution
in a standard fashion, one chemical compound, benzo(a)pyrene (BaP)
was chosen as the indicator because it is a very potent carcinogen. The
problem with choosing this one substance as an indicator is that there
is no correlation between the level of BaP in the air and the level of
other known detectable carcinogens. For instance, car emissions

(gasoline or diesel fuel), coal-fired electric power plants, and oil-fired residential furnaces have low levels of BaP. But forest fires, residential fireplaces, refuse burning and coal burning in older furnaces, and motorcycle emissions produce high levels of BaP. With the new laws from the U.S. Environmental Protection Agency, the level of BaP in cities has dropped dramatically, but permitted levels of other carcinogens have risen. Since the level of BaP does not correlate with other atmospheric carcinogens, a new standard should be devised. This new standard or index should be composed of some number of different carcinogens that would more accurately reflect the total atmospheric carcinogen level. This atmospheric carcinogen index would be much like the pollen count or the Dow Jones Average which is composed of a number of different pollens or stocks, respectively. No accurate statement can be made correlating the number of lung cancer victims and the level of BaP (currently used as the atmospheric carcinogen standard) because BaP levels have decreased while lung cancer cases have increased.

The carcinogens found in the vapor phase include benzene, carbon tetrachloride, chloroform, and vinyl chloride, among others.[5] As you will recall from Table 2.2 in Chapter 2, most of these chemicals are strong human carcinogens. Vapor phase carcinogens are derived from car emissions, industrial activity, burning of solid waste, forest fires, and evaporation of solvents.[6]

Asbestos, a potent carcinogen, can also be found airborne. Persons working with the following may inhale high concentrations of asbestos: asbestos roofing and flooring, car brakes and clutches, dry walls, home heating and plumbing. Family members of persons who work with asbestos or asbestos products are exposed to very high levels of asbestos also. High levels of asbestos are found near asbestos waste dumps; near asbestos mines, mills, and manufacturing plants; near braking vehicles; at demolition areas; and in buildings that were sprayed with asbestos.

Asbestos as a risk factor for lung cancer is well established for those who work with asbestos and for their family members. However, cigarette smoking acts synergistically with asbestos to greatly enhance the risk of lung cancer.

ACID RAIN

In many parts of the world, rain can no longer be regarded as a beneficial occurrence; rather it is thought to be a deadly acidic agent. Acid rain results when sulfur dioxide and nitrogen oxide are released into the atmosphere and converted into sulfuric acid and nitric acid.

The evidence shows that fossil fuel combustion and power plant emissions contribute significantly to the production of acid rain.[7]

Next to carbon dioxide, acid rain ranks second as the most serious global pollution problem in modern time. Many natural habitats in the United States, Norway, Sweden, Scotland, and Canada, and some areas of the Netherlands, Denmark, and Belgium, have been reported to be severely hurt by acid rain. Acid rain has also decreased the amount of fir, spruce, and beech trees in the forests of central Europe.

Normal rain water is slightly acidic. But it is the higher acid content of acid rain that is devastating to human, animal, and plant life. During the past thirty years there has been a substantial increase in the amount of acid precipitation. Three important changes that have enhanced the production of acid rain are : (1) higher chimneys, (2) control of particulate discharge, and (3) a change from seasonal to year-round emission. Two of these were designed by environmentalists to control pollution. The tall chimneys allow the oxides of sulfur and nitrogen to stay longer in the atmosphere and thereby convert more efficiently to the acid.

Because of the increased acid in the atmosphere, there has been a decrease in the fish population and also other forms of animal life and vegetation in the lake areas of Canada, Eastern United States, Sweden, and Norway.[8] Vegetation and some animal forms are affected first; later fish suffer the harmful effects of acid increases.

The lethal effects of acid rain are due not only to the acidity but also to the aluminum and other toxic metals that are mobilized from the soil by the acid. Aluminum is toxic to fish and other life forms.[9] Zinc, nickel, lead, manganese, and cadmium are also increased in water after acid precipitation. Zinc, nickel, and mercury are toxic to aquatic forms of life. The direct toxic effects to man are still being reviewed. Aluminum poisoning is recognized in patients with impaired renal function and in patients with certain neurological diseases like Alzheimer's and amyotrophic lateral sclerosis in Guam.[10,11] Amyotrophic lateral sclerosis is prevalent in areas of Guam, where there is a high acid rain content. Consequently, there is a high aluminum concentration and low calcium level in the drinking water in Guam. Low calcium levels in the body lead to increased absorption of aluminum, which then gets deposited in the brain, causing the neurological disorder. The addition of calcium to the diet can help reverse this problem of increased aluminum absorption.

Another heavy metal of major concern is lead. Most of the lead that enters our bodies comes from food, dust, and air. Combustion of petroleum products is a main source of lead in the air and dust. Acid rain is also a culprit, leaching lead from the soil and putting it in our drinking water. Also mobilized by acid rain is mercury, which is consumed by fish that we in turn consume. And finally, acid rain reduces selenium, leading to selenium deficiencies, which is important in cancer prevention.

Acid rain may also be deposited on the human skin, but there have been no harmful consequences from this. However, people can inhale the sulfuric acid and nitric acid, which inhibit normal functioning of the lungs.

Findings of the United States National Acid Precipitation Assessment Program confirm the following:

- Acid rain adversely affects aquatic life in about 10 percent of Eastern lakes and streams.
- Acid rain decreases the number of red spruce at high elevations.
- Acid rain contributes to the corrosion of buildings and materials.
- Acid rain and other pollutants, especially fine sulfate particles, reduce visibility in the Northeastern states and in parts of the West.

There seems to be no direct correlation between acid rain and the etiology of cancer in humans; however, studies are ongoing. To control acid rain we should remove the sulfuric and nitric acids at their source by switching to fossil fuel with a low sulfur content. The key regions in the United States affected by acid rain are the Northeast, Midwest, and West. Lakes in the Northeast are being acidified by acid rain produced by the high-sulfur coal burned in the large power plants of the industrial Midwest. Low-sulfur fuel can almost completely obviate the production of acid rain, eliminating it as a risk factor for many illnesses.

DIESEL EXHAUST EXPOSURE

Animal studies in rats and mice show a link between exposure of whole diesel exhaust and lung cancer. The lung cancer is associated with diesel exhaust particulates and diesel exhaust gas.

Several human studies have also been done and show an increased risk of death from lung cancer in workers who have been exposed to diesel engine emissions.[12] This, too, is another controllable risk factor, especially emissions from vehicles that are obviously polluting the air.

DEPLETION OF NATURAL UPPER ATMOSPHERIC OZONE

The naturally occurring upper atmospheric ozone layer is crucial to the protection of living organisms because it absorbs harmful ultraviolet radiation. About 3 percent of the sun's electromagnetic output is emitted as ultraviolet radiation, but only a fraction of this reaches the surface of the Earth. Wavelengths of 240–290 are eliminated, and only a portion of the wavelengths at 290–320 penetrate to the Earth. The lower-range ultraviolet light wavelengths destroy DNA, which is the genetic material of all life forms.

Chlorofluorocarbons, commonly known as CFCs, are chemical compounds that have been shown to damage the protective ozone layer. What is of major concern now is the appearance of an actual hole in the ozone layer over Antarctica.[13] The concern here is obvious: what happens if there is a hole in the ozone layer in more densely populated areas of the globe?

Ultraviolet exposure is highly associated with melanoma, basal cell carcinoma, and squamous cell carcinoma of the skin. People with fair skin, blond hair, and blue eyes who also sunburn easily are at highest risk for the development of these skin cancers. Not only does ultraviolet exposure cause cancer, but in most people it causes severe skin damage and ages the skin dramatically. The U.S. Environmental Protection Agency calculates that a 1 percent decrease in the ozone concentration will increase the incidence of most skin cancers by 3–5 percent. The EPA further calculates that for every 2.5 percent increase per year of chlorofluorocarbon, an additional one million skin cancers and 20,000 deaths will occur over the lifetime of the existing United States population. In fact, in 1990 the incidence of skin cancer increased markedly: squamous cell carcinoma rose 3.1 times in women and 2.6 times in men; and melanoma rose 4.6 times in women and 3.5 times in men. By the year 2000, 1 in 75 will develop melanoma.

Effects on other living organisms may be far more important than the actual risk to man. Certain organisms, in particular phytoplankton, zooplankton, and the larval stages of fish, are very sensitive to small increases of ultraviolet exposure. This decrease in the food chain and in the oxygen output from the ocean's plants will have serious and dramatic repercussions on all human life.

Addressing the Problem

A research model indicates that the global ozone will be 6 percent lower in the year 2030 than it was in 1970.[14] This will increase the incidence of nonmelanomatous skin cancer by 12–36 percent and melanoma mortality by 9–18 percent. An assessment by the U.S. National Aeronautics and Space Agency indicates that ozone depletion is occurring globally and is progressing faster than previously realized. What we need to do is minimize the use of chlorofluorocarbons. CFCs are in aerosols, foam blowers for items such as hamburger cartons and drinking cups, refrigerants and cooling systems, and solvents for computer circuits. In most instances, nonchlorinated substitutes are available or can be developed. Some countries are recommending a 20 percent reduction of CFCs; the United States is recommending a 50 percent reduction. However, some CFCs remain in the air for over a century. Halones, used in fire extinguishers throughout the world, are synergistic with CFCs. Once these chemicals are stopped from being used and once the ozone depletion has been resolved, it will be many decades before any useful improvement is seen.

If pentane is used instead of chlorofluorocarbons as the blowing agent to produce foam products, *ozone is produced* both in the stratosphere and at the ground level. Now let's assume that pentane is used to produce a polystyrene drinking cup. Which do you think costs more to your pocketbook and the environment, a paper cup or a polystyrene cup? No, the paper cup costs more by far. A paper cup costs more to make from the standpoint of raw materials (wood, bark, petroleum fractions), finished weight, wholesale price, utilities needed to produce it (steam, power, cooling water), waste products produced, and air emissions (chlorine, chlorine dioxide, reduced sulfides, particulates).[15] The polystyrene cup is easier to recycle and ultimately to dispose. Here again we have the proper technology, we simply need to do something about it.

We can all do something about this major problem. We can write to our senators and congressmen to encourage them to completely ban all chemical compounds that will further deplete the ozone layer. Again, the solution to this problem is totally within our control.

OZONE POLLUTION

Ozone pollution at ground level is different from the naturally occurring protective ozone layer in the upper atmosphere that shields the Earth from harmful ultraviolet rays. Ozone at ground level is the most widespread air pollutant in any industrialized country and is formed when car exhaust and other emissions from industries react with sunlight.

In a study involving children in a summer camp, researchers found that there was enough ozone pollution in the air at ground level to cause significant impairment of lung function in about 70 percent of the campers. The effects of this ozone pollution at ground level persisted for about eighteen hours after exposure, and the suspicion is that even small changes in the lungs' capacity may lead to cell damage and ultimately to chronic respiratory illness.

Ozone pollution is a health hazard, particularly for those with respiratory illnesses and those who exercise out-of-doors. Ozone at ground level has been linked to cancer, lung disease, heart disease, and many other chronic illnesses. In healthy people, ozone impairs the ability of the lungs to absorb oxygen. Repeated exposure to ozone leads to early stages of lung damage similar to that seen from smoking. Respiratory infections are quite common in people who breathe more ozone at ground level than others. People who are asthmatic do much worse when the ozone level is high. Cardiac patients do worse because the amount of oxygen in the air is reduced. The incidence of mortality also is increased in older people who have respiratory illnesses in areas with high levels of sulfur oxides in the air.

Most cities exceed the federal ozone standard. Los Angeles has the most and other cities that have a large amount of ozone smog include New York, Philadelphia, Trenton, Baltimore, Hartford, Chicago, and Houston. Some national parks like Acadia, Shenandoah, and Sequoia National Parks have higher ozone levels than some cities because of their proximity to the major cities with smog and/or the air currents around them.

Ozone forms when certain compounds react with sunlight. These compounds include nitrogen oxides and volatile organic compounds. Nitrogen oxides are derived from motor vehicles as well as industrial plants. Volatile organic compounds come from things like backyard barbecues and dry cleaners.

Smog is derived predominantly from ozone as well as from volatile organic compounds, carbon monoxides, nitrogen oxides, sulfur oxides, and other particulates. These compounds are derived from bakeries during the fermentation process; dry cleaning chemicals; paints; wood-burning stoves and starter fluid used to ignite charcoal; and industries and motor vehicles using fossil fuels. However, ground level ozone is clearly the most widespread air pollution problem we know today.

The Environmental Protection Agency did a study involving non-smoking men in a room where ozone was close to the federal maximum. After five hours of walking and then bicycling, 80 percent of these men began to cough and feel chest pains. In a study of men who exercised for only two hours while breathing ozone that was below the federal maximum but still above the ambient air in very rural settings, 80 percent experienced serious symptoms of the lower airways. The airways were inflamed, and biochemical changes occurred with a subsequent impaired immune response at the local sites of the lung.

Ground level ozone can be controlled. We must insist again that the fuels burned are better and cleaner so that less volatile organic compounds, nitrogen oxides, and other ozone-producing compounds are emitted. And although the 1990 Clean Air Act is thought to be the most expensive environmental legislation ever passed in terms of attaining the new standards, enforcement of these standards must also be rigorous.

ULTRAVIOLET SUNLIGHT

There are two major forms of ultraviolet light emitted from the sun, ultraviolet A (UVA) and ultraviolet B (UVB). The UVB is the more harmful of the two and has wavelengths between 290 and 320 nanometers, whereas UVA has wavelengths between 320 and 400 nanometers, which is where the visible light spectrum begins.

The current package labeling on a sunscreen product states its ability to protect against UVB, the form responsible for causing sunburn and skin cancers. UVA can also cause skin cancer but, in addition, causes skin damage and premature aging of the skin. New labeling regulations by the FDA will reflect the UVA protection as well. You need to have protection from both forms of ultraviolet light.

What type of sunglasses should you use to protect your eyes from the harmful ultraviolet rays of the sun? People frequently ask does the cost of the sunglasses reflect the protection they afford? Thirty different makes and prices of sunglasses were tested for ultraviolet transmission. Each of the sunglasses completely filtered all UVB radiation, hence no danger to the eye would be anticipated if sunglasses were worn. With respect to transmission of UVA to the eye, the results varied greatly but had no relation to price.[16] Hence, when you see a person with a pair of sunglasses costing $200, you can laugh quietly knowing that your $2 sunglasses give you just as much protection.

INDOOR AIR

Indoor air pollution has become a major problem as well, causing both specific illnesses and the minor complaints that now constitute the "sick building syndrome."[17] Indoor accumulation of radon, passive smoking pollutants, combustion pollutants from stoves, chemical emission from plastics, and insulation materials are just a sample of the indoor pollutants that are hazardous.

When radon is present in the soil below buildings, or in surface water or construction materials, particularly granite, the indoor radon concentration will exceed the acceptable standard as set by the Environmental Protection Agency at 4 pCi/liter (pCi are pica Curies).[18] Some homeowners have spent $1,000 to $2,000 to comply with this standard. In 1988, however, Congress passed the Indoor Radon Abatement Act, which forces the EPA to set the standard of indoor radon equal to that of outdoor radon. The average cost to homeowners to comply with the newer standard could be close to $10,000.

Radon has now been implicated in up to 20,000 deaths from lung cancer in the United States.[19] A person living in a house with an indoor radon level of 4 pCi/liter has the same risk of developing lung cancer as a person who smokes half a pack of cigarettes per day.[20] The risk of lung cancer is increased more if people smoke cigarettes and are exposed to radon, as in the case of coal miners.[21]

Freestanding stoves without chimneys increase the indoor air concentration of nitric oxide, benzo(a)pyrene, and sometimes even sulfur dioxide. These pollutants increase respiratory disease. Kerosene stoves also produce many pollutants, several of which are carcinogenic. Heat exchangers, cooling towers, and leaky shower heads provide favorable culture media for many microorganisms. These bacteria and other organisms disperse in droplets and remain airborne by mechanical or thermal air movements. Legionella (Legionnaires' disease) and many other organisms have been detected airborne in closed indoor situations.

Passive smoking is a serious problem in indoor air pollution. Passive smoking is responsible for doubling the lung cancer rate in persons exposed to it as compared to those not exposed to passive smoking.[22] In past years it has been up to the individual to avoid such passive smoking, but things have changed. A nonsmoking Swedish office worker was awarded damages for a lung cancer he developed from breathing other people's tobacco smoke in the office. Now in the United States there are many laws to protect the passive smoker in certain public areas and on domestic airline flights. Hopefully more and more such laws will protect us in *all* public areas.

Other indoor pollutants come from materials that are used in the construction of modern buildings, such as formaldehyde, isocyanates, solvents, and volatile synthetic organic compounds. These are used in the manufacture of insulin, decoration, and equipment. We know that formaldehyde is associated with human cancer.

To protect ourselves against indoor pollutants, we simply need to have adequate ventilation. Studies have been done and show that one or more air changes per hour should be provided and that the carbon dioxide concentration should not exceed 0.5 percent. As we move toward a service-oriented society in America, with more people working in offices, this problem is everyone's concern. However, it can soon be eliminated if we work to modify the environment.

WATER TREATMENT AND POLLUTION

In 1960 W.C. Hueper warned that the drinking water in the United States was contaminated with natural and manmade pollutants and that some of these were potentially carcinogenic.[23] In addition, other reports in the past ten years have shown that there are carcinogens in the drinking water and that in some areas, contaminated water has been associated with an increased cancer risk and other medical problems.

There are several groups of drinking water contaminants that may be carcinogenic. Synthetic organic chemicals comprise the first group, whose carcinogenic potential is of greatest concern. The United States Environmental Protection Agency has found over 700 organic chemicals in our drinking water,[24] and that number probably represents a small fraction of the actual number that exists. Forty of these are carcinogens, and three (benzene, chloromethyl ether, and vinyl chloride) are associated with cancers in man.[25] Drinking polluted water is said by the EPA to be one of the top four health hazards to Americans, but enforcement of existing laws has been poor at best, and enforcement of additional laws and standards will be difficult. The standard set by the EPA allows municipalities to average their water toxicities over a year. For example, much more chlorine is added to water during summer months to hold down microorganisms. In some cities the tap water level of chlorine carcinogens exceeds the standard by 20 percent during these months. The same spike of toxicity holds true for nitrates and pesticides, both used seasonally for lawn beautification and farming.

Water chlorination produces chemical compounds called trihalomethanes, which are the most common organic compounds found in drinking water. These compounds, which include chloroform and bromohalomethane, are associated with a high incidence of gastrointestinal cancers and urinary bladder cancers.[26,27] In fact, a study involving 3,000 people from the U.S. National Cancer Institute suggests that chlorine may double the risk for developing urinary bladder cancer. The EPA's safety limit of chlorine and its harmful associated carcinogens is based on the consumption of two liters a day, and this does not take into account increased consumption in summer, for example, or the fact that these compounds can be absorbed during bathing.

Fewer organic chemicals are found in drinking water that comes from ground water sources than from surface water sources.[28] Chlorinated drinking water from surface sources is linked with gastrointestinal cancers as well as urinary bladder cancers.[29-31]

The second group of water contaminants consists of inorganic chemicals. These are needed for normal biological processes and are found in all natural waters. Some, however, are carcinogenic. Arsenic, chromium, and nickel, each a known carcinogen to man, are found in our drinking water (see Chapter 2, Table 2.2); these can either increase or decrease in concentration during water treatment.[32] Nitrate ions are found in surface or ground waters, and their concentration is not affected by water treatment. As you may recall from Chapter 3, nitrates can be converted to nitrosamines, which are powerful carcinogens. Nitrates are used for fertilizers, and in the early summer, the Corn Belt states' water supply sometimes has a 50 percent higher nitrate content than what is acceptable.

Lead also is a big problem. Lead can impair a child's IQ and attention span. One in six people in the United States drink water with higher than acceptable levels of lead. Chicago has one of the worst lead water pollution problems in the United States. Suppliers were still using lead pipes there until 1986. Lead pipes were used in antiquity in Pompeii; those people later realized that large numbers died up until their lead pipes became calcified with calcium from the water.

The amount of calcium and magnesium in water determines water "hardness." It appears that soft water, that is, water containing lesser amounts of calcium and particularly magnesium, is correlated with a higher incidence of all cardiovascular diseases.[33,34] Low calcium levels are also linked to osteoporosis, hypertension,[35] and even colon cancer.[36,37] No definite conclusions can be made yet as to whether all drinking water should be made "hard" with the addition of more magnesium and/or calcium to modify the risk for cardiovascular diseases and cancer, as well as other illnesses.

Radioactive materials constitute the third group of drinking water contaminants. Their concentration varies with geography, geology, industrial wastes, pharmaceutical use, and nuclear power generation.[38] So far there are no reported cases of human cancer related to different radioactive compounds in drinking water.[39] However, radon gets into ground water, especially in New Jersey, the New England states, and the Rocky Mountain states. Excessive levels of radon are seen in water supplies used for drinking and bathing by more than 17 million people.

Living organisms make up the fourth group. They include bacteria, viruses, and protozoa. Water purification has been effective in removing them from our drinking water. Microorganisms are not believed to be waterborne carcinogens; however, certain viruses cause human cancers. Some microbes resist current water purification, and these are responsible for 33 percent of all gastrointestinal infections in the United States.

The last group of water contaminants is solid particulates. Clays, asbestos particles, and organic particulates comprise this group. Clays absorb and bind carcinogenic agents and hence protect them from water treatment. Asbestos fibers are found naturally in water in many regions of Canada and some parts of the United States. In addition, some asbestos fibers are found where cement and other construction products are made, since asbestos is used in their production. Asbestos fibers can also get into the water supply by release from cement pipes and by processes associated with mining of iron ore. Many studies of the association between waterborne asbestos and human cancer are inconclusive because so many other variables may be interacting. However, one study by M.S. Kanarek has shown that measured concentrations of asbestos in drinking water are associated with lung cancer, gallbladder cancer, pancreatic cancer, and several other cancers.[40]

Our drinking water contains a number of carcinogens, including asbestos, metals, and synthetic organic compounds. Asbestos and nitrates are associated with gastrointestinal cancers; arsenic is associated with skin cancer; and synthetic organic chemicals, especially trihalomethanes, are associated with cancers of the gastrointestinal tract and the urinary bladder.

Who is to blame for the shambles of the water supply? Probably everyone. The standards issued by the EPA in the late seventies double in 1992. James Elder, commissioner of the EPA, says that forty-eight to forty-nine states do not comply with existing standards, or comply by way of loopholes. For example, a loophole permits water suppliers to flush lead-filled water out of plumbing before testing tap water. This loophole will be closed, but the EPA will allow twenty years more for compliance. On the other hand, the EPA has been lax. Studies show that radon increases cancer risk, and more to the point, drinking water with radon increases the risk for certain kinds of cancers. However, the EPA just recently imposed restrictions starting in 1996 for radon in the drinking water. To monitor and remove radon is simple and inexpensive to do, but still no action will be taken until 1996.

Eighty percent of the top 1,000 superfund sites, that is, those designated as containing toxic waste and chemical contaminants, are leaching these toxic substances into the ground water. In many geographic sites in the United States, well water has been contaminated. About 10 percent of all underground tanks, which store gasoline or other hazardous chemicals, leak. Too many pesticides and fertilizers are used by farmers and homeowners. Industries dump chemicals and other harmful pollutants into our water supply, and homeowners dump chemicals into household drains.

What Can Be Done?

One of the major obstacles to our cleaning up America's underground toxic wastes is the unrealistic requirements that have been set by state and county authorities throughout the nation. Although the intentions may often be laudable, the effect of these laws has been to create such enormous costs, for most projects, that the clean-up effort is moving at a snail's pace. For example, a toxic site in Houston has a concentration of, say, 2,000 parts per billion. The local rules require a reduction of 99.99 percent. The problem is that there is no technology available at the present time that can accomplish this without digging up an enormous area of the earth and either processing it on the surface or moving it by rail to some remote location. These are expensive and disruptive operations which are invariably fought by the agencies that are supposed to pay for them. The result is that litigation goes on for years while the people who live in the area are left to their toxic diet. The project, even if completed, will absorb excessive funds that might otherwise be available for many other projects.

The problem is that the objectives are simply too difficult to be accomplished by existing technologies. If the requirement had been to reduce the contaminants from 2,000 parts per billion to, say, 10 parts, it is possible that an in-ground vacuuming technology could have been used, reducing the health hazard by 99.5 percent and leaving limited funds available for twenty or thirty more of the same type of clean-up projects. The trick here is to promote the use of low-cost, in-ground technologies and increase the clean-up rate by 2,000–5,000 percent of the current rate without having to wait for the seemingly impossible dream of getting more funds from government and industry. The most promising development in this area is a new patented vacuuming technology that can "clean" far greater areas than the existing vacuuming technologies for the same cost. This device will be an advance if it can reduce the toxic chemicals to 0.6 parts per billion or less. If it cannot, then we must re-examine the standards set. It is better to clean up all the toxic sites by a significant factor like 99.5 percent than only a few sites by a factor of 99.99 percent and thereby propagate endless litigation.

A number of cities refuse to build costly processing plants and instead choose to pay less expensive fines. The EPA observes that small utilities tend to violate regulations the most, to falsify documents, and even to wash away evidence because of a thirty-day window given them by the state.

Bottled Versus Tap Water

Many people want to know if bottled water is safer than tap water. Recent findings indicate that many bottled waters derived from domestic or international springs or from other water sources contain microorganisms, and/or have contaminants. If you prefer bottled water, look for water derived from such processes as reverse osmosis, distillation, or a combination of reverse osmosis and deionization, which yields the purest form of water. This combined process gets rid of everything in water except H_2O, therefore you should supplement your diet with certain nutrients already discussed in Chapter 6.

There are documented airborne and waterborne carcinogens. As with many carcinogens, the time between exposure to the carcinogen and actual development of cancer may be quite long, and as such, the cause of a cancer initiated by trace amounts of either airborne or waterborne carcinogens years before may be attributed to an unrelated or unknown cause at time of diagnosis. This is the main reason that we must detect and clean our environment of as many carcinogens as possible.

ELECTROMAGNETISM

Non-ionizing electromagnetic radiation has become very important and is generated largely through electrical and magnetic fields that surround us: household wiring, appliances, high-tension wires, radio transmitters, television screens, video display terminals, electric blankets, and even the Earth, which has its own magnetic field. This kind of radiation includes infrared rays, microwaves, radiowaves, and alternating electrical currents. All of these penetrate the body readily except for infrared rays. Beside the vague symptoms of fatigue, nausea, headache, and loss of libido associated with electromagnetism,[41] there is now great concern over whether it can cause cancer.

Many countries like the United States use alternating electric currents that flow back and forth at a frequency of 60 cycles per second. This is within the extremely low frequency range of the electromagnetic spectrum.

An electromagnetic field is created along wires when electricity flows. The strength of the electromagnetic field is measured in gauss. The electromagnetic field is made of two components: the electric field made from the strength of the charge that starts the flow, and the magnetic field that results from the motion of the alternating currents.

The energy needed to make electricity flow is called voltage. More voltage is needed to make electricity go farther. Depending on where electricity is needed to be delivered, voltage is either stepped-up or stepped-down along transmission lines by transformers at substations or on utility poles near homes. Most studies concerning the effects of electromagnetic fields on humans focus on the strength of the field.

The Earth itself has an electromagnetic field covering the largest area. In fact, this electromagnetic field is responsible for making a compass needle point in the direction of north. However, the Earth's electromagnetic fields do a flip flop, the North and South Pole fields trading places at intervals of hundreds of thousands of years. All electrically driven products have electromagnetic fields. The closer you are to a given appliance or other source, the higher is the strength of the electromagnetic field. See Table 15.1 for the strength of the electromagnetic fields of common appliances. This table lists electromagnetic field strength from least to greatest.

Evidence shows almost a direct link between electromagnetic fields and cancer in rats. Researchers at Battell Pacific Northwest Laboratory in Richland, Washington, have shown that electromagnetic fields suppress the levels of a certain hormone called melatonin. Melatonin is produced by the pineal gland in the central part of the brain. It is a regulatory hormone and also modifies the functioning of the immune system. Low levels of melatonin have been linked to breast cancer as well as prostate cancer. Animal studies show that electromagnetic fields produce low melatonin, which, in turn, then increases the incidence of breast cancer and prostate cancer. These animal studies have been repeated and corroborated in multiple centers throughout North America.[42]

High- And Low-Voltage Wires

Many studies of the effects of electromagnetic fields on humans have also been done. Children and adults in Colorado living close to high-tension wires had a definite increase of all cancers. The likelihood of getting cancer is twice as high for children near the power lines.[43,44] A number of other investigations have corroborated these findings and have shown that men exposed to electrical and

Table 15.1 Electromagnetic Fields Of Various Appliances[45]	
Source	Electromagnetic Field Strength* (Milligauss)
Coffee makers	0.7–1.5
Crock pots	0.8–1.5
Refrigerators	<0.1–3
Dryers	0.7–3
Irons	1–4
Toasters	0.6–8
Disposals	8–12
Dishwashers	7–14
Televisions	0.3–20
Washers	2–20
Desk lamps	5–20
Blenders	5–25
Fans	0.2–40
Portable heaters	1.5–40
Fluorescent fixtures	20–40
Ovens	1–50
Ranges	3–50
Microwave ovens	40–90
Hair dryers	<1–100
Shavers	1–100
Mixers	6–150
Vacuum cleaners	20–200
Can openers	30–300
Electric lines on telephone poles	10–600
High-tension transmission electric lines	50–10,000

*At a distance of 30 centimeters

magnetic fields at work have an increased risk of leukemia, especially acute myeloid leukemia, brain tumors, and breast cancer.[46-49] Researchers at the University of California in Riverside confirm these results and say exposure to common sources of low- and high-energy electromagnetic radiation from overhead power lines probably promotes the growth of malignant tumors.[50] Many of these studies involve high-tension wires with 60 Hz (60 electromagnetic cycles per second).

It had been thought that the low-voltage power lines which had low frequencies and thus low energies would be too weak to have any biological effects. However, epidemiological studies show that low-frequency electromagnetic fields produce weak electric fields in our bodies, affecting such biological function as hormone levels, the binding levels of ions to cell membranes, and certain genetic processes inside the cell such as RNA and protein synthesis. Calcium ions in the cell play a major role in cell division, which, in turn, has an important role in cancer promotion.

A study done by Savitz at the University of North Carolina in Chapel Hill measured the proximity of homes to power lines and also the low voltage of electrical and magnetic fields within homes. There was a positive correlation between childhood cancers, including leukemias and brain tumors, and the magnetic fields generated by the power lines. This study is important because it investigated high-voltage lines as well as low-voltage lines, which are on "telephone" poles in our cities. All the childhood cancer studies are significant because they are consistent and have been corroborated. They show an increased incidence of malignancies among people with long-term exposure to electromagnetic fields.

Computer Video Display Monitors

A concern that has commanded major news media coverage in the last several years is computer video display monitors and their potential to cause health problems. The "extremely-low-frequency" magnetic fields produced by these video monitors have been linked to cancers, breast disorders, and other health problems. The United States Environmental Protection Agency recommended that the extremely-low-frequency radiation fields produced by such display monitors be categorized as *probable* human carcinogens. The EPA states that "the findings show a consistent pattern of response that suggests, but does not prove, a causal link" between radiation levels and cancer in people.[51] In March 1990, Dr. William Farland, director of the EPA's Office of Health and Environmental Assessment, ordered that the researchers' recommendation be deleted.

A study by the magazine *MACWORLD* of monitors manufactured by different companies found certain uses to be hazardous and suggested several precautions. Workers should sit at least two feet away from the front of the monitor and stay at least four feet away from the back or sides of a coworker's monitor. The same precautions should be applied to laser printers. Color monitors produce more electromagnetic radiation than do monochrome monitors. The amount of radiation, it was discovered, is always higher at the sides, back and top of the monitor. The more powerful the monitor, the more radiation is emitted.

Some American computer makers already have low-radiation monitors for sale in Europe, where standards set by the government as well as their unions are very strict. IBM sells low-radiation monitors here in America but does not advertise them, perhaps fearing that these would create concern and anxiety about other terminals that the company produces. A review of sixteen studies shows that the preponderance of evidence links video display monitors with a risk of spontaneous abortion.[52]

Magnetic Resonance Imaging Scans

In the last ten years or so, there has been widespread use of magnetic resonance imaging scans (MRI scans). In many instances, MRI scans show more detail and hence give more information on a patient than conventional CT scans. Up until now, MRI scans have been thought to be without risk to the patient, that is, no radiation exposure or other harm. However, the newest and fastest MRI scanners may not be entirely safe.

Patients undergoing MRI scanning are exposed to three types of electromagnetic radiation: static magnetic fields, pulsed radiofrequency (RF) electromagnetic fields, and gradient (time-varying) fields. Atoms of all tissues resonate at specific frequencies within an electromagnetic field and produce radiofrequency signals, which are converted into images by MRI scanners.

The newest and fastest MRI scanners rely on the time-varying fields to obtain large amounts of information in milliseconds compared to the ten minutes or more needed by the conventional MRI scanners. The tremendous speed with which the newest MRI scanners acquire information results in a clearer image—one that is not distorted by patient movement or heartbeat—and a reduction in time for the patient to be in the magnet, which may also reduce the incidence of claustrophobia. However, time-varying fields, unlike static fields used in conventional scanners, produce electric currents in the body. These currents can cause cardiac arrhythmias or peripheral nerve stimulation, the latter of which has already been reported in three patients. There is, then, a potential for problems in patients with existing heart disease or seizure disorders. Only further research will help delineate the potential for harm to the body with the use of these very fast MRI scanners.

Electromagnetic fields have been used therapeutically for years to increase cell activity and heal bone fractures. Researchers report that cancer cells reproduce faster after exposure to electromagnetic fields and that these electromagnetic waves increase the activity of a certain enzyme called ornithine decarboxylase, which is involved in DNA synthesis and cell growth.[53] Certain cancer-promoting chemicals also stimulate the activity of this enzyme, and prior exposure to electromagnetic fields potentiate this effect. Exposure to the electromagnetic fields may alter the cancer cell membranes and make them more resistant to the immune system.[54]

Electromagnetic fields have other health consequences. Microwaves affect our circadian rhythms, which in turn affect our sleep patterns, growth, and repair mechanisms. The waves also affect the results of IQ tests in animals. Still other studies show that electromagnetic fields alter cortisol output, which, when secreted in larger amounts, suppresses the immune system.

With the fixed amount of land in our country and the fact that the population is growing, the demand for electricity will increase by about 40 percent by the year 2000. The proximity between people and high-tension wires will have to lessen to accommodate the increased demand. Utility companies may also choose to increase the voltage of the power lines to meet this growing need. Larger power lines will generate stronger electromagnetic fields and hence pose a greater cancer risk.

Addressing the Problem

There are some simple steps that have been taken to minimize exposure to electromagnetic fields. There is already a way to reduce electromagnetic radiation from video display terminals. There are electric blankets made with reduced electromagnetic field strengths. Or simply use electric blankets only to preheat the bed. Redesign home appliances to minimize or eliminate fields. Move electric alarm clocks as far away from your bed as is practical. Route new transmission lines to avoid developed areas and increase the distance from the lines to the houses. Some utility companies are arranging their high-voltage transmission lines to reduce the magnetic fields. The problem is that little can be done to reduce the electromagnetic fields from the low-voltage lines within our cities.

Electromagnetic waves do, in fact, have health consequences and are probably associated with the development of cancer. We obviously need to be wary about where we live, avoid high-tension wires, and take other common sense precautions.

16
Sedentary Lifestyle

For quite some time we have all accepted that a sedentary lifestyle or lack of exercise is a risk factor for the development of cardiovascular illnesses. Doctors preach it and people generally are aware of it, sometimes even putting on their sneakers to do something about it. Sales of exercise equipment have risen over the past few years, but more often than not, these treadmills, stationary bicycles, and other very expensive equipment remain unused in most people's basements. Now, however, consider this: exercise has been shown in animal studies and in human epidemiological studies to decrease the incidence of cancer.

BENEFITS OF EXERCISE ON THE IMMUNE SYSTEM

There have been a number of human trials looking at the effects of exercise on the immune system.[1-9] These studies examined patients before and after exercise; thus the patients served as their own controls for the experiment. Most of the subjects in the studies were men. The studies included unconditioned people, people who were trained under supervision, and also highly conditioned marathon and cross-country skiers. The amount of time spent exercising varied in these peoples, as did the degree of strenuous activity. In most cases, exercise produced a higher number of white blood cells, specifically the granulocytes that are needed to fight off infections and tumors. The higher count remained elevated for about forty-five minutes. The killing capability of the cells was not much different from that of sedentary individuals. There was no increase or decrease in the amount of antibody or in complement protein levels.

The lymphocyte count also was elevated in people who exercise. Both the B and T cell counts were increased, but the T cell count more so. Again, this elevation was transient and returned to normal. The functioning of the B and T cells when elevated seemed to be no different than when they were at resting levels.

During exercise a person's temperature rises slightly. Accompanying the rise in temperature is the production of something called pyrogen.[10,11] Pyrogen, now known as part of the interleukins,[12,13] is an important protein produced by white blood cells that enhances lymphocyte functions. Fever has been shown to enhance the survival of animals infected with bacteria. High temperatures can also kill viruses—that's one of the major reasons why you run a fever when you have an infection—and high temperatures have also been shown to kill cancer cells.

A significant number of animal studies have shown that exercise can actually inhibit cancer growth.[14,15] These and other animal experiments were set up in similar fashion. Rats were injected in their hind legs with tumors that were allowed to grow. One group of rats was not permitted to exercise; however, the other did exercise. The group that did exercise rejected the tumors uniformly.

A number of human studies have been done which show that increased physical activity promotes health with less disease in general, and a longer life.[16] One of the largest human studies looking at the relationship between exercise and cancer was done at the Harvard School of Public Health in Boston in 1985. Almost 5,400 women were involved, all of whom were college graduates during the years 1925–1981. Their ages ranged from 21 to 80, and more than half of them had been college athletes. To be classified as an athlete, the woman had to have played for at least one year in intramural or varsity sports, which included basketball, field hockey, softball, tennis, volleyball, dance and other sports, or she had to have earned a college letter. This study showed that women who did participate as college athletes had a lower incidence of cancers of the uterus, ovary, cervix, vagina, and breast than did their classmates who did not participate in exercise.[17] The study showed that the risk of developing breast cancer was 1.86 times higher for nonathletes than it was for athletes, and the risk of developing cancers of the reproductive system was 2.5 times higher for nonathletes than it was for athletes.

EXERCISE AND BREAST CANCER

Another similar study from the University of Southern California also showed that regular vigorous physical activity led to a reduced risk of getting breast cancer in women. Women who trained regularly, such as runners who ran at least two miles a day, five times a week, were deemed to be athletes. The investigators of this study suggest that longer menstrual cycles, characteristic of these physically active women, confer a protective effect against the development of breast cancer. Other studies confirmed these findings: female athletes, who usually have irregular menstrual patterns, have been found to have lower breast cancer rates than their nonexercising colleagues. Females who begin training in ballet, swimming, or running before puberty are more likely to begin menstruating at a later age and have longer intermittent menstrual cycles than other girls. Earlier studies showed that women with breast cancer had significantly shorter menstrual cycles than women without cancer. Women with shorter cycles also had fewer days between menses and ovulation, the time period when breast tissue is least active and at least risk for cancer development. Longer cycles imply more days during the low-risk interval.

EXERCISE AND COLON CANCER

Colon cancer, the second most common cancer, has also been studied in relation to exercise.[18] Men who had sedentary jobs had a 1.6 higher risk of developing colon cancer than their colleagues who had more active jobs. Workers having sedentary jobs included accountants, lawyers, musicians, and bookkeepers. Those who were classified as having active jobs included carpenters, plumbers, gardeners, and mail carriers. It was found that men who had sedentary jobs had more cancer in parts of the large intestine further away from the rectum and sigmoid area, such as in the cecum, the ascending colon, and the transverse colon, whereas the active employees had a low rate of cancer in those anatomical areas. The sedentary individuals had a threefold increase in cancer of the descending colon over their active counterparts. The decreased incidence of colon cancer in men with active jobs is probably related to the fact that increased physical activity causes more motility of the gastrointestinal tract and more frequent evacuation of the colon. The longer the stool remains in the colon, the longer a carcinogen in the stool called fecapentaene has to exert its effect on the colon, and consequently the higher is the risk for cancer in the various parts of the colon with which the stool is in contact.

The same relationship between colon cancer and a sedentary job was examined at the State University of New York at Buffalo. The risk of developing colon cancer increased significantly with time spent in jobs that involved sedentary or very light work. The risk of getting colon cancer was twice as high for people who worked at a sedentary job for more than 40 percent of their work years than it was for those who never worked at a sedentary job.[19]

A Swedish study involving nineteen years of follow-up and over 1.1 million men confirmed the two preceding studies. The risk of getting colon cancer was 1.3 times higher for those in sedentary jobs than for those in active jobs.[20]

FUTURE PROJECTIONS

What will happen to future generations as our jobs become more service related? Children of today are much less physically active and physically fit than their counterparts of twenty or even ten years ago. Forty percent of children aged 5–8 exhibit signs of obesity, elevated blood pressure, and high cholesterol levels, according to a survey conducted by the American Alliance for Health, Physical Education, Recreation and Dance. The physical fitness of American public school children has shown no improvement in the last ten years and, in many cases, has greatly deteriorated according to a nationwide survey conducted by the President's Council on Physical Fitness and Sports. Part of the responsibility of getting our children into shape rests with the schools. However, only four states require all students to take a specific amount of physical education in all grades, kindergarten through twelfth: Illinois, New Jersey, New York, and Rhode Island. Only Illinois requires that all students take physical education classes every day. With a decrease in exercise, an increase in obesity, an increase in junk food, and the other risk factors that we have already discussed and will discuss, the incidence of cancer will continue to spiral with each succeeding generation unless we dramatically alter our lifestyles.

BEGINNING AN EXERCISE PROGRAM

The United States Preventive Services Task Force has shown that exercise and physical activity is helpful in cardiovascular disease, hypertension, diabetes, osteoporosis, obesity, mental health, mental depression, musculoskeletal disorders, cancer, immunological abnormality, and others already listed.[21] Everyone, young or old, should be on an exercise program; however, you must begin your exercise program slowly and cautiously work up to the desired level.

The main risk of beginning an exercise program is sudden death. Most reported cases of sudden death are older persons who had several cardiac risk factors. Among the non-life-threatening adverse effects of jogging and running are those ranging from blister formation to bursitis, Achilles tendonitis to stress fracture, and possibly early osteoarthritis, a wearing out of bones. Long-distance runners can transiently have blood in their urine. Other problems associated with jogging include heat stroke and problems related to breast connective tissue support.

Because of a risk of sudden death associated with beginning to exercise, anyone 35 years or older, or under 35 with cardiac risk factors, should be medically screened. This screening should include a full history and physical examination by a physician, and a resting electrocardiogram (ECG). An exercise electrocardiogram is indicated if the person has symptoms of heart disease.

An exercise program should be individualized for each person because abilities and motivations differ. Activities that offer a constant and sustained exertion, like fast walking, running, and swimming, may offer physiological advantages over activities with varying levels of exertion, like volleyball and tennis. Your exercise program should start slowly and then gradually build up to the desired level. Your heart rate should be monitored. The safest training program is one in which training lasts twenty to forty minutes per day, three to four times a week, while maintaining the heart rate during exercise at 50 percent of the predicted maximum heart rate for your age.[22] Of course, you should be warned to stop exercising immediately if you experience chest pain, severe shortness of breath, palpitations, or other cardiac symptoms. You should contact your physician at once if any of these occur.

About how many people are engaged in an exercise program? The Perrier Survey interviewed 1,510 adults at random and found that 59 percent of them were actively exercising in one form or another, but only 15 percent spent more than five hours per week exercising— equivalent to about 1,500 calories per week. Running was ranked sixth in popularity behind walking, swimming, calisthenics, bicycling, and bowling. Not all would be likely to improve cardiovascular fitness. Only about 5 percent of the adults were doing meaningful exercises that would actually improve cardiac fitness. The survey concluded that the one most important factor likely to initiate and increase a person's physical activity was his physician's recommendation.[23]

The new athlete often consults with his physician about matters that are related to exercise and nutrition. Young and old athletes alike realize that proper nutrition plays a big role in their performance. Over 7 million high-school athletes are in an age group that has the highest risk of nutritional deficiencies.[24] An adequate diet, with the proper vitamin and mineral supplementation if necessary, is a must for all athletes. Athletes who are their ideal weight may require additional calories for the extra energy they need. They can monitor this by weighing themselves regularly to see if their daily dietary intake meets the needs of routine activities plus training requirements. Do not increase muscle mass by taking any hormones like testosterone, which is a risk factor for cancer. Exercising your muscles will increase your muscle mass.

Research from an important study shows that even a modest improvement in fitness among the most unfit people confers to them a very substantial health benefit.[25] The same study showed that people who were exercising routinely or only moderately did not have a corresponding "health gain" if they increased their exercising a little bit more. However, people who did not exercise and then started to exercise only a little bit increased their health benefit markedly. In this study lower mortality rates among exercisers were seen for cardiovascular disease as well as cancer sites. High levels of physical fitness appeared to delay mortality from all causes, primarily due to the lower rates of cancer as well as cardiovascular disease.

Here again people who are exercising even moderately are subsidizing the health care costs for those who do not exercise. Fewer than 10 percent of Americans older than 18 years meet the criteria for exercise proposed in the 1990 objectives for physical fitness and exercise.[26] These guidelines have said that 60 percent of Americans between 18 and 65 years old should engage in regular vigorous physical exercise. An inactive individual should find walking a very acceptable form of exercise. Brisk walking will afford this person a substantial health benefit. Low-intensity activities are more likely to be done since they are more comfortable, convenient, and affordable, as well as safer. A minimal exercise program alone has also been shown to reduce borderline or mild hypertension.[27]

You have already learned that exercise can reduce your risk for colon cancer, stroke, and hypertension, and assist in the management of diabetes, depression, and obesity. My recommendations for your exercise program are simple: brisk walking and stair climbing. There can be no excuse for not doing these—they require no fancy warm-up suits, no fancy leotards, and no membership fees, and in inclement weather, you simply go to a shopping mall to walk. Walking can be done by virtually anybody. With recent findings about the health benefits of lifelong exercise, walking should be done on a daily basis.

It is used to improve aerobic capacity as well as to lose weight, and few injuries, if any, are ever incurred. You can burn more calories while walking if you carry weights on the extremities and swing the arms up high. Brisk walking has also been shown to reduce anxiety and tension, and is an adequate training stimulus for young and old.[28] Both age groups benefited from brisk walking as long as they increased their heart rate by 50–60 percent of their normal resting heart rate.[29]

Stair climbing is another simple but very beneficial exercise. Provided you do stair climbing for 15–20 minutes at a time, you will derive benefit. Going up one flight of stairs and then performing a task on that floor without continuous exertion is better than nothing, but it simply does not give you the cardiovascular benefit seen with continuous and repetitive stair climbing. During repetitive stair climbing, each individual step increases life by about four seconds.[30]

Four decades ago people were amazed by the idea of cardiac patients' exercising, but now rehabilitation programs are common for cardiac patients. The same should be true for patients with cancer. Cancer patients ask their physicians about the types of activities that might be beneficial, as well as the recommended duration of exercise. In most instances, walking can be tolerated by all.[31]

The benefits of exercise are numerous. As mentioned, exercise is associated with a lower incidence of cancer for a number of reasons. The immune system is enhanced. There is an increase in gastrointestinal motility, resulting in quicker elimination of stools and carcinogens. And importantly, the person who is exercising is also aware of other risk factors and tends to be less obese, to eat more fiber foods, to eat less fatty foods, and to consume vitamins and minerals, in addition to not smoking or drinking. Exercisers also tend to be of better mental health[32] and have a lower risk of developing other diseases like diabetes[33,34] and cardiovascular illness.

There is no excuse for not walking or stair climbing. Check with your physician first and work into an exercise program gradually and slowly, but do exercise four times a week, at least twenty-five minutes at a time so that your heart rate gets up to about 50 to 60 percent of its normal resting level. Again this is another risk factor over which you have absolute control. If you are not currently exercising, you can easily modify your life to include walking, stair climbing, or other forms of exercise.

17
Stress

As early as the second century, Galen said that psychological factors contributed greatly to the development of cancer. He believed that melancholic women were more likely to develop cancer than those who were not. A number of physicians of the eighteenth and nineteenth centuries stated that there was a relationship between emotional trauma and the development of cancer. In fact, highly respected cancer specialists of that time, who were not quacks or charlatans, considered this relationship between stress and cancer to be very real. They based their conclusions on clinical observations.[1]

Over the last seventy-five years, many reports—some anecdotal, others more rigorously scientific—have suggested that psychological factors, such as stress, influence a person's immune response and hence his susceptibility to infectious disease as well as cancer.[2] Until recently, there was a missing link needed to explain how the nervous system and immune system communicated. Special neuroendocrine cells have been found in all important immune structures, and specialized T cells have been found at the ends of large peripheral nerves.[3]

We now know not only that the nervous system can influence the immune response but also that the immune response, in turn, can alter nerve cell activities. Cells from the immune system can act as sensors to send messages to the brain, relaying information about invading microorganisms or other problems that might not otherwise be detected by the classical nervous sensory system.

The nervous system sends fibers to the thymus gland, the immune organ in which T lymphocytes are matured. The nerve fibers form a very specific pattern in this organ.[4] The spleen, lymph nodes, and bone marrow also contain very specific patterns of nerve fibers. The nerve follows the blood vessels into the organ and branches out into the fields of lymphocytes. Interestingly, the ends of the nerve are in regions containing T cells and not in areas that contain B cells.

The nervous system can modulate the immune system with nerve chemicals and also with its influence on specific areas of the brain. Likewise, the immune system has the potential to influence the nervous system. Work done at the Swiss Research Institute has shown that the firing rate of brain nerves is altered during immune responses. It is thought that the brain is informed by the immune system about the invasion of foreign invaders. Several cellular products that lymphocytes manufacture, such as interferon and interleukin, are probably responsible for informing the nervous system about these kinds of changes. One of the hormones produced by the immune system, called thymosin alpha 1, acts on the hypothalamus and pituitary gland to increase production of cortisol. Cortisol depresses the immune system by decreasing the number of lymphocytes, decreasing the mass of the spleen, and decreasing the size of the peripheral lymph nodes, among other things.[5] Early in life thymosins are important because they protect T lymphocytes from the immunosuppressive effects of cortisol and allow them to mature. This mechanism is a normal regulation of the immune response.

EFFECTS OF STRESS ON IMMUNE RESPONSE

Other immunological parameters including those of lymphocytes have been studied. Lymphocytes are one of the front line defenses against tumors, among other things. In 1977 lymphocytes from 29 patients whose spouses had died six weeks earlier were studied. In this group of patients, lymphocytes did not function properly.[6] This study has since been repeated several times with very similar findings in hospitalized patients admitted for depression.[7-10] These studies reveal that regardless of the other aspects of a patient's condition, depression alone was enough to produce abnormal lymphocyte testing.

Even mild forms of stress and loneliness can depress the immune response. A study of medical students both a month before final exams and on the day of the exam itself was conducted at Ohio State University School of Medicine. Multiple changes in cellular immunity were seen the day the exam was to be taken, especially in those who were seen the day the exam was to be taken, especially in those who were most distressed and unable to cope well. Medical students more than other students should be well accustomed to taking tests, but immunological changes occurred in them nonetheless: a reduction in the helper T cell, and decreased activity of the natural killer cell, which is the immune cell needed to destroy cancer cells. Although these changes were more prominent the day of the test, they were also abnormal one month prior to the test, indicating that a generally higher stressed life or loneliness can lead to the development of these abnormal immune parameters.

Natural killer cell activity was also found to be depressed in other students who experienced stress but were unable to handle it effectively. These students subsequently had a great deal of distress and poor coping mechanisms. Natural killer cell activity was normal in good copers—those who had high levels of stress but low levels of distress.[11] In another college student study, those who perceived themselves to be psychologically unhealthy also had depressed natural killer cell activity.[12]

Antibody production in those who experience stress has also been measured and studied. It has been found that dental students produced less antibodies during the more stressful parts of their academic year than at other times.[13]

A curious set of findings evolved from the University of Rochester School of Medicine in 1975.[14] The researchers were studying conditioned taste aversion in rats. Animals were first given a saccharin solution to drink from and then the drug called cyclophosphamide, a commonly used chemotherapeutic agent today that also has immunosuppressant properties. In the experiment, however, the drug was used to induce nausea. The rats learned to avoid drinking the saccharin and hence avoided the nausea from the cyclophosphamide. Cyclophosphamide was then not given to the animals in the later phases of the experiment. The rats forgot the taste aversion but were still dying at a very high rate. The unconditioned animals, the control group, which preferred the saccharin solution to plain water did not die. The researchers concluded that the rats were conditioned to associate the taste of the saccharin with immunosuppression and were, in fact, suppressing their own immune responses when they drank the saccharin solution.

Stress + Inability to Cope = Depressed Immune System

It has been clearly documented that emotional stress from whatever cause accompanied by poor coping ability is associated with the depression of animal and human immune systems. Human immune responses have also been depressed by hypnosis[15] and meditation.[16]

The largest groups of studies linking cancer to psychological stress are retrospective studies. These studies show that stressful events frequently precede several forms of cancer.[17,18] Children who developed cancer had a significant stressful change a year before, including personal injury and/or change in the health of a family member. In adults, the incidence of cancer was higher among people who experienced the loss of a loved one.[19,20] The incidence of cancer has also been higher in people who were widowed, divorced, or separated;[21-23] individuals who have expressed a sense of loss and hopelessness; and those who have an inability to cope with the stress of separation. A higher incidence of cancer is seen in people who are unable to express negative emotions and who also have reduced aggressive behavior.[24-26] Sometimes it is seen in those with masochistic personality as well.

Detection of a cancer occurs several years after the time the first cell changed into a cancer. So when a person is asked about a stressful event in his past after he has already been told that he does have cancer, his perception of that stressful event may be very different from what actually happened. However, prospective studies show the same relationship: an inability to cope with stress leads to a higher incidence of human cancer.[27-29]

Using several psychological tests to define the patient's inability to cope, several investigations have predicted subsequent development of cancer in people who had precancerous conditions,[30] or were able to predict recurrence in patients who were having difficulty in adjusting to their illness prior to surgery.[31] In other studies, patients who expressed high levels of anger toward their disease survived longer than those who did not.[32] There are clear psychological differences between women with benign and malignant breast tumors, and their psychological reaction to the diagnosis of breast cancer was strongly predictive of the survival for the next five years.[33,34]

A prospective randomized epidemiological study of 2,020 middle-aged men who were followed for seventeen years found that those who scored as being depressed by the psychological test MMPI had a twofold greater chance of dying from cancer. In this study, all other cancer risk factors, like alcohol consumption, tobacco use, family history, and occupation, were controlled. Another interesting study reported an unexpected lack of closeness to parents seen in male medical students in their late twenties and early thirties who later developed cancers primarily in their forties.[35] This and other prospective studies indicate a good correlation between stress and cancer and are compatible with such an effect via the immune system.[36-39]

The medical community regards stress as a risk factor for cardiovascular illness. I am convinced that stress is also one of many risk factors for the development of cancer. By itself, stress causes immunological depression; coupled with other risk factors a person might have, it can contribute to the development of cancer. We are all confronted with stress on a daily basis. Some stresses, however, present us with a feeling of distress or of being unable to cope.

Is there a cancer-prone personality? The evidence suggests that a person who is unable to cope with stress may have a higher risk for the development of cancer. Those who can cope better have less of a risk. Therefore, learn to cope, learn techniques like meditation and biofeedback, and use any other techniques that you think will make you better able to cope and deal with stress.

RELAXATION TECHNIQUE

Get into a very comfortable lounging position. Concentrate on "feeling" with your mind every part of your body. You can begin by thinking about your right foot, then your right ankle, right leg, right thigh, then left foot, etc.; then from your hands up to your shoulders and neck, and so on. Now, start to tense specific muscle groups as hard as you can, hold them tense for twenty to thirty seconds, then relax them. Again, start with your foot muscles (tense, relax), the leg muscles (tense, relax), and so on. You can repeat the entire sequence once or twice. While you are doing this, tell yourself that you are tightening your muscles each time you do so, and, provided that your effort is exhausting, you will look forward to relaxing each muscle group. While this is happening, you can also think of a pleasant place that invokes fond memories. This sequence should produce relief and relaxation, and decrease your anxiety levels. Stress is another risk factor over which you have a great deal of control. Seize control of stress!

PART FOUR

Diseases

18
Breast Cancer

One woman in nine will develop breast cancer during her lifetime. It is the second leading cause of death in women with cancer in the United States; 29 percent of the cancers that women develop are breast cancers. In 1995 the number of new cases of breast cancer in the United States is about 183,400: 182,000 in women and 1,400 in men. Total deaths from breast cancer in 1995 are estimated to be 46,300: 46,000 females and 300 males. Black women are less likely to develop breast cancer than white women. However, black women have not done as well as white women once breast cancer has developed. This could be related to the extent of spread of the cancer (known as stage): it is usually more widespread in blacks than in whites at the time of diagnosis. Physicians use the term "stage of disease" to denote the extent to which a cancer has spread. The stage of breast cancer at diagnosis profoundly influences survival. There are three general terms to describe the stage:

1. Localized—cancer is in its primary site of the breast.
2. Regional—cancer has spread to lymph nodes in the region of the breast.
3. Distant—cancer has spread to other parts of the body.

The prognosis worsens with each higher stage.

Breast cancer is more fatal in white men than in white women. Of all those who survive for five years after the diagnosis has been made, 65 percent are women and 53 percent are men. This is because most people think that breast cancer is a woman's disease, and therefore when men get a lump in their breast or other symptoms related to their breasts, they tend to ignore it or dismiss it as not possibly being cancer. For all white breast cancer victims (both male and female) from 1960 to 1973, the length of time that most people survived from initial diagnosis was six years and seven months, compared to three years and eight months for blacks. While several cancers, such as cancers of the uterus, stomach, and liver, have decreased in women from 1930 to 1991, there has been little or no change in the death rate (survival rate) for breast cancer patients. For this very reason it is important to understand what role nutrition and other risk factors play in the development of breast cancer so that you can modify them accordingly wherever possible. For example, a diet that is high in fat is a risk factor that can be modified. Simply reduce the amount of fat in your diet. An example of a risk factor that cannot be modified is your genetic makeup (there are inherited risk factors that contribute to the development of breast cancer in a small percentage of patients). Age is another risk factor that cannot be modified. See Figure 18.1 for the age-related incidence of breast cancer.

THE RISK FACTORS

Nutrition

Human breast cancer is associated with a high-fat diet, particularly animal fat.[1-4] Almost forty years ago A. Tannenbaum showed that dietary fat significantly favored the development and growth of both spontaneous and induced breast cancer in animals.[5] Since then, a high-animal-fat diet has been associated with human breast cancer, colon cancer, and coronary heart disease, suggesting that similar modifications of the diet will be beneficial in decreasing the risks of developing all these major diseases. Over the past half century Americans have been consuming more fat, more cholesterol, more animal protein, more sugar, and less fiber and less starch. Likewise, there is a higher incidence of cancer and heart disease in the United States for the same time period.

Epidemiological studies are important to assess cancer trends. They show that there is a sixfold variation in breast cancer incidence in different parts of the world. High-risk countries like the United States are characterized by high standards of living with diets rich in cholesterol and animal fat. In high-risk countries there is a constant

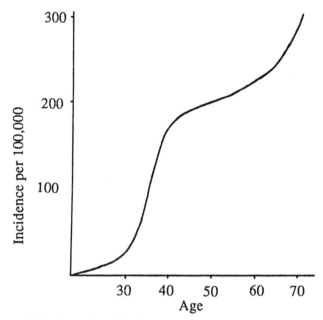

Figure 18.1   Age-related incidence of breast cancer.

rate of increase in the rate of breast cancer development with age, but in low-risk countries the rate decreases after menopause.

Other epidemiological investigations have associated not only dietary fat but also total caloric intake (obesity) with the incidence of breast cancer.[6-8] Obesity is a risk factor; breast cancer patients tend to be heavier and slightly taller than the average. Tannenbaum was one of the first investigators to show that the restriction of calories decreased the incidence of spontaneous breast cancers in mice. If calories were reduced by 30 percent from the carbohydrate fraction of the daily diet, cancer formation was inhibited.

A population of great interest, in studying the incidence of breast cancer, is the Seventh-Day Adventists in the United States. About half of them follow a vegetarian diet, and most do not eat pork. Breast cancer mortality is one half to two thirds of the breast cancer mortality seen in the general U.S. population.[9] R.L. Phillips has shown that the frequencies of eating five food items were associated with breast cancer: fried potatoes, hard fat (butter and margarine) for frying, all fried foods, some dairy products, and white bread. All these foods, except white bread, represent excellent sources of dietary fat.

In Japan, only 20 percent of the calories in the daily diet come from fat, compared to 40 percent in the United States. The incidence of colon and breast cancer is low in Japan and high in the United States. Japanese who come to the United States and adopt American customs and eating habits have the same incidence of colon cancer as Americans after living here for twenty years, and have the same incidence of breast cancer as Americans after only two generations.[10,11] Obviously nutrition is one major factor that accounts for these differences.

Another study shows that breast cancer mortality significantly correlates with an intestinal enzyme called lactase.[12] Lactase is responsible for the digestion of the milk sugar lactose. The enzyme is present in all mammals at birth and then starts to decrease after weaning, so that the adult human usually is incapable of digesting milk and many milk products. Exceptions to this pattern include populations of northwestern European origin (including the United States, Australia, and Canada) and scattered groups in other areas of the world in whom the enzyme is still present in varying amounts. These people historically consume a large amount of dairy products compared to other populations. Asians, Africans, and Mexicans, on the other hand, rarely have the enzyme lactase after childhood, and breast cancer mortality is only a small fraction of that seen in peoples who originate from northwestern Europe. This same study confirmed the findings of other investigations showing that breast cancer mortality is closely associated with the consumption of animal fat, milk, butter, and total calories.

Milk may be related to cancer in several ways. Milk consumption may contribute to the production of carcinogenic estrogens and other carcinogens by changing the type of bacteria in the intestine (more anaerobes) or by increasing the amount of cholesterol and bile acids available for the production of estrogens and other carcinogens. Also, it is known that mouse milk harbors a certain virus that can cause breast cancer in mice. When mouse milk is fed to baby mice, the cancer-producing virus is passed along and causes breast cancer. Milk from cows with leukemia harbors a cancer-producing virus that is infectious for several species. It is altogether possible, but not proven, that a cancer-producing virus in cow's milk may be passed along to humans who consume milk. Virus particles that can cause cancer have been found in human milk. In addition, a person is exposed to other contaminants in milk. For example, DES (diethylstilbestrol) is used as a growth promoter for cattle. The amount of DES in milk is very small and probably cannot cause human breast cancer. However, there is no information concerning chronic low-level exposure to DES and its effect on cancer development. Additional contaminants that may inadvertently be included in milk are pesticides, industrial contaminants, and heavy metals.

A high-animal-fat diet can favor the development of breast cancer for many reasons. First, the typical high-fat American diet produces large amounts of sterol chemicals and bile acids in the intestine. Bacteria that normally live in our intestines can alter the sterol chemicals and bile acids produced by a high-fat diet in such a way to produce certain carcinogenic estrogens and other carcinogens affecting the breast.[13-15] This fact is supported by a great amount of research that has been reviewed by S.H. Brammer and colleagues.[16]

Second, large amounts of fatty tissue in the breasts may lead to greater amounts of estrogens in these tissues locally, which can be carcinogenic. An increased incidence of breast cancer is seen in heavier women who tend to have larger breasts and subsequently more fatty tissue in them.

Third, it has been shown that dietary polyunsaturated fats enhance cancer development. They do so more than saturated fats, presumably by increasing the hormone called prolactin.[17] A woman who eats a high-fat diet, especially high in unsaturated fats, has a very high blood prolactin level.[18] High prolactin levels are also found in women who have their first pregnancies late in life; this may account for the high risk of developing breast cancer in these women.

Polyunsaturated fats not only increase prolactin levels but can also be easily attacked by chemical-free radicals. As we discussed in Chapter 5, this is another mechanism by which polyunsaturated fats can lead to the development of cancer. Furthermore, polyunsaturated fatty acids in the serum may inhibit the normal function of the immune system and thus favor cancer development. And finally, the more polyunsaturated fats there are in cell membranes, the more susceptible the cell is to carcinogenic agents.

Substances in breast fluid may also have an influence on the development of breast cancer. Breast fluid secretion occurs in most women, but in varying amounts. For example, Oriental women have much less breast fluid secretion than white women, and they also have a lower incidence of breast cancer. Breast fluid bathes the ductal cells of the breast gland. Many of the breast cancers originate in the ductal cells of the gland, so the fluid that bathes the cells may have an effect on the development of cancer. A study involving 252 Finnish women revealed that about one third of them had very high prolactin levels in their breast fluid compared to the amount in their blood. However, this study by P. Hill has not yet been extended for a long enough period of time to determine whether this group will eventually develop breast cancer. The prolactin content of breast fluid from Oriental women has not yet been determined, so no conclusion can be made concerning breast fluid prolactin level and its effect on the development of breast cancer.

A chemical substance derived from cholesterol called cholesterol epoxide has been found in human breast fluid.[19] The higher the blood cholesterol level, the higher the cholesterol epoxide level in breast fluid. Cholesterol epoxide is carcinogenic in animals. Its carcinogenic potential in humans is very real. Hence, this is another reason to keep your blood cholesterol level low—so that your breast fluid level of cholesterol epoxide is also low and lessens the potential risk of cancer development.

Nicotine and its close relative cotinine have been shown to appear in breast fluid within five minutes after smoking.[20] So far no studies have shown a conclusive relationship between smoking and the development of breast cancer. However, it is well known that there are fifteen carcinogens derived from smoking. And the fact that nicotine can be detected in breast fluid indicates that many other environmental factors may be present, many of which may be carcinogenic. Chemicals may be held in breast fluid longer than in the blood because there are more lipids inside the breast. Therefore, known risk factors for cancer in general, such as tobacco smoking, should be eliminated altogether because carcinogens get into breast fluid, bathe breast tissue for long periods of time, and may lead to the development of cancer.

Trauma

Perhaps one of the worst misconceptions about the development of breast cancer is trauma. Trauma, such as a bump into the car steering wheel or a blow to the breast, will not cause breast cancer. Likewise, fondling or caressing the breast will not cause breast cancer.

Age

Age is a risk factor for breast cancer. Generally, the longer an individual lives, the more likely it is that the person will develop cancer. The incidence of breast cancer rises rapidly when a woman enters her forties, levels off between forty-five and fifty-five, then rises again more slowly during the postmenopausal years. Age is a risk factor that one can do little about.

Family History of Breast Cancer

If a woman has had breast cancer once, she has an increased risk of developing cancer again, either in the same breast or in the opposite breast. Ten to 25 percent of women with breast cancer in one breast also have it in the other. There is a two- to threefold increased risk of breast cancer in women who have a sister or mother diagnosed with breast cancer.

Hormonal Factors

A woman's reproductive history can be a risk factor for breast cancer. (For a complete review of hormonal risk factors, see Chapter 14.) Women with a long menstrual history, characterized by beginning menstrual cycles early in life and starting menopause very late in life, are at an increased risk for developing breast cancer when compared to others. Women are less at risk for developing breast cancer if they have had a natural early menopause, or if they have had their ovaries removed and hence had an early menopause artificially. The older a woman is at the time of her first pregnancy, the higher is her risk for developing breast cancer. A woman who delivers her first child after the age of 35 has a threefold higher risk of breast cancer than a woman who bears her first child before the age of 18. The number of pregnancies does not seem to have much effect on the risk. Women who have never been pregnant have the same risk as women who became pregnant late in life.

Fibrocystic breast disease, a benign disorder that affects almost 50 percent of all women during some time of their lives, is a risk factor for breast cancer. This increased risk persists for as long as thirty years after diagnosis has been made. The more abnormal and the more enlarged (atypia and hyperplasia) the fibrocystic breast cells are at the time of diagnosis, the higher is the risk of developing breast cancer in the future.

Exogenous estrogens (estrogens taken by mouth) affect some cells' division and may make them abnormal. Normally the hormones produced by the body are in a very delicate balance. If you take additional hormones, the tissues that respond to them may become abnormal and cancerous. In an extensive review of the literature, it was shown that estrogens taken by mouth increase the risk of cancer of the endometrium (uterus lining).[21] In addition to an increased risk of cancer of the endometrium, exogenous estrogens are also implicated in an increased incidence of breast cancer. Exogenous estrogens administered in large amounts have been associated with breast cancer in male transsexuals[22-24] as well as in male heart and ulcer patients.[25,26] The use of estrogens by postmenopausal women to relieve menopausal symptoms seems to increase the risk of developing breast cancer in these women;[27-29] some other studies show no such effect, however.

A subject of great controversy is whether oral contraceptives can cause breast cancer. Several very compelling and clear studies show that oral contraceptives do cause an increase in the incidence of breast cancer in women regardless of whether they have had benign cystic breast disease or not,[30-33] although other studies show no increased risk. The study by M.C. Pike and colleagues also showed that a first-trimester abortion before a first full-term pregnancy causes a substantial increase in risk of developing breast cancer.[34] The controversy about whether the Pill causes breast cancer will probably continue for some years, but current evidence indicates that it does cause an increased risk. The United States Food and Drug Administration now requires that package inserts of oral contraceptives warn consumers of the suspected link to breast cancer.[35]

Approximately 2 million women took DES (diethylstilbestrol) to avert miscarriages in the 1940s and 1950s. These women and their children add up to about 4–6 million people exposed to DES. There is ample evidence now indicating that daughters of women who were exposed to DES have a higher incidence of cancer of the vagina, cervix, endometrium, and breast. Sons of DES-exposed mothers may have reproductive and urinary-tract abnormalities. One of these abnormalities in men is undescended testicles, which, if uncorrected before the age of six, is a risk factor for the development of cancer of the testicles. This information is derived from a recent study that compiled data from 1950 to 1952 concerning mothers who were in a randomized clinical trial—50 percent were given DES and 50 percent were given a placebo (reported by the National Cancer Institute in *The Breast Cancer Digest* in December 1979). Besides informing your physician, the following are recommendations by the research task force for women who were exposed to DES.

1. Tell your daughter or son about your DES exposure.

2. Try to obtain the details of your DES dosage and the duration you took it.

3. Have an annual physical examination (the same type of examination all women should have if they are over 20 or sexually active). The examination should include:

- A pelvic examination with a Pap smear.
- A breast examination by a physician.
- Mammography (X-ray study of the breast) under the following conditions *if you have no symptoms of breast cancer*: no mammog-

raphy under the age of 35; mammography annually if you are over 50.

4. Practice breast self-examination every month. Report anything suspicious to your doctor. Eighty percent of all breast lumps are not cancer, however.

5. Report any unusual bleeding or discharge from the vagina to a physician immediately.

6. Avoid exposure to other estrogens. This includes oral contraceptives, estrogens as a "morning-after" pill, and estrogens used as replacement therapy during or after menopause.

The recommendations for a daughter of a DES-exposed mother are similar:

- If unusual bleeding or discharge occurs from the vagina at any age, see your physician immediately.
- If you have no symptoms, you should have a pelvic examination including a Pap smear at least once a year starting at age 14 or when you begin to menstruate—whichever is first.
- During the pelvic exam, the vaginal walls should be temporarily stained so the physician can see any abnormalities.
- Follow-up examinations are most important.

The recommendations for sons of DES-exposed mothers are that they should see a physician to check their reproductive and urinary systems to make certain there are no abnormalities.

Radiation

Radiation exposure is another risk factor for breast cancer. An increased number of breast cancer cases were found in Japanese people who were exposed to radiation in the bombing of Hiroshima. Women with tuberculosis who had multiple chest X rays following treatment have had substantially increased incidence of breast cancer.[36] Women who received radiation to their thymus gland in infancy also have had a higher risk of developing breast cancer,[37] as have those who received radiation to their scalp as children.[38] And finally, there have been reports that show a slightly increased risk of developing breast cancer in the opposite breast of women treated with radiation therapy for a breast cancer.[39-41] Other studies do not demonstrate this finding, however.

Viruses

There is no evidence thus far indicating viruses as a cause of breast cancer. Virus particles similar to the mouse breast cancer virus have been found in human breast milk. It appears that these virus particles may be more prevalent in women who have a family history of breast cancer. These virus particles have been detected frequently in Parsi women, a group in India that has a very high incidence of breast cancer. A normally functioning immune system, plus good nutrition with the proper vitamins and minerals, will in part safeguard against viruses and other dietary risk factors.

Breast Implants

A long-time concern is whether breast implants can lead to the development of cancer. It has been known that implants hinder the detection of cancer by mammography and cause pain and hardening of the breast tissue around the implant. There have also been reports that implants have been associated with cases of lupus, or scleroderma. But when it was learned that animal studies showed a relationship between implant material and cancer, the FDA issued a warning to all makers of breast prostheses to prove that the devices were safe and clinically effective or remove them from the market. Usually, a product has to be shown to be safe and effective before it is released on the market.

Since the silicon gel filled prostheses became available in 1962, about 2 million American women have had augmentation mammoplasty, about 400,000 of these after mastectomy. These devices were in use before the FDA began regulation of medical devices in 1976.

Isolated reports linked breast implants to cancer, specifically a type of sarcoma. Now, however, recent evidence suggests that the polyurethane coating on the implants can break down in the body and continuously release small amounts of a carcinogen called 2-toluene diamine (TDA). The polyurethane coating is used because it decreases the scar tissue around the implant. The estimated risk of developing cancer from breast implants is one in fifty.[42]

PREVENTIVE MEASURES

Having any or all of the risk factors does not necessarily mean that a woman will actually develop breast cancer. However, women who are included in any of the three major risk categories should practice breast self-examination and should consider other detection techniques such as mammography according to the criteria already discussed. The three major risk groups are:

1. Advanced age.
2. Previous personal history of breast cancer.
3. Mother or sister who had breast cancer.

The following categories are also risk factors for the development of breast cancer:

- High dietary intake of animal fat.
- Obesity.
- History of breast cancer in your grandmother or aunt (father's or mother's sister).
- History of fibrocystic breast disease.
- First baby born after age 30.
- Never been pregnant.
- Abortion in first trimester before a full-term pregnancy.
- Early start of menses and late onset of menopause.
- Excessive exposure to radiation.
- History of cancer of the endometrium, ovary, or colon.
- Estrogen therapy for menopause or birth control (oral contraceptives).

Breast Cancer Detection

Since breast cancer mortality is directly related to how extensive the disease is at time of diagnosis, it seems reasonable then to advocate methods of early detection. One such method, breast self-examination, can be performed by every woman after being properly taught. About 90 percent of breast cancer symptoms are found by women themselves, either accidentally or by self-examination. Although 96 percent of women surveyed by the National Cancer Institute were aware of breast self-examination, only 40 percent actually did it. It is important to learn this technique properly, otherwise a woman who examines her breasts incorrectly may have a false sense of security when she finds no masses. A recent study revealed that only 20 percent of women (161 in the group studied by H. Howe) were proficient at detecting about half of the lumps in a model of a breast with seven lumps in it. As you can tell from this, a woman who actually goes through the motions of breast self-examination every month may not be able to find the cancer mass in her breast. Therefore, breast examinations should be done in conjunction with a yearly physical examination by a qualified physician.

Breast self-examination should be done a few days after your menstrual period because your breasts are not swollen or tender at that time. After menopause you should pick a particular day each month, like the first Monday of the month, to examine your breasts.

The first step in breast self-examination is to stand in front of the mirror without clothing from your waist up. You must look for any changes in the shape or size of your breasts, for discharge from the nipples, for pulling inward of the nipples, or for changes in the appearance of the skin, like dimpling or an orange-peel appearance. Since changes in the breast may be accentuated by changing the position of your body and arms, you should lean forward next and observe; then put your hands behind your head and observe; and finally, observe after you place your hands on your hips, pushing inward on your hips with your hands.

The next few steps begin by lying on your back and placing a folded towel under your right shoulder first. The towel acts to raise the breast and allows for easier examination. Now put your right hand and arm behind your head. With your left hand, move your fingers in a circular motion around your breast, working in from the outer edge of the breast to the nipple, in order to explore for masses. Do not pinch your breast between your thumb and fingers because this may give you the false impression of a mass. Feel gently but firmly. Thoroughly examine the area between your breast and axilla (armpit) because this is the location of some of the lymph nodes that drain the breast. Repeat the process now on the opposite side.

If you think anything is abnormal, contact your physician. You can write to the National Cancer Institute in Bethesda, Maryland, for information on free classes about breast self-examination in your area, or call toll-free (800) 638-6694.

Mammography is a sensitive X-ray technique that helps to detect breast masses. The current National Cancer Institute criteria for using mammography have already been outlined in this chapter.

A woman with one or more of the risk factors for breast cancer should probably be seen by a physician twice a year, have a mammography if indicated according to the accepted criteria, and perform monthly breast self-examinations. If a woman has none of the risk factors for breast cancer, she should practice breast self-examination monthly, have a physical examination yearly, and obtain a mammography according to the criteria already outlined.

In this chapter we have examined the risk factors associated with breast cancer. Some of them can be modified and others cannot. Nutrition appears to play an important role, and these dietary factors (high animal fat, obesity, etc.) should be eliminated or modified substantially to reduce the associated risk. By modifying all the risk factors that you can, you lessen your overall risk of developing this number-one female cancer killer. It is just good common sense!

19
Gastrointestinal Cancers

Gastrointestinal cancers are the second leading cause of death among all cancer victims. The death rate for cancer of the colon and rectum has been about the same for the past half century. Death due to cancer of the pancreas has increased slightly, while the mortality rate from stomach cancer has decreased substantially over this same period for both men and women. The total number of new gastrointestinal cancer cases estimated for 1993 was 240,800; the total number of deaths from gastrointestinal cancer is about 123,000. Nutrition appears to play a dominant role in this group of cancers.

COLON AND RECTAL CANCER

Together, colon and rectal cancers are the most frequently diagnosed cancers in the United States with the exception of skin cancer. Because of this, it is important to make an early diagnosis, and even more important to eliminate all known risk factors. A major risk factor involved in the development of colon/rectal cancer is the food you eat. Red meat, cholesterol, animal fat, and low fiber consumption are very closely correlated with the development of colon cancer.

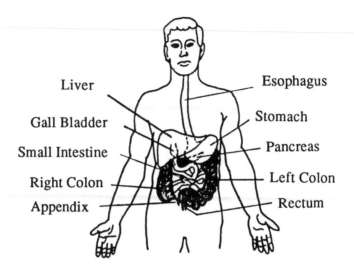

Figure 19.1. Representation of the gastrointestinal tract.

There are major differences in death rates from colon cancer in different parts of the world, and epidemiological studies show that dietary factors account for the different incidence rates. The more industrialized a country, the higher the rate of colon cancer (two exceptions are Japan and Finland), because the people in an industrialized country usually eat more animal fat, beef, and cholesterol-containing foods than do people in nonindustrialized countries. The highest colon cancer incidence rates are found in Western Europe and in English-speaking countries; the lowest incidence rates are found in Asia, Africa, and South America (with the exception of Uruguay and Argentina, where the rates are similar to those of North America). In countries with a high incidence of colon cancer, most of the cancers are located in the left colon and rectum, whereas in countries with a low incidence, most of the cancers are in the right colon. Dr. Denis Burkitt offers the following analogy for this distribution of cancer since carcinogens become progressively more concentrated at the end of the gastrointestinal tract (left colon and rectum). While a man proceeds down a path carrying a leaky pot of water containing a tablet of dye that is gradually dissolving, the water becomes more deeply colored because the volume will be progressively reduced and the dye more concentrated, and more dye will be progressively dissolved.

If persons emigrate from a country with a low incidence rate of colon cancer to a country with a high rate, the higher cancer rate shows up within the first generation. Before World War II, the Japanese got the bulk of their calories from rice, and the incidence of colon cancer was then very low. Among the Japanese who immigrated to Hawaii and California after the war, a significant increase of colon cancer was seen in the first generation and more particularly in the second generation. The main reason for this was the consumption of Western foods such as milk, eggs, and beef. The incidence of colon cancer is rising now in Japan, especially among young Japanese whose diets are more like Western diets.

A population group at high risk for the development of colon/rectal cancer is American-born Jews of European descent living in Israel. However, a twenty-year study has shown that a diet high in fiber, with polyunsaturated fats and supplemented with vitamin C, substantially reduces the number of colon/rectal cancer cases in this group.[1] Seventh-Day Adventists and Mormons have a substantially lesser incidence of colon cancer than the general population.[2,3] Both groups consume a lot of dietary fiber and little or no beef and animal fat. People in Finland have a low incidence of colon cancer, but they have a high fat intake. However, the bulk of their fat calories are derived from dairy products rather than beef. They also consume a great amount of fiber in their diet, which may play a protective role. Other studies also suggest that a high intake of animal fat, high consumption of red meat, and low intake of dietary fiber have a strong association with colon cancer.[4-7] Beef is a high-fat meat contributing about 40 percent of the total fat calories consumed by the American population. People who consume large amounts of animal fat usually eat very little fiber.

The largest prospective study done concerning the relationship between a high-fat, low-fiber diet and colon cancer was published in December 1990.[8] The study involved over 89,000 subjects and found that the more red meat and animal fat people ate, the more likely they were to develop colon cancer. No surprise.

How do red meat, animal fat, cholesterol, and low fiber in your diet relate to the development of colon cancer? The answers are to be found in the contents of the colon itself. The intestine is lined with billions of various bacteria that help to digest our food, produce certain vitamins, and perform several other functions. There are two main groups of bacteria: those that need oxygen to live, called aerobes, and those that do not need oxygen, called anaerobes. What you eat greatly influences the type of bacteria in the intestine. Dietary fat determines the amount of acid and neutral sterol chemicals in the colon as well as the type of bacteria that acts on those chemicals.

Carcinogens and cocarcinogens may exist in food products as well as in fungus and its possible toxic substances. Bacteria and their products are yet another source of potential carcinogens and cocarcinogens, which are formed by bacteria from acid and neutral sterol chemicals in the colon. Some bacterial products include actinomycin D and mitomycin C, potential carcinogens, and streptozotocin, which causes cancer of the renal cortex of the kidney.[9]

Stools from persons in the United States and Britain, where the incidence of colon cancer is very high, have much higher counts of anaerobic bacteria (non-oxygen users) than those from people in Uganda or South India, where the incidence of the disease is low. In another study, the International Agency for Research on Cancer found in 1977 that Danes in Copenhagen had ten times more anaerobic bacteria and a higher incidence of colon cancer than Finns in Kuopio, who have a low incidence of colon cancer and ten times less anaerobic bacteria in their colon.

Dietary animal fat substantially increases the number of anaerobic bacteria, which produce carcinogens. B. Maier et al. found that ten American students who ate absolutely no meat for four weeks had a very high amount of aerobic bacteria and lower levels of anaerobic bacteria. When the same students were fed red meat, many more anaerobic bacteria grew.[10] Certain strains of an anaerobic bacteria called clostridia are capable of producing carcinogens from bile acids. An experiment using rats showed that if one group of rats was fed dietary fatty foods and also had all their gastrointestinal bacteria eliminated, the incidence of gastrointestinal cancer was much lower than the incidence of cancers seen in animals that were fed the same dietary fat but retained their gut bactria.[11] Together, the dietary animal fat and anaerobic bacteria, which produce carcinogens and other chemicals, develop more colon cancer than just the dietary fat alone. It seems prudent therefore to decrease or eliminate beef and other sources of dietary animal fat so that the number of anaerobic bacteria is kept normal and your risk of developing colon cancer is thereby decreased.

It is also known that certain enzymes are made by bacteria in response to dietary beef and animal fat. These enzymes are made to aid in the digestion of beef, but they also can convert cocarcinogens into carcinogens. These enzymes include nitroreductase, azoreductase, and beta-glucuronidase.

Dietary animal fats also increase bile-acid production; bile acids are excreted from the gallbladder into the gastrointestinal tract. They get mixed with the stools and travel along the colon where they are converted into carcinogens and cocarcinogens by colonic bacteria.[12-16] The more beef and animal fat you eat, the greater is the potential for the production of more carcinogens in the colon.

A certain amount of time is required by the colon bacteria to convert bowel contents into carcinogens. The longer the stools stay in the colon, the greater is the potential for an increased production of carcinogens and their buildup. And the longer the carcinogens touch the inside of the colon, the greater is the risk for the development of colon cancer. Hence, a more rapid transit time should be associated with a decreased risk of developing colon cancer. Transit time is the amount of time required by food to travel through the gastrointestinal tract from the mouth to the anus.

People in agricultural societies have a rapid transit time. Several studies have shown that a rapid transit time, which is associated with a diet high in indigestible fiber, is protective against the development of colon cancer.[17, 18] Another study supporting this finding involves the epidemiological investigation of Finns and Americans in New York City.[19] Finns in Kuopio, Finland, are a low-risk population for the development of colon cancer, and North Americans are a high-risk group. The major part of the Finns' dietary fat comes from milk and other dairy products, whereas the major source of dietary fat for Americans is beef and animal fat. Finns consume low amounts of meat and high amounts of cereal compared to Americans. The daily output of stools (by weight) is three times greater by Finns than by Americans. Bile acids, carcinogens, and carcinogen-producing enzymes were detected in both groups' stools, but much less so in the stools of the Finns because the great volume of their daily stools simply dilutes all the carcinogens (and those carcinogens that are there are moved out of the colon much more quickly). Hence, both the large volume of the stool and the increased transit time contribute to the Finns' decreased risk of colon cancer.

Fiber

Fiber is a complex carbohydrate consisting of a polysaccharide and a lignin substance that provides the structure of the plant cell. It is undigested residue that reaches the end of the small intestine. There are three groups of dietary fiber types: vegetable fibers, which are highly fermentable and have a low undigested content; bran, which is less fermentable; and purified fibers such as cellulose, which are much less fermentable and have a high undigested content.

Recently the subject of dietary fiber has been reviewed extensively.[20] This complex substance can act as a "glue" for certain chemicals. For instance, unconjugated bile acids that are produced by the body can be adsorbed to fiber in the colon and passed out in the stool without intestinal bacteria forming carcinogens from those bile acids.[21] In addition some fiber binds to cholesterol and lipids, nitrogen, and certain minerals, and eliminates them in the stool. This action in essence lowers the blood concentration of cholesterol and certain other lipids, nitrogen, and some minerals such as zinc, calcium, and iron.[22] (The effects of fiber on cholesterol and lipids will be discussed in Chapter 21.) Also, B.H. Ershoff has shown that various poisons added to food can be neutralized if fiber-rich foods are eaten.[23] Fiber holds a great deal of water, and this is responsible for the increased weight and amount of stool excreted every day. If 16 grams of cellulose or bran are added to a normal diet every day, stool weight will almost double because of the increased water content. Moreover, without fiber, solids move down the tract more slowly than water and that is the common problem in people who have diverticular disease.

George Oettle in 1960 was the first person to associate dietary-fiber consumption with a low risk of developing colon cancer. He noted that the Bantu tribe, living in the rural areas of South Africa, had a very low incidence of colon cancer. Also, they excreted large piles of feces, which was related to the great amount of fiber they ate. Another student of Africa, Denis Burkitt, wrote about Oettle's observation. Burkitt stated that a high-fiber diet results in a rapid transit time for solid material to pass through the gastrointestinal tract and also increases the amount of stool. And these two variables are associated with a decreased risk of colon cancer as described by Oettle, Burkitt, and others.[24-31] Other nutritional factors have been reviewed in Chapter 8. Diet in rural Africa and in other similar locations provides about 25 grams of crude fiber daily, whereas Western diets provide less than 5 grams of fiber daily. Patients who have diverticular disease consume about 3.5 grams of fiber per day.[32] With a more rapid transit time, bile acids and other carcinogens produced by anaerobic intestinal bacteria (fostered by dietary fat) move out of the gastrointestinal tract more quickly. Furthermore, since the volume of feces is increased, those carcinogens that are produced pass through the gut more diluted. Hence, if more dietary fiber is eaten, carcinogens pass out of the gut more quickly and there are fewer carcinogens per square inch.

Table 23.1 in Chapter 23 lists various foods and their fiber content. Bran, carrots, oranges, apples (pectin), Brussels sprouts, and cabbage are the best fiber sources that bind water. Alfalfa, wheat straw, and some other fibers bind considerable amounts of bile acids that otherwise could promote colon cancer. Chlorophyll was recently shown to be the major factor in wheat sprout that inhibits carcinogens requiring metabolic activation.[33]

In a prospective study involving patients recovering from colon or rectal cancer, it was found that a diet of wheat bran cereal (13.5 grams a day for only eight weeks) protected these patients against the recurrence of cancerous growths.[34] This is one of the first human prospective trials that shows a high-fiber diet will protect the high-risk patient who has had colon or rectal cancer from having a recurrence.

Besides colon cancer, some studies reviewed by Burkitt postulate that dietary fiber may play a protective role in diverticular disease, diabetes, heart disease, obesity, gallbladder disease, and peptic ulcer disease.[35,36] Future studies need to be carried out using standard types of fiber so that results of the studies will be more meaningful.

Other Risk Factors for Colon Cancer

Other risk factors for colon/rectal cancer include:

- Familial polyposis—multiple polyps in the colon.
- Ulcerative colitis (inflammation of the colon) for more than ten years.
- Gardner's syndrome.
- Cholesterol greater than 250 mg/dl.
- Elevated intake of calories and total protein.[37]
- Asbestos exposure.

Colon Cancer Detection

Screening for colon cancer in persons 40 years old or older who have no symptoms whatsoever should include an annual physical examination with a rectal exam and a stool examination for traces of blood. Blood in the stool, unnoticed by the eye, may be an early warning signal for an otherwise undetected colon cancer. In this situation, the stool would look normal to you if there were only traces of blood in it. In addition, you should have a sigmoidoscopy done. A sigmoidoscope is a tubelike device 25 centimeters long with a light on the end. It is placed in the anus by a physician as far as its length. The physician can then directly visualize the rectum and a portion of the sigmoid colon. Fifty-five percent of all large-bowel cancers occur in this very short segment of the colon (25 centimeters). Therefore, if this area is routinely checked and a cancer is detected in a person who has no symptoms, therapy can begin sooner. Removal of all ployps detected by sigmoidoscopy sharply reduces the incidence of cancer in this area of the colon.[38,39]

For persons with a high risk of developing colon/rectal cancer, a sigmoidoscopy should be done annually. High-risk patients include those whose diets are high in beef, animal fat, and cholesterol, and low in fiber, and those who have the risk factors listed above. Persons 40 years old or older who are not at high risk and who have no symptoms should have a sigmoidoscopy every two years or so.[40]

MOUTH AND ESOPHAGUS CANCER

An association has been made between the Plummer-Vinson syndrome (anemia and epithelial lesions) and cancer of the mouth (hypopharynx) in Swedish women. Iron deficiency, as well as some vitamin deficiencies, may be responsible for this syndrome.[41] Improved nutrition and health care lead to a decreased incidence of the syndrome and cancer.[42] Other risk factors associated with the development of cancer of the mouth and pharynx are alcohol, tobacco, and nutritional deficiencies. There is a precancerous lesion that can be found in the mouth, called leukoplakia—a thin white area of mucosa that cannot be rubbed off. This should be biopsied and followed by a physician.

The incidence of cancer of the esophagus differs greatly in different parts of the world by as much as a factor of 500. Soviet central Asia, northern Iran, northern China, and southern and eastern Africa have the highest incidence of esophageal cancer. Curiously, less than 500 miles from each of these areas is an area of low or moderate incidence of esophageal cancer.

There are several major risk factors for the development of esophageal cancer. Tobacco smoking and excessive alcohol consumption are two main risk factors in the United States, Brittany, and Normandy. However, there are areas of the world that have high incidence of esophageal cancer and where the use of alcohol is forbidden by religious teachings. Tobacco contains sixteen known carcinogens. A recent study by T. Hirayama showed that people who both drank and smoked every day had five times the normal rate of cancers of the mouth cavity and three times the rate for esophageal cancer. All alcoholic beverages increased the number of cancer cases of the esophagus, but different percentages of alcohol content produced different cancer incidence rates. For example, beer drinkers had the lowest rate of esophageal cancers compared to the other alcohol consumers. The risk increases with saki and then whiskey. In addition, the study shows that bracken fern, a plant from certain areas of the world, when eaten by humans is a risk factor for esophageal cancer.[43]

Another risk factor is long-term irritation of the esophageal mucosa, the cells that line the inner surface of the esophagus on which food passes to the stomach. Swallowing lye is one such irritation that

To safeguard against the potential of developing gallbladder cancer, you must modify the known risk factors. The diet should be appropriately modified by reducing cholesterol-containing foods, eliminating animal fat, avoiding estrogens, and reducing your weight if you are obese. Patients with gallbladders loaded with calcified gallstones should have the gallbladder removed if they are in good physical condition, because the risk of developing gallbladder cancer is very high, varying from 12 to 62 percent depending on what study you read.[51]

In some parts of the world, parasite infections of the gallbladder and ducts are thought to be responsible for causing gallbladder cancer: liver-flukes in the Orient, *Clonorchis sinensis* and *Opisthorchis felineus* in Asia, and *O. viverrini* in Thailand and Malaysia. The diet of Thais contains a great deal of nitrosamines, the potent carcinogen. This may help promote cancer in a gallbladder that has already been assaulted by a parasitic infection.

There may be carcinogens that affect workers in rubber plants and automotive plants since there is a higher incidence of gallbladder cancer in these workers than in the normal population.[52] However, the specific carcinogen(s) have not yet been identified.

PANCREATIC CANCER

Cancer of the pancreas has been steadily increasing since 1930. It is the fourth most common fatal cancer in the United States. There are about 28,200 estimated deaths in 1993 from pancreatic cancer, far more than the number of deaths from either stomach cancer, esophageal cancer, or small-intestine cancer. The reasons for this are unclear, but excessive alcohol consumption throughout life is an important risk factor. Many alcoholics at one time or another have had pancreatitis (inflammation of the pancreas) resulting from alcohol. When the pancreas tries to heal itself after repeated assaults, abnormal cells could result and lead to the development of cancer. Other investigators feel differently, however.

Poor dietary factors have been implicated as a risk factor for pancreatic cancer, particularly a high-fat diet.[53] This is certainly true of alcoholics who live on alcohol as their only source of calories. Smoking is also a risk factor, a fact that is very consistent in many studies.

A study showed that drinking coffee may also be a risk factor for pancreatic cancer.[54] The study showed that drinking two cups of coffee every day increases the risk of developing pancreatic cancer by a factor of 1.8. Considerable doubt has been cast upon this study.[55,56]

WHAT CAN BE DONE?

All of the risk factors for gastrointestinal cancers can be modified. A few changes in your diet, cessation of smoking, and reduction of alcohol consumption are good first steps. Also, do not use exogenous hormones.

20
Other Cancers

Other cancers are also associated with dietary and nutritional factors. Besides breast cancer and colon/rectal cancers, prostate and endometrial cancers are two cancers in which nutritional factors have been implicated. These four cancers represent the number two, three, four, and five cancers in America. Other cancers will be explored in this chapter.

PROSTATE CANCER

In 1995, about 40,400 men will die of prostate cancer, now the number one cancer in America. The death rate is higher in American blacks than American whites, and even higher than the death rate seen in blacks in Nigeria. Nutrition and hormones are risk factors in this cancer.

There is a four- to fivefold increased risk for the development of prostate cancer in men who have enlarged prostates, a condition known as benign prostatic hypertrophy.[1] This benign condition is very common in older men and may be the result of a high-cholesterol, high-fat diet. Cancer of the prostate is higher in immigrant Japanese living in Hawaii than in Japanese living in Japan. A major difference between the two groups is the diet, the former group eating an "American" diet, which is high in animal fat and cholesterol. A number of studies confirm that dietary factors are associated with prostate cancer.[2] A variety of mechanisms have been proposed.

After age 50, male hormones start to decrease. But in many men with prostate cancers, testosterone levels are the same as the levels seen in men with benign prostatic hypertrophy. The continued presence of the hormone may also be an activating factor for prostate cancer. Receiving testosterone injections to restore or rejuvenate potency in older men who have become impotent due to low hormone levels may be dangerous, because testosterone could activate a dormant prostatic cancer.

ENDOMETRIAL CANCER

There are a number of risk factors associated with endometrial cancer. Endometrial cancer is a cancer of the lining of the internal aspect of the uterus. Women who are obese, who have diabetes mellitus and/or hypertension, and who had early menarche or late menopause are at high risk for the development of endometrial cancer. Each of these high-risk factors is related directly to nutritional factors.[3-5]

High estrogen levels increase the risk of endometrial cancer, and obesity increases the production of a certain kind of estrogen called estrone. Estrone is carcinogenic. It is because of the increased estrone in overweight women that menopausal symptoms are usually very much lessened.

The endometrium of women having early menarche or later onset of menopause has been stimulated with hormones for a long time. The incidence of endometrial cancer has been increasing over the last twenty years, which could be related to dietary factors or to increased usage of estrogens for birth control or for symptoms of menopause. This tumor is more associated with fat consumption than sugar consumption. Women who are vegetarians and only slightly less obese have a lower mortality from the disease than women in general. These vegetarian women secrete less estrogen as well.

URINARY BLADDER CANCER

In 1895 a German urologist named L. Rehn observed a relationship between urinary bladder cancer and certain dyes in industry. Presently about 20 percent of bladder cancers can be attributed to chemicals in industry. Beta-naphthylamine was the first chemical found to produce human bladder cancer. Compounds with aromatic amines have been implicated as well.

In 1950 dietary tryptophan and its breakdown products were found to be a risk factor for bladder cancer.[6] Tryptophan-rich foods include cow's milk, human milk, wheat (white flour), maize, beef, and eggs. Since then other dietary risk factors have been found. In 1977 there was a flurry of reports concerning artificial sweeteners as risk factors for bladder cancer. Other more recent studies show that artificial sweeteners pose no increased risk for bladder cancer.[7,8] A similar story is seen with cyclamate use. The implication of coffee as a bladder carcinogen was made while A. B. Miller was studying bladder cancer patients.[9] However, there is not enough conclusive evidence to point to coffee as a risk factor yet.

Bracken fern (*Pteridium aquilinum*) is a naturally occurring bladder carcinogen. In certain parts of the world, this plant is eaten by cattle that later develop bladder cancer. This carcinogen is found in cow's milk, which is drunk by humans there. So far no increased evidence of bladder cancer is reported, but these people do have a much higher rate of esophageal cancer.[10]

Since the bladder's function is to hold water for long periods of time, any carcinogens that do get into the urine will also affect the bladder wall. Investigators are now looking at the nitrate and nitrite content of the water we drink, which can form nitrosamine. It has already been reported that some bladder cancer patients have high levels of N-butyl-N-(hydroxybutyl) nitrosamine, but it has not yet been established whether this chemical has come from the water supply. Other risk factors for bladder cancer are smoking and a high-animal-fat diet.[11,12]

There are several protective measures you can take to reduce your risk for urinary bladder cancer. Obviously, the first thing to do is to eliminate the risk factors. Also, 25 milligrams of pyridoxine (vitamin B6) per day can decrease the risk of tryptophan's effects[13] and diminish the frequency of "recurring" bladder cancers.[14] Finally, vitamin A may have an inhibitory effect on bladder carcinogens.

THYROID CANCER

Dietary iodine has been associated with thyroid cancer. Iodine deficiency has been associated with follicular carcinoma of the thyroid in humans as well as in animals. The data accumulated from the United States Third National Cancer Survey have suggested that a high alcohol intake is also associated with thyroid cancer. Alcohol increases the secretion of thyrotropin, a hormone from the pituitary gland of the brain. This increase in secretion correlates with the higher incidence of thyroid cancer.

Inflammation of the thyroid, as in Hashimoto's thyroiditis, seems to be another risk factor for the development of thyroid lymphoma, another cancer. Some Japanese studies show that Hashimoto's thyroiditis leads to a higher risk of developing breast cancer as well as lung cancer.

OVARIAN CANCER

The studies that have linked dietary factors with cancers of the breast and colon have also shown a correlation between dietary factors and ovarian cancer. The higher the fat content of the diet, the higher the risk of developing ovarian cancer. Galactose consumption also increases the risk of developing ovarian cancer. Galactose is commonly seen in dairy products, which have not only galactose but also fat.[15]

Although fat consumption is implicated in ovarian cancer, obesity does not seem to be a strong risk factor. Other studies have shown similar findings with no effect of height or weight on the incidence of ovarian cancer. Patients with ovarian cancer are much more likely to get a second new and unrelated cancer in the uterus, colon, or breast. This information simply supports the fact that these tumors have dietary risk factors in common.

LUNG CANCER

The number one cancer in our country is lung cancer. The number one risk factor for this tumor is cigarette smoking (discussed in Chapter 12), and occupational exposures contribute substantially to this cancer in men and women.

In animal studies, the development of lung cancer was inhibited by vitamin A. A large number of human studies have now been done showing that foods with high amounts of carotene, vitamin A, vitamin E, vitamin C, and other nutrients have a protective effect against lung cancer.[16-18] As you may recall from Chapter 6, smoking depletes the body of vitamins C, E, and B6; folic acid; and beta-carotene. The incidence of lung cancer is increased dramatically in heavy smokers when there are low levels of vitamin A, carotene, vitamin C, or other nutrients. It would be prudent not only to stop smoking but also to supplement the diet with certain vitamins and minerals.

All these risk factors *can be modified* by you: avoid beef and animal fat; eat low-cholesterol-containing foods; eat fiber-rich foods daily; eat green vegetables daily; stop smoking; drink alcohol in moderation; and do not take exogenous hormones (oral contraceptives, etc.). Finally, take the proper amount of vitamins and minerals as a food supplement. Antioxidants and vitamin A have been shown to be protective in colon cancers and other cancers.[19]

21

Cardiovascular Disease

Risk Factors In Common With Cancer

Cardiovascular disease is the leading cause of death in the United States. About 30 million Americans suffer from heart or blood vessel disease and as many as 27 million from high blood pressure. In 1991, 765,500 people died of heart disease and 190,000 died of stroke and other vascular complications—a total of 400 deaths per 100,000 people—and the death rate has increased since then. Cardiovascular disease accounts for 45 percent of all deaths in this country, compared to 22 percent caused by cancer. A quarter of the people who have a heart attack die within three hours of the first symptoms. Many don't even reach a hospital. Another 25 percent die within the first few weeks after a heart attack. Advances in intensive-care facilities throughout the United States probably will not significantly reduce the death rate from sudden death and can only partially affect patients in the hospital during the heart-attack episode and convalescence. Furthermore, cardiovascular diseases cost the people and government of the United States over $65 billion a year; and more than $38 billion of this cost is related to premature death, or death before the age of 65. Once again we must learn about the risk factors involved and modify or eliminate them. We cannot cure the disease; we must try to prevent it. Nutrition has a great deal to do with heart disease, and many other risk factors for cancer are also risk factors for heart disease.

Most industrialized nations, except for Japan, have populations with a high incidence of heart disease. Japan, as we discussed in Chapters 19 and 20, has had one of the lowest incidences of breast, colon, and prostate cancers in the world compared to other industrialized nations. A major risk factor for these cancers is nutrition: a high-animal-fat, high-cholesterol, low-fiber diet. Nutrition presents the same risk factor in heart disease: eating a low-animal fat, low-cholesterol, high-fiber diet will decrease your risk of developing heart disease as well as breast, colon, and prostate cancers. It is known that atherosclerosis begins in childhood, so dietary modification and education should begin then also.

Atherosclerosis is responsible for the majority of all cardiovascular diseases (see pages 23–24). It is a disease that narrows the inside diameter of an artery. The first step in this narrowing is the manufacture of cells that line the inside of the artery. Then cholesterol gets deposited in these cells; this is called a plaque. Certain carcinogens can start the manufacture of these cells from a single cell. This process is called cloning, and it is a form of cancer. These carcinogens are hydrocarbons; they are carried in the blood by low-density lipoproteins (LDLs), which also carry cholesterol. LDLs are thought to be the initiators of the process of atherosclerosis. Therefore, if we eat food contaminated with hydrocarbons or are otherwise exposed to them so that they can get into our bloodstream, atherosclerosis may

Figure 21.1　Progression of plaque formation.

begin. If the blood cholesterol is high, a plaque will form and begin to narrow the artery (see Figure 21.1).

These are the major risk factors for cardiovascular diseases:

- High blood cholesterol.
- High blood lipids (triglycerides).
- High blood pressure.
- Smoking.
- Age greater than 55.
- Obesity.
- Diabetes.
- Positive family history of *early* heart disease.
- Little or no physical activity.
- Exogenous estrogens (oral contraceptives, etc.).
- High stress levels.

Do any of these risk factors look familiar? Ten of the eleven cardiac risk factors are cancer risk factors as well.

Nutrition and Cardiovascular Disease

Dietary factors play a major role in determining the blood level of cholesterol and triglycerides. The Keys study was the first to show the correlation between heart disease and high cholesterol and lipids.[1] Since then eight or more international studies have confirmed this finding, including the recent Western Electric and Norwegian studies.[2,3] Another interesting study involved strict vegetarians who were asked to eat beef every day for two weeks. At the end of those two weeks, their blood cholesterol had risen significantly, by 19 percent, and their blood pressure had risen slightly; both parameters returned to their normally low levels when the vegetarians resumed their meatless diet.[4]

As dietary factors demonstrate pronounced differences for cancer incidence in immigrant populations, so do dietary factors alter their cardiac disease rates. Japanese men living in Japan show a lower incidence of cardiovascular disease than Japanese-Americans in Hawaii or California, because of a lower blood cholesterol.

The Framingham study showed that the average intake of cholesterol was 650 milligrams per day for American men and 750 milligrams per day for American women.[5] Most of these people had cardiac disease.

Cholesterol is one of the three most important cardiac risk factors. Cholesterol is an important part of the atherosclerotic plaque. Animals fed high-cholesterol diets develop atherosclerosis. Regression of atherosclerosis in experimental animals is seen if they are fed a low-cholesterol diet. There are certain inherited forms of high blood cholesterol seen in a very few people; all these people have *early* heart disease. High blood lipids also contribute to heart disease. Eat low-animal-fat, low-cholesterol diets! I do not recommend lowering a high blood cholesterol level by eating more polyunsaturated fats. Polyunsaturated fats do have a lowering effect on the level of blood cholesterol, but, as we saw in Chapter 5, high levels of polyunsaturated fats in cell membranes can easily be attacked by free radicals and lead to the development of cancer.

In the past several years, there has been a lot of talk that low blood cholesterol is a risk factor for cancer. There is very little evidence to support this statement, however. It is true that one study showed a low blood cholesterol level in persons who also had cancer,[6] but four other studies showed no such correlation.[7] In fact, when information from six additional studies was reviewed, a low blood cholesterol level was associated with a very low risk of death from colon cancer.[8] There are more plausible reasons for the association of a low blood cholesterol level with cancer. First, the low blood cholesterol probably reflects the advanced degree of cancer rather than indicating a cause of cancer.[9] Second, people with colon cancer break down cholesterol, and these breakdown products are excreted through the colon with the stool, so that the blood cholesterol level is low.[10]

Some foods may have a protective role in cardiovascular disease as well as in cancer. The fatty acid eicosapentaenoic acid (EPA), which is found in most cold-water fish, especially salmon, and possibly in seaweed, lowers blood cholesterol and triglycerides and also reduces the tendency for blood-clot formation. This finding has been confirmed[11-14] and suggests that fish should become a regular part of your diet. Dietary fiber also plays a protective role in cardiovascular disease as well as in cancer. South African Bantu blacks were studied and found to have a much lower incidence of heart disease than white South Africans, probably because of their massive daily consumption of crude fiber.[15] As you will recall, these same Bantu peoples were studied by Oettle and were found to have a very low incidence of gastrointestinal cancer. Certain types of fiber, pectin, psyllium mucilloid, alfalfa, and guar gum cause decreases in blood cholesterol much more than do bran and other more crude fiber sources. Guar gum is derived from *Cyamopsis tetragonoloba* and lowers the blood cholesterol level by an average of 13 percent, lowers the LDL level without altering the HDL level (high-density lipoproteins are believed to be protective), and lowers the blood glucose level.[16] Cholestyramine, a drug commonly used to treat patients with high blood cholesterol, was not tolerated as well as guar gum nor did it lower the blood cholesterol level to the same low degree as guar gum.[17] Psyllium mucilloid and pectin (apples are its best source) lower the cholesterol level but do not lower the LDL level. How fiber works is not clear, but many grains and fibers bind, or act as a glue for, bile acids. When the bile acids are bound, cholesterol cannot be absorbed from the gastrointestinal tract, because bile salts are needed for the transport of cholesterol from the gut to the blood. Therefore, dietary fiber should be eaten to decrease your risk of developing heart disease as well as cancer. Once again, we see the benefit of a low-animal-fat, low-cholesterol, high-fiber diet.

High Blood Pressure

Hypertension, or high blood pressure, is another of the three major cardiac risk factors and a major risk factor for stroke. It also is a risk factor for breast and colon cancer. Blood pushes against your arteries as your heart beats. Sometimes this push is too great, and high blood pressure is the result. Hypertension is defined as having a blood pressure greater than 150/90. Two numbers make up the blood pressure. If either number or both are elevated consistently above those defined levels on more than three different office visits, a person then has hypertension by definition and should be treated on a daily basis. Hypertension represents an increased risk for stroke as well as heart disease. Of the people with hypertension, 95 percent have primary hypertension, the cause of which is unknown. The use of oral contraceptives is the second most common cause of high blood pressure.

High blood pressure increases with age and is 50 percent more likely to occur in American blacks than American whites. It affects over 35 million Americans and costs you and the government almost $30 billion per year. Adding salt (sodium chloride) to your food has been shown to increase the blood pressure by inducing a hormone called natriuretic to increase and thereby cause hypertension. Some studies show that adding salt to food may itself cause hypertension. In populations with low sodium intakes, hypertension is rare. Therefore, add minimal salt, if you must, to food while it is cooking. After the food is served, do not add more salt. Sodium is present in many beverages (soft drinks), processed foods, pickled foods, and sandwich meats. Americans consume about two teaspoons of salt per day, most of which is hidden in prepared foods, perservatives, and flavorings. Read food labels. Limit your intake of salty foods such as potato chips, pretzels, nuts, cheese, pickled foods, and cured meat.

Smoking

Smoking is an extremely important risk factor for heart disease. Since the Surgeon General's Report in 1964, there has been little doubt or controversy about the role of cigarette smoking in the development of heart attacks and cardiovascular disease. There is also little doubt concerning smoking as a risk factor for cancer.

Middle-aged adults have greatly reduced their cigarette smoking, but smoking among women as a whole and among teenagers has increased dramatically. The more a person smokes, the more likely he or she is to have a heart attack. A person who smokes two packs of cigarettes a day is more at risk than someone who smokes one pack a day, and both are more likely to have a heart attack than a person who does not smoke at all. The likelihood of developing heart complications is greatly reduced when smoking is stopped. The Framingham study showed that heart disease is half as common among former smokers as among those who continue to smoke.[18] But more importantly, former smokers who haven't smoked for more than ten years seem to have the same risk as those who never smoked at all. (This does not apply to smokers who quit after the age of 65.) The risk of heart disease for a person who smokes forty cigarettes a day is four times greater than the risk for a nonsmoker.

Smoking is a manmade cardiovascular and cancer risk factor and thus can be modified. If you are presently smoking, it's up to you to stop! Smoking is one risk factor that will produce substantial results if modified.

Age

Age is another risk factor for cardiovascular disease, but one that cannot be modified. We mentioned premature cardiac disease, which is inherited more often than not. However, the older you get past the age of 55, the greater is your risk for cardiovascular disease if you have been eating the typical American diet all your life: high animal fat, high cholesterol, low fiber.

Obesity

Obesity together with one or more other risk factors seems to be a risk factor for cardiovascular disease. Several studies show that obesity by itself, without other concomitant factors like hypertension or diabetes, is a major risk factor. In fact, central obesity, a "beer belly," is even more of a risk.[19,20]

Diabetes

Diabetes, another risk factor, is high blood sugar. About 80 percent of patients with both juvenile and adult onset diabetes die of some form of premature cardiovascular disease, usually heart attack. Diabetic men have twice as many cardiovascular problems as do nondiabetics, and diabetic women have three times as many. Diabetes is thought to adversely affect the blood-vessel walls over the course of many years.

Family History

A person is at increased risk for heart disease if his mother, father, brother, or sister died of heart problems or heart attack before age 65. Of course, this is a risk factor that you can do very little about. You cannot pick and choose your parents. In addition to family history, males usually have a higher cardiac risk than females.

Physical Activity

It is widely thought that a less active person, especially in adult years, is more likely to have a heart attack. Physical fitness does correlate with systolic blood pressure, lung capacity, and blood lipid levels (exercise raises the blood level of HDL, which is thought to be protective in heart disease[21]).

Although physical fitness is important, exercise itself can be dangerous. Anyone over the age of 35, or under the age of 35 with cardiac risk factors, should seek medical advice before beginning an exercise program.

Personality Factor

The role of stress is poorly understood in relation to cardiovascular disease. However, several studies show that an individual can be at risk for cardiac disease if he has a particular behavior or emotional lifestyle. This person is known as Type A personality, characterized by relentless drive, competitiveness, impatience, and being easily provoked. But these traits are difficult to quantitate, and hence studies of this type are difficult to interpret meaningfully.

Other Risk Factors

Oral hypoglycemic pills, which are medications other than insulin used to reduce blood sugar, seem to be a risk factor for cardiovascular disease, but this finding is very controversial. Women who use oral contraceptives have a three- to fourfold increased rate of heart attack,

254 Cancer and Nutrition

stroke, thrombophlebitis, and blood clots in the lung compared to women who never used them.[22] This risk is doubled in women who also smoke. Also there is a two- to threefold higher risk of having a heart attack even after a woman has stopped using oral contraceptives for five years or longer.[23]

Alcohol and caffeine play a role in cardiovascular disease as well. One large study done in 1977, the Cooperative Lipoprotein Phenotyping study, which included 3,806 people, has presented information that moderate consumption of alcohol may increase the HDL level (the cardiovascular protective lipoprotein).[24] The study shows that the HDL level increases modestly if a person consumes either a 12-ounce can of beer a day (0.60 ounces of 100 percent alcohol), a 4-ounce glass of wine a day (0.67 ounces of 100 percent alcohol), or a cocktail a day (0.69 ounces of 100 percent alcohol). Other studies have shown similar findings.[25-27] One additional study shows that persons who exercise vigorously every day, which alone will raise the HDL level, and consume a modest amount of alcohol daily will have a higher HDL level independent of the exercise factor.[28] Hence moderate amounts of alcohol alone will raise the HDL level whether a person exercises or not. These studies do not and cannot say that consuming this amount of these different drinks will decrease your risk of developing heart disease. It remains to be seen if such moderation in alcohol consumption will have any positive impact on heart disease. Excessive alcohol consumption is very harmful. It can directly produce an irreversibly enlarged heart and is related to several different cancers as well as many other complications of alcoholism. Caffeine can stimulate the heart to beat faster, which is harmful for a person who has coronary artery disease.

Many of these risk factors can be and should be modified; this will lessen your risk of developing cardiovascular disease. The Arizona Heart Institute has a "Cardiovascular Risk Factor Analysis." (See Table 22.1.) This consists of a list of risk factors, each followed by statements from which you choose one, and a score associated with the statement. After going through the questionnaire, add up your numerical score.

Table 21.1	Cardiovascular Risk Factor Analysis	
Risk Factor	Statement	Score
Age	Over 55 years of age	Score 1
	Under 55 years of age	Score 0
Gender	Male	Score 1
	Female	Score 0

Table 21.1   Cardiovascular Risk Factor Analysis—*continued*

Risk Factor	Statement	Score	
Family History	If one or more close family members had heart attack before age 60	Score 12	
	If one or more had heart attack after age 60	Score 6	
	No family history	Score 0	___
Personal History	If you had heart attack, stroke, or heart or blood-vessel surgery before age 50	Score 20	
	If you had the above after age 50	Score 10	
	If you had none	Score 0	___
Diabetes	Onset before age 40 using insulin	Score 10	
	Onset after 40 using insulin or pills	Score 5	
	No diabetes, or diet controlled	Score 0	___
Smoking	Smoke 2 packs or more per day	Score 10	
	Smoke 1–2 packs or quit less than a year ago	Score 6	
	Smoke less than 1 pack or quit 1–10 years ago	Score 3	
	Never smoked or quit 10 years ago	Score 0	___
Cholesterol	Blood level over 275	Score 10	
	Level between 225 and 275	Score 5	
	Level below 225	Score 0	___
Diet	One serving of red meat daily, 7 eggs a week, and butter, milk, and cheese daily	Score 8	
	Red meat 5–6 times a week, 4–7 eggs a week, margarine, low-fat dairy products, and some cheese	Score 4	
	Little or no red meat, but rather poultry and fish, 3 eggs or less, margarine, skim milk, and skim-milk products	Score 0	___
Hypertension	Pressure above 160 over 105	Score 8	
	Between 140 to 160 over 90 to 105	Score 4	
	Lower than 140 over 90	Score 0	___

Risk Factor	Statement	Score	
Weight	Ideal weight for men should be 110 pounds plus 5 lbs. per inch over 5 ft. For women, ideal weight is 100 lbs. plus 5 lbs. per inch over 5 ft.		
	If you are 25 lbs. overweight	Score 4	
	If you are 10-25 lbs. over	Score 2	
	If you are less than 10 lbs. over	Score 0	_____
Exercise	Briskly walk, jog, bicycle, swim, etc., for 15 minutes		
	only, once a week	Score 4	
	Those exercises twice a week	Score 2	
	Those exercises 3 or more times a week	Score 0	_____
Stress	If you are frusterated waiting in line, easily angered, or irritable	Score 4	
	Occasionally harried or moody	Score 2	
	Comfortable when waiting, easygoing	Score 0	_____
		TOTAL POINTS	_____

Table 21.1   Cardiovascular Risk Factor Analysis—*continued*

The Arizona Heart Institute defines risk for having cardiovascular disease based on the following total point score:

High Risk   Score of 40 or over
Medium Risk   Score of 20 to 39
Low Risk   Score of 19 or under

A high score does not mean a person will develop heart disease; the test only indicates that a person with a high score is more at risk than a person with a low score.

CAN YOU REVERSE EXISTING CARDIOVASCULAR DISEASE?

The short answer is yes. A prospective study over the course of a year involving patients with coronary heart disease who started on a low-fat diet, did not smoke, exercised moderately, and followed a stress-management program showed that 82 percent of them had regression of their diseased arteries as documented by coronary angiography.[29] Other studies showed similar angiographic regression of coronary artery disease in patients who used various doses of niacin.[30,31]

It has also been documented that if you lower your cholesterol even after a heart attack, either by diet or by using a medicine, you can reduce your risk of future cardiovascular problems, including a second heart attack.[32-36] Medicine should be used to reduce cholesterol only after dietary changes fail to do so. With minimal exercise you can also get your blood pressure to normal if you have borderline or mild hypertension.[37]

How much should you lower the fat content of your diet? Remember, not long ago the government and also the American Heart Association recommended that Americans include less fat in their diet, from 40 to 30 percent of dietary calories. This new recommendation still does not go far enough.[38] In fact, some studies show that people with coronary artery disease continue to have progression of the disease while on a 30 percent-fat diet.[39,40]

The bottom line is this: yes, you can still help yourself even after you have had a heart attack by following our Ten-Point Plan. Since 1981, I have recommended that only 20 percent of your dietary calories be from fat, not 40 percent and not 30 percent. See Chapter 23 for dietary modifications.

PART FIVE

Simone Plan for Risk Factor Modification

22

The Simone
Ten-Point Plan

Cancer, the most dread of all diseases, will affect one out of every three Americans. Eighty to 90 percent of all cancers are related to nutritional factors (a high-animal-fat, high-cholesterol, low-fiber diet), lifestyle (tobacco smoking, excessive alcohol consumption), the environment (chemical carcinogens, ozone, air pollution, industrial exposure), and some hormones and drugs. As we have learned, many of these cancer risk factors are risk factors for developing and worsening cardiovascular diseases as well. Since we can now identify many of these factors, we should modify them accordingly to lessen our risk of developing cancer and cardiovascular diseases. The likelihood of drastically increasing the number of cancer cures by conventional cancer therapies in the foreseeable future is not great, even though some of the very best American minds and technologies are involved in cancer research.

Cancer is the most complex group of diseases known, and there are many different causes. We must all do our part to try to *prevent* cancer because that is how the number of new cancer cases can be substantially reduced. Americans need to know the risk factors for cancer and cardiovascular diseases. Adults who become aware of these risk factors and then modify their diet and lifestyle accordingly will reduce their risk of developing cancer and cardiovascular diseases. Table 22.1 is helpful because it provides a check list of the risk factors for cancer and heart disease that you can control and cannot control. As you now know, you have direct control over the majority of them.

Children will benefit the most from properly modified nutritional factors and daily habits. Nutrition education should be part of a

Table 22.1   Controllable Risk Factors for Cancer and Heart Disease

Risk Factors	Controllable
• Nutritional	Yes
Fat Intake	Yes
Fiber Intake	Yes
Vitamin/Mineral Intake	Yes
Food Additives/Contaminants	Yes
Caffeine Intake	Yes
• Obesity	Yes
• Tobacco Use	Yes
• Alcohol Use	Yes
• Drug Use	Yes
• Pesticides	Yes
• Environmental Factors	
Air Pollution (Outdoor, Ozone Depletion, Acid Rain)	Yes
Indoor Pollution	Yes
Water Treatment and Pollution	Yes
Electromagnetic Fields	Yes
• Radiation	
Sun Exposure	Yes
Suntanning Booths	Yes
Multiple Unnecessary X Rays	Yes
• Sexual-Social	
Female Promiscuity	Yes
Male Promiscuity	Yes
AIDS Spread	Yes
• Hormonal Factors	
Menstrual History (fats trigger early menarche)	Yes/No
First Pregnancies	Yes
Abortion First Trimester, First Pregnancy	Yes
Benign Breast Disease	Yes
Repair of Undescended Testicle	Yes
DES	Yes
Oral Contraception	Yes
Estrogen Use	Yes
Androgen Use	Yes
• Sedentary Lifestyle	Yes
• Stress	Yes
• Occupational Factors	Yes
• High Blood Pressure	Yes
• Age	No
• Physical Examination	Yes

child's education throughout the school years, because nutritional practices and habits are easily modified in youth. Nutrition is a topic of intense interest to teachers and parents as well. The main risk factors for the development of cancer and cardiovascular disease are nutrition and tobacco smoking. If parents set the example of correct nutritional practices, no smoking, and very modest alcohol consumption, their children will continue these practices throughout their own lives. There will be a consequent decrease in the incidence of cancer and cardiovascular disease.

What can you do to help yourself? My recommendations to modify your risk factors for cancer as well as cardiovascular disease will not be anything like the popular fad diets purported to cure diseases or the crash schemes for weight reduction. Primary prevention and early detection are the goals of my plan for risk-factor modification. Simply, I have presented the current body of scientific information concerning cancer and cardiovascular-disease risk factors, and now will discuss how those risk factors can be modified. The more closely you adhere to my recommendations, the better off you will be. The preponderance of information suggests the following Simone Ten-Point Plan for prevention of cancer and heart disease.

POINT 1: NUTRITION

Maintain an ideal weight. Remember, repeated fluctuations in your weight can, per se, increase your risk for heart disease and death. You will find several medically sound weight-reduction diets in the next chapter, along with a table of foods and their compositions.

Consume a low-animal-fat, low-cholesterol diet. Eating the recommended foods under this heading will provide you with more than enough fats necessary for all bodily functions and at the same time modify disease risks.

Eat poultry. White meat is best. Remove all skin before cooking. Chicken, turkey, Cornish hen, and game birds are good. Do not eat any fatty poultry like goose or duck.

Eat fish. All fish are recommended except shellfish, sardines, mackerel, and fish canned in oil, which are high in fat or cholesterol.

Limit red meat. Eat only lean red meat and limit consumption to about once every ten days. Eliminate all fatty meats like bacon, fatty hamburger, spareribs, sausage, luncheon meats, sweetbreads, hot dogs, kidney, brains, liver, etc. Do not eat smoked or salt-cure foods. Limit the amount of barbecued and charcoal-broiled foods.

Simone Ten-Point Plan to Decrease Your Risk of Cancer and Heart Disease

POINT 1: NUTRITION.

- Maintain an ideal weight. Lose weight even if it is just 5 or 7 pounds.

- Decrease the number of daily calories.

- Eat a low-fat, low-cholesterol diet: fish, especially those rich in omega-3 fatty acids; poultry without skin; and skim-milk products (not whole, 2 percent, or 1 percent milk). Limit red meat, including luncheon meat. Limit oils and fats.

- Eat lots of fiber (25 to 30 grams a day). Include fruits, vegetables, cereals, and a supplement of fiber to obtain a consistent amount each day (guar gum, bran, etc.). High-fiber cereals are the best.

- Supplement your diet with certain vitamins and minerals in the proper dosages and combinations for your lifestyle.

- Eliminate salt and food additives.

- Limit barbecued, smoked, or pickled foods.

- Avoid caffeine.

POINT 2: TOBACCO.   Do not smoke, chew, or snuff. Do not inhale other people's smoke.

POINT 3: ALCOHOL .   Avoid all alcohol or consume *only* minimal amounts (less than one drink per week).

POINT 4: RADIATION.   Have X rays taken only when needed. Use a sunscreen with an SPF of at least 15 when sunbathing.

POINT 5: ENVIRONMENT.   Keep air, water, and work place clean. Regulate electromagnetic fields.

POINT 6: SEXUAL-SOCIAL, HORMONES, DRUGS.   Avoid promiscuity, hormones, and any unnecessary drugs.

POINT 7: LEARN THE SEVEN EARLY WARNING SIGNS.

- Lump in breast.
- Change in wart or mole.
- Nonhealing sore.
- Change in bowel or bladder habits.
- Persistent cough or hoarseness.
- Indigestion or trouble swallowing.
- Unusual bleeding or discharge.

POINT 8: RETAKE SELF-TEST (see inset in Chapter 2). Note your disease risk factors and symptoms that may indicate cancer or heart disease.

POINT 9: EXERCISE AND RELAX REGULARLY.

POINT 10: TAKE EXECUTIVE PHYSICAL YEARLY.

- *Limit dairy products.* Only nonfat products should be eaten: skim milk, skim powdered milk, evaporated skim milk, nonfat yogurt and buttermilk, and cheeses made only with skim milk. Eat only a few egg whites per week or a cholesterol-free egg substitute a couple of times a week. Eliminate whole and low-fat milk and the products made from them, cream, half and half, all cheeses containing greater than 0 percent fat, whipped cream, etc. Do not eat whole eggs.
- *Eliminate all oils and fats* including butter, margarine, meat fat, lard, and all oils. Both saturated and polyunsaturated fats are detrimental.
- *Watch garnishes and sauces.* Use products that do not have fats, oils, or egg yolks. Dry white wine may be used in cooking, and you can also use ketchup and vinegar. Do not use salad dressings, pickle relish, prepared gravies and sauces, mayonnaise, sandwich spreads, or other products containing fats, oils, or egg yolks.

Eat a high-fiber diet. Consume foods that will give you 25 to 30 grams of fiber per day. Consult Chapter 23 for the fiber content of foods. As you will learn, it is very easy to choose foods that will give you a total of 30 grams of fiber a day. High-fiber cereals are the best.

Vegetables of the Brassicaceae family provide fiber and induce enzymes to destroy certain carcinogens. These include Brussels sprouts, broccoli, and cabbage. You can eat whole or lightly milled grains like rice, barley, and buckwheat. Whole wheat bread and whole wheat pasta, cereals, crackers, and other grain products can also be eaten. Unsweetened fruit juices and unsweetened cooked, canned, or frozen fruit can also be eaten.

Do not eat cooked, canned, or frozen fruit with added sugar, all jams and jellies, fruit syrups with added sugar, fruit juices with added sugar, bleached white flour, and grain products made with added fats, oils, or egg yolks. Avoid butter rolls, commercial biscuits, muffins, doughnuts, sweet rolls, cakes, egg bread, cheese bread, and commercial mixes containing dried eggs and whole milk.

Vitamins and minerals. You should supplement your balanced diet with vitamins and minerals in the proper dosages and combinations so that risks are even further modified. The formulations I have developed are outlined in Chapter 6. They contain effective doses of all the vitamins and minerals, especially antioxidants. For more information, see Afterword.

Salt. Eliminate table salt. Add only a minimal amount of salt while cooking. Most condiments, pickles, dressings, prepared sauces, canned vegetables, bouillon cubes, pot pies, popcorn, sauerkraut, and caviar have high amounts of salt in them.

Food additives. Avoid all foods containing nitrates, nitrites, or other harmful additives, or that were processed using a harmful technique.

Snacks and desserts. Acceptable snacks or desserts include fresh fruit and canned fruit without added sugar, water ices, gelatin, and (sparingly) puddings made with skim milk. Do not eat commercial cakes, pies, cookies, doughnuts, and mixes; coconut or coconut oil; frozen cream pies; potato chips and other deep-fried snacks; whole-milk puddings; ice cream; candy; chocolate; or gum with sugar.

Beverages. Acceptable beverages are skim milk or nonfat buttermilk, mineral water, unsweetened fruit juices, and vegetable juices. Avoid caffeine-containing beverages—coffee, tea, cola, etc.

Dining out. Call the restaurant to see if they can accommodate your needs as outlined here. Airlines and ocean liners will also help you. Request that the chef not cook with any salt products (Chinese food is high in sodium). Use lemon juice or vinegar on your salad.

POINT 2: TOBACCO

Do not smoke! Do not chew or snuff tobacco. If you are smoking, quit now. There is no easy, painless way to quit. The best way is simply to go "cold turkey" without tapering off or using any of those expensive smoke-ending courses.

The American Lung Association can help you. Call this organization. Remember, cigarette smoke also endangers the health of non-smokers.

As a nonsmoker, demand that smokers not smoke in your presence, especially in a public or work-related area.

POINT 3: ALCOHOL

Abstain from alcohol consumption or reduce to a minimum (less than one drink per week). Remember, consumption of even modest amounts of alcohol in a week is a risk factor for breast cancer and other cancers.

POINT 4: RADIATION

X-ray exposure (ionizing). X-ray pictures are certainly needed in many circumstances and should be taken when a physician recommends it. The equipment is getting better and less radiation is delivered to a person per film now. However, there are hypochondriacs who want X-ray studies, and some people involved in motor-vehicle accidents also want X rays done for possible legal purposes. These people receive unnecessary radiation exposure.

See a physician if you had radiation to your head and neck as a child.

Sunlight. Sunscreens should be used when you sunbathe. Remember, sunlight causes skin cancer and ages skin rapidly. Avoid suntanning booths.

POINT 5: ENVIRONMENTAL EXPOSURE

Environmental protection standards for air, water, and the work place should be rigorously observed.

Several specific industries, such as the manufacturing of boots, shoes, furniture, and cabinets, are risk factors for the development of cancer of the nasal sinuses. Other industries that use certain chemicals (see Chapter 2, Table 2.2) pose an increased risk for persons working with those chemicals. All these industries have safety standards that should be strictly observed. For instance, a person working with asbestos (insulation, brake lining, etc.) should wear a mask to protect the respiratory and gastrointestinal systems. Frequently, workers find a mask to be a nuisance and will not wear one, especially on hot days. This simply increases their risk of developing cancer. Firefighters are indirectly exposed to many of these chemicals when objects made from them burn.

Avoid prolonged exposure to household cleaning fluids, solvents, and paint thinners. Some may be hazardous if inhaled in high concentrations. Pesticides, fungicides, and other home garden and lawn chemicals are also potentially dangerous.

The dangers of electromagnetic force fields need to be addressed. "Safe distance" codes should be established for housing, offices, hotels, etc.

POINT 6: SEXUAL-SOCIAL FACTORS, HORMONES, AND DRUGS

Female promiscuity. The earlier the age of starting sexual intercourse and the more male sexual partners a female has (particularly uncircumcised partners), the higher is her risk of developing cancer of the cervix.

Hygiene in uncircumcised males. Bathe frequently. Poor hygiene may lead to cancer of the penis.

Male homosexuality and promiscuity. Practice "safe" sex.

Benign breast disease. Take steps to minimize your risk by following this Ten-Point Plan.

Birth control pills. Birth control pills should not be used, nor should estrogens be used to treat other conditions. Other means of birth control should be sought.

DES exposure. Report to a physician if you yourself were exposed to DES, or if you are the daughter or son of a DES-exposed mother.

Androgens. Androgens (those substituted with a methyl compound in the seventeenth position) should not be used for body building or any other purpose. Build your body by working out.

Drugs. Avoid all unnecessary drugs. Take drugs only when they are prescribed by your physician. Check to see if the drug interferes with vitamin function.

POINT 7: LEARN THE SEVEN CANCER WARNING SIGNS

- A lump or thickening in breast.
- A change in a wart or mole.
- A sore that does not heal.
- A change in bowel or bladder habits.
- A persistent cough or hoarseness.
- Constant indigestion or trouble swallowing.
- Unusual bleeding or discharge.

If any of these signs appear, contact your physician immediately.

POINT 8: CANCER QUESTIONNAIRE*

If, after answering these questions, you find you have three or more, or all, of the possible "yes" answers in any one category, consult your physician.

	No	Yes
General		
1. Have you ever been told by a physician that you had cancer?	___	___
If yes, cancer of what?_____		
2. Have any of your blood relatives had cancer?	___	___
If yes, cancer of what?_____		
3. Have you lost 10 to 15 pounds over the past 6 months without knowing why?	___	___

*Adopted from Cancer Prevention and Detection Screening Program.

	No	Yes

Lungs
4. Have you coughed up blood in the past several weeks? ___ ___
5. Have you had a chronic daily cough? ___ ___
6. Have you been told that you have emphysema? ___ ___
7. Have you had pneumonia twice or more in the
    past year? ___ ___
8. Have you ever smoked? ___ ___
9. Did you quit smoking less than 15 years ago? ___ ___
10. Do you smoke now? ___ ___
    Cigarettes: Number of packs/day ___.
    　　　　　　Number of years ___.
    Cigars:　　Number of cigars/day ___.
    Pipe:　　　Number of bowls/day ___.
11. Do you inhale others' smoke for one or more
    hours/day? ___ ___

Larynx (voice box)
12. Have you had persistent hoarseness? ___ ___

Mouth and Throat
13. Have you had any of the following symptoms
    lasting more than a month?
    Pain or difficulty swallowing ___ ___
    Pain or tenderness in the mouth ___ ___
    A sore or white spot in your mouth ___ ___
14. Do you drink more than 4 oz. of wine, 12 oz.
    of beer, or 1 ½ oz. of whiskey every day? ___ ___

Stomach
15. Have you vomited blood in the past month? ___ ___
16. Have you had black stools in the past 6 months? ___ ___
    Does this happen only when you are taking pills with
    iron in them? ___ ___
17. Have you had a stomach pain several times a week? ___ ___
18. Has a physician told you that you had stomach
    growths called polyps or an ulcer? ___ ___

Large Intestine and Rectum
19. Have you had a change in your usual bowel habits? ___ ___
20. Has your stool been becoming more narrow
    in diameter? ___ ___
21. Does this happen with every bowel movement? ___ ___
22. Have you had bleeding from the rectum, either with
    bowel movements or at other times? ___ ___
23. Have you had mucus in your stool every time you had
    a bowel movement? ___ ___
24. Have you been told that you had a polyp in the
    large intestine? ___ ___
25. Have you had ulcerative colitis? ___ ___

	No	Yes

Breasts

26. Do you self-examine your breasts? ____ ____
27. Do you have a lump in either breast? ____ ____
28. Have you had breast pain recently? ____ ____
    If yes, is this only at time of menstruation? ____ ____
29. Has there been discharge or bleeding from your
    nipples, or have they begun to pull in (retract)? ____ ____
30. Are there any changes in the skin of your breasts? ____ ____
31. Have you ever had a breast biopsy? ____ ____

Cervix, Uterus, and Vagina

32. Do you have vaginal bleeding or spotting? ____ ____
    If yes:
      Is it between periods? ____ ____
      Is it after sexual intercourse? ____ ____
      Is it after menopause? ____ ____
33. Have you stopped having your periods? ____ ____
    At what age? _____
    Since then, have you ever had hormone therapy? ____ ____
    Have you had a hysterectomy? ____ ____
34. Have you ever had sexual intercourse? ____ ____
    Did you first have intercourse before age 16? ____ ____
35. Did your mother use the hormone DES when
    she was pregnant with you? ____ ____

Skin

36. Has there been bleeding or a change in a mole on
    your body? ____ ____
37. Do you have a mole on your body where it may be
    irritated by underwear, a belt, etc.? ____ ____
38. Do you have a sore that does not heal? ____ ____
39. Do you have a severe scar from a burn? ____ ____
40. Do you have fair skin and sunburn easily? ____ ____
41. Do you sunbathe for long hours or use a
    suntanning booth? ____ ____

Thyroid

42. Can you see or feel a lump in the lower front of
    your neck? ____ ____
43. Did you have X-ray treatment to your face for
    acne, tonsil enlargement, or other reasons? ____ ____

Kidney and Urinary Bladder

44. Have you had blood in your urine? ____ ____

POINT 9: EXERCISE AND STRESS

Everyone should start a program of exercise, but see a physician before doing so if you have risk factors of cardiovascular disease. Initially the exercising should start out slowly, then increase to a comfortable level. Fast walking is a good form of exercise and should be done as part of your program. Two miles would be a satisfactory distance to briskly walk four out of seven days. I stress fast walking because it is easier to do than other forms of exercise—no equipment to buy, no change of clothing, no one to rely on except yourself. You can walk in a shopping mall in inclement weather. Calisthenics should also be done to firm up abdominal-wall muscles and decrease that "spare tire." Five to ten sit-ups, with knees bent, can readily be done at home every day. Lower back pain is one of the most common pains in America. Simple stretching and flexing exercises will prevent and treat lower back pain.

Remember, the data show that some amount of exercise is better than none for those who do not do any. Just a little exercise every day will benefit you enormously. Choose an exercise program that you are likely to follow, and continue to stick with your exercise routine.

In addition to exercising, learn to control stress by whatever means you can. Self-hypnosis, meditation, biofeedback, or other methods are beneficial if they work for you. Some people use music or recreation to relax. Stress is a killer! So deal with it.

POINT 10: EXECUTIVE PHYSICAL

It is well known that persons with localized cancer are potentially curable and live longer than those with widespread cancer. Hence everyone age 35 and older should have an annual comprehensive executive-type history and physical examination with appropriate laboratory studies in order to prevent or detect early cancer or heart disease. What is certain is that if a physician looks for early cancer, he will probably find it if it is there.

A thorough history should include questions about all the risk factors for cancer that are listed in Chapter 2, as well as a review of the questions outlined in Point 8 of this modification plan. Also, questions should be asked concerning the risk factors of cardiovascular disease as well as other routine questions designed to pick up additional medical abnormalities.

The physical examination is important and should be complete, starting at the scalp and finishing at the toes. One capable, highly trained specialist should perform the entire examination, rather than your gynecologist doing the Pap smear and breast exam, your cardiologist checking the heart, your dentist looking in your mouth, and so on. The examining physician can then ask for consultation in certain circumstances.

Laboratory tests are the third major part of a person's workup. Little more than one ounce of blood and urine is taken and assayed for chemical tests. Table 22.2 lists the laboratory tests, the normal range values of the tests, and the functions tested.

Table 22.2	Laboratory Tests for the Executive Physical	
Function Tested	Laboratory Test	Normal Range
Bleeding from gut	Stool for occult blood	Negative
Blood count	Hemoglobin	Male: 13–16; Female: 12–15
	Hematocrit	Male 42–50; Female: 40–48
	White blood cells	5,000–10,000
	Platelet count	145,000–365,000
Blood lipids	Cholesterol	160–260
	HDL cholesterol	25–90
	Triglycerides	10–150
Blood proteins	Total protein	6.1–7.7
	Albumin	3.8–4.9
Blood sugar	Glucose	70–120
Electrical function of cells	Calcium	4.5–5.3
	Phosphate	3.0–4.5
	Magnesium	1.3–2.1
	Sodium	137–145
	Chloride	100–110
	Potassium	3.3–4.6
	CO_2	23–33
	Uric acid	3–7
Kidney function	Blood urea nitrogen	7–23
	Creatinine	.7–1.6
	Urinalysis	—
Liver function and enzymes	Alkaline phosphatase	30–85
	SGPT	3–44
	SGOT	8–31
	LDH	133–248
	Total bilirubin	.2–1.5

Table 22.3   Cancer Detected By Each Part of Executive Examination

Part of Executive Examination	Cancer Detected
Medical history	Most cancers with local or generalized symptoms
Executive physical examination	Skin, lymphoma, mouth, thyroid, breast, abdomen, uterus, vagina, rectum, penis, testicle
Chest X ray	Lung, pleura, central chest, bone
Colonoscopy	Colon, sigmoid, rectum
Complete blood count	Leukemias, multiple myeloma, cancers that produce abnormal red and white counts
Blood chemistries	Liver and associated cancer, kidney
Urinalysis	Kidney, bladder
Stool occult blood	Gastrointestine
Papanicolaou smear	Uterine cervix
Sputum cytology	Lung
Mammography	Breast
Sigmoidoscopy	Rectum and sigmoid colon
Direct laryngoscopy	Larynx
Toluidine blue mouth rinse	Mouth

Testing the stool for trace amounts of blood is another important laboratory examination. Trace amounts of blood in the stool could result from some lesion(s) in the gastrointestinal tract, which could be a gastrointestinal cancer. To detect the reason for the blood, the gastrointestine should then be appropriately worked up by doing a colonoscopy. It is important to completely avoid all red meat for three entire days prior to and during the collection of the stool specimens, because red meat contains animal blood, which will produce a positive result in the test. All other instructions must also be followed for this test.

Certain fiberoptic procedures should be done when indicated. By using a fiberoptic laryngoscope, we have found many lesions of the nasopharynx and larynx when examining patients who have been exposed to passive smoke for several hours a day, patients who have been hoarse for two weeks or more, or other high-risk patients.

Indications for doing a fiberoptic colonoscopy to examine the colon are:

1. To evaluate the colon when an abnormality was found with a barium enema.

2. To discover and excise polyps.

3. To evaluate unexplained bleeding:
   - A positive occult blood stool test (detection of blood in the stool that could not be seen by the eye).
   - Bleeding from the rectum.

4. An unexplained iron deficiency anemia.

5. A survey for colon cancer:
   - A strong family history of colon cancer.
   - To check entire colon in a patient with a treatable cancer or polyp.
   - A follow-up after resection of polyp or cancer at 18- to 36-month intervals, depending on the clinical circumstances.
   - In a patient with ulcerative colitis.

6. Chronic inflammatory bowel disease.

7. To control bleeding.

An annual chest X ray should be done in high-risk patients. A person's lung function can be readily assessed by pulmonary function testing—a series of tests that determine the quantity and speed of the air moving in and out of the lungs, the volumes of the lungs, etc. Also, routine examination of the sputum (excretions brought up from the lungs) will detect certain lung cancers earlier.

A resting electrocardiogram can also be done as part of a routine examination. If the resting ECG is abnormal or if the patient has cardiac symptoms, an exercise or stress electrocardiogram should be done by a competent specialist.

If a bruit (pronounced brew-ee) is heard in a person's neck and the person has no strokelike symptoms from this abnormality, special tests should be done to determine if the all-important carotid arteries are severely narrowed. A bruit is a sound in an artery usually produced by obstructions caused by plaques in the arteries.

Self-examinations of the breasts should be performed once a month by all women. Because men can also get breast cancer, they should examine their breasts as well. Self-examinations of the testicles should also be performed by men, especially between the ages of 20 and 40.

If you are leery about the executive physical, review Table 22.3 on page 273, which shows which cancer(s) can be detected in each part of the executive examination. As you can see, it will be well worth the time.

FOOD FOR THOUGHT

A number of studies have shown that people who abuse their bodies, like smokers, alcohol users, those who eat poorly, those who don't exercise, and so forth, do not pay enough dollars to health-care or other insurance premiums to adequately offset the much higher number of health-care dollars or other insurance dollars they consume. As always, those who are health conscious and who take care of themselves have to subsidize those who do not.

I propose that this injustice stop! I propose that those who consume products that increase the risk of illness should pay a tax on those products right at the point of sale. Differential health insurance premiums can be established to reward those who follow healthy lifestyles by allowing them to pay lower premiums, and properly reflect the higher costs associated with caring for individuals who do not follow healthy lifestyles by imposing higher premiums. You can control the destiny of your health and should be able to control its cost!

23
Diet Plan to Modify Risks

I will outline several easy-to-follow diets for weight reduction. Remember, it is not enough just to adhere to a good diet; you must also initiate some form of exercise, because you must use up more calories than you consume in order to lose weight. You must burn off 3,500 calories to lose one pound. This means that if you are consuming 1,000 calories per day and you burn off 1,500 calories per day, you lose a total of 500 calories a day, and therefore it will take seven days to lose one pound. (See Table 9.1 in Chapter 9 for the effectiveness of different forms of exercise.) I recommend that initially you lose two to four pounds per week to get down to your ideal weight. Once you attain your weight goal, you must modify your eating habits and lifestyle *permanently*. By adhering to the overall plan outlined in Chapter 22—eating a low-cholesterol, very low-fat, high-fiber diet, exercising moderately, and following all the other points listed—you will find that you will keep extra weight off and at the same time substantially reduce all risks for cancer and cardiovascular disease.

The types of food you eat are important, but often it is the amount of food that will determine your ultimate weight. Table 23.1 lists food groups—milk, vegetable, fruit, meat and fish, bread, and fat—and

Group 7 is miscellaneous. Starchy vegetables are listed in the bread group because, per serving, they contain the same amount of carbohydrate and protein as one slice of bread. In each group various foods are listed with their cholesterol content, calories, and fiber content, if known. In the recommended diets you will be able to "trade," or exchange, one food item for another in the same group; they are listed in portions that are approximately equivalent in calories and nutritional content. This trading will reduce the tediousness and take the chore out of dieting.

Table 23.1 Cholesterol, Calorie, and Fiber Content of Foods				
Group 1. Milk Group				
Food	Serving	Cholesterol (mg)†	Calories	Fiber (gm)††
Cheeses:				
*American	1 oz	25	105	0
Cottage, 1% fat	½ cup	15	100	0
*Cheddar	1 oz	28	115	0
Monterey	1 oz	—	105	0
*Mozzarella	1 oz	30	80	0
Mozzarella, skim	1 oz	18	70	0
*Muenster	1 oz	25	105	0
Parmesan	1 oz	14	110	0
*Provolone	1 oz	28	100	0
Ricotta, skim	1 oz	14	171	0
*Swiss	1 oz	35	95	0
Cream:				
Light	1 tbs	10	32	0
*Half and half	1 tbs	6	20	0
*Heavy	1 tbs	20	53	0
*Ice cream, vanilla	½ cup	29	135	0
*Ice cream, chocolate	½ cup	30	140	0
Ice milk	½ cup	13	90	0
Milk, 2% fat	1 cup	22	120	0
Pudding: chocolate, vanilla, butterscotch, or banana, made with 2% milk	½ cup	16	175	0
Sherbet	½ cup	—	135	0
Skim milk	1 cup	5	85	0
*Whole milk	1 cup	34	150	0
Yogurt, *whole milk, unflavored	1 cup	28	140	0
*whole milk, flavored	1 cup	24	250	0
low-fat, unflavored	1 cup	17	125	0
low-fat, flavored	1 cup	15	225	0

†Data for all food groups from Feeley, R. M., et al. 1972. Cholesterol content of food. *J. Am. Diet. Assoc.* 61:134.
*These foods are to be avoided.

Group 2. Vegetable Group

Food	Serving	Cholesterol (mg)	Calories	Fiber (gm)
Artichoke, cooked	1 bud	0	44	—
Asparagus	4 spears	0	10	.9
Asparagus, boiled, cut	½ cup	0	15	1.1
Avocado, fresh	½ whole	0	240	2.2
Bean sprouts	½ cup	0	5	1.6
Beets, boiled or sliced	½ cup	0	35	2.1
Broccoli, boiled and drained	½ cup	0	15	3.2
Brussels sprouts, boiled	½ cup	0	15	2.3
Cabbage,shredded, boiled	½ cup	0	10	2.0
Carrots				
boiled,drained	½ cup	0	15	2.3
1 raw	7½ "	0	20	2.3
Cauliflower, boiled, drained	½ cup	0	5	1.1
Celery, raw	1 stalk	0	5	.7
	½ cup	0	5	1.1
Coleslaw	½ cup	0	60	1.7
Cucumber				
raw	6 slices	0	5	.1
1 small	6⅜"	0	5	.6
Dandelion green, cooked	½ cup	0	35	—
Eggplant, peeled, cooked	½ cup	0	15	2.5
Green beans, boiled	½ cup	0	5	2.0
Green pepper	2 rings	0	5	0.2
1 medium	2¾"	0	15	0.8
Lettuce	⅙ head	0	10	1.4
	6 leaves	0	5	0.7
Mushrooms, raw	½ cup	0	5	0.9
Okra	½ cup	0	15	2.6
Onions				
raw, sliced	½ cup	0	15	0.7
boiled	½ cup	0	15	1.4
green	2 medium	0	10	0.9
Peas, boiled and drained	½ cup	0	40	4.2
Pickle, dill	3¾ " x 1¼"	0	5	1.1
Pumpkin	½ cup	0	40	0.5
Radishes	10 medium	0	10	0.5
Sauerkraut, solid and liquid	½ cup	0	20	3.3
Spinach, boiled and drained	½ cup	0	25	5.7
Tomato				
raw	2½ "	0	20	2.0
juice	½ cup	0	25	0
sauce	½ cup	0	115	2.6
Turnips, boiled and mashed	½ cup	0	15	3.2
Watercress, cut	½ cup	0	5	0.6
Zucchini	½ cup	0	15	

††Data for all food groups from McCance, R.A., and W. Widdowson. 1968. The composition of foods. London:Elsevier/North Holland Biomedical Press.
—Denotes no determined values.

Group 3. Fruit Group

Food	Serving	Cholesterol (mg)	Calories	Fiber (gm)
Apple, with peel	2½ "	0	50	2.1
Apple juice	⅓ cup	0	40	0
Applesauce, unsweetened	½ cup	0	40	2.6
Apricots	2	0	20	1.6
Banana	½ small	0	40	1.6
Blackberries	½ cup	0	42	7.3
Blueberries	½ cup	0	45	—
Cantaloupe	¼	0	40	1.6
Cherries, sweet	10	0	30	1.2
Cranberries	½ cup	0	22	4.2
Dates, dried	2	0	18	0.8
Fig	1 medium	0	40	2.4
Fruit salad with syrup	¼ cup	0	60	1.4
Grapefruit, fresh	½ whole	0	20	0.6
canned, syrup packed	¼ cup	0	35	0.25
Grapefruit juice, sweet	⅓ cup	0	35	0.0
Grapes, seedless	12	0	20	0.3
Honeydew melon	⅒ melon	0	30	1.3
Lemon, fresh	1 slice	0	0	0.5
Lemon juice	1 tbs	0	5	0
Lemonade, frozen	¼ cup	0	30	0
Lychees	5	0	50	0.3
Mango	½	0	60	1.5
Nectarine	2½ "	0	70	3.0
Olives	10	—	50	2.1
Orange	2½"	0	40	2.4
Orange juice	½ cup	0	55	0
Oranges, mandarin	½ cup	0	55	0.3
Papaya	½ of 3½"	0	60	—
Peach				
fresh	2½"	0	35	1.4
canned, light syrup	¼ cup	0	35	0.6
Pear, fresh	2½"	0	45	2.6
Pineapple				
fresh	½ cup	0	35	0.9
*canned, heavy syrup	¼ cup	0	50	0.6
juice, unsweetened	¼ cup	0	35	0
Plums, fresh	1"	0	10	0.4
Prunes				
uncooked	2	0	20	2.0
stewed without sugar	½ cup	0	80	7.8
Raisins	2 tbs	0	45	1.2
Raspberries	½ cup	0	15	4.6
Rhubarb, stewed with sugar	½ cup	0	55	2.8
Strawberries	½ cup	0	20	1.7
Tangerine	2½"	0	30	1.6
Watermelon	1 cup	0	40	—

Group 4. Meat and Fish Group

Food	Serving	Cholesterol (mg)	Calories	Fiber (gm)
Beef:				
Broth	1 cube	0	6	0
*Hamburger	3 oz	77	245	0
Pot pie, commercial	2 oz	9	109	0
*Rib roast	1 oz	26	69	0
Roast	1 oz	26	58	0
Flank steak, lean	1 oz	28	58	0
Vegetable stew,canned	1 cup	36	194	0
*Brains, raw	½ cup	2000	110	0
*Chicken, dark, with skin	3 oz	82	150	0
*Chicken, white, with skin	3 oz	69	140	0
Chicken pot pie, commercial	2 oz	8	125	0
Chicken, roasted, no skin:				
1 drumstick	1.3 oz	39	70	0
½ thigh	1 oz	24	48	0
¼ breast	1 oz	24	45	0
Chicken salad	⅓ cup	50	260	0.3
Egg:				
*Whole	1 large	252	82	0
White	1 large	0	17	0
*Yolk	1 large	252	72	0
Fish:				
*Caviar, sturgeon	1 tbs	48	113	0
Clams	1 oz	14	21	0
Cod	1 oz	16	36	0
Crabs, steamed	2 oz	25	52	0
Flounder	1 oz	17	40	0
Haddock	1 oz	20	50	0
Halibut	1 oz	20	40	0
Herring	1 oz	30	75	0
Lobster, fresh	2 oz	31	54	0
Oysters, raw	1 oz	15	20	0
Salmon, broiled	2 oz	40	105	0
*Sardines, drained	1 oz	43	102	0
Scallops	1 oz	15	32	0
Shrimp, raw	1 oz	50	37	0
Trout	1 oz	20	40	0
*Tuna, in oil	2 oz	40	112	0
Tuna, in water	2 oz	32	70	0
Tuna salad	1 oz	18	70	0.5
Fish cakes	1 oz	—	55	0
Fish sticks, breaded	1 oz	—	70	0
*Hot dog	2 oz (1)	34	175	0
*Ham, boiled	3 oz	75	200	0
*Kidneys	8 oz	1125	90	0
Lamb,⅓ chop	1 oz	30	55	0
Lamb, roast	1 oz	30	60	0
*Liver, beef	3 oz	372	150	0
*Liver, calf	3 oz	372	165	0

Group 4. Meat and Fish Group—*continued*

Food	Serving	Cholesterol (mg)	Calories	Fiber (gm)
Meat loaf, lean	1 oz	28	55	0
Pork:				
⅓ chop	1 oz	25	80	0
*Loin	3 oz	72	215	0
*Sausage	1 link	34	60	0
Turkey, roasted, no skin:				
Dark meat	1 oz	30	60	0
White meat	1 oz	22	50	0
Turkey pot pie, commercial	2 oz	10	80	0
Veal cutlet, lean	1 oz	28	62	0

Group 5. Bread Group

Food	Serving	Cholesterol (mg)	Calories	Fiber (gm)
Breads:				
Cracked wheat	1 slice	0	55	2.1
English muffin	½	0	50	0.9
Pumpernickel	1 slice	0	55	1.2
Raisin	1 slice	0	65	0.4
Rye	1 slice	0	60	1.2
White	1 slice	0	65	0.8
Whole wheat	1 slice	0	50	2.1
Dinner roll	1	0	75	0.8
Hot dog roll	½	0	60	0.6
Hamburger roll	½	0	60	0.6
Pancake, mix/egg/milk	4" diameter	54	60	0.5
Taco shell	1	0	45	0
Waffle, mix/egg/milk	4" diameter	60	61	0.6
Cereals and Grains:				
All-Bran	⅓ cup	0	70	9.0
40% Bran Flakes	⅓ cup	0	90	4.0
Cornflakes	⅓ cup	0	92	4.0
Grape-Nuts	⅓ cup	0	63	2.3
Puffed Wheat	⅓ cup	0	104	5.1
Rice Krispies	⅓ cup	0	124	1.2
Shredded Wheat	⅓ cup	0	108	4.1
Special K	⅓ cup	0	122	1.8
Sugar Puffs	⅓ cup	0	116	2.1
Corn flour	3½ oz	58	354	—
*Flour, white	3½ oz	—	337	3.0
Pasta:				
Noodles	3½ oz	101	100	—
Macaroni with cheese	3½ oz	21	370	—
Spaghetti with meatballs/ tomato sauce	3½ oz	75	378	—
Rice	3½ oz	2	361	2.4
*Cakes:				
Angel food	1/12 10"	0	120	0.1

Group 5. Bread Group—*continued*

Food	Serving	Cholesterol (mg)	Calories	Fiber (gm)
Cakes (cont.)				
Chocolate,chocolate frosting				
homemade	1/16 9"	32	288	2.4
box mix	1/16 9"	33	294	2.4
Coffee cake	3" x 2" x 1½"	—	230	0.7
Cupcake, frosted	2½"	24	130	0.9
Fruitcake	2" x 2" x ½"	7	115	3.4
Gingerbread	1/9 8"	trace	373	1.3
Sponge cake	1/12 12"	162	120	1.0
*Cookies:				
Brownies with nuts	1¾"	17	128	—
Ladyfinger	4	157	170	0
Crackers:				
Rye wafers	3 3½ "	0	65	2.3
Saltines	4	0	50	0
Vanilla wafers	4	0	75	0
Starchy vegetables:				
Baked beans	½ cup	—	95	11.0
Chili	½ cup	—	175	8.6
Corn:				
solid	1/3 cup	—	40	3.1
on the cob	1 ear	—	155	5.9
popped	1 cup	—	40	0.4
Potato				
baked, with skin	2½ "	—	130	3.0
boiled, peeled	2½ "	—	105	2.7
mashed with milk	½ cup	—	125	0.9
sweet	5" x 2"	—	130	3.5
Soups:				
Lentil, homemade	1 cup	—	240	5.5
Minestrone	1 cup	—	55	1.2

Group 6. Fat Group

Food	Serving	Cholesterol (mg)	Calories	Fiber (gm)
*Bacon, cooked and drained	1 strip	40	47	0
*Butter	1 pat (1 tsp)	35	35	0
Cheese sauce	¼ cup	14	130	0
Cooking or salad oil	1 tbs	—	120	0
Cream cheese	1 tbs	16	50	0
Dressings:				
French, low calorie	1 tbs	7	15	0
*French, regular	1 tbs	10	65	0
Italian, low calorie	1 tbs	6	10	0
*Italian, regular	1 tbs	9	85	0
*Margarine				
animal/vegetable	1 pat (1 tsp)	35	102	0
all vegetable	1 pat (1 tsp)	0	35	0

Group 6. Fat Group—*continued*

Food	Serving	Cholesterol (mg)	Calories	Fiber (gm)
Mayonnaise, low calorie	1 tbs	5	47	0
Peanut butter, smooth	2 tbs	—	200	2.4
Peanuts, roasted and salted	¼ cup	—	205	2.9
Peanuts, Spanish	20	—	160	0.7
Sour cream	1 tbs	8	25	0
Tartar sauce				
low calorie	1 tbs	6	30	0
*regular	1 tbs	7	75	0
Walnuts				
chopped	¼ cup	—	160	1.6
halves	¼ cup	—	130	1.3
White sauce	¼ cup	9	100	0

Group 7. Miscellaneous

Food	Serving	Cholesterol (mg)	Calories	Fiber (gm)
Beverages:				
Alcoholic				
Beer, regular	12 oz	0	151	—
light	12 oz	0	96	—
Gin, rum, whiskey				
80 proof	1½ oz	0	97	—
100 proof	1½ oz	0	124	—
Wines				
dessert	4 oz	0	164	—
table	4 oz	0	100	—
Other beverages:				
Club soda	12 oz	0	0	0
Cola	12 oz	0	144	0
Cream soda	12 oz	0	160	0
Ginger ale	12 oz	0	113	0
Coffee	1 cup	0	2	0
Tea	1 cup	0	0	0
Gelatin	½ cup	—	70	0
*Honey	2 tbs	0	90	0
*Jelly	1 tsp	—	20	0
Ketchup	1 tbs	0	15	0
*Maple syrup	1 tbs	0	50	0
Mustard	1 tsp	—	5	0
*Sugar	1 tsp	0	15	0
Vinegar	1 tbs	0	0	0

The foods of each group make a specific nutritional contribution. No one group can supply all the nutrients required for a well-balanced diet. However, the foods marked with an asterisk (*) are to be avoided because they have too high a total fat content (cholesterol is one component of the total fat content), or too much concentrated sugar and may be too high in calories to be safe in your diet.

The grid below is an example of the way the diets are structured. This one is for dinner only. The numbers inside the grid represent the number of portions of a food in a particular group. One portion is the exact quantity listed under "Serving" in Table 23.1. In the milk group (Group 1), you are allowed to take one half of the portion listed in Table 23.1 for skim milk, which turns out to be ½ cup. Next, you are allowed one portion of any food in the vegetable group (Group 2). Referring to Table 23.1, this means that you could have 4 spears of asparagus, or ½ cup of bean sprouts, or ½ cup of green beans, and so on. Moving on, you are allowed one of any food in the fruit group (Group 3), again exactly as listed in the table. You can choose a small apple, half of a banana, half a grapefruit, ½ cup of fresh pineapple, ½ cup of raspberries, and so on. Next, you may eat three portions of any food listed in the meat group. That means you can have a chicken thigh and leg without skin, or 3 ounces of cod, or one whole pork chop, and so on. Nothing is listed in the bread or fat groups, so you cannot have any of these foods for this hypothetical dinner.

	Milk Group 1	Veg. Group 2	Fruit Group 3	Meat Group 4	Bread Group 5	Fat Group 6
Breakfast						
Lunch						
Dinner	½ skim	1	1	3	—	—

In the following Sample Diet, the approximate number of grams of protein, fat, and carbohydrate are given for one portion, or "trade," in the six major food groups. The total energy in calories for each portion is also shown. These values for calories are obtained by multiplying 4 times the number of grams of protein (1 gram of protein = 4 kcal), 9 times the number of grams of fat (1 gram of fat = 9 kcal), and 4 times the number of grams of carbohydrate (1 gram of carbohydrate = 4 kcal), and then adding up these answers for the total amount of calories for one portion. You can now see why you can lose much more weight and maintain that loss if you decrease the amount of fat in your diet, because there are over twice as many calories in 1 gram of fat as there are in either 1 gram of protein or 1 gram of carbohydrate.

While dieting to lose weight you should always:

• Take a multiple vitamin/mineral complex daily.
• Eat foods that are high in potassium, which include apricots,

bananas, berries, grapefruit, grapefruit juice, mangoes, cantaloupes, honeydews, nectarines, oranges, orange juice, and peaches.
• Remember, the more vegetables you eat, the more gas you will have, because of the intestinal bacteria's action on the complex carbohydrates in vegetables. Don't despair; your system will adjust. The following *raw* vegetables may be used as desired: carrots, celery, chicory, Chinese cabbage, cucumbers, endive, escarole, lettuce, parsley, radishes, scallions, and watercress.

Sample Diet					
Milk Group 1 portion	Veg. Group 1 portion	Fruit Group 1 portion	Meat Group 1 portion	Bread Group 1 portion	Fat Group 1 portion
Protein	8 gm	2 gm	0	7 gm	2 gm	0
Fat	10 gm	0	0	5 gm	0	5 gm
Carbohydrate	12 gm	7 gm	10 gm	0	15 gm	0
Calories	170	36	40	73	68	45

• Look at the fiber content of the foods listed in Table 23.1 and try to choose a daily combination that will give you 25 to 30 grams of fiber. Choose cereals and breads with high fiber content. You can increase the fiber value of your breakfast by adding fruit to the cereal.
• Drink as much water, bouillon without fat, and salt-free club soda as you desire. Consume tea and coffee in moderation—they do not have any calories.
• Use freely the following seasonings: paprika, garlic, parsley, nutmeg, lemon, mustard, vinegar, mint, cinnamon, and lime. Use salt only while actually cooking. Do not use salt at the table.

Diets #1 and #2 contain approximately 1,000 calories. You can see that the first diet has five meat trades and the second has four, but with an increase in vegetables and fruits. Either can be used, depending upon your taste for meat or vegetables. It also doesn't matter *when* you take the five meat trades in the first diet. For example, you may want one egg in the morning, which then would leave four meat trades for the rest of the day. The same interchanging can be applied within any of the food groups of each diet; the breakfast/lunch/dinner designations aren't rigid.

Don't forget, these diets are designed only for weight loss, not maintenance. Once your weight goal is attained, you will have to increase the protein content somewhat in your daily diet. If you stick to these 1,000-calorie-per day diets and exercise, you will lose a great deal of weight.

Diets #3 and #4 provide an additional 200 calories per day.

Diet #1: 997.5 Calories Per Day

	Milk Group 1	Veg. Group 2	Fruit Group 3	Meat Group 4	Bread Group 5	Fat Group 6
Breakfast	1 skim		1		1	½
Lunch		2	2	2	1	
Dinner		2	1	3		

Protein: 55 grams per day
Fat: 37.5 grams per day
Carbohydrate: 110 grams per day

Diet #2: 1,000.5 Calories Per Day

	Milk Group 1	Veg. Group 2	Fruit Group 3	Meat Group 4	Bread Group 5	Fat Group 6
Breakfast	1 skim		1		1	½
Lunch		2	2	2	1	
Dinner		3	2	2		

Protein: 50 grams per day
Fat: 32.5 grams per day
Carbohydrate: 127 grams per day

Diet #3: 1,218.5 Calories Per Day

	Milk Group 1	Veg. Group 2	Fruit Group 3	Meat Group 4	Bread Group 5	Fat Group 6
Breakfast	1 skim		1		1	½
Lunch		2	2	2	2	
Dinner		3	1	3	1	
Snack			1			

Protein: 61 grams per day
Fat: 37.5 grams per day
Carbohydratee: 157 grams per day

Diet #4: 1,255.5 Calories Per Day

	Milk Group 1	Veg. Group 2	Fruit Group 3	Meat Group 4	Bread Group 5	Fat Group 6
Breakfast	1 skim		1		1	½
Lunch		2	1	3	1	
Dinner		3	1	3	1	
Snack	½		1			

Protein: 70 grams per day
Fat: 47.5 grams per day
Carbohydrate: 138 grams per day

If you don't want to follow the tables, eat a high-fiber cereal twice a day and one sensible meal a day. Exercise twenty minutes a day, four days a week. Avoid fats. You will lose 1–2 pounds a week, and you will keep it off.

Afterword

You have read quite a bit of information. But you should come away with a single important thought. You have almost total control over the destiny of your health. The work in the prevention of disease is exploding. More and more people realize that by controlling risk factors, especially the major ones like nutrition, tobacco use, and alcohol, you can control your well-being.

You now have the knowledge and the tools to modify your lifestyle to optimize your health and the health of your loved ones. You have the chance for a rendezvous with your well-being. Determine your own health's destiny. Seize this opportunity! Do it now!

For more information, please send a stamped, self-addressed envelope to:

Charles B. Simone, M.D.
Simone Cancer Center
123 Franklin Corner Road
Lawrenceville, NJ   08648

NOTES

Introduction

1. U.S. Department of Health and Human Services, Public Health Service. 1988. The Surgeon General's Report on Nutrition and Health. Washington, D.C., U.S. Government Printing Office.
2. Boring, et al. 1992. Cancer statistics, 1992. *Ca–A Cancer J for Clinicians* 43 (1):7–26.
3. Bailar, J., and E. Smith. 1986. Progress against cancer? *NEJM* 314 (19):1226–32.
4. Boyd, J., ed. 1985. NCAB approves year 2000 report. *The Cancer Letter* 11(28):1–6.
5. Kolata, G. 1985. Is the war on cancer being won? *Science* 229:543–44.
6. Boffey, P. 1984. Cancer progress: Are the statistics telling the truth? *New York Times* (Sept 18): C1.
7. Bush, H. 1984. Cancer cure. *Science 84* 34–35.
8. Blonston, G. 1984. Cancer prevention. *Science 84* 36–39.
9. Marshall, E. 1990. Experts clash over cancer data. *Science* 250:900–902.
10. Simone, C.B. 1983. *Cancer and Nutrition*. McGraw-Hill: 1–237.
11. National Academy of Sciences, National Research Council, Food and Nutrition Board. 1989. *Diet and health: Implications for reducing chronic disease risk*. Washington, D.C.: National Academy Press.
12. The Surgeon General's Report on Nutrition and Health. 1988.
13. Butrum, et al. 1988. NCI dietary guidelines: Rationale. *Am J Clin Nutrition* 48: 888–95.
14. U.S. Bureau of Vital Statistics from 1900 to present.
15. *Ca–A Cancer J for Clinicians*. Years 1962–1993.

Chapter 1
The Scope of Cancer

1. Bertino, J.R. 1977. Principles of neoplasia. In *Harrison's Principles of Internal Medicine*, 8th ed., ed. G.W. Thorn, R.D. Adams, E. Braunwald, et al. New York: McGraw-Hill.

2. Boring, et al. 1992. Cancer statistics, 1992. *Ca–A Cancer J for Clinicians* 43(1):7–26.
3. Silverberg, E. 1984. Cancer statistics, 1984. *Ca–A Cancer J for Clinicians* 34(1):7.
4. U.S. National Center for Health Statistics and the U.S. Bureau of the Census. 1980.

Chapter 2
Risk Factors—An Overview

1. The National Academy of Sciences. 1982. *Nutrition, diet, and cancer.*
2. Wynder, E.L., and G.B. Gori. 1977. Contribution of the environment to cancer incidence: An epidemiologic exercise. *J Natl Cancer Inst* 58:825.
3. Workshop on Fat and Cancer. September 1981. Supplement to *Cancer Res* 41(9):3677.
4. Mulvihill, J.J. 1977. Genetic repertory of human neoplasia. In *Genetics of human cancer*, ed. J.J. Mulvihill, R.W. Miller, and J.F. Fraumeni. New York: Raven Press, 137.
5. Armstrong, B., and R. Doll. 1975. Environmental factors and cancer incidence and mortality in different countries, with special reference to dietary practices. *Intl J Cancer* 15:617.
6. Bjarnason, O., N. Day, G. Snaedal, and H. Tilinus. 1974. The effect of year of birth on the breast cancer age incidence curve in Iceland. *Intl J Cancer* 13: 689.
7. Miller, A.B. 1980. Nutrition and cancer. *Prev Med* 9:189.
8. Eskin, B.A. 1978. Iodine and mammary cancer. In *Inorganic and nutrition aspects of cancer*, ed. G.H. Schrauzer. New York: Plenum Press, 293–304.
9. Upton, A.C. 1980. Future directions in cancer prevention. *Prev Med* 9:309.
10. Alpert, M.E., M.S.R. Hutt, G.N. Wogan, et al. 1971. Association between aflatoxin content of food and hepatoma frequency in Uganda. *Cancer* 28:253.
11. Shank, R.C., G.N. Wogan, J.B. Gibson, et al. 1972. Dietary aflatoxins and human liver cancer.II. Aflatoxins in market foods and foodstuffs of

Thailand and Hong Kong. *Food Cosmet Toxicol* 10:61.

12. MacMahon, B., S. Yen, D. Trichopoulos, et al. 1981. Coffee and cancer of the pancreas. *NEJM* 304:630.

13. Feinstein, A.R., R.I. Horwitz, W.O. Spitzer, and R.N. Battista. 1981. Coffee and pancreatic cancer. *JAMA* 246:957.

14. Goldstein, H.R. 1982. No association found between coffee and cancer of the pancreas. *NEJM* 306:997.

15. Tomatis, L., C. Agthe, H. Bartsch, et al. Evaluation of the carcinogenicity of chemicals: A review of the monograph program of the International Agency for Research on Cancer. *Cancer Res* 38:877.

16. Wattenberg, L.W. 1978. Inhibitors of chemical carcinogenesis. *Adv Cancer Res* 26:197.

17. Pierce, R.C., and M. Katz. 1975. Dependency of polynuclear aromatic hydrocarbons on size distribution of atmospheric aerosols. *Environ Sci Technol* 9:347.

18. U.S. Environmental Protection Agency. 1975a. Preliminary assessment of suspected carcinogens in drinking water. Report to Congress. Environmental Protection Agency, Washington, D.C.

19. Harris, R.H., T. Page, and N.A. Reiches. 1977b. Carcinogenic hazards of organic chemicals in drinking water. In *Book A. Incidence of cancer in humans*, ed. H.H. Hiatt, et al. Cold Spring Harbor Lab.

20. Gardner, M.J., et al. 1990. Results of case-control study of leukemia and lymphoma among young people near Sellafield nuclear plant in West Cumbria. *BMJ* 300:423–29.

21. Wing, S., et al. 1991. Mortality among workers at Oak Ridge National Laboratory: Evidence of radiation effects in follow-up through 1984. *JAMA* 265:1397–1408.

22. Jablon, S., et al. 1991. Cancer in populations living near nuclear facilities. *JAMA* 265:1403–8.

23. International Agency for Research on Cancer. 1980. Annual Report. World Health Organization. Lyon, France.

24. Fox, A.J., E. Lynge, and H. Malker. 1982. Lung cancer in butchers. *Lancet* i:156.

25. Johnson, E.S., and H.R. Fischman. 1982. Cancer mortality among butchers and slaughterhouse workers. *Lancet* i:913.

26. Miller, D.G. 1980. On the nature of susceptibility to cancer. *Cancer* 46:1307.

27. Walford, R.L. 1969. *The immunological theory of aging.* Munksgaard, Copenhagen.

28. Kahn, H.A. 1966. The Dorn study of smoking and mortality among U.S. veterans: Report on eight and one-half years of observation. In *Epidemiological study of cancer and other chronic diseases.* Natl. Cancer Inst. Mono. 19. Washington, D.C. U.S. Government Printing Office. 1.

29. Kahn. The Dorn study.

30. Benditt, E.P., and J.M. Benditt. 1973. Evidence for a monoclonal origin of human atherosclerotic plaques. *Proc Natl Acad Sci USA* 70:1753.

31. Shu, H.P., and A.V. Nichols. 1979. Benzo(a)pyrene uptake by human plasma lipoproteins *in vitro. Cancer Res* 39:1224.

32. Pero, R.W., C. Bryngelsson, F. Mitelman, et al. 1976. High blood pressure related to carcinogen induced unscheduled DNA synthesis, DNA carcinogen binding, and chromosomal aberrations in human lymphocytes. *Proc Natl Acad Sci USA* 73:2496.

33. de Waard, F., E.A. Banders-van Halewijn, and J. Huizinga. 1964. The bimodal age distribution of patients with mammary cancer. *Cancer* 17:141.

34. Dyer, A.R., J. Stamler, A.M. Berkson, et al. 1975. High blood pressure: A risk factor for cancer mortality. *Lancet* 1:1051.

35. Paffenbarger, R.S., E. Fasal, M.E. Simmons, et al. 1977. Cancer risk as related to use of oral contraceptives during fertile years. *Cancer Res* 39:1887.

36. Pike, M.C., H.A. Edmondson, B. Benton, et al. 1977. Origins of human cancer. In *Book A. Incidence of cancer in humans.* Cold Spring Harbor Lab., 423–27.

37. Wobbes, T., H.S. Koops, and J. Oldhoff. 1980. The relation between testicular tumors, undescended testes, and inguinal hernias. *J Surg Onc* 14:45.
38. Armstrong and Doll. Environmental factors.
39. Bjarnason, Day, et al. Effect of year of birth.
40. de Waard, F. 1975. Breast cancer incidence and nutritional status with particular reference to body weight and height. *Cancer Res* 35:3351.
41. Gray, G.E., M.C. Pike, and B.E. Henderson. 1979. Breast cancer incidence and mortality rates in different countries in relation to known risk factors and dietary practices. *Br J Cancer* 39:1.
42. Miller, A.B. 1978. An overview of hormone-associated cancers. *Cancer Res* 38:3985.
43. Monson, R.R., S. Yen, and B. Mac-Mahon. 1976. Chronic mastitis and carcinoma of the breast. *Lancet* 2:224.
44. Leis, H.P., and C.S. Kwon. 1979. Fibrocystic diseases of the breast. *J Reprod Med* 22:291.
45. Narayana, A.S., et al. 1982. Carcinoma of the penis. *Cancer* 49:2185.
46. Hymes, K.B., et al. 1981. Kaposi's sarcoma in homosexual men—a report of eight cases. *Lancet* 19:598.
47. Thomsen, H.K., et al. 1981. Kaposi's sarcoma among homosexual men in Europe. *Lancet* 21:688.
48. Goedert, J.J., et al. 1982. Amyl nitrite may alter T lymphocytes in homosexual men. *Lancet* 20:412.
49. Daling, J.R., et al. 1982. Correlates of homosexual behavior and the incidence of anal cancer. *JAMA* 247:1988.
50. Gottleib, M.S., et al. 1981. *Pneumocystis carinii* pneumonia and mucosal candidiasis in previously healthy homosexual men. *NEJM* 305:1425.
51. Siegal, F.P., et al. 1981. Severe acquired immunodeficiency in male homosexuals, manifested by chronic perianal ulcerative herpes simplex lesions. *NEJM* 305:1439.
52. Goedert, et al. Amyl nitrite.
53. Wallace, J.I., et al. 1982. T cell ratios in homosexuals. *Lancet* 17:908.

Chapter 3
The Backbone of Nutrition

1. Brock, J.F., and M. Autret. 1952. *Kwashiorkor in Africa.* WHO Monograph Series. No. 8. Geneva: WHO.
2. Consalazio, C.F., H.L. Johnson, R.A. Nelson, J.G. Dramise, and J.H. Shala. 1975. Protein metabolism during intensive physical training in the young adult. *Am J Clin Nutr* 28:29.
3. Harrison, F.C., and A.D. King-Roach. 1976. Cell size and glucose oxidation rate in adipose tissue from non-diabetic and diabetic obese human subjects. *Clin Sci Mol Med* 50:171.

Chapter 4
Nutrition, Immunity, and Cancer

1. Cannon, P.R. 1942. Antibodies and protein reserves. *J Immunol* 44:107.
2. Chandra, R. 1989. *Nutrition and immunology.* New York: Alan R. Liss, Inc. Press.
3. Rous, P. 1914. The influence of diet on transplanted and spontaneous mouse tumors. *J Exp Med* 20:433.
4. Tannenbaum, A. 1940. The initiation and growth of tumors. Introduction I. Effects of underfeeding. *Am J Cancer* 38:335.
5. Simone, C.B., and P.A. Henkart. 1980. Permeability changes induced in erythrocyte ghost targets by antibody-dependent cytotoxic effector cells: Evidence for membrane pores. *J Immunol* 124:954.
6. Burnet, F.M. 1970. *Immunological surveillance.* Oxford: Pergamon Press.
7. Kersey, J.H., G.D. Spector, and R.A. Good. 1973. Primary immunodeficiency diseases and cancer: The immunodeficiency-cancer registry. *Intl J Cancer* 12:333.
8. Spector, G.D., G.S. Perry III, R.A. Good, and J.H. Kersey. 1978. Immunodeficiency diseases and malignancy. In *The immunopathology of lymphoreticular neoplasms*, ed. J.J. Twomey, and R.A. Good. New York: Plenum Publishing, 203.
9. Penn, I. 1970. *Malignant tumors in organ transplant recipients.* New York: Springer-Verlag.

10. Birkeland, S.A., E. Kemp, and M. Hauge. 1975. Renal transplantation and cancer. The Scandia transplant material. *Tissue Antigens* 6:28.
11. Chandra, R. *Nutrition and immunology.*
12. Dworsky, et al. 1983. *JNCI* 71:265.
13. Delafuente, et al. 1988. *J Am Geriat Soc* 36:733.
14. Lichenstein, et al. 1982. *J Am Geriat Soc* 30:447.
15. Rosenkoetter, et al. 1983. *Cell Immunol* 77:395.
16. Halgren, et al. 1983. *J Immunol* 131:191.
17. Delafuente, and Panush. 1990. Potential of drug-related immunoenhancement of the geriatric patient. *Geriatric Med* 9 (4):32–40.
18. Aschekenasy, A. 1975. Dietary protein and amino acids in leucopoiesis. *World Rev Nutri Diet* 21:152.
19. Jose, D.G., and R.A. Good. 1971. Absence of enhancing antibody in cell-mediated immunity to tumor homografts in protein deficient rats. *Nature* 231:807.
20. Passwell, J.H., M.W. Steward, and J.F. Soothill. 1974. The effects of protein malnutrition on macrophage function and the amount and affinity of antibody response. *Clin Exp Immunol* 17:491.
21. Van Oss, C.J. 1971. Influence of glucose levels on the *in vitro* phagocytosis of bacteria by human neutrophils. *Infect Immunol* 4:54.
22. Perille, P.E., J.P. Nolan, and S.C. Finch. 1972. Studies of the resistance to infection in diabetes mellitus: Local exudative cellular response. *Lab Clin Med* 59:1008.
23. Bagdade, J.D., R.K. Root, and R.J. Bulger. 1974. Impaired leukocyte function in patients with poorly controlled diabetes. *Diabetes* 23:9.
24. Stuart, A.E., and A.E. Davidson. 1976. Effect of simple lipids on antibody formation after ingestion of foreign red cells. *J Pathol Bacteriol* 87:305.
25. Santiago-Delpin, E.A., and J. Szepsenwol. 1977. Prolonged survival of skin and tumor allografts in mice on high fat diets. *J Natl Cancer Inst* 59:459.
26. DiLuzio, N.R., and W.R. Wooles. 1964. Depression of phagocytic activity and immune response by methyl palmitate. *Am J Physiol* 206:939.
27. Clausen, J., and J. Moller. 1969. Allergic encephalomyelitis induced by brain antigen after deficiency in polyunsaturated fatty acids during myelination. *Int Arch Allergy Appl Immunol* 36:224.
28. Meade, C.J., and J. Mertin. 1976. The mechanism of immunoinhibition by arachidonic and linoleic acid. Effects on the lymphoid and RE systems. *Int Arch Allergy Appl Immunol* 51:2.

Chapter 5
Free Radicals

1. Weves, R., D. Roos, R.S. Weening, et al. 1976. An EPR study of myeloperoxidase in human granulocytes. *Biochem Biophys Acta* 421:328.
2. Tam, B.K., and P.B. McKay. 1970. Reduced triphosphopyridine nucleotide oxidase-catalysed alterations of membrane phospholipids, III. Transient formation of phospholipid peroxides. *J Biol Che* 245:2295.
3. Reich, L., and S.S. Stivala. 1969. *Autoxidation of hydrocarbons and polyoletins.* New York: Dekker.
4. Lundberg, W.O. 1961. *Autoxidation and antioxidants.* Vol. I. New York: Wiley.
5. Pryor, W.A. 1971. Background radiation. *Chem Eng News* 49:34.
6. Wills, E.D. 1970. *Int J Rad Res* 17:229.
7. Norins, A.L. 1962. Free radical formation in skin following exposure to ultraviolet light. *J Invest Dermatol* 39:445.
8. Urbach, F., J.H. Epstein, and P.D. Forbes. 1974. *Sunlight and man*, ed. M.A. Pathak, et al. Tokyo: Univ. Tokyo Press, 259.
9. Zelac, R.E., H.L. Cromroy, W.E. Bloch, et al. 1971. Inhaled ozone as a mutagen. I. Chromosome aberration induced in Chinese hamster lymphocytes. *Environ Res* 4:262.
10. Pryor, W.A. 1973. Free radical reactions and their importance in biochemical systems. *Fed Proc, Amer Soc Exp Biol* 32:1862.

11. Slater, T.F. 1972. *Free radical mechanism in tissue injury.* London: Pion, Ltd.
12. Recknagel, R.O. 1967. Carbon tetrachloride hepatoxicity. *Pharmacol Rev* 19:145.
13. Cross, et al. 1987. Oxygen radicals and human disease. *Ann Int Med* 107:526–45.
14. Southorn, P., and Powis. 1988. Free radicals in medicine, chemical nature and biological reactions. *Mayo Clin Proc* 63:381–389.
15. Saul, et al. 1987. Free radicals, DNA damage, and aging. In *Annals: Modern biological theories of aging.* New York: Raven Press, 113–29.
16. Cerutti. 1985. Pro-oxidant states and tumor promotion. *Science* 227:375–82.
17. Vuillaume, M. 1987. Reduced oxygen species, mutation, induction and cancer initiation. *Mutat Res* 186:43–72.
18. Halliwell, et al. 1985. *Free oxygens in biology and medicine.* Oxford: Clarion Press.
19. Draper, et al. 1984. Anti-oxidants and cancer. *J Agri Food Chem* 32:433–35.
20. Rubanyi. 1988. Vascular effects of oxygen-derived free radicals. *Free Rad Bio Med* 4:107–20.
21. Hennig and Chow. 1988. Lipid peroxidation and endothelial cell injury: Implications in atherosclerosis. *Free Rad Bio Med* 4:99–106.
22. Re-profusion injury after thrombolytic therapy for acute myocardial infarction. 1989. *Lancet* (Sept 16):655–57.
23. McCord. 1985. Oxygen derived free radicals in post ischemic tissue injury. *NEJM* 312:159–63.
24. Fridovich, I. 1975. Superoxide dismutases. *Ann Rev Biochem* 44:147.
25. Ogura, Y. 1955. Catalase activity at high concentrations of hydrogen peroxide. *Arch Biophys* 57:228.
26. Christopherson, B.O. 1969. Reduction of linoleic acid hydroperoxide by a glutathione peroxidase. *Biochem Biophys Acta* 176:463.
27. Wattenberg, W.L., W.O. Loub, L.K. Lam, and J.L. Speier. 1976. Dietary constituents altering the response to chemical carcinogens. *Fed Proc* 35:1327.

Chapter 6
Vitamins, Minerals, and Other Nutrients
1. Pietrzik, K. 1985. Concept of borderline vitamin deficiencies. *Int J Vit Nutr Res Suppl* 27:61–73.
2. Brin, M. 1972. Dilemma of marginal vitamin deficiency. *Proc 9th Int Cong Nutrition, Mexico* 4:102–115.
3. U.S. Department of HEW. 1974. HANES: Health and Nutrition Examination Survey, Publication No. 74-1219-1. Rockville, Maryland.
4. U.S. Department of HEW. 1970. Ten State Nutrition Survey, Publication No. 72-8130 to 8134. Washington, D.C.
5. Baker, H., and O. Frank. 1985. Subclinical vitamin deficits in various age groups. *Int J Vit Nutr Res Suppl* 27:47–59.
6. Christakis, G. 1980. *Socio-economic and long term effects of teenage nutrition: Threat or threshold to a healthy adult life.* New York: Elsiever Publishing.
7. McGanity, W. 1980. *Why it is important at teenage nutrition: Threat or threshold to a healthy adult life.* New York, New York.
8. Brin, M., M.V. Dibble, A. Peel, E. McMullen, A. Bourquin, and N. Chen. 1965. Some preliminary findings on the nutritional status of the aged in Onondaga County, NY. *Am J Clin Nutr* 17:240–58.
9. Brin, M., S.H. Schwartzberg, and D. Arthur-Davies. 1964. A vitamin evaluation program as applied to 10 elderly residents in a community home for the aged. *J Am Geriat So* 12:493–99.
10. Davis, T.R.A., S.N. Gershoff, and D.F. Gamble. 1969. Review of studies of vitamin and mineral nutrition in the United States (1950-1968). *J Nutr Edn* suppl. 1:410–57.
11. Dibble, M.V., M. Brin, E. McMullen, A. Peel, and N. Chen. 1965. Some preliminary findings on the nutritional status of Syracuse and Onondaga County, New York Junior High School children. *Am J Clin Nutr* 17:218–239.
12. Thiele, V.F., M. Brin, and M.V. Dibble. 1968. Preliminary biochemical findings in Negro migrant workers at King Ferry, New York. *Am J Clin Nutr* 21:1229–38.

13. Vitamins and Health, Man and Molecules. 1977. American Chemical Society, Script #852, Washington, D.C. (April).
14. Proposed fortification policy for cereal-grain products, food and nutrition board. 1974. Divsn. of Biol. Sci. Ass. of Life Sci., Natl. Research Council, Nat'l. Acad. of Sci. Washington, D.C.
15. U.S. Dept. of Agriculture. 1980. USDA Household Food Consumption Survey. Family Economics Research Group. Science and Education Administration. Hyattsville, Maryland 20782.
16. U.S. Dept. of Agriculture, Human Nutrition Information Service, 1985. Nationwide Food Consumption Survey, Continuing Survey of Food Intakes by Individuals. Women 19-50 Years and Their Children 1-5 Years, 4 Days. NFCS, CSFII Report No. 85-4.
17. Ten State Nutrition Survey, Publ. No. 72-8130 to 8134. 1970. Washington, D.C.: United States Dept. of Health, Education, and Welfare.
18. Brin, M. Marginal deficiency and immunocompetence. Presented at *American Chemical Society Symposium,* Las Vegas, NV, Aug. 1980.
19. Schumann, I. Preoperative measures to promote wound healing. *Nursing Cl. of N.A.* (Dec 1979) 14:4.
20. Statistical Abstracts of the United States, 1980. U.S. Dept. of Commerce, Bureau of the Census, Washington, D.C.
21. Sheils, M. 1983. Portrait of America. *Newsweek* Special Report (Jan 17).
22. U.S. Dept. of Agriculture. Nationwide Food Consumption Survey.
23. Pao, E.M., and S.M. Mickle. Nutrients from meals and snacks consumed by individuals. Family Economics Review, U.S. Dept. of Agriculture, Science and Education Administration, Beltsville, MD.
24. Sheils, M. Portrait of America.
25. Pao and Mickle. Nutrients from meals and snacks consumed by individuals.
26. Ideas for better eating. 1981. Menus and recipes to make use of the dietary guidelines. Science and Education Administration/Human Nutrition. U.S. Dept. of Agriculture (January).
27. Dietary intake source data. United States 1976-80. Data from the National Health Survey, Series 11, No. 231, DHHS Publication No. (PHS) 83-1681 (March 1983).
28. U.S. Dept. of Agriculture. Nationwide Food Consumption Survey.
29. Leevy, C.M., L. Cardi, O. Frank, et al. 1965. Incidence and significance of hypovitaminemia in a randomly selected municipal hospital population. *Am J Clin Nutr* 17:259.
30. Sheils, M. Portrait of America.
31. Pao, E. and S. Mickle. 1981. Problem nutrients in the United States. *Food Technology* (September).
32. Krehl, W.A. 1981. The role of nutrition in preventing disease. Presented at Davidson Conference Center for Continuing Education. Univ. of Southern California School of Dentistry. (Feb. 29).
33. Roe, D. 1976. *Drug-induced nutritional deficiencies.* Connecticut: The AVI Publishing Company, Inc.
34. Leevy, C.M., and H. Baker. 1968. Vitamins and alcoholism. *Am J Clin Nutr* 21:11.
35. Lieber, C.S. Alcohol and malnutrition in the pathogenesis of liver disease and nutrition. Veterans Administration Hospital and Department of Medicine. Mt. Sinai School of Medicine of the City University of New York, Bronx, NY. (Sept 1975).
36. Baker, H., O. Frank, R.K. Zetterman, K.S. Rajan, W. ten Hove, and C.M. Leevy. 1975. Inability of chronic alcholics with liver disease to use food as a source of folates, thiamine and vitamin B6. *Amer J Clin Nutr* 28:1377–1380.
37. Payne, I.R., G.H.Y. Lu, and K. Meyer. 1974. Relationships of dietary tryptophan and niacin to tryptophan metabolism in alcoholics and nonalcoholics. *Am J Clin Nutr* 27:572–579.
38. Lumeng, L., and T.K. Li. 1974. Vitamin B6 metabolism in chronic alcohol abuse. *J of Clin Investigation* Vol. 53.
39. Hines, J.D. and D.H. Cowan. 1970. Studies on the pathogenesis of alcohol-induced sideroblastic bone-marrow abnormalities. *NEJM* 238:9.
40. Leevy, C.M., H. Baker, W. ten Hove, O. Frank, and G.R. Cherrick. 1965. B-

complex vitamins in liver disease of the alcoholic. *Amer J Clin Nutr* 16:4.

41. Lieber, C.S., E. Baraona, M.A. Leo, and A. Garro. 1987. Metabolism and metabolic effects of ethanol, including interaction with drugs, carcinogens and nutrition. *Mutat Res* 186:201–233.

42. Halsted, C.H., and C. Heise. 1987. Ethanol and vitamin metabolism. *Pharmac Ther* 34:453–464.

43. Aoki, K., Y. Ito, R. Sasaki, M. Ohtani, N. Hamajima, and A. Asano. 1987. Smoking, alcohol drinking and serum carotenoids levels. *Jpn J Cancer Res Gann* 78:1049–1056.

44. Fazio, V., D.M. Flint, and M.L. Wahlqvist. 1981. Acute effects of alcohol on plasma ascorbic acid in healthy subjects. *Am J Clin Nutr* 34:2394–2396.

45. Pelletier, O. 1975. Vitamin C and cigarette smokers. Second Conference on Vitamin C. *Ann NY Acad Sci* 258:156–166.

46. U.S. Department of Health, Education and Welfare. The health consequences of smoking. January 1973.

47. Hornig, D.H., and B.E. Glatthaar. 1985. Vitamin C and smoking: Increased requirement of smokers. *Int J Vit Nutr Res Suppl* 27:139–155.

48. Menkes, M.S., G.W. Constock, J.P. Vuilleumier, K.J. Helsing, A.A. Rider, and R. Brookmeyer. 1986. Vitamin C is lower in smokers. *NEJM* 315:1250–4.

49. Chow, C.K., R.R. Thacker, C. Changchit, R.B. Bridges, S.R. Rehm, J. Humble, and J. Turbek. 1986. Lower levels of vitamin C and carotenes in plasma of cigarette smokers. *J Am Coll Nutr* 5:305–312.

50. Witter, F.R., D.A. Blake, R. Baumgardner, E.D. Mellits and J.R. Niebyl. 1982. Folate, carotene, and smoking. *Am J Obstet Gynecol* 144:857.

51. Gerster, H. 1987. Beta-carotene and smoking. *J Nutr Growth Cancer* 4:45–49.

52. Pacht, E.R., H. Kaseki, J.R. Mohammed, D.G. Cornwell, and W.B. Davis. 1986. Deficiency of vitamin E in the alveolar fluid of cigarette smokers: Influence on alveolar macrophage cytotoxicity. *J Clin Invest* 77:789–796.

53. Serfontein, W.J., J. B. Ubbink, L.S. DeVilliers, and P.J. Becker. 1986. Depressed plasma pyridoxal-5'-phosphate levels in tobacco-smoking men. *Atherosclerosis* 59:341–346.

54. Who's dieting and why. A.C. Nielsen Co. 1978.

55. Welsh, S.O., and R.M. Marston. 1982. Review of trends in food used in the United States, 1909 to 1980. *J A Dietetic Assn* August 1982.

56. Kasper H. 1964. Vitamins in prevention and therapy: Recent findings in vitamin research. Fortschritte der Medizin 82:22. Institute for Nutritional Sciences. Justus–Liebig University, Giessen, Germany.

57. Horo, E.H., M. Brin, and W.W. Faloon. Fasting in obesity: Thiamine depletion as measured by erythrocyte activity changes. *The Archives of Internal Medicine* 117:175–81.

58. Fisher, M.C. and P.A. Lachance. 1985. Nutrition evaluation of published weight-reducing diets. *J Am Diet Assoc* 85:450–454.

59. Bristrian, Bruce, et al. 1976. Prevalence of malnutrition in general medical patients. *JAMA* (Apr. 12) 235 (15).

60. Lemoine et al. 1980. Vitamin B1, B2, B6 and status in hospital inpatients. *Am J Clin Nutr* (December): 33.

61. Leevy, et al. 1965. Incidence and significance of hypovitaminemia in a randomly selected municipal hospital population. *Amer J Clin Nutr* (Oct. 17).

62. Driezen, S. 1979. Nutrition and the immune response—a review. *Internat J Vit Nur*, Res. 49.

63. Beisel, et al. 1981. Single-nutrient effects on immunologic functions. *JAMA* (Jan. 2.) 245 (1).

64. Leevy C.M. 1972. Vitamin therapy: It means more than simply giving vitamins. *Drug Therapy* (February).

65. Pollack, S.V. 1979. Nutritional factors affecting wound healing. *J Dermatol Surg Oncol* (August):5:8.

66. Kaminsky, M.V. and Allan Windborn. 1978. Nutritional assessment guide. Midwest Nutrition, Educational and Research Foundation, Inc.

67. Pao and Mickle. Problem nutrients in the United States.

68. Nationwide Food Consumption Sur-

vey, Spring 1980. U.S. Dept of Agriculture, Science and Education Administration, Beltsville, MD.

69. Dietary intake source data. United States 1976-80.

70. Kirsch, A. and W.R. Bidlack. 1987. Nutrition and the elderly: Vitamin status and efficacy of supplementation. *Nutr* 3:305–314.

71. Baker, H., S.P. Jaslow, and O. Frank. 1978. Severe impairment of dietary folate utilization in the elderly. *J Am Geriatrics Soc* 26:218–221.

72. Pao and Mickle. Problem nutrients in the United States.

73. U.S. Department of Agr. Nationwide Food Consumption Survey.

74. First Health and Nutrition Examination Survey. 1971. U.S. Public Health Service. Health Resources Administration. U.S. Dept. of Health, 72.

75. Connelly, T.J., A. Becker, and J.W. McDonald. 1982. Bachelor scurvy. *Intl J Dermatol* 21:209–211.

76. Schorah, C.J. 1978. Inapproprate vitamin C reserves: Their frequency and significance in an urban population. In *The importance of vitamins to health*, ed. T.G. Taylor. Lancaster, England: MTP Press, 61–72.

77. Garry, P.J., J.S. Goodwin, W.C. Hunt, E.M. Hooper, and A.G. Leonard. 1982. Nutritional status in a healthy elderly population: Dietary and supplemental intakes. *Am J Clin Nutr* 36:319–331.

78. Pao and Mickle. Problem nutrients in the United States.

79. Clark, A.J., S. Mossholder, and R. Gates. 1987. Folacin status in adolescent females. *Am J Clin Nutr* 46:302–306.

80. Sumner, S.K., M. Liebman, and L.M. Wakefield. 1987. Vitamin A status of adolescent girls. *Nutr Rep Intl* 35:423–431.

81. Lee, C.J. 1978. Nutritional status of selected teenagers in Kentucky. *Am J Clin Nutr* 31:1453–1464.

82. Saito, N., M. Kimura, A. Kuchiba, and Y. Itokawa. 1987. Blood thiamine levels in outpatients with diabetes mellitus. *J Nutr Sci Vitaminol* 33:421–430.

83. Mooradian, A.D., and J.E. Morley. 1987. Micronutrient status in diabetes mellitus. *Am J Clin Nutr* 45:877–895.

84. Pao and Mickle. Problem nutrients in the United States.

85. Vobecky, J.S., and J. Vobecky. 1988. Vitamin status of women during pregnancy. In *Vitamins and minerals in pregnancy and lactation*, ed. H. Berger. Nestle Nutrition Workshop Series, Vol. 16. Nestec Ltd. New York: Vevey/Raven Press, Ltd., 109–111.

86. Shenai, J.P., F. Chytil, A. Jhaveri, and M.T. Stahlman. 1981. Plasma vitamin A and retinol-binding protein in premature and term neonates. *J Pediatr* 99:302–305.

87. Heinonen, K., I. Mononen, T. Mononen, M. Parviainen, I. Penttila, and K. Launiala. 1986. Plasma vitamin C levels are low in premature infants fed human milk. *Am J Clin Nutr* 43:923–924.

88. Vitamin E status of premature infants. 1986. *Nutr Rev* 44:166–167.

89. Dietary intake source data. United States 1976-80.

90. Pao and Mickle. Problem nutrients in the United States.

91. First Health and Nutrition Examination Survey. U.S. Public Health Service.

92. Pao and Mickle. Problem nutrients in the United States.

93. Peterkin, B.B., R.L. Kerr, and M.Y. Hama. Nutritional adequacy of diets of low income households. *J Nut Ed* 14(3):102.

94. Roe, D.A. 1985. *Drug-Induced Nutritional Deficiencies*, 2nd ed. Westport, CT: AVI Publishing Company, Inc., 1–87.

95. Brin, M. 1978. Drugs and environmental chemicals in relation to vitamin needs. In *Nutrition and Drug Interrelations*, ed. J.N. Hathcock and J. Coon. New York: Academic Press, 131–150.

96. Driskell, J.A., J.M. Geders, and M.C. Urban. 1976. Vitamin B6 status of young men, women, and women using oral contraceptives. *J Lab Clin Med* 87:813–821.

97. Prasad, A.S., K.Y. Lei, D. Oberleas, K.S. Moghissi, and J.C. Stryker. 1975. Effect of oral contraceptive agents on nutrients: II. Vitamins. *Am J Clin Nutr* 28:385–391.

98. Rivers, J.M., and M.M. Devine. 1972. Plasma ascorbic acid concentrations and oral contraceptives. *Am J Clin Nutr* 25:684–689.

99. Truswell, A.S. 1985. Drugs affecting nutritional state. *Br Med J* 291:1333–1337.

100. Benton and Roberts. 1988. Effect of vitamin and mineral supplementation on intelligence of a sample of school children. *Lancet* (Jan. 23):140–144.

101. Campbell, et al. 1988. Vitamins, minerals, and I.Q. *Lancet* (Sept 24):744–745.

102. Letters to the Editor. 1988. Vitamin/mineral supplementation and non-verbal intelligence. *Lancet* (Feb. 20):407–409.

103. Grantham-McGregor, S.M., et al. 1991. Nutritional supplementation, psychosocial stimulation, and mental development of stunted children: The Jamaican study. *Lancet* 338:1–5.

104. Brown, et al. 1972. *J Pediatrics* 81:714.

105. Webb and Oski. 1973. Iron deficiency and IQ. *J Pediatr* 82:827–30.

106. Grantham-McGregor, et al. Nutritional supplementation, psychosocial stimulation, and mental development.

107. Brown, et al. 1972.

108. Benton, et al. 1987. Glucose improves attention and reaction. *Biol Psychol* 24:95–100.

109. Benton. 1981. Influence of vitamin C on psychological testing. *Psychopharmacology* 75:98–99.

110. Pfeiffer and Braverman. 1982. Zinc, the brain and behavior. *Biol Psychiat* 17:513–31.

111. Brin. 1973. Behavioral effects of protein and energy deficits. DHEW (NIH) publication No:79-1966. Washington, D.C.

112. Nutrition: A study of consumers: Attitudes and behavior toward eating at home and out of home. 1978. First Woman's Day/FMI Family Food Study, conducted by Yankelovich, Skelly and White, Inc.

113. Peto, R., R. Doll, J.D. Buckley,and M.B. Sporn. 1981. Can dietary beta-carotene materially reduce human cancer rates? *Nature* 290:201.

114. Bendich, A. 1989. *Antioxidant vitamins and their function in immune responses.* New York: Plenum Publishing Corp.

115. World Health Organization. 1974. Technical Report. Ser. No. 557.

116. Dietary intake of carotenes and the carotene gap. 1988. *Clin Nutri* (May-June).

117. Bendich, A. 1988. Safety of beta-carotene. Review. *Nutr Cancer* 11:207–214.

118. Meltzer, M.S., and B.E. Cohen. 1974 Tumor regression by Mycobaterium-bovis (strain BCG) enhanced by vitamin A. *J Natl Cancer Inst* 53:585.

119. Kurata, T., and M. Micksche. 1977. Immunoprophalaxis in Lewis lung tumor with vitamin A and BCG. *Sci* 5:277.

120. Lotan, R. 1979. Different susceptibilities of human melanoma and breast carcinoma cell lines to retinoic acid-induced growth inhibition. *Cancer Res* 39:1014.

121. Lotan, R. Different susceptibilities.

122. Micksche, M., C. Cerni, O. Kokron, et al. 1977. Stimulation of immune response in lung cancer patients by vitamin A therapy. *Oncology* 34:234.

123. Mettlin, C., S. Graham, and M. Swanson. 1979. Vitamin A and lung cancer. *J Nat Cancer Inst* 62:1435.

124. Krishnan, S., U.N. Bhuyan, et al. 1974. Effect of vitamin A and protein calories undernutrition on immune response. *Immunol* 27:383.

125. Genta, V.M., D.G. Kaufmann, C.C. Harris, et al. 1974. Vitamin A deficiency enhances binding of benzo(a)pyrene to tracheal epithelial DNA. *Nature* 247:48.

126. Rosenberg, H., and A.N. Felzman. 1974. In *The book of vitamin therapy.* New York: Berkley Publishing Corp.

127. *A pharmacological basis of therapeutics.* 1977. 5th ed., ed. L.S. Goodman, and A. Gilman. New York: Macmillan.

128. Bendich and Langseth. 1989. Safety of vitamin A. *Am J Clin Nutr* 49:358-371.

129. Vitamin D: New perspective. 1987. *Lancet* (May 16):1122–1123.

130. Reitsma, et al. 1983. Regulation of

myc gene expression. *Nature* 306:492–495.

131. Reichel, et al. 1989. Role of vitamin D in the endocrine system in health and disease. *NEJM* 320:980–991.
132. Garland, et al. 1989. Serum vitamin D and colon cancer—8 year prospective study. *Lancet* (Nov. 18):1176–1178.
133. Rosenberg and Felzman. In *Book of vitamin therapy*.
134. Jaffe, W. 1946. The influence of wheat germ on the production of tumors in rats by methylcholanthrene. *Exp Med Surg* 4:278.
135. Haber, S.L., and R.W. Wissler. 1962. Effect of vitamin E on carcinogenicity of methylcholanthrene. *Proc Soc Exp Biol Med* 111:774.
136. Harman, D. 1969. Dibenzanthracene induced cancer: Inhibition effect of dietary vitamin E. *Clin Res* 17:125.
137. Monson, R.R., S. Yen, and B. Mac-Mahon. 1976. Chronic mastitis and carcinoma of the breast. *Lancet* 2:224.
138. Leis, H.P., and C.S. Kwon. 1979. Fibrocystic disease of the breast. *J Reprod Med* 22:291.
139. London, R., D. Solomon, E. London, et al. 1978. Mammary dysplasia: Clinical response and urinary excretion of 11-desoxy 17 keto-steroids and pregnandiol following alpha-tocopherol therapy. *Breast, Diseases of the Breast* 4(2):19.
140. London, R., G.S. Sundaram, M. Schultz, et al. 1981. Alpha-tocopherol, mammary dysplasia and steroid hormones. *Cancer Res.*
141. Ceriello, et al. 1991. Vitamin E reduction of protein glycosylation in diabetics. *Diabetes Care* 14:68–72.
142. Bendich and Machlin. 1988. Safety of oral intake of vitamin E: A Review. *Am J Clin Nutr* 48:612–9.
143. Vitamin E. 1989. Tenth Edition of Recommended Dietary Allowances. National Research Council. National Academy Press. Washington D.C.
144. Bendich and Machlin. Safety of oral intake of vitamin E.
145. Guggenheim, K., and E. Buechler. 1946. Thiamine deficiency and susceptibility of rats and mice to infection with Salmonella typhimurium. *Proc Soc Exp Biol Med* 61:413.
146. Yunis, J. 1984. Fragile sites and predisposition to leukemia and lymphoma. *Cancer Genetics and Cytology* 12:85–88.
147. Yunis and Soreng. 1984. Constitutive fragile sites and cancer. *Science* 226:1199–1204.
148. Morgan, A.F., M. Groody, and H.E. Axelrod. 1946. Pyridoxine deficiency in dogs as affected by level of dietary protein. *Am J Physiol* 146:723.
149. National Heart, Lung, and Blood Institute: Report of the National Cholesterol Education Program: Expert panel on detection, evaluation, and treatment of high blood cholesterol levels in adults. 1988. *Arch Intern Med* 148:36–69.
150. Morgan, Groody, and Axelrod. Pyridoxine deficiency.
151. Robson, L.C., and M.R. Schwartz. 1975. Vitamin B6 deficiency and the lymphoid system. I. Effects on cellular immunity and *in vitro* incorporation of ^{3}H-uridine by small lymphocytes. *Cell Immunol* 16:145.
152. Kamm, J.J., T. Dashman, A.H. Conney, and J.J. Burns. 1973. Protective effects of ascorbic acid on hepatotoxicity caused by sodium nitrite plus aminopyrine. *Proc Natl Acad Sci* 70:743.
153. Weisburger, J.H. 1979. Mechanism of action of diet as a carcinogen. *Cancer* 43:1987.
154. Pipkin, G.E., R. Nishimura, L. Banowsky, and J.U. Schlegel. 1967. Stabilization of urinary 3 hydroxyanthranilic acid by oral administration of L-ascorbic acid. *Proc Soc Exp Biol Med* 126:702.
155. Schlegel, J.U. 1975. Proposed uses of ascorbic acid in prevention of bladder carcinoma. *Ann NY Acad Sci* 258:423.
156. Gluttenplan, J.B. 1978. Mechanism of inhibition of ascorbate of microbial mutagenesis induced by N-nitroso compounds. *Cancer Res* 38:2018.
157. Pauling, L. 1972. Preventive nutrition. *Medicine on the Midway* 27:15.
158. Cameron, E. 1966. In *Hyaluronidase and cancer*. New York: Pergamon Press.
159. Bendich. Antioxidant vitamins and their function in immune response.

160. Herbert, V.D. 1977. *Contemp Nutr* 2(10).
161. Hoffer, A. 1971. Ascorbic acid and toxicity. *NEJM* 285:635.
162. Klenner, F.R. 1971. Vitamin C and toxicity. *J Appl Nutr* 23:61.
163. Schrauzer, G.N., and D.A. White. 1978. Selenium in human nutrition: Dietary intakes and effects of supplementation. *Bioinorganic Chem* 8:303.
164. Schrauzer, G.N., D.A. White, and C.J. Sneider. 1977. Cancer mortality correlation studies. III. Statistical associations with dietary selenium intakes. *Bioinorganic Chem* 7:23–34, 35–56.
165. Shamberger, R.J. 1966. Protection against cocarcinogenesis by antioxidants. *Experientia* 22:116.
166. Shamberger, R.J., and C. Willis. 1971. Selenium distribution and human cancer mortality. *Clin Lab Sci* 2:211.
167. Shamberger and Willis. Selenium distribution and human cancer mortality.
168. Ip, C., D.K. Sinha. 1981. Enhancement of mammary tumorigenesis by dietary selenium deficiency in rats with a high polyunsaturated fat intake. *Cancer Res* 41:31.
169. Medina, R., et al. 1981. Editorial. Selenium may act as cancer inhibitor. *JAMA* 246:1510.
170. Kurkela, P. 1977. The health of Finnish diet. 22nd Gen. Conf. Internat. Fed. of Agricultural Producers. Helsinki, Finland.
171. Chinese Academy of Medical Sciences. 1977. Keshan Disease Group. Beijing. Epidemiologic studies on the etiologic relationship of selenium and Keshan disease. *Chin Med J* 92:477.
172. Schrauzer, White, and Sneider. Cancer mortality.
173. Young, V.R., and D. Richardson. 1979. Nutrients, vitamins, and minerals in cancer prevention. Facts and fallacies. *Cancer* 43:2125.
174. Sakurai, H., and K. Tsuchiya. 1975. A tentative recommendation for the maximum daily intake of selenium. *Environ Physiol Biochem* 5:107.
175. Danbolt, N., and K. Closs. 1942. Akrodermatitis enteropathica. *Acta Derm Venereol* 23:127.
176. Good, R.A., G. Fernandes, et al. 1979. Nutrition, immunity, and cancer—a review. *Clin Bull* 9:3–12, 63–75.
177. McMahon, L.J., D.W. Montgomery, A. Guschewsky, et al. 1976. *In vitro* effects of $ZnCl_2$ on spontaneous sheep red blood cells (E) rosette formation by lymphocytes from cancer patients and normal subjects. *Immunol Commun* 5:53.
178. Frost, P., J.C. Chen, I. Rabbini, et al 1977. The effects of zinc deficiency on the immune response. *Proc Clin Biol Res* 14:143.
179. Lennard, E.S., A. B. Bjornson, et al. 1974. An immunologic and nutritional evaluation of burn neutrophil functions. *J Surg Res* 16:286.
180. McCarron, et al. 1985. Blood pressure response to oral calcium in persons with mild to moderate hypertension. *Ann Intern Med* 103:825.
181. Garland, et al. 1985. Dietary vitamin D and calcium and risk of colorectal cancer: A 19 year prospective study in men. *Lancet* i:307.
182. Rozen, et al. 1989. *Gut* 30:650–655.
183. Deary, et al. 1986. Calcium and Alzheimer's disease. *Lancet* (May 24):1219.
184. Dawson-Hughes, et al. 1990. A controlled trial of the effect of calcium supplementation on bone density in postmenopausal women. *NEJM* 323:878–883.
185. Prince, et al. 1991. Prevention of postmenopausal osteoporosis. *NEJM* 325:1189–1195.
186. Recommended Dietary Allowances. 1989. 10th Edition. National Research Council. National Academy Press. Washington, D.C.
187. Sheik, et al. 1990. Calcium bioavailability from two calcium carbonate preparations. *NEJM* 323:921.
188. Bigg, et al. 1981. Magnesium deficiency: Role in arrhythmias complicating acute myocardial infarction. *Med J Aust* i:346–48.
189. Heptinstall, et al. 1986. Letters to the Editor. *Lancet* (March 8):551–552.

190. Flink. 1985. Hypomagnesemia in the patient receiving digitalis. *Arch Int Med* 145:625–626.
191. Paolisso, et al. 1989. Improved insulin response and action by chronic magnesium administration in aged NIDM subjects. *Diabetes Care* 12:265–269.
192. Riggs, et al. 1990. Effect of fluoride treatment on fracture rate in osteoporosis. *NEJM* 322:802–809.
193. Simonen, et al. 1985. Does fluoridation of drinking water prevent bone fragility and osteoporosis? *Lancet* (August 24): 432–434.
194. Farley, et al. 1983. Fluoride directly stimulates proliferation of bone forming cells. *Science* 222:330–332.
195. Muenier, et al. 1989. Increased vertebral bone density in heavy drinkers of mineral water rich in fluoride. *Lancet* (January 21): 152.
196. Newell, et al. 1986. Lack of association between fluoridation and cancer. *Text Med* 82:48–50.
197. Tenth Edition Recommended Dietary Allowances. 1989. National Research Council.
198. Myers, Gianni, and Simone. 1982. Oxidative destruction of membranes by Doxorubicin-iron complex. *Biochemistry* 21:1707–1713.
199. Stevens, et al. 1988. Body iron stores and the risk of cancer. *NEJM* 319:1047–1052.
200. Basu, T.K. 1976. Significance of vitamins in cancer. *Oncology* 33:183.
201. Bertino, J.R. 1979. Nutrients, vitamins, and minerals as therapy. *Cancer* 43:2137.

Chapter 7
Disease Prevention and Treatment Using Nutrients

1. Greenwald. 1984. Manipulation of nutrients to prevent cancer. *Hospital Practice*. (May): 119–134.
2. Menkes, et al. 1986. Serum beta carotene, vitamins A and E, Selenium, and the risk of lung cancer. *NEJM* 315:1250–4.
3. Greenwald, et al. 1989. Chemoprevention of lung cancer. *Chest* 96:14S–17S.
4. Cougeia J., G. Mathe, T. Hercend, et al. 1982. Degree of bronchial metaplasia in heavy smokers and its regression after treatment with a retinoid. *Lancet* 1:710–12.
5. Misset J.L., G. Mathe, G. Santelli, et al. 1985. Regression of bronchial epidermoid metaplasia in heavy smokers with etretinate treatment. *Acta Vitaminol Enzymol* 7:21–25.
6. Heimburger, D.C., C.B. Alexander, R. Birch, C.E. Butterworth, W.C. Bailey and C.L. Krumdieck. 1988. Improvement in bronchial squamous metaplasia in smokers treated with folate and vitamin B12; report of a preliminary randomized, double-blind intervention trial. *J Am Med Assoc* 259:1525–1530.
7. Heimburger, et al. 1988. Improvement in bronchial squamous metaplasia in smokers treated with folate and vitamin B12. *JAMA* 259:1525–1530.
8. Hennekens, et al. 1984. Micronutrients and cancer chemoprevention. *Cancer Detect Prev* 7:147–58.
9. Peto, et al. 1981. Can dietary beta-carotene materially reduce human cancer rates? *Nature* 290:201–8.
10. Hennekens. 1986. Vitamin A analogs in cancer chemoprevention. In *Important Advances in Oncology*. Philadelphia: J. Lippincott, 23–35.
11. Celentano, D.D., A.C. Klassen, C.S. Weisman, and N.B. Rosenhein. 1989. Duration of relative protection of screening for cervical cancer. *Preventive Med* 18:411–22.
12. Romney, S.L., P.R. Plana, C. Duttagupta, et al. 1981. Retinoids and the prevention of cervical dysplasia. *Am J Obstet Gynecol* 14:890–94.
13. Wylie-Rossett, J.A., S.L. Romney, S. Slagle, et al. 1984. Influence of vitamin A on cervical dysplasia and carcinoma in situ. *Nutr Cancer* 6:49–57.
14. Harris, R.W.C., D. Forman, R. Doll, M.P. Vessey and N.J. Wald. 1986. Cancer of the cervix uteri and vitamin A. *Br J Cancer* 53:653–59.
15. Palan, R.R., S.L. Romney, M. Mikhail, J. Basu and S.H. Vermund. 1988. Decreased plasma beta carotene levels in women with uterine cervical dysplasia and cancer. *J Natl Cancer Inst* 80:454–55.
16. Brock, K., G. Berry, P.A. Mock, R.

MacLennan, A.S. Truswell and L.A. Brinton. 1988. Nutrients in diet and plasma and risk of *in situ* cervical cervical cancer. *J Natl Cancer Inst* 80:580–85.

17. Wassertheil-Smoller, S., S.L. Romney, J. Wylie-Rosett, et al. 1981. Dietary vitamin C and uterine cervical dysplasia. *Am J Epidemiol* 114:714–24.

18. Romney, S.L., C. Duttagupta, J. Basu, et al. 1985. Plasma vitamin C and uterine cervical dysplasia. *Am J Obstet Gynecol* 151:976–80.

19. Marshall, Jr., S. Graham, T. Byers, M. Swanson and J. Brasure. 1983. Diet and smoking in the epidemiology of cancer of the cervix. *J Natl Cancer Inst* 70:847–51.

20. LaVecchia, C., S. Franceschi, A. Decarli, A. Gentile, M. Fasoli, S. Pampallona, and G. Togoni. 1984. Dietary vitamin A and the risk of invasive cervical cancer. *Int J Cancer* 34:319–22.

21. Verreault, F., J. Chu, M. Mandelson, and K. Shy. 1985. A case-control study of diet and invasive cervical cancer. *Int J Cancer* 43:1050–54.

22. Bjelke, E. 1974. Epidemiologic studies of cancer of the stomach, colon and rectum with special emphasis on the role of diet. *Scan J Gastroenterol* (Suppl) 9:1–235.

23. Stahelin, H.B., F. Rosel, E. Buess and G. Brubacher. 1984. Cancer, vitamins and plasma lipids: Prospective Basel study. *J Natl Cancer Inst* 73:1463–68.

24. Correa, P., Cuello, L.F. Fajardo, W. Haenszel, et al. 1983. Diet and gastric cancer: Nutrition survey in a high-risk area. *J Natl Cancer Inst* 70:673–78.

25. Risch, H.A., M. Jain, N.W. Choi, et al. Dietary factors and the incidence of cancer of the stomach. *Am J Epidemiol* 122:947.

26. Trichopoulos, D., G. Ouranos, N.E. Day, et al. 1985. Diet and cancer of the stomach: A case-control study in Greece. *Int J Cancer* 36:291–97.

27. LaVecchia, C., E. Negri, A. Decarli, et al. 1987. A case-control study of diet and gastric cancer in Northern Italy. *Int J Cancer* 40:484–89.

28. Burr, M.L., I.M. Samloff, C.J. Bates, and R.M. Holliday. 1987. Atrophic gastritis and vitamin C status in two towns with different stomach cancer rates. *Br J Cancer* 56:163–67.

29. You, W.C., W.J. Blot, Y.S. Change, et al. 1988. Diet and high risk of stomach cancer in Shandong, China. *Cancer Res* 48:3518–23.

30. Buiatti, E., D. Palli, A. Decarli, et al. 1989. A case-control study of gastric cancer and diet in Italy. *Int Cancer* 44:611–16.

31. Graham, S., A.M. Lillienfeld, and J.E. Tidings. 1967. Dietary and purgation factors in the epidemiology of gastric cancer. *Cancer* 20:2224–34.

32. Correa, P. 1985. Mechanism of gastric carcinogenesis. In *Diet and Human Carinogenesis*, ed. J.V. Joossens, M.J. Hill, and J. Geboers. New York: Elsevier Science Publishers B.V., 109–15.

33. Sipponen, P., K. Sepala, M. Aarynen, T. Helske, and P. Kettunen. 1989. Chronic gastritis and gastroduodenal ulcer: A case-control study on risk of coexisting duodenal or gastric ulcer in patients with gastritis. *Gut* 30:922–29.

34. Rathbone, B.J., A.W. Johnson, J.I. Wyatt, et al. 1989. Ascorbic acid: A factor concentrated in human gastric juice. *Clin Sci* 76:237–41.

35. Sobala, G.M., C.J. Schorah, M. Sanderson, et al. 1989. Ascorbic acid in the human stomach. *Gastroenterol* 97:357–363.

36. Fontham, E., D. Zavala, P. Correa, et al. 1986. Diet and chronic atrophic gastritis: A case-control study. *J Natl Cancer Inst* 76:621–27.

37. Sobala, Schorah, Sanderson, et al. Ascorbic acid in the human stomach.

38. Haenszel, W.P., et al. 1985. Serum micronutrient levels in relation to gastric pathology. *Int J Cancer* 36:43–48.

39. Schwartz, J., D. Suda, and G. Light. 1986. Beta carotene is associated with the regression of hamster buccal pouch carcinoma and induction of tumor necrosis factor in macrophages. *Biochem Biophys Res Communic* 136:1130–35.

40. Shklar, G., J. Schwartz, D. Grau, et al. 1980. Inhibition of hamster buccal pouch carcinogenesis by 13-cis

retinoic acid. *Oral Surg* 50:45–52.

41. Shklar, G., P. Marefat, A. Kornhauser, et al. 1980. Retinoid inhibition of lingual carcinogenesis. *Oral Surg* 49:325–332.

42. Shklar, G. 1982. Oral mucosal in hamsters: Inhibition by vitamin E. *JNCL* 68:791–97.

43. Odukoya, O., F. Hawach, and G. Shklar. 1984. Retardation of experimental oral cancer by topical vitamin E. *Nutrition and Cancer* 6:98–104.

44. Suda, D., J. Schwartz, and G. Shklar. 1986. Inhibition of experimental oral carcinogenesis by topical beta carotene. *Carcinogenesis* 7:711–15.

45. Koch, H.J. 1978. Biochemical treatment of precancerous oral lesions; the effectiveness of various analogues of retinoic acid. *J Maxillofac Surg* 6:59–63.

46. Koch, H.J. 1981. Effects of retinoids on precancerous lesions of oral mucosa. In *Retinoids: Advances in Basic Research and Therapy*, ed. C.E. Orfanos, O. Braun-Falco, E.M. Barber, et al. Berlin: Springer-Verlag, 307–312.

47. Shah, J.P., E.W. Strong, J.J. DeCosse, et al. 1983. Effect of retinoids on oral leukoplasia. *Am J Surg* 146:466–70.

48. Hong, W.K., J. Endicott, L.M. Itrl, et al. 1986. 13-cis retinoic acid in the treatment of oral leukoplakia. *NEJM* 315:1501–5.

49. Stich, H.P., M.P. Rosin, A.P. Hornby, B. Mathew, R. Sankarangrayanan, et al. 1988. Remission of oral leukoplakias and micronuclei in tobacco/betal quid chewer treated with beta carotene and with beta carotene plus vitamin A. *Int J Cancer* 42:195–99.

50. Stich, H.F., A.P. Hornby, B. Mathew, et al. 1988. Response of oral leukoplakias to the administration of vitamin A. *Cancer Letters* 40:93–101.

51. Stich, H.F., W. Stich, M. Rosin, and M. Valletera. 1984. Use of the micronucleus test to monitor the effect of vitamin A, beta carotene and canthaxanthin on the buccal mucosa of betel nut/tobacco chewers. *Int J Cancer* 34:745–50.

52. Stich, H.F., A.P. Hornby, and B.P. Dunn. 1985. A pilot beta carotene intervention trial with insults using smokeless tobacco. *Int J Cancer* 36:321–27.

53. Garewal, H.S., V. Allen, D. Killen, et al. Beta carotene (BC) is an effective, nontoxic agent for the treatment of premalignant lesions of the oral cavity. *J Clin Onco* (in press).

54. Garewal, et al. 1991. Response of oral leukoplakia to beta-carotene. *J Clin Oncol.*

55. Xu, et al. 1990. Effect of chronic oral administration of B-carotene on plasma tocopherol concentration in normal subjects. *Proc Am Assoc Cancer Res* 31:126.

56. Meyskens, F. 1990. Coming of age—the chemoprevention of cancer. *NEJM* 323:825–27.

57. Wattenberg. 1985. Chemoprevention of cancer: A review. *Cancer Research* 45:1–8.

58. Sporn. 1983. Retinoids and suppression of carcinogens. Hospital practice. *National Cancer Institute* (October): 83–98.

59. Goodman. 1984. Vitamin A and retinoids in health and disease. *NEJM* 310:1023–1031.

60. Pryor. 1987. Views on wisdom of using antioxidant vitamin supplements. *Free Rad Bio Med* 3:189–191.

61. Bieri. 1987. Are the recommended allowances for dietary antioxidants adequate? *Free Rad Bio Med* 3:193–197.

62. Draper and Byrd. 1987. Micronutrients and cancer prevention. *Free Rad Bio Med* 3:203–207.

63. Bertram, et al. Rationale and strategies for chemoprevention of cancer in humans. *Cancer Research* 47:3012–31.

64. Wood. 1985. Possible prevention of adriamycin induced allopecia by tocopherol. *NEJM* 312:1060.

65. Jialal, I., et al. 1990. Physiologic levels of ascorbate inhibit the oxydative modification of low density lipoprotein. *Atherosclerosis* 82:185–191.

66. Steinberg, D., et al. 1989. Beyond cholesterol, modifications of low density lipoprotein that increase its atherogenecity. *NEJM* 320(14):1915–24.

67. Frei, B., et al. 1989. Ascorbate is an outstanding antioxidant in human blood plasma. *Proc Natl Acad Sci* 86:6377–6381.

68. Coetzee, W.A. 1990. Reperfusion damage: Free radicals mediate delayed membrane changes rather than early ventricular arrhythmias. *Cardiovasc Res* 24:156–64.
69. Editorial. 1991. Myocardial stunning. *Lancet* 337:585–86.
70. Riemersma, et al. Risk of angina pectoris and plasma concentrations of vitamins A, C, and E, and carotene. *Lancet* 337:1–6.
71. Smithells. 1983. Vitamin supplementation for prevention of neural tube defect. *Lancet* 1:1027–1031.
72. Mulinare, et al. 1988. Periconceptual use of multivitamins and neural tube defects. *JAMA* 260:3141–3145.
73. MRC Vitamins Study Research Group. 1991. Prevention of neural tube defects: Results of the medical research council vitamin study. *Lancet* 338:131–137.
74. Dearden. 1985. Ischemic brain. *Lancet* (Aug 3): 255–260.
75. Lohr, et al. 1987. Vitamin E in tardive dyskinesia. *Lancet* (April 18): 913–914.
76. Traber, et al. 1987. Lack of tocopherol in peripheral nerves in peripheral neuropathy. *NEJM* 317:262–266.
77. Editorial. 1988. Does topical tretinoin prevent cutaneous aging? A review. *Lancet* (April 30): 977–978.
78. Gaby and Machlin. 1991. Vitamin E. In *Vitamin Intake and Health, A Scientific Review*. New York: Marcel Dekker, Inc., 85–87.
79. Taylor. 1992. Effect of nutrition on cataract and macular degeneration. In *Beyond Deficiency: New Views on the Function and Health Effects of Vitamins*. New York: New York Academy of Sciences, 10.
80. Jacques, P.F., et al. 1988. Antioxidant status in persons with and without senile cataract. *Arch Opthalmol* 106:337–340.
81. Leske, M.C., et al. 1991. The lens opacities case-control study: risk factors for cataract. *Arch Opthalmol* 109:244–255.
82. Hankinson, S., et al. 1992. Nutrient intake and cataract extraction in women: A prospective study. *Br Med J* 305:335–339.
83. Salim. 1989. Scavenging free radicals to prevent stress induced gastric mucosal injury. *Lancet* (Dec 9): 1390.

84. Rahmathullah, et al. Reduced mortality among children in southern India receiving a small weekly dose of vitamin A. *NEJM* 323:929–35.
85. Hussey, et al. 1990. A randomized controlled trial of vitamin A in children with severe measles. *NEJM* 323:160–64.
86. Keusch, G. 1990. Vitamin A supplements—too good not to be true. *NEJM* 323:985–86.
87. Editorial. 1990. Vitamin A and malnutrition/infection complex in developing countries. *Lancet* 336:1349–50.
88. West, K., et al. 1991. Efficacy of vitamin A in reducing preschool child mortality in Nepal. *Lancet 338: 67–71*.
89. Cohn and Bone. 1992. New strategies in nonantibiotic treatment of gramnegative sepsis. *Cleveland Clinic J Med* 59(6): 608–615.
90. Delmi, et al. 1990. Dietary supplementation in elderly patients with fractured neck of femur. *Lancet* 335:1013–1016.
91. Kragballe, et al. 1991. Double blind, right/left comparison of calcipotriol and betamethasone valerate in treatment of *psoriasis vulgaris*. *Lancet* 337: 193–196.
92. Editorial. 1988. Retinoids and control of cutaneous malignancy. *Lancet* (Sept 3): 545–547.
93. Kessler, et al. 1983. Treatment of cutaneous T cell lymphoma with cis-retinoic acid. *Lancet* (June 18): 1345–1348.
94. Degos, et al. 1990. Treatment of first relapse in acute promyelocytic leukemia with all-trans retinoic acid. *Lancet* 336:1440–41.
95. Hong, et al. 1990. Prevention of second primary tumors with isotretinoin in squamous cell carcinoma of the head and neck. *NEJM* 323:795–801.
96. Lippman, S.M., et al. 1991. Vitamin A and interferon effective against skin cancer. *Oncology* 5(9):72.
97. Warrell, R.P., et al. 1991. Differentiation therapy of acute promyelocytic leukemia with tretinoin (all trans-

retinoic acid) *NEJM* 324 (20):1385–93.

98. LoCoco, R., et al. 1991. Molecular evaluation of response to all-trans retinoic acid therapy in patients with acute promylelocytic leukemia. *Blood* 77:1657–59.

99. Mehta, et al. 1984. Treatment of advanced myelophystic syndrome. *Lancet* (Sept 29): 761.

100. Greenberg, P.L. 1991. Treatment of myelodysplastic syndromes. *Blood Rev* 5(1):42–50.

101. Speyer, et al. 1988. Protective effect of ICRF-187 against doxorubicin induced cardiac toxicity in women with breast cancer. *NEJM* 319:745–752.

102. Filppi and Enck. 1990. A review of ADR-529: A new cardioprotective agent. *Clin Oncology* 16–18.

103. Speyer, J., et al. 1992. Cumulative dose-related doxorubicin cardiotoxicity can be prevented by ICRF-187. *Cancer Investigation* 10(1):26.

104. Carlson, R. 1992. Reducing the cardiotoxicity of the anthracyclines. *Oncology* 6(6):95–108.

105. Taper, H., et al. 1989. Potentiation of chemotherapy *in vivo* in an ascitic mouse liver tumor, and growth inhibition *in vitro* in 3 lines of human tumors by combined vitamin C and K3 treatment. European Association for Cancer Research Tenth Biennial Meeting. Sept. Galway, Ireland. p. 72.

106. Shimpo, et al. 1991. Ascorbic acid and adriamycin toxicity. *Am J Clin Nutr* 54:1298S–1301S.

107. Ripoll, E.A., et al. 1986. Vitamin E enhances the chemotherapeutic effects of adriamycin on human prostatic carcinoma cells in vitro. *J Urol* 136(2):529–531.

108. Pieters, R., et al. 1991. Cytotoxic effects of vitamin A in combination with vincristine, daunorubicin and 6-thioguanine upon cells from lymphoblastic leukemic patients. *Jap J Cancer Res* 82(9): 1051–1055.

109. Van Vleet, et al. 1980. *Cancer Treat Reports* 64:315.

110. Singal, P.K., et al. 1988. *Molecular and Cellular Biology* 84:163.

111. Wang, Y.M., et al. 1980. Effect of vitamin E against adriamycin-induced toxicity in rabbits. *Cancer Res* 40:1022–1027.

112. Milei, J., et al. 1986. Amelioration of adriamycin-induced cardiotoxicity in rabbits by prenylamine and vitamins E and A. *Am Heart J* 111:95.

113. Svingen, B., et al. 1981. Protection against adriamycin-induced skin necrosis in the rat by dimethyl sulfoxide and alpha-tocopherol. *Cancer Research* 41:3395–3399.

114. Mills. 1982. Retinoids and cancer. *Soc R Radiotherap and Congress* (May 13).

115. Okunieff, P. 1991. Interactions between ascorbic acid and the radiation of bone marrow, skin, and tumor. *Am J Clin Nutr* 54:1281S–1283S.

116. Meadows, G., et al. 1991. Ascorbate in the treatment of experimental transplanted melanoma. *Am J Clin Nutr* 54:1284S–1291S.

117. Taper, H.S., et al. 1987. Non-toxic potentiation of cancer chemotherapy by combined C and K3 vitamin pre-treatment. *Int J Cancer* 40:575–579.

118. Crary, E.J., et al. 1984. *Medical Hypothesis* 13:77.

119. Sprince, H., et al. 1975. *Agents and Actions* 5(2):164.

120. Poydock, E. 1984. *IRCS Medical Science* 12:813.

121. Holm, et al. 1982. Tocopherol in tumor irradiation and chemotherapy—experimental studies in the rat. Feb 12 Linderstrom-Lang Conference. Selenium, Vitamin E and Glutathioperoxidase (June 25). Icelandic Biochemical Society, p. 118.

122. Kagerud, A., et al. 1980. Effect of tocopherol in irradiation of artificially hypoxic rat tumours. Second Rome International Symposium: Biological Bases and Clinical Implications. Sept. 21. pp. 3–9.

123. Kagerud, A., and Peterson. 1981. Tocopherol in tumour irradiation. *Anticancer Res* 1:35–38.

124. Shen, et al. 1983. Antitumour activity of radiation and vitamin A used in combination on Lewis lung carcinoma. Thirty-first Annual Meeting of the Radiation Research Society. Feb. 27. San Antonio, p. 145.

125. Seifter, et al. 1983. C3HBA tumor therapy with radiation, beta-carotene and vitamin A. A two year follow-up. *Fed Proc* 42:768.
126. Williamson, J.M., et al. 1982. Intracellular cysteine delivery system that protects against toxicity by promoting glutathione synthesis. *Proc Natl Acad Sci* 79:6246–6249.
127. Ohkawa, K., et al. 1988. The effects of co-administration of selenium and cisplatin on cis-platin induced toxicity and antitumour activity. *Br J Cancer* 58:38–41.
128. Waxman, S., et al. 1982. The enhancement of 5-FU antimetabolic activity by leucovorin, menadione, and alpha-tocopherol. *Eur J Cancer Clin Oncol* 18(7): 685–692.
129. Watrach, A.M., et al. 1984. Inhibition of human breast cancer cells. *Cancer Letters* 25:41–47.
130. DeLoecker, W., et al. 1993. Effects of vitamin C and vitamin K3 treatment on human tumor cell growth *in vitro*. Synergism with combined chemotherapy action. *Anticancer Res* 13(1):103–106.
131. Ferrero, D., et al. 1992. Self-renewal inhibition of acute myeloid leukemia clonogenic cells by biological inducers of differentiation. *Leukemia* 6(2):100–106.
132. Schwartz, J.L., et al. 1992. Beta-carotene and/or vitamin E as modulators of alkylating agents in SCC-25 human squamous carcinoma cells. *Canc Chemo and Pharma* 29(3):207–213.
133. Zhang, L., et al. Induction by bufalin on human leukemic cells HL60 . . . and synergistic effect in combination with other inducers. *Cancer Res* 52(17):4634–4641.
134. Hofsli and Waage. 1992. Effect of pyridoxine on tumor necrosis factor activities *in vitro*. *Biotherapy* 5(4):285–290.
135. Petrini, et al. 1991. Synergistic effects of interferon and D3. *Haematologica* 76(6): 467–471.
136. Saunders, et al. 1992. Inhibition of ovarian carcinoma cells by taxol combined with vitamin D and adriamycin. *Proc Ann Meet Am Assoc Cancer Res.* 33:A2641.
137. Ermens, A.A., et al. 1987. Enhanced effect of MTX and 5FU on folate metabolism of leukemic cells by B12. *Proc Ann Meet Am Assoc Cancer Res.* 28:275.
138. Dimery, et al. 1992. Reduction in toxicity of high-dose 13-cis-retinoic acid with vitamin E. *Proc Ann Meet Am Soc Clin Oncol.* 11:A399.
139. Wood, L.A. 1985. *NEJM* April 18.
140. Komiyama, et al. 1985. Synergistic combination of 5FU, vitamin A, and cobalt radiation for head and neck cancer. *Auris, Nasus, Larynx* 12 S2:S239–S243.
141. Israel, L., et al. 1985. Vitamin A augmentation of the effects of chemotherapy in metastatic breast cancers after menopause. Randomized trial in 100 patients. *Annales De Medecine Interne* 136(7):551–554.
142. Nagourney, et al. 1987. Menadiol with chemotherapies: feasibility for resistance modification. *Proc Ann Meet Am Soc Clin Oncol.* 6:A132.
143. Ladner, H.L., et al. 1986. In *Vitamins and Cancer*, ed. F.L. Meyskens. Clifton, NJ: Humana Press, 429.
144. Sakamoto, A., et al. 1983. In *Modulation and Mediation of Cancer by Vitamins*. Karger, Basel, 330.
145. Schein, P. 1992. Results of chemotherapy and radiation therapy protection trials with WR-2721. *Cancer Investigation* 10(1):24–26.
146. Santamaria, Benazzo, et al. First clinical case-report (1980–88) of cancer chemoprevention with beta-carotene plus canthaxanthin supplemented to patients after radical treatment.
147. Jaakkola, et al. 1992. Treatment with antioxidant and other nutrients in combination with chemotherapy and irradiation in patients with small cell lung cancer. *Anticancer Res* May–June 12(3): 599–606.
148. Henriksson, et al. 1991. Interaction between cytostatics and nutrients. *Med Oncol Tumor Pharmacother* 8(2):79–86.
149. Simone, C.B. 1992. Use of therapeutic levels of nutrients to augment oncology care. Adjuvant Nutrition in Cancer Treatment Symposium. Nov. 6–7. Tulsa, OK, 72.

Chapter 8
Nutritional Factors

1. Wynder and Gori. 1977. Contribution of the environment to cancer incidence: An epidemiologic exercise. *JNCI* 58:825.

2. The National Academy of Sciences. 1982. *Nutrition, Diet, and Cancer.*

3. Simone, C.B. 1983. *Cancer and Nutrition: A Ten-Point Plan to Reduce Your Chances of Getting Cancer.* New York: McGraw-Hill Book Co.

4. Moody. 1973. *Aboriginal Health.* Canberra, Australia: Australian National University Press, 92.

5. Truswell and Hansen. 1976. Medical research among the Kung. In Lee and DeVore Ed S. Kalahari *Hunter-Gatherers.* Cambridge, Mass: Harvard University Press.

6. Eaton, Konner. 1985. Paleolithic nutrition. *NEJM* 312 (5):283–289.

7. Tannenbaum, A. 1942. The genesis and growth of tumors. III. Effects of a high-fat diet. *Cancer Res* 2:468.

8. Rosen, P., S.M. Hellerstein, and C. Horwitz. 1981. The low incidence of colorectal cancer in a "high-risk" population. *Cancer* 48:2692.

9. Wydner, E.L., et al. 1969. Environmental factors of cancer of the colon and rectum. II. Japanese epidemiological data. *Cancer* 32:1210.

10. Phillips, R.L. 1975. Role of life-style and dietary habits in risk of cancer among Seventh-Day Adventists. *Cancer Res* 35:3513.

11. Lyon, J.L., J.W. Gardner, M.R. Klauber, and C.R. Smart. 1977. Low cancer incidence and mortality in Utah. *Cancer* 39:2608.

12. Baptista, J., W.R. Bruce, I. Gupta, J. Krepinsky, R. Van Tassell, T.D. Wilkins. 1984. On distribution of different fecapentaenes, the fecal mutagens, in the human population. *Cancer Letters* 22:299.

13. Bruce, W.R., A.J. Varghese, and R. Farrer. 1977. A mutagen in the feces of normal humans. In *Origins of Human Cancer,* ed. H.H. Hiatt, J.D. Watson, and J.A. Winsten, Cold Spring Harbor Laboratory, Cold Spring Harbor, NJ, 1641–44.

14. Drori, D., and Y. Folman. 1976. Environmental effects on longevity in the male rat: Exercise, mating, castration, and restricted feeding. *Exp Gerontol* 11:25.

15. Jose, D.G., and R.A. Good. 1973. Quantitative effects of nutritional protein and caloric deficiency upon the immune response to tumors in mice. *Cancer Res* 33:807.

16. Kraybill, H.F. 1963. Carcinogenesis associated with foods, food additives, food degradation products and related dietary factors. *Clin Pharmacol Ther* 4:73.

17. Ross, M.H., and G. Bras. 1971. Lasting influence of early caloric restriction on prevalence of neoplasms in the rat. *J Natl Cancer Inst* 47:1095.

18. Tannenbaum, A. 1959. Nutrition and cancer. In *Physiopathy of Cancer*, 2nd ed., ed. F. Homberger. New York: Hoeber-Harper, 517–62.

19. Armstrong, B., and R. Doll. 1975. Environmental factors and cancer incidence and mortalities in different countries with special reference to dietary practices. *Int J Cancer* 15:617.

20. Gaskill, S.P., et al. 1979. Breast cancer mortality and diet in the United States. *Cancer Res* 39:3628.

21. de Waard, F., and E.A. Baanders-van Halewign. 1974. A prospective study in general practice on breast cancer risk in postmenopausal women. *Int J Cancer* 14:153–160.

22. Hin, T.M., K.P. Chen, and B. MacMahon. 1971. Epidemiologic characteristics of cancer of the breast in Taiwan. *Cancer* 27:1497–1504.

23. Mirra, A.P., P. Cole, and B. MacMahon. 1971. Breast cancer in an area of high parity–Sao Paolo, Brazil. *Cancer Res* 31:77–83.

24. Lew, E.A., and L. Garkinkel. 1979. Variations in mortality by weight among 750,000 men and women. *J Chronic Dis* 32:563–576.

25. Aries, V.C., J.S. Growther, B.S. Drasar, M.J. Hill, and F.R. Ellis. 1971. The effect of a strict vegetarian diet on the fecal flora and fecal steroid concentration. *J Pathol* 103:54.

26. Burkitt, D. 1984. Etiology and prevention of colorectal cancer. *Hospital Practice* (Feb.), vol. 67.

27. *Nutrition and Cancer*, ed. DeWys, W.D. 1983. Seminars in Oncology. 10 (3):255–364.

28. Maier, B., M.A. Flynn, G.C. Burton, R.K. Tsutakawa, and D.J. Hentges. 1974. Effect of high-beef diet on bowel flora: A preliminary report. *Am J Clin Nutr* 27:1470.

29. Jacobs, L. 1987. Effect of dietary fiber on colon cell proliferation. *Prev Medicine* 16:566–571.
30. McKeown-Eyssen, G. 1987. Fiber intake in different populations and colon cancer risk. *Prev Medicine* 16:532–539.
31. McPherson-Kay, R. 1987. Fiber, stool bulk, and bile acid output: Implications for colon cancer risk. *Prev Medicine* 16:540–544.
32. Wynder, E.L., and G.B. Gori. 1977. Contribution of the environment to cancer incidence: An epidemiologic exercise. *J Natl Cancer Inst* 58:825.
33. Wynder, E.L., and B.S. Reddy. 1974. The epidemiology of cancer of the large bowel. *Digestive Diseases* 19:937.
34. *Nutrition and Cancer*, ed. W.D. DeWys. 1983. Seminars in Oncology. 10 (3):1–367.
35. Workshop on Nutrition in Cancer Causation and Prevention. *Cancer Research Supplement.* 1983. 43:2386–2519.
36. Willett and MacMahon. 1984. Diet and cancer: An overview. *NEJM* 310:633–638, 697–703.
37. Diet and Human Carcinogenesis Proceedings. 1986. *Nutrition and Cancer* 8 (1):1–71.
38. Rivlin, et al. 1983. Nutrition and cancer. *Am J Med* 75:843–854.
39. Executive Summary. Diet, Nutrition, and Cancer. 1983. *Cancer Research* 43:3018–3023.
40. Beardshall, et al. 1989. Saturation of fat and pancreatic carcinogenesis. *Lancet* (October 28): 1008–1010.
41. Cohen, L. 1987. Diet and cancer. *Scientific American* 257(5):42–48.
42. Insull, W. 1987. Dietary fats and carcinogenesis. *Prev Medicine* 16:481–484.
43. Reddy, B. 1987. Dietary fat and colon cancer. *Prev Medicine* 16:460–467.
44. Proceeding of a Workshop. 1987. Dietary fat and fiber in carcinogenesis. *Prev Medicine* 16:449–527.
45. National Research Council. 1982. *Diet, Nutrition and Cancer.* Washington, D.C.: National Academy Press.
46. Alcantara, E.N., and E.W. Speckman. 1976. Diet, nutrition, and cancer. *Am J Clin Nutr* 29:1035.
47. Carroll, K.K. 1975. Experimental evidence of dietary factors and hormone dependent cancers. *Cancer Res* 35:3374.
48. Carroll, K.K., E.B. Gammel, and E.R. Plunkett. 1968. Dietary fat and mammary cancer. *Can Med Assoc J* 98:590–594.
49. Drasar, B.S., and D. Irving. 1973. Environmental factors and cancer of the colon and breast. *Br J Cancer* 27:167.
50. Kent, S. 1979. Diet, hormones, and breast cancer. *Geriatrics* 34:83.
51. Paptestas, A.E., D. Panvelliwalla, P. Tartter, S. Miller, D. Pertsemlidis, and A. Aufses. 1982. Fecal steroid metabolites and breast cancer risk. *Cancer* 49:1201.
52. Kolonel, L.N., J.H. Hankin, J. Lee, S.Y. Chu, A.Y. Nomura, and M. Word-Hinds. 1981. Nutrient intakes in relation to cancer incidence in Hawaii. *Br J Cancer* 44:332–339.
53. Gregorio, D.I., L.J. Emrich, S. Graham, J. Marshall, and T. Nemoto. 1985. Dietary fat consumption and survival among women with breast cancer. *JNCI* 75:37–41.
54. Morrison, A.S., C.R. Lowe, B. MacMahon, B.R. Ravnihar, and S. Yuasa. 1977. Incidence, risk factors and survival in breast cancer: Report on five years of follow-up observation. *Europ J Cancer* 13:209–214.
55. Wynder, E.L., T. Kajatani, J. Kuno, J.C. Lucas, Jr., A. DePalo, and J. Farrow. 1963. A comparison of survival rates between American and Japanese patients with breast cancer. *Surg Gynecol Obstet* 117:196–200.
56. Armstrong and Doll. Environmental factors and cancer incidence.
57. Carroll, K.K. Experimental evidence of dietary factors and hormone dependent cancers.
58. Donegan, W.L., A.J. Hartz, and A.A. Rimm. 1978. The association of body weight with recurrent cancer of the breast. *Cancer* 41:1590–1594.
59. Morrison, A.S., C.R. Lowe, B. MacMahon, B. Ravnihar, and S. Yuassa. 1977. Some international differences in treatment and survival in breast cancer. *Int J Cancer* 18:269–273.
60. Tartter, P.I., A.E. Papatestas, J. Ioannovich, M.N. Mulvihill, G. Lesnick, and A.H. Aufses. 1981. Cholesterol and obesity as prognostic factors in breast cancer. *Cancer* 47:2222–2227.

61. Wynder, E.L., F. MacCornack, P. Hill, L.A. Cohen, P.C. Chan, and J.H. Weisburger. 1976. Nutrition and the etiology and prevention of breast cancer. *Cancer Detection and Prevention* 1:293–310.

62. Kolonel, Hankin, Lee, Chu, Nomura, and Word-Hinds. Nutrient intakes in relation to cancer incidence in Hawaii.

63. Nemoto, T., T. Tominago, A. Chamberlain, Z. Iwasa, H. Koyama, M. Hama, I. Bross, and T. Dao. 1977. Differences in breast cancer between Japan and the United States. *J Natl Cancer Inst* 58:193–197.

64. Wynder and Reddy. The epidemiology of cancer of the large bowel.

65. Abe, R., N. Kumagai, M. Kimura, A. Hirosaki, and T. Nakamura. 1976. Biological characteristics of breast cancer in obesity. *Tohoku J Exp Med* 120:351–359.

66. Ward-Hines, M., L.N. Kolonel, A.M.Y. Nomura, and J. Lee. 1982. Stage-specific breast cancer incidence rates by age among Japanese and Caucasian women in Hawaii, 1960-1979. *Br J Cancer* 45:118–123.

67. Boyd, N.F., J.E. Campbell, T. Germanson, D.B. Thomson, D.J. Sutherland, and J.W. Meakin. 1981. Body weight and prognosis in breast cancer. *J Natl Cancer Inst* 67:785–789.

68. Kwa, H.G., R.D. Bulbrook, F. Cleton, et al. 1978. An abnormal early evening peak of plasma prolactin in nulliparous and obese postmenopausal women. *Int J Cancer* 22:691–693.

69. deWaard and Baanders-van Halewign. A prospective study in general practice on breast cancer risk in postmenopausal women.

70. McDonald, R., J. Grodin, and P. Sitteri. 1969. The utilization of plasma androstenedione for estrone production in women in endocrinology. *Excerpta Med Int Congr Ser* 184:770–776.

71. O'Dea, J., R. Wieland, M. Hallberg, L.A. Llerena, E.M. Zorn, and S.M. Genuth. 1979. Effect of dietary weight loss on sex steriod binding, sex steroids and gonadotropins on obese postmenopausal women. *J Lab Clin Med* 93:1004–1008.

72. Goldin, B.R., H.A. Adlercreutz, S.L. Gorbach, J.H. Warren, J.T. Dwyer, L. Swenson, and M.N. Woods. 1982. Estrogen excretion patterns and plasma levels in vegetarian and omnivorous women. NEJM 307(25):1542–47.

73. Santiago-Delpin, E.A., and J. Szepsenwol. 1977. Prolonged survival of skin and tumor allografts in mice on high-fat diets. *J Natl Cancer Inst* 59:459.

74. Stuart, A.E., and A.E. Davidson. 1976. Effect of simple lipids on antibody formation after ingestion of foreign red cells. *J Pathol Bacteriol* 87:305.

75. Burkitt, D. Etiology and prevention of colorectal cancer.

76. Goldin, Adlercreutz, Gorbach, Warren, Dwyer, Swenson, and Woods. Estrogen excretion patterns and plasma levels.

77. *American Journal of Clinical Nutrition.* 1978. Supp No. 31 (Oct. 31).

78. Miller, J.A., and E. C. Miller. 1969. The metabolic activation of carcinogenic aromatic amines and amides. *Prog Exp Tumor Res* 11:273.

79. Haung, C., B.S. Gopalakrishna, and B.L. Nichols. 1978. Fiber, intestinal steroid, and colon cancer. *Am J Clin Nutr* 31:512.

80. Phillips, R.L. Role of life-style and dietary habits in risk of cancer.

81. Rosen, Hellerstein, and Horwitz. The low incidence of colorectal cancer in a "high-risk" population.

82. Lyon, Gardner, Klauber, and Smart. Low cancer incidence and mortality in Utah.

83. Wynder and Reddy. The epidemiology of cancer of the large bowel.

84. Goldin, Adlercreutz, Gorbach, Warren, Dwyer, Swenson, and Woods. Estrogen excretion patterns and plasma levels.

85. Burkitt, D.P. 1975. Large-bowel cancer: An epidemiological jigsaw puzzle. *Natl Cancer Inst* 54:3.

86. MacDonald, I.A., R. Webb, and D.E. Mahony. 1978. Fecal hydroxysteroid dehydrogenase activities in vegetarian Seventh-Day Adventists, control subjects, and bowel cancer patients. *Am J Clin Nutr* 31:S233.

87. Graham, S., and C. Mettlin. 1979. Diet and colon cancer. *Am J Epidemiol* 109:1.

88. Roth, H.P., and M. Hehlman. 1978. Role of dietary fiber in health. Symposium. *Am J Clin Nut* 31(Suppl):51–5191.

89. Hirayama, T. 1979. Diet and cancer. *Nutrition and Cancer* 1(3):67.

90. Kritchevsky, D., and J. Story. 1974. Binding of bile salts in vitro by non-nutritive fiber. *J Nutr* 104:458.

91. MacLennan, M.B., O.M. Jensen, J. Mosbech, and H. Vuoris. 1978. Diet, transit time, stool weight, and colon cancer in two Scandinavian populations. *Am J Clin Nutr* 31:S239.

92. Jain, M., et al. 1980. A case control study of diet and colo-rectal cancer. *Int J Cancer* 26:757.

93. Tannenbaum, A. 1940. The initiation and growth of tumors. Introduction I. Effects of underfeeding. *Am J Cancer* 38:335.

94. Armstrong and Doll. Environmental factors and cancer incidence and mortalities in different countries.

95. Tannenbaum, A. Nutrition and cancer.

96. Kolonel, Hankin, Lee, Chu, Nomura, and Word-Hinds. Nutrient intakes in relation to cancer incidence in Hawaii.

97. Knox, E.G. 1977. Foods and diseases. *Br J Prev Soc Med* 31:71–80.

98. Armstrong and Doll. Environmental factoros and cancer incidence and mortalities in different countries.

99. Jain, M., et al. A case control study of diet and colo-rectal cancer.

100. Drasar and Irving. Environmental factors and cancer of the colon and breast.

101. Hems, G. 1978. The contribution of diet and childbearing to breast cancer rates. *Br J Cancer* 37:974–982.

102. Ames, B.N. 1983. Dietary carcinogens and anticarcinogens. *Science* 221:1256.

103. Ashwood-Smith, M.J., and G.A. Poulton. 1981. *Mutat Res* 85:389.

104. Concon, J.M., D.S. Newburg, and T.W. Swerczek. 1979. Black pepper (piper nigrum):Evidence of carcinogenesis. *Nutr Cancer* 1(3):22.

105. Hirayama, T., and Y. Ito. 1981. Diet and cancer. *Prev Med* 10:614.

106. Tazima, Y. 1982. *Environmental mutagenesis, carcinogenesis, and plant biology*, Vol. 1, ed. E.J. Klekowski, Jr. New York: Praeger, 68–95.

107. Toth, B. 1979. *Naturally occurring carcinogens-mutagens and modulators of carcinogenesis*, ed. E.C. Miller. Tokyo and Baltimore: Japan Scientific Societies Press and University Park Press, 57–65.

108. Tomatis, L., C. Agthe, J. Bartsch, J. Huff, Montesano, R. Saracci, E. Walker, and J.

Wilbourn. 1978. Evaluation of the carcinogenicity of chemicals: A review of the monograph program of the International Agency for Research on Cancer. *Cancer Res* 38:877.

109. Ames, B.N. Dietary carcinogens and anticarcinogens.

110. Stich, H.F., M.P. Rosin, C.H. Wu, and W.D. Powrie. 1981. A comparative genotoxicity study of chlorogenic acid. *Mutat Res* 90:201.

111. Delaney Clause, Sec. 401(a)(2)(C) and Sec. 409(C)(1)(A). Congressional Record.

112. Harris, M. 1983. The revolutionary hamburger. *Psychol Today* 17:6–8.

113. Stafford and Wills. 1989. Consumer demand for increasing convenience food products. *Nat Food Rev* 6:15.

114. Heaney, R., et al. 1982. Calcium, nutrition and bone health in the elderly. *Am J Clin Nutr* 36:supp 5:986–1013.

115. Massachusetts Medical Society Committee on Nutrition. 1989. Fast-food fare: Consumer guidelines. *NEJM* 321:752–756.

116. Young, et al. 1986. Fast-foods. 1986: Nutrient Analysis Diet Curr 13:25–36.

117. Pennington and Church. 1985. *Bowes's and Church's Food Values of Portions Commonly Used*, 14th ed. Philadelphia: J.B. Lippincott.

118. Burr, et al. 1989. Effects of changes in fat, fish, and fiber intakes on death and heart attack. September 30. *Lancet* 757–761.

Chapter 9
Obesity

1. Hannon, B.M., and T.G. Lohman. 1978. The energy cost of overweight in the United States. *Am J Public Health* 68:8.

2. McCay, C.M., M.F. Crowell, and L.A. Maynard. 1935. The effect of retarded growth upon the length of lifespan and upon the ultimate size. *J Nutr* 10:63.

3. Jose, D.G., and R.A. Good. 1973. Quantitative effects of nutritional protein and caloric deficiency upon the immune response to tumors in mice. *Cancer Res* 33:807.

4. Jose, D.G., O. Stutman, and R.A. Good. 1973. Good, long term effects on immune function of early nutritional deprivation. *Nature* 241:57.

5. Manson, et al. 1987. Body weight and longevity: A review. *JAMA* 257:353–358.

6. Tannenbaum, A. 1959. Nutrition and cancer. In *Physiopathy of Cancer*, 2nd ed., ed. F. Homberger. New York: Hoeber-Harper, 517–62.

7. Kraybill, H.F. 1963. Carcinogenesis associated with foods, food additives, food degradation products and related dietary factors. *Clin Pharmacol Ther* 4:73.

8. Jose and Good. Quantitative effects.

9. Drori, D., and Y. Folman. 1976. Environmental effects on longevity in the male rat: Exercise, mating, castration, and restricted feeding. *Exp Gerontol* 11:25.

10. Ross, M.H., and G. Bras. 1971. Lasting influence of early caloric restriction on prevalence of neoplasms in the rat. *J Natl Cancer Inst* 47:1095.

11. National Dairy Council. 1975. Nutrition, diet, and cancer. *Dairy Council Digest* 46(5):25.

12. Gaskill, S.P., W.L. McGuire, et al. 1979. Breast cancer mortality and diet in the United States. *Cancer Res* 39:3628.

13. Sylvester, P.W., et al. 1981. Relationship of hormones to inhibition of mammary tumor development by underfeeding during the "critical period" after carcinogen administration. *Cancer Res* 41:1384.

14. Newberne, P.M., and G. Williams. 1979. Nutritional influences on the cause of infection. In *Resistance to Infectious Diseases*, ed. R.H. Dunlop, and H.W. Moon. Saskatoon: Saskatoon Modern Press.

15. Leonard, P.J., and K.M. MacWilliam. 1964. Cortisol binding in the serum in kwashiorkor. *J Endocrinol* 29:273.

16. Manson, et al. 1990. A prospective study of obesity and risk of coronary heart disease in women. *NEJM* 322:882–889.

17. Donahue, et al. 1987. Central obesity and coronary heart disease in men. *Lancet* (April 11):821–823.

18. Harris, et al. 1988. Body mass index and mortality among nonsmoking older persons. *JAMA* 259:1520–1524.

19. Sims, et al. 1982. Obesity and hypertension. *JAMA* 247:49–52.

20. MacMahon, et al. 1986. The effect of weight reduction on left ventricular mass. *NEJM* 314:334–339.

21. Hall, et al. 1986. Smoking cessation and weight gain. *J Consult Clin Psychol* 54:342–346.

22. Perkins, et al. 1989. The effect of nicotine on energy expenditure during light physical activity. *NEJM* 320:898–903.

23. Hamm, P.B., et al. 1989. Large fluctuations in body weight during young adulthood and twenty-five year risk of coronary death in men. *Am J Epidemiol* 129:312–18.

24. Hamm, P.B., et al. Large fluctuations in body weight during young adulthood.

25. Lissner, L., et al. 1989. Body weight variability and mortality in the Gothenburg Prospective Studies of men and women. In *Obesity in Europe 88: Proceedings of the First European Congress on Obesity*, ed. P. Bjorntorp, and S. Rossner. London: Libbey, 55–60.

26. Lissner, L., et al. 1991. Variability of body weight and health outcomes in the Framingham population. *NEJM* 324:1839–1844.

Chapter 10
Food Additives and Contaminants

1. Resin, A., and H. Ungar. 1957. Malignant tumors in the eyelids and the auricular region of thiourea treated rats. *Cancer Res* 17:302.

2. Nelson, A.A., and G. Woodward. 1953. Tumors of the urinary bladder, gall bladder, and liver in dogs fed o-aminoazotoluene or p-dimethyl-amino-azobenzene. *J Nat Cancer Inst* 13:1497.

3. Witschi, H., D. Williamson, and S. Lock. 1977. Enhancement of urethan tumorigenesis in mouse lung by butylated hydroxytoluene. *J Nat Cancer Inst* 58:301.

4. Wattenberg, L.W. 1978. Inhibition of chemical carcinogenesis. *J Nat Cancer Inst* 60:11.

5. Munro, E.C., C. Moodie, D. Krewski, et al. 1975. A carcinogenicity study of commercial saccharin in the rat. *Toxicol Appl Pharmacol* 32:513.

6. Kessler, I. 1976. Non-nutritive sweeteners and human bladder cancer: Preliminary findings. *J Urol* 115:143.

7. Shubik, P. 1979. Food additives (natural and synthetic). *Cancer* 43:1982.

8. Sen, N.P. 1972. The evidence for the presence of dimethylnitrosamine in meat products. *Food Cosmet Toxicol* 10:219.

9. Newberne, P.M. 1979. Nitrite promotes lymphoma incidence in rats. *Science* 204:1079.
10. Shubik, P. 1980. Food additives, contaminants, and cancer. *Prev Med* 9:197.
11. Toth, B., and D. Nagel. 1978. Tumors induced in mice by N-methyl-N-formylhydrazine of the false moral *Gyromitra esculenta. J Nat Cancer Inst* 60:201.
12. Lijinsky, W., and P. Shubik. 1964. Benzo(a)pyrene and other polynuclear hydrocarbons in charcoal broiled meats. *Science* 145:53.
13. Lijinsky and Shubik. Benzo(a)pyrene and other polynuclear hydrocarbons.

Chapter 11
Pesticides

1. Jeyaratnam, J. 1985. Health problems of pesticide usage in the Third World. *Br J Indust Med* 42:505–6.
2. California State Health and Welfare Agency, Interagency Pesticide Training Coalition. 1981. Pesticide training: Course syllabus and manual for health personnel. Berkeley, Ca.
3. Pimentel, D., and J. Perkins. 1980. *Pest Control: Cultural and Environmental Aspects.* Boulder, Colorado: Westview Press.
4. Pimentel, D., et al. 1983. Energy efficiency and farming systems organic and conventional agriculture. *Agriculture, Ecosystems and the Environment* 9:359–72.
5. Pimentel and Perkins, *Pest Control: Cultural and Environmental Aspects.*
6. Wong, K., et al. 1985. Potent induction of human placental mono-oxygenase activity by previous dietary exposure to polychlorinated biphenyls and their thermal degradation products. *Lancet* (March 30): 721–724.
7. Biscardi, S. 1991. Pesticides linked to breast cancer? *Oncology Times* (February):36.
8. Bocchatta, A., and G.U. Corsini. 1986. Parkinson's disease and pesticide. *Lancet* (November 15):1163.
9. Peters, et al. 1987. *JNCI.*
10. Pimental and Perkins. *Pest Control: Cultural and Environmental Aspects.*
11. Watterson, Andrew. 1988. Pesticide user's health and safety handbook: An international guide. New York: Van Nostrand Reinhold, 420.
12. Richards, et al. 1987. *Nature* 327:129.
13. Council on Scientific Affairs. 1982. Health effects of Agent Orange and dioxin contaminants. *JAMA* (October 15) 248(15):1895–1897.
14. Sterling, T.D., A.V. Arundel. 1986. Health effects of phenoxy herbicides: A review. *Scand J Work Environ Health* 12:161–173.
15. Advisory Committee on Pesticides. 1980. Further review of the safety of the use of herbicides 2,4,5-T. H.M. Stationary Office.
16. Hardell, L., et al. 1979. Case-control study: Soft-tissue sarcomas and exposure to phenoxyacetic acids or chlorophenols. *Br J Cancer* 39:711–7.
17. Eriksson, M., et al. 1981. Exposure to dioxins as a risk factor for soft tissue sarcoma: A population-based case-control study. *Br J Ind Med* 38:27–33.
18. Hardell, L., et al. Case-control study: Soft-tissue sarcomas and exposure to phenoxyacetic acids or chlorophenols.
19. Eriksson, M., et al. Exposure to dioxins as a risk factor for soft tissue sarcoma.
20. Hardell, L., et al. 1988. The association between soft tissue sarcomas and exposure to phenoxyacetic acids: A new case-referent study. *Cancer* 62:652–56.
21. Hardell, L., et al. 1983. Epidemiologic study of socioeconomic factors and clinical findings in Hodgkin's disease, and reanalysis of previous data regarding chemical exposure. *Br J Cancer* 48:217–25.
22. Hardell, L., et al. 1981. Malignant lymphoma and exposure to chemicals, especially organic solvents, chlorophenols and phenoxy acids: A case-control study. *Br J Cancer* 43:169–76.
23. Woods, J.S., et al. 1987. Soft tissue sarcoma and non-Hodgkin's lymphoma in relation to phenoxyherbicide and chlorinated phenol exposure in western Washington. *J Natl Cancer Inst* 78:899–910.
24. Persson, B., et al. 1989. Malignant lymphomas and occupational exposures. *Br J Ind Med* 46:516–20.

25. Axelson, O., et al. 1980. Herbicide exposure and tumor mortality: An updated epidemiologic investigation on Swedish railroad car workers. *Scand J Work Environ Health* 6:73–9.

26. Thiess, A.M., et al. 1982. Mortality study of persons exposed to dioxin in a trichlorophenol-process accident that occurred in the BASF AG on November 17, 1953. *Am J Ind Med* 3:179–89.

27. Hardell, L., et al. 1982. Epidemiological study of nasal and nasopharyngeal cancer and their relation to phenoxy acid or chlorophenol exposure. *Am J Ind Med* 3:247–57.

28. Kociba, R., et al. 1982. Results of a two-year chronic toxicity and oncogenicity study of 2, 3, 7, 8-tetrachlorodibenzo-p-dioxin in rats. *Toxicol Appl Pharmacol* 46:279–303.

29. National Toxicology Program (NTP). Carcinogenesis bioassay of 2, 3, 7, 8-tetrachlorodibenzo-p-dioxin (CAS No. 1746-01-6) in Osborne-Mendel rats and B6C3F1 mice (gavage study) 1982. Washington, D.C.: Government Printing Office, 1982. (DHHS publication no. (NIH) 82-1765.)

30. Smith, A.H., et al. 1984. Soft tissue sarcoma and exposure to phenoxyherbicides and chlorophenols in New Zealand. *J Natl Cancer Inst* 73:1111–17.

31. Wiklund, K., and L. Holm. 1986. Soft tissue sarcoma risk in Swedish agriculture and forestry workers. *J Natl Cancer Inst* 76:229–34.

32. Pearce, N.E., et al. 1987. Non-Hodgkin's lymphoma and farming: An expanded case-control study. *Int J Cancer* 39:155–61.

33. Wilkund K., et al. 1987. Risk of malignant lymphoma in Swedish pesticide appliers. *Br J Cancer* 56:505–8.

34. Olsen, J.H., and O.M. Jensen. 1984. Nasal cancer and chlorophenols. *Lancet* 2:47–8.

35. Hardell, L., et al. 1984. Aetiological aspects on primary liver cancer with special regard to alcohol, organic solvents and acute intermittent porphyria—an epidemiological investigation. *Br J Cancer* 50:389–97.

36. Fingerhut, et al. 1991. Cancer mortality in workers exposed to 2, 3, 7, 8-tetrachlorodibenzo-p-dioxin. *NEJM* 324(4):212–218.

37. Bailer, J.C. 1991. How dangerous is dioxin? *NEJM* 324(4):260–262.

38. Borzsonyi, M., et al. 1984. Agriculturally related carcinogen at risk. International Agency for Research on Cancer. *Science Publication* 56:465–486.

39. National Toxicology Program: Fourth Annual Report on Carcinogens: Summary, 1985. Publication NTP 85-002. U.S. Department of Health and Human Services.

40. Vainio, H., et al. 1985. Data on the carcinogenicity of chemicals in the IARC monographs programme. *Carcinogenesis* 6:1653–1665.

41. Environmental Protection Agency. Carcinogens. 1986. Federal Register (September 24).

42. Brand, O. 1990. Pesticide regulation. *Newsweek* (April 23):17.

43. Hopmann, C. 1990. (reporter-no title) *Newsweek* (April 23):17.

44. *Handbook on Pest Control.* 1991. Boca Raton, FL: CRC Press.

Chapter 12
Smoking—A Slow Suicide

1. Conference. Smoking and health. 1990. *Lancet* (April 28):1026.

2. Conference. Smoking and health.

3. Public Health Service. 1979. Smoking and health, a report of the surgeon general. U.S. Dept. of HEW.

4. Fielding. 1985. Smoking: Health effects and control. *NEJM* 313:491–498.

5. Shackney, S.E. 1982. Carcinogenesis and tumor cell biology. 1982 Surgeon General's Report.

6. Hirayama, T. 1979. Diet and cancer. *Nutrition and Cancer* 1(3):67.

7. Winn, D.M., W.J. Blot, et al. 1981. Snuff dipping and oral cancer among women in the southern United States. *NEJM* 304:745.

8. Slattery, et al. 1989. Cigarette smoking and exposure to passive smoke are risk factors for cervical cancer. *JAMA* 261:1593–1598.

9. Trevathan, et al. 1983. Cigarette smoking and dysplasia and carcinoma in situ of the uterine cervix. *JAMA* 250:499–502.

10. Nakayama, et al. 1985. Cigarette smoke induces DNA single-stranded breaks in human cells. *Nature* 314:462.

11. Pic, A. 1981. Heavy smoking and exercise can trigger MI. *Int Med News* 14(9):3.

12. Abbott, et al. 1986. Risk of stroke in male cigarette smokers. *NEJM* 315:717–720.

13. Wolf, et al. 1988. Cigarette smoking as a risk factor for stroke. *JAMA* 259:1025–1029.

14. Colditz, et al. 1988. Cigarette smoking and risk of stroke in middle-aged women. *NEJM* 318:937–941.

15. Rogers, et al. 1985. Abstention from cigarette smoking improves cerebral perfusion among the elderly chronic smokers. *JAMA* 253:2970–2974.

16. Baird, et al. 1985. Cigarette smoking associated with delayed conception. *JAMA* 253:2979–2983.

17. Stjernfeldt, et al. 1986. Maternal smoking during pregnancy and risk of childhood cancer. *Lancet* (June 14):1350–1352.

18. Hopkin, J.M., and H.J. Evans. 1980. Cigarette smoke induced DNA damage and lung cancer risks. *Nature* 283:388.

19. Evans, H.J., et al. 1981. Sperm abnormalities and cigarette smoking. *Lancet* (March):627.

20. Finch, et al. 1982. Surface morphology and functional studies of human alveolar macrophages from cigarette smokers and nonsmokers. *J Reticuloendothel Soc* 32:1–23.

21. Cantin and Crystal. 1985. Oxidants, antioxidants, and the pathogenesis of emphysema. *Eur J Respir Dis* 139:7–17.

22. Bridges, et al. 1985. Effect of smoking on peripheral blood leukocytes and serum antiproteases. *Eur J Respir Dis* 139:24–33.

23. Ginns, et al. 1982. Alterations in immunoregulatory cells in lung cancer and smoking. *J Clin Immunol 3 Suppl:* 90S–94S.

24. Miller, et al. 1982. Reversible alterations in immunoregulatory T cells in smoking. *Chest* 82:526–529.

25. Nguyen and Keast. 1986. Effects of chronic daily exposure to tobacco smoke on the high leukemic AKR strain of mice. *Cancer Res* 46(7):3334–40.

26. Hersey, et al. 1983. Effects of cigarette smoking on the immune system. *Med J Aust* 2(9):425–9.

27. Burrows, et al. 1983. Interactions of smoking and immunologic factors in relation to airway obstruction. *Chest* 84(6):657–61.

28. Burrows, et al. Interactions of smoking and immunologic factors.

29. McSharry, et al. 1985. Effect of cigarette smoking on antibody response to inhaled antigens. *Clin Allergy* 15:487–94.

30. Department of Health and Human Services. Health consequences of smoking: Chronic obstructive lung disease: A report of the surgeon general. Washington, D.C. Government Printing Office. 1984. PHS: 84-50205.

31. Idem. health consequences of involuntary smoking: A report of the surgeon general. Washington, D.C. GPO. 1986. Publication No. 87-8398.

32. National Research Council, committee on passive smoking. Environmental tobacco smoke: Measuring exposures and assessing health effects. 1986. Washington, D.C. National Academy of Press.

33. National Research Council, committee on passive smoking.

34. Uberla. 1987. Lung cancer from passive smoking: Hypothesis or convincing evidence? *Ant Arch Occupa Environ Health* 59:421–37.

35. Jaherich, et al. 1990. Lung cancer and exposure to tobacco smoke in the household. *NEJM* 323(10):632–36.

36. Slattery, et al. 1989. Cigarette smoking and exposure to passive smoke are risk factors for cervical cancer. *JAMA* 261:1593–1598.

37. Stjernfeldt, et al. 1986. Maternal smoking during pregnancy and risk of childhood cancer. *Lancet* (September 20):687–689.

38. Kabat, et al. 1986. Bladder cancer in nonsmokers. *Cancer* 57:362–367.

39. Light and Foreb. 1980. Small airway dysfunction in non-smokers chronically exposed to tobacco smoke. *NEJM* 302:720–3.

40. Rubin, et al. 1986. Effect of passive smoking on birth weight. *Lancet* (August 23):415–417.

41. Harlap and Davies. 1974. Infant admissions to hospital and maternal smoking. *Lancet* 1:529–32.

42. Black. 1985. Etiology of glue ear—A case control study. *Int J Pediatric Otorhinolaryngology.* 9:121–33.
43. Fielding and Phenow. 1988. Health effects of involuntary smoking. *NEJM* 319:1452–1460.
44. Hermanson, B., et al. 1988. Beneficial six year outcome of smoking cessation in older men and women with coronary heart disease: Results from the CASS registry. *NEJM* 319:1365–9.
45. LaCroix, A., et al. 1991. Smoking and mortality among older men and women in three communities. *NEJM* 324:1619–25.
46. Williamson, D.F., et al. 1991. Smoking cessation and severity of weight gain in a national cohort. *NEJM* 324:739–45.

Chapter 13
Alcohol and Caffeine

1. Shaw, S., and C.S. Lieber. 1977. Alcoholism. In *Nutritional Support of Medical Practice.* New York: Harper and Row, 202–21.
2. Rosenberg, L., D. Sloan, S. Shapiro, et al. 1982. Breast cancer and alcoholic consumption. *Lancet* 30:267.
3. Schatzkin, et al. 1987. Alcohol consumption and breast cancer in the epidemiologic follow-up study of the first NHANES. *NEJM* 316:1169–1180.
4. Graham, S. 1987. Alcohol and breast cancer. *NEJM* 316:1211–1212.
5. Longnecker, et al. 1988. A meta-analysis of alcohol consumption in relation to risk of breast cancer. *JAMA* 260:652–656.
6. Editorial. 1985. Does alcohol cause breast cancer? *Lancet* (June 8): 1311–12.
7. Stampfer, et al. 1988. A prospective study of moderate alcohol consumption and the risk of coronary heart disease and stroke in women. *NEJM* 319:267–273.
8. Gill, et al. 1986. Stroke and alcohol consumption. *NEJM* 315:1041–1046.
9. Simon, D., S. Yen, and P. Cole. 1975. Coffee drinking and cancer of the lower urinary tract system. *J Natl Cancer Inst* 54(3):587.
10. Mulvihill, J. 1973. Caffeine as teratogen and mutagen. *Teratology* 8:69.
11. Weinstein, D., I. Mauer, and H. Solomon. 1972. The effects of caffeine on chromosomes of human lymphocytes. *Mutat Res* 16:391.
12. Soyka, L.F. 1979. Effects of methylxanthines on the fetus. *Clinics in Perinatol* 6(1):37.
13. Weathersbee, P.S., L.K. Olsen, and J.R. Lodge. 1977. Caffeine and pregnancy. *Postgrad Med* 62(3):64.
14. LaCroix, et al. 1986. Coffee consumption and the incidence of coronary heart disease. *NEJM* 315:977–982.

Chapter 14
Sexual-Social and Hormonal Factors

1. Slattery, et al. 1989. Cigarette smoking and exposure to passive smoke are risk factors for cervical cancer. *JAMA* 261(11):1593–1598.
2. Greene, W. 1991. The molecular biology of human immunodeficiency virus type 1 infection. *NEJM* 324(5):308–317.
3. HIV transmission via skin and mucous membranes. 1987. *Lancet* (June 6): 1329.
4. Leads from the MMWR. 1987. Update: Human immunodeficiency virus infections in health care workers exposed to blood of infected patients. *JAMA* 257:3032–3039.
5. *Cope* Magazine. 1987. (April): 60.
6. Aoun, H., et al. 1991. Issues raised by the possible transmission of HIV from a dentist to a patient. *NEJM* 324(4):265–66.
7. Niedecken, et al. 1987. Langerhans cell as primary target and vehicle for transmission of HIV. *Lancet* (August 29): 519–20.
8. Colebunders, et al. 1988. Breast feeding and transmission of HIV. *Lancet* (December 24): 1487.
9. Goldberg, et al. 1988. HIV and oral-genital transmission. *Lancet* (December 10): 1363.
10. Rozenbaum, et al. 1988. HIV transmission by oral sex. *Lancet* (June 18): 1395.
11. Haverkos, and Edelman. 1988. The epidemiology of acquired immunodeficiency syndrome among heterosexuals. *JAMA* 260:1922–1929.
12. Donahue, et al. 1990. Transmission of HIV by transfusion of screened blood. *NEJM* 323(24):1709.
13. Greenhouse. 1987. Female to female transmission of HIV. *Lancet* (August 19): 401.

14. Transmission of HIV by human bite. 1987. *Lancet* (August 29): 522.

15. Blaser, M. 1986. Insect-borne transmission of AIDS. *JAMA* 255:463–464.

16. Vittecoq, et al. 1989. Acute HIV infection after acupuncture treatments. *NEJM* 320:250–251.

17. Conacher. 1988. AIDS, condoms, and prisons. *Lancet* (July 2): 41–42.

18. Wahn, et al. 1986. Horizontal transmission of HIV infection between two siblings. *Lancet* (September 20): 694.

19. Quinn, A.G., et al. 1991. Long-lasting viability of HIV after patient death. *Lancet* 338:63.

20. Grossman, C. 1985. Interactions between the gonadal steroids and the immune system. *Science* 227:257–261.

21. Pike, et al. 1981. Oral contraceptive use and early abortion as risk factors for breast cancer in young women. *Br J Cancer* 43:72–76.

22. Donegan, W.L. 1983. Cancer and pregnancy. *Ca–A Cancer Journal for Clinicians* 33(4):194–214.

23. Orr, J.W., and H.M. Shingleton. 1983. Cancer in pregnancy. *Current problems in cancer.* Yearbook Medical Publishers 8(1):3–50.

24. Haagensen, C.D. 1986. *Disease of the Breast.* New York: W.B. Saunders Co.

25. Boyd, N.F., et al. 1988. Effect of low fat, high carbohydrate diet on symptoms of cyclical mastopathy. *Lancet* (July 16): 128–129.

26. Wobbes, et al. 1980. Relation between testicular tumors, undescended testes and inguinal hernias. *J Surg Onc* 14:45–51.

27. Batata, et al. 1980. Cryptorchidism and testicular cancer. *J Urology* 124:382–387.

28. Henderson, et al. 1982. Endogenous hormones as a major factor in human cancer. *Cancer Research* 42:3232–3239.

29. Musey, et al. 1987. Long term effect of a first pregnancy on the secretion of prolactin. *NEJM* 316:229–234.

30. Herbst, et al. 1971. Adenocarcinoma of the vagina. *NEJM* 284:878–81.

31. Robboy, S.J., et al. 1984. Increased incidence of cervical and vaginal dysplasia in 3980 diethylstilbesterol exposed young women. *JAMA* 252:2979–2990.

32. Greenberg, et al. 1984. Breast cancer in mothers given DES in pregnancy. *NEJM* 311:1393–1398.

33. Bibbo, et al. 1978. A twenty-five year follow up study of women exposed to DES during pregnancy. *NEJM* 298:763–7.

34. Melnick, et al. 1987. Rates and risk of DES related clear cell adenocarcinoma of the vagina and cervix. *NEJM* 316:514–516.

35. Conley, et al. 1983. Seminoma and epididymal cysts in a young man with known DES exposure in utero. *JAMA* 249:1325–1326.

36. Loizzo, et al. 1984. Italian baby food containing DES: Three years later. *Lancet* (May 5): 1013–1014.

37. Centers for Disease Control cancer and steroid hormone study: Long term oral contraceptive use and the risk of breast cancer. 1983. *JAMA* 249:1591–1595.

38. Pike, M.C., et al. 1983. Breast cancer in young women and use of oral contraceptives: Possible modifying effect of formulation and age at use. *Lancet* (October 22): 926–930.

39. McPherson, et al. 1983. Oral contraceptives and breast cancer. *Lancet* ii:1414–1415.

40. UK National Case Control Study Group. Oral contraceptive use and breast cancer risk in young women. 1989. *Lancet* (May 6): 973–982.

41. Rosenberg, L., et al. 1984. Breast cancer and oral contraceptive use. *Am J Epidemiol* 119:167–76.

42. Olsson, et al. 1985. Oral contraceptive use and breast cancer in young women in Sweden. *Lancet* i:748–49.

43. Kalach, et al. 1983. Oral contraceptives and breast cancer. *Br J Hosp Med* 30:278–83.

44. Royal College of General Practitioners. 1981. Breast cancer and oral contraceptives in the royal college of general practitioners study. *Br Med J* 282:2089–93.

45. Vessey, et al. 1983. Neoplasia of the cervix uteri and contraception: A possible adverse effect of the pill. *Lancet* (October 22): 930–934.

46. Neuberger, et al. 1986. Oral contraceptives and hepatocellular carcinoma. *Br Med J* 292:1355–1361.

47. Cancer and steroid hormone study for CDC. 1987. Combination oral contraceptive use and the risk of endometrial cancer. *JAMA* 257:796–800.
48. Cancer and steroid hormone study of the CDC. 1987. Reduction in the risk of ovarian cancer associated with oral contraceptive use. *NEJM* 316:650–655.
49. Liange, et al. 1983. Risk of breast, uterus, and ovarian cancer in women receiving medroxyprogesterone injections. *JAMA* 249: 2909–2912.
50. WHO collaborative study of neoplasia and steroid contraceptives. 1984. Breast cancer, cervical cancer, and depot medroxy progesterone acetate. *Lancet* (Nov. 24): 1207–1208.
51. Schwarz, Barry. 1981. Does estrogen cause adenocarcinoma of the endometrium. *Len Ob Gyn* 24:243–251.
52. Henderson, et al. 1975. Elevated serum levels of estrogen and prolactin in daughters of patients with breast cancer. *NEJM* 293:790–795.
53. Kirk, M.E. 1979. Tumorogenic aspects. *Int J Gyn OBS* 16:473–478.
54. Colditz, et al. 1990. Prospective study of estrogen replacement therapy and risk of breast cancer in postmenopausal women. *JAMA* 264(20):2648–2653.
55. Henderson, et al. 1982. Endogenous hormones as major factor in human cancer. *Cancer Research* 42:3232–3239.

Chapter 15
Environmental Factors—Air, Water, and Electromagnetism

1. Buell, P. 1967. Relative impact of smoking and air pollution on lung cancer. *Arch Environ Health* 15:291–297.
2. Cederlof, R., et al. 1975. The relationship of smoking and social covariables to mortality and cancer mortality, a ten year follow up in a probability sample of 55,000 Swedish subjects age 18-69. Stockholm. Department of Environmental Hygiene. The Karolinska Institute.
3. Dean, G. 1966. Lung cancer and bronchitis in Northern Ireland. *Br Med J* 1:1506.
4. Lee, M.L., N. Novotny, and K.D. Bartle. 1976. Gas chromatography/mass spectometric and nuclear magnetic resonance determination of polynuclear aromatic hydrocarbons in airborne particulates. *Anal Chem* 48:1566.
5. Hoffmann, D., I. Schmeltz, S.S. Hecht, et al. 1976. Volatile carcinogens. Occurence, formation, and analysis. In *Prevention and Detection of Cancer*. Part 1. Prevention. Vol. 2. Etiology, prevention methods, ed. H.E. Nieburgs. New York and Basel: Marcel Dekker, Inc. 1943-1959.
6. National Research Council. 1976. Vapor-phase organic pollutants. Committee on medical and biological effects of environmental pollutants. National Academy of Sciences, Washington, D.C.
7. Committee on the Atmosphere and Biosphere, National Research Council. *Atmosphere biosphere interactions: Toward a better understanding of the ecological consequences of fossil fuel combustion.* 1981. Washington, D.C.: National Academy Press.
8. Luoma, J.R. 1984. *Troubled Skies, Troubled Waters.* New York: Viking Press.
9. Cronan, C.S., et al. 1979. Aluminum leaching response to acid precipitation: Effects on high elevation water sheds in the northeast. *Science* 204:304–306.
10. Perl, D.P., et al. 1982. Intraneuronal aluminum accumulation in amyotrophic lateral sclerosis and parkinsonism in Guam. *Science* 217:1053–1055.
11. Shore, D., et al. 1983. Aluminum and Alzheimer's disease. *J Nerv Ment Dis* 171:553–558.
12. U.S. Department of Health and Human Services, National Institute for Occupational Safety and Health. 1988. Carcinogenic effects of exposure to diesel exhaust. Current intelligence bulletin No. 50. (August).
13. Geophysical research letters. 1986. Vol. 13. (November).
14. Isaksen, I. 1986. Ozone perturbations studies in a two dimensional model in a feedback on the stratosphere included UNEP workshop.
15. Hocking, M. 1991. Paper versus polystyrene: A complex choice. *Science* 251:504–505.
16. Blumthaler and Ambach. 1991. How well do sunglasses protect against ultraviolet radiation? *Lancet* 337:1284.

17. World Health Organization. 1983. Indoor air pollutants: Exposure and health effects assessment. Reports No. 78. Nordlingen Copenhagen: WHO.
18. National Council on Radiation Protection and Measurements. 1984. Exposures from the uranium series with emphasis on radon and its daughters. Bethesda, Maryland. *NCRP* March 15, 1984.
19. Nero, AV. 1983. Indoor radon exposures from radon and its daughters. *Health Physics* 45:277–88.
20. Abelson, P. 1990. Uncertainties about health effects of radon. *Science* 250:353.
21. *Health risks of radon and other internally deposited alpha emitters*, BEIR IV. 1988. Washington, D.C.: National Academy Press.
22. Repace, J.L. 1984. Consistency of research data on passive smoking and lung cancer. *Lancet* i:506.
23. Hueper, W.C. 1960. Cancer hazards from natural and artificial water pollutants. In *Proceedings, Physiological Aspects of Water Quality*, ed. H.A. Farber, and J.L. Bryson. Washington, D.C., Public Health Service, 181–193.
24. U.S. Environmental Protection Agency. 1975a. Preliminary assessment of suspected carcinogens in drinking water. Report to Congress. Environmental Protection Agency, Washington, D.C.
25. Harris, R.H., T. Page, and N.A. Reiches. 1977b. Carcinogenic hazards of organic chemicals in drinking water. In *Book A. Incidence of Cancer in Humans*, ed. H.H. Hiatt, J.D. Watson, and J.A. Winsten. Cold Spring Harbor Laboratory.
26. Hogan, M.D., et al. 1979. Association between chloroform and various site-specific cancer mortality rates. *J Environ Pathol Toxicol* 2:873.
27. Cantor, K.P., et al. 1978. Associations of cancer mortality with halomethanes in drinking water. *JNCI* 61:979.
28. National Research Council. 1978a. Chloroform, carbon tetrachloride, and other halomethanes—an environmental assessment. Washington, D.C. National Academy of Sciences.
29. Rafferty, P.J. 1978. Public health aspects of drinking water quality in North Carolina. Masters thesis, Department of En-

vironmental Sciences and Engineering, School of Public Health, University of North Carolina, Chapel Hill, North Carolina.
30. Spivey, G.H., et al. 1977. Cancer and chlorinated drinking water. Final report. EPA contract No. CA-6-99-3349-J. Cincinnati, Ohio. U.S. Environmental Protection Agency.
31. Tuthill, R.W., et al. 1978. Chlorination of public drinking water supplies and subsequent cancer mortality: An ecological-time lag study. Final report. EPA contract No. EPA-68-03-1200. Cincinnati, Ohio. U.S. Environmental Protection Agency.
32. U.S. Environmental Protection Agency. 1975a. Preliminary Assessment.
33. Comstock, G. 1980. The epidemiologic perspective: Water hardness and cardiovascular disease. *J Environ Path Toxicol* 4-2, 3:9.
34. Hewitt, D., et al. 1980. Development of the water story: some recent Canadian studies. *J Environ Path Toxicol* 4-2, 3:51.
35. McCarron, et al. 1985. Blood pressure response to oral calcium in persons with mild to moderate hypertension. *Ann Intern Med* 103:825.
36. Garland, et al. 1985. Dietary vitamin D and calcium and risk of colorectal cancer: A 19-year prospective study in man. *Lancet* 1:307.
37. Rozen, et al. 1989. Calcium supplements protect against colorectal cancer. *Gut* 30:650–655.
38. U.S. Atomic Energy Commission. 1974. Plutonium and other transuranium elements; Sources, environmental distribution and biomedical effects. Washington, D.C., WASH-1359.
39. National Research Council. 1977. Drinking water and health. Safe drinking water committee, NAS. Washington, D.C. National Academy of Sciences.
40. Kanarek, M.S. 1978. Asbestos in drinking water and cancer incidence in the San Francisco Bay Area. Ph.D. Dissertation, Department of Epidemiology, School of Public Health, University of California, Berkeley, California.
41. Bonnell, J.A. 1982. Effects of electric fields near power transmission plant. *J Roy Soc Med* 75:933–44.

42. Pool, Robert. 1990. Electromagnetic fields: The biological evidence. *JAMA* 249:1378–1381.

43. Wertheimer, and Leeper. 1979. Electrical wiring configurations in childhood cancer. *Am J Epidemiol* 109:273–84.

44. Wertheimer, and Leeper. 1982. Adult cancer related to electrical wires near the home. *Int J Epidemiol* 11:354–55.

45. Gauger, J.R. 1985. Household appliance magnetic field survey. IEEE Trans PAS-104, No. 9. In *Epidemiological studies relating human health to electric and magnetic fields; criteria for evaluation, 1988.* International Electricity Research Exchange (June 22): 26.

46. Milham. 1982. Mortality from leukemia in workers exposed to electrical and magnetic fields. *NEJM* 307:249.

47. Wright, et al. 1982. Leukemia in workers exposed to electrical and magnetic fields. *Lancet* ii:1160–61.

48. McDowall. 1983. Leukemia mortality in electrical workers in England and Wales. *Lancet,* 246.

49. Tynes and Anderson. 1990. Electromagnetic fields and male breast cancer. *Lancet* 336:1596.

50. University of California News Service. 1988. 63:13.

51. Worries about radiation continue, as do studies. 1990. *The New York Times* (July 8).

52. Worries about radiation continue, as do studies. 1990.

53. *J Electro Anal Chem.* 1986. 211:447–456.

54. *Immunol Lett.* 1986. 13:295–299.

Chapter 16
Sedentary Lifestyle

1. Tomasi, et al. 1982. Immune parameters in athletes before and after strenuous exercise. *J Clin Immunol* 2:173–178.

2. Soppi, et al. 1982. Effect of strenuous physical stress on circulating lymphocyte number and function before and after training. *J Clin Lab Immunol* 8:43–46.

3. Robertson, et al. 1981. The effect of strenuous physical exercise on circulating blood lymphocytes and serum cortisol levels. *J Clin Lab Immunol* 5:53–57.

4. Hanson, et al. 1981. Immunological responses to training in conditioned runners. *Clin Soc* 60:225–228.

5. Green, et al. 1981. Immune function in marathon runners. *Ann Allergy* 47:73–75.

6. Busse, W.W., et al. 1980. The effect of exercise on the granulocyte response to isoproterenol in the trained athlete and unconditioned individual. *J Allergy Clin Immunol* 65: 358–364.

7. Eskola, et al. 1978. Effect of sport stress on lymphocyte transformation and antibody formation. *Clin Exp Immunol* 32:339–345.

8. Yu, et al. 1977. Effect of corticosteroid on exercise induced lymphocytosis. *Clin Exp Immunol* 28:326–331.

9. Hedfors, et al. 1976. Variations of blood lymphocytes during work studied by cell surface markers, DNA synthesis and cytotoxicity. *Clin Exp Immunol* 24:328–335.

10. Cannon and Kluger. 1983. Endogenous pyrogen activity in human plasma after exercise. *Science* 220:617–619.

11. Dinarello and Wolff. 1982. Molecular basis of fever in humans. *Am J Med* 72:799–819.

12. Dinarello. 1984. *Rev Infect Dis* 6:51–94.

13. Cannon and Dinarello. 1984. Interleukin I activity in human plasma. *Fed Proc* 43:462.

14. Gershbein, L.L., et al. 1974. An influence of stress on lesion growth and on survival of animals bearing parental and intracerebral leukemia. L 1210 and Walker Tumors. *Oncology* 30:429.

15. DeRosa, G., and N.R. Suarez. 1980. Effect of exercise on tumor growth and body composition of the host. *Fed Am Soc Exp Biol,* 1118.

16. Paffenbarger, R., et al. 1986. Physical activity, all cause mortality, and longevity of college alumni. *NEJM* 314:605–613.

17. Frisch, R.E., et al. 1985. Lower prevalence of breast cancer in cancers of the reproductive system among former college athletes compared to non-athletes. *Br J Cancer* 52:885–891.

18. Garabrant, D.H., et al. 1984. Job activity and colon cancer risk. *Am J Epidemiol* 119(6):1005–1014.

19. Vena, J.E., et al. 1985. Lifetime occupational exercise and colon cancer. *Am J Epidemiol* 122(3):357–365.

20. Gerhardsson, M., et al. 1986. Sedentary jobs and colon cancer. *Am J Epidemiol* 123(5):775–780.
21. Harris, S.S., et al. 1989. Physical activity counseling for healthy adults as a primary preventive intervention in the clinical setting report for the U.S. Preventive Services Task Force. *JAMA* 261:3590–3598.
22. Pollack, M.L. 1973. The quantification and endurance training programs. In *Exercise and sport sciences reviews*, vol. I, ed. J.H. Wilmore. New York: Academic Press.
23. Louis Harris and Associates, Inc. 1978. Perrier survey of fitness in America. Study No. S 2813. New York, NY.
24. Heald, F. 1975. Adolescent nutrition. *Med Clin North Am* 59:1329.
25. Blair, et al. 1989. Physical fitness an all cause mortality. *JAMA* 262:2395–2401.
26. Centers for Disease Control. Progress toward achieving the 1990 national objectives for physical fitness and exercise. 1989. *MMWR* 38:449–453.
27. Somers, V.K., et al. 1991. Effects of endurance training on baroreflex sensitivity and blood pressure in borderline hypertension. *Lancet* 337:1363–68.
28. Rippe, James M., et al. 1988. Walking for health and fitness. *JAMA* 259:2720–2724.
29. Porcari, J., et al. 1987. Is fast walking an adequate aerobic training stimulus for 30-69 year old men and women? *Physician and Sports Medicine* 15(2):119–129.
30. Petty, B.G., et al. 1986. Physical activity and longevity of college alumni, letter. *NEJM* 315(6):399.
31. Winningham, M.L., et al. 1986. Exercise for cancer patients: Guidelines and precautions. *Physician and sports medicine* 14(10):125–134.
32. Medical News and Perspectives. 1991. Exercise, health links need hard proof, say researchers studying mechanisms. *JAMA* 265 (22):2928.
33. Horton, E. 1991. Exercise and decreased risk of NIDDM. *NEJM* 325(3): 196–97.
34. Helmrich, S., et al. 1991. Physical activity and reduced occurrence of non-insulin-dependent diabetes mellitus. *NEJM* 325(3):147–52.

Chapter 17
Stress

1. LeShan, L.L. 1959. Psychological states as factors in the development of malignant disease: A critical review. *JNCI* 22:1–18.
2. *Psychoneuroimmunology*, ed. R. Ader. 1981. New York: Academic Press.
3. Angeletti, R., W. Hickey. 1985. A neuroendocrine marker in tissues of the immune system. *Science* 230:89–90.
4. Bulloch, K. 1985. *Neuralmodulation of Immunity*. New York: Raven Press, 111.
5. Riley, V. 1981. Psychoneuroendocrine influences on immunocompetence and neoplasia. *Science* 212:1100–1109.
6. Bartrop, R., et al. 1977. Depressed lymphocyte function after bereavement. *Lancet* i:834–836.
7. Schleifer, S.J., et al. 1983. Suppression of lymphocyte stimulation following bereavement. *JAMA* 250:374–377.
8. Kronfol, Z., et al. 1983. Impaired lymphocyte function in depressive illness. *Life Science* 33:241–247.
9. Schleifer, S.J., et al. 1984. Lymphocyte function in major depressive disorder. *Arch Jen Psychiatry* 41:484–486.
10. Schleifer, S.J., et al. 1985. Lymphocyte function in ambulatory depressed patients, hospitalized schizophrenic patients, and patients hospitalized for herniorrhaphy. *Arch Jen Psychiatry* 42:129–133.
11. Locke, S., et al. 1984. Life change stress, psychiatric symptoms, and natural killer cell activity. *Psychosomatic Med* 46:441–453.
12. Heisel, J.S., et al. 1984. Natural killer cell activity and MMPI scores of a cohort of college students. *Am J Psychiatry* 143:1382–86.
13. Jemmott, J.B., et al. 1983. Academic stress, power motivation and decrease in secretion rate of salivary secretory immunoglobulin A. *Lancet* ii:1400–1402.
14. Ader, R., N. Cohen. 1975. Behaviorally conditioned immunosuppressant. *Psychosomatic Medicine* 37:333–340.
15. Black, S., et al. 1963. Inhibition of mantoux reaction by direct suggestion under hypnosis. *Br Med J* i:1649–1652.
16. Smith, G.R., et al. 1985. Psychological modulation of human immune response to varicella zoster. *Arch Intern Med* 145:2110–2112.

17. Horne, R.L. and R.S. Picard. 1979. Psychosocial risk factors for lung cancer. *Psychosomatic Medicine* 41:503–514.

18. Jacobs, T.J. and E. Charles. 1980. Life events and the occurrence of cancer in children. *Psychosomatic Medicine* 42:11–24.

19. Bloom, B.L., et al. 1978. Marital disruption as a stressor: A review and analysis. *Psychological Bulletin* 85:867–894.

20. Fox, B.H. 1978. Premorbid psychological factors as related to cancer incidence. *Journal of Behavioral Medicine* 1:45–133.

21. Bloom, B.L., et al. 1978. Marital disruption as a stressor: A review and analysis. *Psychological Bulletin* 85:867–894.

22. LeShan, L.L. 1966. An emotional life history pattern associated with neoplastic disease. *Ann NY Acad Sci* 125:780–793.

23. Ernster, B.L., et al. 1979. Cancer incidence by marital status: U.S. third national cancer survey. *J Natl Cancer Inst* 63:567–585.

24. Mastrovito, R.C., et al. 1979. Personality characteristics of women with gynecological cancer. *Cancer Detection and Prevention* 2:281–287.

25. Stavraky, K.C., et al. 1968. Psychological factors in the outcome of human cancer. *Journal of Psychosomatic Research* 12:251–259.

26. Bacon, C.L., et al. 1952. A psychosomatic survey of cancer of the breast. *Psychosomatic Medicine* 14:453–560.

27. Greer, S., and T. Morris. 1975. Psychological attributes of women who develop breast cancer: A controlled study. *Journal of Psychosomatic Research* 19:147–153.

28. Horne, R.L., and R.S. Picard. 1979. Psychosocial risk factors for lung cancer. *Psychosomatic Medicine* 41:503–514.

29. Paykel, E.S. 1979. Recent life events in the development of depressive disorders. In *The Psychobiology of the Depressive Disorders*, ed. R.A. Depue. New York: Academic Press.

30. Schmale, et al. 1966. The psychological setting of the uterine cervical cancer. *Ann NY Acad Sci* 125:807–813.

31. Rogentine, et al. 1979. Psychological factors in the prognosis of malignant melanoma. *Psychosomatic Medicine* 41:647–655.

32. Derogatis, et al. 1979. Psychological coping mechanisms and survival time in metastatic breast cancer. *JAMA* 242:1504–1508.

33. Greer, et al. 1979. Psychological response to breast cancer: Effect on outcome. *Lancet* ii:785–787.

34. Greer, H.S., and Morris. 1975. Psychological attributes of women who develop breast cancer. *Journal of Psychosomatic Research* 19:147–153.

35. Thomas, C.B., et al. Family attitudes reported in youth as potential predictors of cancer. *Psychosomatic Medicine* 41:287–302.

36. *Impact of psychoendocrine systems in cancer and immunity*, ed. Fox, Newberry. 1984. Lewiston, New York: C.J. Hogrefe.

37. Bahnson. 1981. Stress and cancer: The state of the art. *Psychosomatics* 22(3):207–220.

38. Visintainer, et al. 1982. Tumor rejection in rats after inescapable or escapable shock. *Science* 216:437–439.

39. Sklar and Anisman. 1979. Stress and coping factors influence tumor growth. *Science* 205:513–515.

Chapter 18
Breast Cancer

1. Goodwin and Boyd. 1987. *JNCI* 79:473–485.

2. Ip, et al. 1986. *Dietary Fat and Cancer*. New York: Alan R. Liss, Inc.

3. Alcantara, E.N., and E.W. Speckman. 1976. Diet, nutrition and cancer. *Am J Clin Nutr* 29:1035.

4. Wynder, E.L. 1979. Dietary habits and cancer epidemiology. *Cancer* 43:1955.

5. Tannenbaum, A. 1942. The genesis and growth of tumors. III. Effects of a high fat diet. *Cancer Res* 2:468.

6. Carroll, K.K., E.B. Gammel, and E.R. Plunkett. 1968. Dietary fat and mammary cancer. *Can Med Assoc J* 98:590.

7. Drasar, B.S., and D. Irving. 1973. Environmental factors and cancer of the colon and breast. *Br J Cancer* 27:167.

8. Hems, G. 1970. Epidemiologic characteristics of breast cancer in middle and late age. *Br J Cancer* 24:226.

9. Phillips, R.L. 1975. Role of life-style and dietary habits in risk of cancer among Seventh-Day Adventists. *Cancer Res* 35:3513.

10. Kent, S. 1979. Diet, hormones, and breast cancer. *Geriatrics* 34:83.

11. Haenzel, W., et al. 1973. Large bowel cancer in Hawaiian Japanese. *J Natl Cancer Inst* 51:1765.
12. Gaskill, S.P., et al. 1979. Breast cancer mortality and diet in the United States. *Cancer Res* 39:3628.
13. Reddy, B.S., Mastromarino A., and E. Wynder. 1977. Diet and metabolism: Large bowel cancer. *Cancer* 39:1815.
14. Reddy, B.S., and E. Wynder. 1977. Metabolic epidemiology of colon cancer. *Cancer* 39:2533.
15. Paptestas, A.E., et al. 1982. Fecal steroid metabolites and breast cancer risk. *Cancer* 49:1201.
16. Brammer, S.H. and R.L. DeFelice. 1980. Dietary advice in regard to risk for colon and breast cancer. *Prev Med* 9:544.
17. Chan, P.C., J.F. Head, L.A. Cohen, et al. 1977. Effect of high fat diet on serum prolactin levels and mammary cancer development in ovariectomized rats. *Proc Am Assoc Cancer Res* 18:189.
18. Brammer and DeFelice. Dietary advice.
19. Petrakis, N.L., L.D. Gruenke, and J.C. Craig. 1981. Cholesterol and cholesterol epoxide in nipple aspirate of human breast fluid. *Cancer Res* 41:2563.
20. Wynder. Dietary habits.
21. Schwarz, B.E. 1981. Does estrogen cause adenocarcinoma of the endometrium? *Clin Obst Gyn* 24:243.
22. Orentreich, N., and N.P. Durr. 1974. Mammogenesis in transsexuals. *J Invest Dermatol* 63:142.
23. Symmers, W.S. 1968. Carcinoma of the breast in transsexuals. *Br Med J* 1:83.
24. Treves, N., and A. Holleb. 1955. Cancer of the male breast. *Cancer* 8:1239.
25. Orentreich and Durr. Mammogenesis in transsexuals.
26. Treves and Holleb. Cancer of the male breast.
27. Hoover, R., L.A. Gray, and B. MacMahon. 1976. Menopausal estrogens and breast cancer. *NEJM* 295:401.
28. Casagrande, J., U. Gerkins, et al. 1976. Exogenous estrogens and breast cancer in women with natural menopause. *J Natl Cancer Inst* 56:839.
29. Burch, J., et al. 1975. The effects of long term estrogen therapy, estrogen in the postmenopause. *Front Horm Res* 3:208.
30. Pike, M.C., et al. 1981. Oral contraceptive use and early abortion as risk factors for breast cancer in young women. *Br J Cancer* 43:72.
31. Paffenberger, R.S., et al. Cancer risk as related to use of oral contraceptives during fertile years. *Cancer* 39:1887.
32. Lees, A.W., et al. 1978. Oral contraceptives and breast disease in premenopausal Northern Alberta women. *Int J Cancer* 22:700.
33. Brinton, L.A., et al. 1979. Breast cancer risk factors among screening program participants. *J Natl Cancer Inst* 62:37.
34. Pike, et al. Oral contraceptive use.
35. Food and Drug Administration. 1978. Drugs for human use: New drug requirements for labeling directed to the patient. *Federal Register* (Jan 31) 43:4212.
36. Miller, et al. 1989. Mortality from breast cancer after irradiation during fluoroscopic examination in patients being treated for tuberculosis. *NEJM* 321:1285–1289.
37. Hildreth, et al. 1989. The risk of breast cancer after irradiation of the thymus in infancy. *NEJM* 321:1281–1284.
38. Modan, et al. 1989. Increased risk of breast cancer after low-dose irradiation. *Lancet* (March 25), 629–632.
39. Harvey, et al. 1985. Second cancer following cancer of the breast in Conn. 1935-82. *NCI Monograph* 68:99–112.
40. Hankey, et al. 1983. A retrospective analysis of second breast cancer risk for primary breast cancer patients with an assessment of the effect of radiation therapy. *JNCI* 70:797–804.
41. Kurtz, et al. 1988. Contralateral breast cancer and other second malignancies in patients treated by breast conserving therapy with radiation. *Int J Radiat Oncol Biol Phys* 15:277–284.
42. Weiss, R. 1991. Implants: How big a risk? *Science* 252:1059–60.

Chapter 19
Gastrointestinal Cancers

1. Rosen, P., S.M. Hellerstein, et al. 1981. The low incidence of colorectal cancer in a "high-risk" population. *Cancer* 48:2692.
2. Phillips, R.L. 1975. Role of life-style and dietary habits among Seventh-Day Adventists. *Cancer Res* 35:3513.

3. Lyon, J.L., J.W. Gardner, et al. 1977. Low cancer incidence and mortality in Utah. *Cancer* 39:2608.

4. Wynder, E.L., et al. 1969. Environmental factors of cancer of the colon and rectum. II. Japanese epidemiological data. *Cancer* 32:1210.

5. Armstrong, B., and R. Doll. 1975. Environmental factors and cancer incidence and mortalities in different countries with special reference to dietary practices. *Int J Cancer* 15:617.

6. Burkitt, D.P. 1975. Large-bowel cancer: An epidemiological jigsaw puzzle. *J Natl Cancer Inst* 54:3.

7. Haenszel, W.M., et al. 1973. Large bowel cancer in Hawaiian Japanese. *J Natl Cancer Inst* 51:1765.

8. Willett, et al. 1990. Relation of meat, fat, and fiber intake to the risk of colon cancer in a prospective study among women. *NEJM* 323:1664–72.

9. Miller, J.A., and E.C. Miller. 1969. The metabolic activation of carcinogenic aromatic amines and amides. *Prog Exp Tumor Res* 11:273.

10. Maier, B., M.A. Flynn, et al. 1974. Effects of a high-beef diet on bowel-flora: A preliminary report. *Am J Clin Nutr* 27:1470.

11. Reddy, B.S., and T. Ohmori. 1981. Effect of intestinal microflora and dietary fat of 3,2,1-dimethyl-4-aminobiphenyl-induced colon carcinogenesis in F344 rats. *Cancer Res* 41:1363.

12. Wynder, E.L. and B.S. Reddy. 1974. The epidemiology of cancer of the large bowel. *Digestive Diseases* 19:937.

13. Berg, J.W., M.A. Howell, and S.J. Silverman. 1973. Dietary hypothesis and diet related research in the etiology of colon cancer. *Health Serv Reports* 88:915.

14. Hill, M.J., Drassar, et al. 1975. Fecal bile acids and clostridia in patients with cancer of the large bowel. *Lancet* 2:806.

15. Aries, V.C., et al. 1971. The effect of a strict vegetarian diet on the fecal flora and fecal steroid concentration. *J Pathol* 103:54.

16. MacDonald, I.A., et al. 1978. Fecal hydroxysteroid dehydrogenase activities in vegetarian Seventh-Day Adventists, control subjects, and bowel cancer patients. *Am J Clin Nutr* 31:S233.

17. Burkitt, D.P. 1971. Epidemiology of cancer of the colon and rectum. *Cancer* 28:3.

18. Hill, M.J., J.S. Crowther, et al. 1975. Bacteria and oetiology of cancer of the large bowel. *Lancet* 1:95.

19. Reddy, B.S., A.R. Hedges, et al. 1978. Metabolic epidemiology of large bowel cancer. Fecal bulk and constituents of high risk North American and low risk Finnish population. *Cancer* 42:2832.

20. *American Journal of Clinical Nutrition* 31 Suppl (Oct. 1978):512–20.

21. Eastwood, M.A. 1978. Fiber in the gastrointestinal tract. *Am J Clin Nutr* 31:30.

22. *Am J Clin Nutr*, 31.

23. Ershoff, B.H. 1974. Antitoxic effects of plant fiber. *Am J Clin Nutr* 27:1395.

24. Phillips. Role of life-style and dietary habits.

25. Lyon, Gardner, et al. Low cancer incidence.

26. Burkitt. Large-bowel cancer.

27. Wynder and Reddy. Epidemiology of cancer.

28. Berg, Howell, and Silverman. Dietary hypothesis.

29. Hill, Drassar, et al. Fecal bile acids.

30. MacLennan, M.B., et al. 1978. Diet, transit time, stool weight, and colon cancer in two Scandinavian populations. *Am J Clin Nutr* 31:S239.

31. Graham, S., and C. Mettlin. 1979. Diet and colon cancer. *Am J Epidemiol* 109:1.

32. Kritchevsky, D., and J. Story. 1974. Binding of bile salts *in vitro* by nonnutritive fiber. *J Nutr* 104:458.

33. Lai, C. 1978. Chlorophyll: The active factor in wheat sprout extract inhibiting the metabolic activation of carcinogens *in vitro*. *Nutr Cancer* 1(3):19.

34. Ramanujam, et al. 1990. Wheat bran diet protects against recurrence of colorectal cancer. *Oncology* 4(7):139.

35. *Am J Clin Nutr* 31.

36. Burkitt, D. 1978. Colonic-rectal cancer: Fiber and other dietary factors. *Am J Clin Nutr* 31:S58.

37. Jain, M., et al. 1980. A case control study of diet and colo-rectal cancer. *Int J Cancer* 26:757.

38. Gilbertsen, V.A., and J. M. Nelms. 1978. The prevention of invasive cancer of the rectum. *Cancer* 41:1137.

39. Gilbertsen, V.A. 1974. Protosigmoidoscopy and polypectomy in reducing the incidence of rectal cancer. *Cancer* 34:939.

40. Carroll, R.L., and M. Klein. 1980. How often should patients be sigmoidoscoped? *Prev Med* 9:741.

41. Larrson, L.A., A. Sandstrom, and P. Westling. 1975. Relationship of Plummer-Vinson disease to cancer of the upper alimentary tract in Sweden. *Cancer Res* 35:3308.

42. Larrson, Sandstrom, and Westling. Relationship of Plummer-Vinson disease to cancer of the upper alimentary tract in Sweden.

43. Hirayama, T. 1979. Diet and cancer. *Nutrition and Cancer* 1(3):67.

44. Suzuki, K., and T. Mitsuoko. 1981. Increase in fecal nitrosamines in Japanese individuals given a Western diet. *Nature* 294:453.

45. Lee, D.H.K. 1970. Nitrates, nitrites, and methemoglobinemia. *Environ Res* 3:484.

46. Suzuki and Mitsuoko. Increase in fecal nitrosamines.

47. Hirayama. Diet and cancer.

48. Kriebel, D., and D. Jowett. 1980. Stomach mortality in the north central states: High risk is not limited to the foreign born. *Nutrition and Cancer* 1(2):8.

49. Armstrong and Doll. Environmental factors.

50. Armstrong and Doll. Environmental factors.

51. Polk, H.C. 1966. Carcinoma and the calcified gall bladder. *Gastroenterology* 50:582.

52. Bismuth, H., and R.A. Malt. 1979. Carcinoma of the biliary tract. *NEJM* 301:704.

53. Armstrong and Doll. Environmental factors.

54. MacMahon, B., S. Yen, et al. 1981. Coffee and cancer of the pancreas. *NEJM* 304:630.

55. Feinstein, A.R., et al. 1981. Coffee and pancreatic cancer. *JAMA* 246:957.

56. Goldstein, H.R. 1982. No association found between coffee and cancer of the pancreas. *NEJM* 306:997.

Chapter 20
Other Cancers

1. Armenian, H.K., et al. 1975. Epidemiologic characteristics of patients with prostatic neoplasms. *Am J Epidemiol* 102:47.

2. Armstrong, and Doll. 1975. Environmental factors and cancer incidence and mortality in different countries with reference to dietary practice. *Int J Cancer* 15:617–631.

3. Dunn, L.J., and J.T. Bradbury. 1967. Endocrine factors in endometrial carcinoma. *Am J Obstet Gynecol* 97:465.

4. Armstrong and Doll. Environmental factors.

5. Armstrong. 1977. The role of diet in human carcinogenesis with special reference to endometrial cancer. In *Origins of Human Cancer*. New York: Cold Spring Harbor Laboratory, 557–565.

6. Dunning, W.F., M.R. Curtis, and M.E. Maun. 1950. The effect of added dietary tryptophan on the occurrance of 2-acetylaminofluorene-induced liver and bladder cancers in rats. *Cancer Res* 10:454.

7. Morrison, A.S., and J.E. Buring. 1980. Artificial sweeteners and cancer of the lower urinary tract. *NEJM* 302:537.

8. Hoover, R.N., and P.H. Strasser. 1980. Artificial sweeteners and human bladder cancer. *Lancet* (April): 837.

9. Miller, A.B. 1977. The etiology of bladder cancer from the epidemiologic viewpoint. *Cancer Res* 37:2929.

10. Hirayama. Diet and cancer.

11. Armstrong and Doll. Environmental factors.

12. Friedell, G.H., et al. 1979. Nutritional factors that may be involved in cancer of the bladder. *Nutrition and Cancer* 1(2):82.

13. Price, J.M. 1971. Etiology of bladder cancer. In *Benign and Malignant Tumors of the Urinary Bladder*, ed. E. Maltry, Jr. Flushing, N.Y.: Med. Examination Publishing Co., Inc., 189–261.

14. Byar, D., and C. Blackard. 1977. Comparison of placebo, pyridoxine, and topical thiotepa in preventing recurrence of stage I bladder cancer. *Urology* 10:556.

15. Cramer, et al. 1989. Galactose consumption and metabolism in relation to the risk of ovarian cancer. *Lancet* (July 8): 66–72.

16. Bjelke. 1975. Dietary vitamin A and human lung cancer. *Int J Cancer* 15:561–565.

17. MacLennan, R., et al. 1977. Risk factors for lung cancer in Singapore Chinese, a population with high female incidence rates. *Int J Cancer* 20:854–860.
18. Hirayama. *Diet and Cancer*.
19. Weisburger, J.H. 1979. Mechanism of action of diet as a carcinogen. *Cancer* 43:1987.

Chapter 21
Cardiovascular Disease

1. Keys, A. 1970. Coronary heart disease in seven countries. *Circulation* 41(S):211.
2. Shekelle, R.B., et al. 1979. Diet, serum cholesterol, and death from coronary heart disease. *NEJM* 304:65.
3. Hjerman, I., et al. 1981. Effect of diet and smoking intervention on the incidence of coronary heart disease: Report from the Oslo study group of a randomized trial in healthy men. *Lancet* 2:1303.
4. Sacks, F.M., et al. 1981. Effect of ingestion of meat on plasma cholesterol of vegetarians. *JAMA* 246:640.
5. Gordon, T. 1970. The Framingham Diet Study: Diet and regulation of serum cholesterol. In *The Framingham Study: An Epidemiological Investigation of Cardiovascular Disease* (Section 24), ed. W.B. Kannel, and T. Gordon. Washington, D.C.: Government Printing Office.
6. Pearce, M.L., and S. Dayton. 1971. Incidence of cancer in men on a diet high in polyunsaturated fat. *Lancet* i:464.
7. Ederer, F., P. Laren, et al. 1971. Cancer among men on cholesterol lowering diets. *Lancet* ii:203.
8. Rose, G., H. Blackburn, et al. 1974. Colon cancer and blood cholesterol. *Lancet* i:181.
9. Cambien, F., P. Ducimetetiere, and J. Richard. 1980. Total serum cholesterol and cancer mortality in a middle aged male population. *Am J Epidemiol* 112:388.
10. Jain, M., et al. 1978. A case-control study of diet and colo-rectal cancer. *Int J Cancer* 26:757.
11. Dyerberg, J., H. O. Bang, et al. 1978. Eicosapenteanoic acid and prevention of thrombosis and atherosclerosis? *Lancet* 2:117, and *Lancet* 1980, 1:199.
12. Dyerberg, J., and H.O. Bang. 1979. Hemostatic function and platelet polyun-

saturated fatty acids in Eskimos. *Lancet* 2:433.
13. Kobayashi, S., A. Hirai, et al. 1981. Reduction in blood viscosity by eicosapentaenoic acid. *Lancet* 2:197.
14. Conner, W.E., et al. 1981. The effects of eicosapentaenoic acid on blood lipids. *JAMA* 246:29.
15. Walker, A.R., and U.B. Arvidsson. 1954. Fat intake, serum cholesterol concentration and atherosclerosis in the South African Bantus. *J Clin Invest* 33:1366.
16. Jenkins, D.J., et al. 1980. Dietary fiber and blood lipids: Treatment of hypercholesterolemia with guar crispbread. *Am J Clin Nutr* 33:575.
17. Jenkins, et al. Dietary fiber and blood lipids.
18. Gordon, T. The Framingham Diet Study.
19. Keys, A., C. Arvanis, et al. 1972. Coronary heart disease: Overweight and obesity as risk factors. *Ann Int Med* 77:15.
20. Dyer, A.R., J. Stamler, et al. 1975. Relationship of relative weight and body mass index to 14 year mortality in the Chicago People's Gas Co. study. *J Chron Dis* 28:109.
21. Leon, A.S., and H. Blackburn. 1977. The relationship of physical activity to coronary heart disease and life expectancy. *Ann NY Acad Sci* 301:561.
22. Stadel, B.V. 1981. Oral contraceptives and cardiovascular disease. *NEJM* 305:612.
23. Slone, D., et al. 1981. Risk of myocardial infarction in relation to current and discontinued use of oral contraceptives. *NEJM* 305:420.
24. Castelli, W.P., J.T. Doyle, et al. 1977. Alcohol and blood lipids. The Cooperative Lipoprotein Phenotyping Study. *Lancet* 2:153.
25. Yano, K., et al. 1977. Coffee, alcohol, and risk of coronary heart disease among Japanese men living in Hawaii. *NEJM* 297:405.
26. Henze, K., et al. 1977. Alcohol intake and coronary risk factors in a population group in Rome. *Nutr Metab* 21 Suppl 1:157.
27. Hulley, S.B., et al. 1977. Plasma high-density lipoprotein cholesterol level: Influence of risk factor intervention. *JAMA* 238:2269.

28. Willett, W., et al. 1980. Alcohol consumption and high-density lipoprotein cholesterol in marathon runners. *NEJM* 303:1159.
29. Ornish, D., et al. 1990. Can lifestyle changes reverse coronary heart disease? *Lancet* 336:129–133.
30. Ost, et al. 1967. Regression of peripheral atherosclerosis during therapy with high doses of nicotinic acid. *Scand J Clin Lab Invest Suppl* 99:241–5.
31. Blankenhorn, et al. 1987. Beneficial effects of combined colestipol-niacin therapy on coronary atherosclerosis and coronary venous bypass grafts. *JAMA* 257:3233–40.
32. Brown, et al. 1990. Regression of coronary artery disease as a result of intensive lipid-lowering therapy in men with high levels of apolipoprotein B. *NEJM* 323:1295–98.
33. Rossouw, et al. 1990. The value of lowering cholesterol after myocardial infarction. *NEJM* 323:1112–19.
34. Buchwald, et al. Effect of partial ileal bypass surgery on mortality and morbidity from coronary heart disease in patients with hypercholesterolemia: report of POSCH. *NEJM* 323:946–55.
35. Loscalzo, J. 1990. Regression of atherosclerosis. *NEJM* 323:1337–1339.
36. Leaf and Ryan. 1990. Prevention of coronary artery disease. *NEJM* 323:1416–19.
37. Somers, V.K., et al. 1991. Effects of endurance training on baroreflex sensitivity and blood pressure in borderline hypertension. *Lancet* 337:1363–68.
38. Ornish, et al. 1990. Lifestyle changes and heart disease. *Lancet* 336:741–42.
39. Blankenhorn, et al. Beneficial effects of combined colestipol-niacin therapy.
40. Brown, et al. 1989. Niacin or lovastatin, combined with colestipol, regress coronary atherosclerosis and prevent clinical events in men with elevated apolipoprotein B. *Circulation* 80:II–266.

About the Author

Dr. Charles B. Simone is a nationally renowned Medical Oncologist, Immunologist, and Radiation Oncologist with a practice in Princeton, New Jersey. He graduated from Rutgers College of Medicine with both a Masters of Medical Science (M.MS.), and a Medical Degree (MD). After training in Internal Medicine at the Cleveland Clinic, Dr. Simone was offered a position as Clinical Associate in the Immunology Branch and Medicine Branch of the National Cancer Institute in Bethesda, MD. Later, he became an Investigator in the Pharmacology Branch and Medicine Branch of the NCI. While at the NCI, he trained in medical oncology (chemotherapy) and clinical immunology.

In 1982, he accepted a position in the Department of Radiation Therapy at the University of Pennsylvania, Philadelphia; and in 1985, he became an Associate Professor in the Department of Radiation Therapy and Nuclear Medicine at Thomas Jefferson University, Philadelphia. Since 1989, he has worked to establish the Simone Prevention Center, a multifunctional facility dedicated to comprehensive patient care.

In addition, Dr. Simone has served as a consultant to the American Cancer Society, major corporations, foreign countries, and has advised many prominent figures, including former President Ronald Reagan, on the principles of cancer prevention.

Index

Acid rain, 185–187
Acquired Immune Deficiency
  Syndrome (AIDS)
  and cancer, 172
  mode of spread, 173–175
Acrylonitrile, 17
Additives. *See* Food additives.
Aflatoxin, 15, 141
Age as a risk factor, 4, 16, 21–22,
  69, 224, 252
Agent Orange. *See* Dioxin.
AIDS. *See* Acquired Immune
  Deficiency Syndrome.
Air pollution. *See* Pollution, air;
  Pollution, indoor air.
Alcohol, 4, 16, 19, 54, 67, 266
  and cancer and other diseases,
  167–168
  and cardiovascular disease,
  254
  and immunity, 166–167
  nutrition and alcoholism, 166
  price of abuse, 165–166
Allergies and passive smoking,
  160

American Cancer Society, 3, 100,
  113, 117
American Lung Association, 183,
  266
Amyl nitrite, 25
Androgens, 182, 268
Aniline, 17
Antibodies, 44–45
Antioxidants
  and chemotherapy, 109
  as supplements in atherosclerosis prevention, 102–103
  protecting individual with
  cardiovascular disease, 105–
  106
  protecting smokers from free
  radicals, 104–105
  See also Atherosclerosis;
  Cardiovascular disease; Free
  radicals.
Arsenic, 18
Artificial sweeteners, 245
Asbestos, 18, 19, 20, 267
Ascorbic acid, 60, 61, 62, 64, 66,
  67, 68, 69, 70, 71, 74, 83–84, 86,